I0639291

# Black Sun

## Legacy of the Predecessors

Daniel Crux

INKWELL BOOKS

Writing-Publishing-Printing

Copyright 2021
By Daniel Crux
All Rights Reserved.


No part of this book may be reproduced, stored in a retrieval
system, or transmitted by any means, electronic, mechanical,
photocopying, recording, or otherwise, without written
permission from the publisher.

ISBN 978-0-9814648-5-5
Library of Congress 2020948934

Published by Inkwell Books
10632 North Scottsdale Road, Unit 695
Scottsdale, AZ 85254
Tel. 480-315-3781
E-mail info@inkwellbooksLLC.com
Website www.inkwellbooksLLC.com

**INKWELL BOOKS**
Writing-Publishing-Printing

# <u>Acknowledgments</u>

My loving family, who continue to support my dreams even in the most trying of times.

# **<u>Contents</u>**

*Upon the twilight of the First Age of Terra, the Age of Progression, a series of great and cataclysmic wars would erupt between its human inhabitance and a mysterious race of invaders from the stars. The consequences of such devastating conflicts were far-reaching. The invaders were eventually defeated and repelled, but in the aftermath of these End Wars, governments would collapse, and humanity would face widespread starvation and extinction.*

*Thus would begin Terra's Second Age, the Age of Desolation or, as it is more commonly known, the Thousand Year Darkness.*

*For seeming eternity, the human race would endure a dark age of utter chaos, a period of everlasting ruin and strife in which only the strongest and most capable survived. Through this desolation, a lone warrior would rise up from the shadows. Seeking to reestablish order, this warrior would utilize a combination of hopeful words, what military power he held at his disposal and, most importantly, lessons learned from civilizations past to bring humanity's remnants under his banner.*

*Though this warrior's crusade would last many lifetimes, the human race, for the first time since its birth, would, at last, become united under a single cause and purpose. From this, order and culture would be revitalized across the ravaged earth, giving rise to a power that would rule over all, the Terran Empire.*

*With the Empire's birth and the warrior's coronation as the first Emperor, human civilization had officially been reborn, thus beginning the Third Age, the Age of Ascension.*

*But even with this Rebirth of Humanity, Terra itself remained broken and devastated, possessing few remaining resources to sustain its inhabitance. For humanity's continued survival, the Empire would turn its attention toward the final conquest, Space.*

*The foundations of this new age are marked solely by humanity's intent of settling its own star system. Once space itself was reached, the Empire's first act was to establish space colonies in geosynchronous orbits around its homeworld. After vast expenditures of funds and manpower, the colonies would become the agricultural centers of this newborn nation, ending all lingering traces of the Darkness virtually overnight.*

*Even so, humanity continued to look to the stars, and soon lunar colonies were also developed for the purpose of industry.*

*Additional colonization and space exploration would continue unabated, with new settlements established on nearly all planetary bodies in the Sol System, from Mercury to the moons of Neptune.*

*Mining adventures, agricultural experiments, terraforming projects, and other endeavors were developed upon these colonies. Technologies that would also come to be used upon Terra itself, transforming the planet from a dark wasteland into a reborn blue and fertile world. New natural resources would also be discovered throughout, further nourishing humanity's growing empire as it began to transcend the borders of the Sol System.*

*Not long after the establishment of these colonies did Terran scientists finally make the discovery of faster than light travel in the form of the Arc Engine. With this breakthrough, humanity became further enamored with exploring the universe around them and expanding their reach throughout, establishing their beloved Empire's rule to the very borders of the galaxy. Seemingly, their only hindrance would be the various "alien" civilizations, which would inevitably seek to impede their progress, perhaps even attempt to subjugate them as those invaders had so long ago.*

*With that in mind, the Emperor would declare the formation of the Imperial Starfleet, the military arm that would defend humanity from its future enemies. It would not be long before the Imperial fleets and armies became as countless as the stars themselves.*

*Well into the Age of Ascension's third century, humanity would make first contact with an alien civilization in the further reaches of space. Unexpectedly, this civilization and many following it would turn out to be far more primitive than humanity had come to believe, varying from cave dwelling races akin to the ancient Neanderthals to some relatively advanced races that were equal to humanity's development in the midst of its First Age.*

*Even so, fearing the potential threat of these races, the Empire fell upon these worlds with great fervor, conquering in the name of humanity's progress while adapting whatever technology and advancement they found along the way. Not even the more advanced societies were capable of defending themselves against the mighty warships and combat ready men and women under the Emperor's service. Thus, humanity's dominion would spread vastly and rapidly throughout the Milky Way, challenged only by twelve others of similar power.*

*And yet even with the rebirth and growth of human civilization, the freedom offered by space also led to the establishment of much darker enterprises. As humanity expanded further into the darkness without end, its ability to maintain order throughout its colonies continued to wane. The equally continued usage of merchant lines to resupply settlements with whatever necessary resources made attractive targets to those who operated outside civilization's law.*

*Piracy had at last emerged.*

*Despite every effort to prevent its growth, piracy would soon become abundant throughout the galaxy. Men and women of all races and backgrounds would commit themselves to the dream of vast power and wealth, utilizing knowledge of the space around them to exploit shipping lines and plunder and pillage in reflection of the ancient Terran buccaneers. Amongst that number, the most successful in these endeavors would come to form the infamous Pirate Clans, establishing their own dominions over the stars. All while retaining no mercy for those who may oppose them.*

*It is now the ninth century of humanity's Third Age. The galaxy progresses on as Terra, and the other twelve Galactic Powers struggle and conflict amongst themselves, each vying for complete domination. All throughout, piracy retains its sway, innumerable renegades sailing under the Jolly Roger's shadow.*

*This is a tale set upon one such band...*

# <u>Chapter XXXI: Lamentations</u>

## Imperial *Superior*-class battleship *Subjugator*
## Arcspace

*How intriguing...* Drake observed as he gazed over the star map on the bridge viewscreen, which displayed the *Black Sun*'s current course. *To think it shall end where it all began.*

Leaning back in his chair, a malicious smile forming on his lips, Drake supposed there could not have been a more ideal location for Arcadia's resting place, but a lone planet orbiting a lone star in one of the more isolated parts of the galaxy. A part of him wondered if the Predecessors had specifically chosen that world for those factors. Just as another part of him wondered if there had been more to Morganna Flint's own journey to Ephesus than a simple voyage.

Despite his intrigue with both considerations, he ultimately decided that there was no way of discerning the truth for either. All that mattered now was, with or without the cooperation of the good Captain Flint and his ever-vigilant crew, the prize would soon be his.

He need only follow his prey in.

On that part, Drake once again reflected upon one of his personal philosophies, one that he had even gone as far as to record in his book; sometimes, the smallest acts made the biggest differences. In this case, his small act was to have a tracking beacon placed upon the Kite that Captain Flint and his "date" had utilized to reach Bonham IV. Namely a "smart" beacon that had been programmed to link into the Black Sun's navigation system, which for all that made it cutting edge was still of Imperial design, and then transmit the findings back to the Subjugator. Admittedly it was a bit of a gambit since Drake's infiltration team had only planted one such device, as any more would have increased the likelihood of detection, but that gambit appeared to be working.

Of course, given all that occurred around Bonham, Drake doubted anyone in the *Black Sun*'s crew had even conceived they were being tracked that way. In fact, he surmised that the pirates were now in a collective state of shock. Not demoralized per se, but rather overwhelmed with the knowledge that their captain and his brother had been bested, their beloved matron had been so elaborately outmaneuvered and, perhaps most of all, they were now under pursuit by one of Starfleet's best commanders. Hardly a state of mind to be extra observant, even when their opponent had a reputation for meticulousness.

But those were all just minor details as far as Drake was concerned. Once more, what really mattered was that Drake now knew the location of Arcadia, and, given his orders to the *Subjugator*'s helmsman to keep to the *Black Sun*'s course, he would be there in a few days to claim the prize. Sure, the *Black Sun* had a head start on him, but that hardly mattered. In races such as this, it wasn't the one who reached the finish line first, but rather the one who was left standing that gained the full victory.

In a good mood, he decided to have a little fun with one of his subordinates. "What do you think?" he posited the question toward the *Subjugator*'s captain.

Realizing instantly that he was put into the spotlight, the captain, while professionally holding himself in, answered his superior's question.

"I think that it is indeed Arcadia's final resting place. Or at least the pirates think it is," the captain answered. "They would have no other reason to turn to that system."

"*Return*," Drake corrected. "At least for some of them."

Knowing what Drake meant, the captain nodded in response. "As you say, sir," he replied. "But all the same, I hold to my explanation."

"Are you sure, Captain?" Drake playfully inquired further. "Wouldn't it be even more likely for them to go to ground? Or perhaps, on the possibility that they know they're being tracked, to set up a trap for us?"

Despite the Admiral's pressing, the captain remained resolute. "As I said, sir. They have no reason to *return* there. Especially given the personal history for a certain number of their members."

"I see," Drake responded, nodding in approval. He had made the same estimates himself; he just wanted to hear a second opinion back them up. That along with some basic amusement.

And so, keeping all of his present considerations in mind, Drake rose from his chair. "Well then," he said as he straightened out his uniform. "That will be enough for now, Captain. I believe I've seen everything that I need to."

The *Subjugator*'s captain could do nothing but nod. "As you wish sir," he replied dutifully. "Will you be retiring for the evening?"

Usually, it was a bad career move for those of lesser rank to make assumptions, even likely ones, of their commanders. However, Drake wasn't that type of admiral, and the captain, besides being a good man, had intended no hidden meaning behind his inquiry.

"Indeed I will," he confirmed before moving toward the turbolift. "I'm afraid I'm still a little strained from the earlier battle."

"Yes, sir," the captain replied again, this time with a mixture of sympathy and pride. The latter emotion became especially prevalent amongst the bridge crew upon his duel with the Flints being mentioned. It had been a while since they had seen their commander in direct action. "Would you like me to reach the galley...?"

"That won't be necessary, but I appreciate the thought," Drake countered as he noted the crew's newfound state. He nodded his gratitude before, at last, adding, "Inform me if anything worthwhile comes up."

With that, Drake stepped into the turbolift and allowed the doors to close behind him. As he reached out to tap the side panel, bringing the turbolift into motion, Drake nearly stumbled, such that he had to momentarily rebalance himself. Though the captain and the bridge crew might have taken it as an exaggeration, Drake had not been lying when he said he was still a "little" strained. The battle, as much as he dominated throughout, had taken much out of him. And not merely because the Flints were much younger.

*They are indeed formidable opponents,* he thought as he steadied himself, his characteristic smile appearing across his lips. Not quite as much as their legendary mother was, but the Flints lived up to their family name and reputation regardless. In turn, making the race, and eventual second battle of Ephesus all the more invigorating. Drake wouldn't have had it any other way.

As he awaited the turbolift to reach the deck that contained his quarters, the Admiral felt his thoughts drift off toward that particular ship and its crew. Yes, their objectives were clear, and they were quite intent on following them in the meantime, but he couldn't help but wonder, what were they doing now? Were they preparing for the inevitable battle, perhaps having one last, solemn drinking event before putting their lives on the line, or were they continuing to work under bated breath as their captain was put under the proverbial knife? After some estimation, Drake decided it was all three during separate time periods, but most of it based around the latter most possibility.

With that last thought, Drake's smile grew ever bolder. He knew all too well that, as severely wounded as Jonathan Flint had ended up, he was not in any real danger of dying. Yes, he had been brought quite close to death during the battle against him, but the elder Flint wasn't close enough to actually die just yet. After all, he had taken extra steps to ensure the pirate's survival and eventual recovery. Perhaps not in time for the final battle at Ephesus, something that only the *Black Sun*'s CMO could decide, assuming he or she had the skills for it, but the good Captain Flint would indeed live to fight another day.

*Unless I blow his ship out from under him,* Drake continued to think. It was admittedly an all too likely, if somewhat regrettable possibility. Just like when he had cornered the *Morgan le Fay*, Drake intended to hold nothing back over Ephesus. When the battle at last sounded, the Flints and their crew, and even *she* would not just be fighting for their possession of Arcadia, but also their very lives. Just as he and his own crew, and by extension, his fleet, would be doing against them.

*Whatever happens...* he thought, his smile taking on a lighter, but no less emboldened tone. *you and I are now even, Nimitz.*

Exhaustion taking hold, Drake thought of nothing else. Instead, he waited for the turbolift to at last reach the appropriate deck. When the doors opened again, the Admiral continued on to his personal dwellings.

All while the *Subjugator*, and the rest of her all too recently assembled fleet, continued their journey through arcspace...

## Flint Pirates umbra *Black Sun*
## Arcspace

Within the silence of the observation deck, with the stars in front of him and the darkness around him, Barbarossa found himself in a strangely similar peace that he usually only felt within his quarters. There was just something about the great abyss and the stars within, even when they were streaking by via arcspace, that brought the mind and body to ease and made Barbarossa appreciate the genius that Aslan had applied to creation. Indeed, it was truly magnificent how a great nothingness filled with the smallest forms of light could not only bring peace to the weariest soul but also reinforce one's belief in the almighty.

*And with belief in the almighty comes belief in salvation,* Barbarossa thought as the stars continued to streak past. Such had been claimed by Amir Hassan during one of the greatest tribulations Aslan had ever placed upon his followers. Barbarossa had always considered the heart of the message, that faith in Aslan meant faith in His salvation, one to remember during the most trying times. Thus, as Barbarossa solemnly reflected, it was all too fitting for the present, in which the shadow of Bonham still held sway.

Compared to the joyousness and exuberance the *Black Sun* had experienced before its arrival to Bonham IV, the last three days, and all too likely those that would follow, had been far less serene. Whatever energy was not being spent on keeping the ship moving was instead being utilized toward preparation for their arrival. Weapons and tactical systems were continuously being calibrated, maintenance cycles were doubled, and the raiders were forever honing their already impressive fighting skills for the inevitable confrontation. Whatever wasn't tied down was in constant motion and whatever crewmen attempted to step out of line, which fortunately had been few in number, was staunchly dealt with. All as if the *Black Sun* had never left Starfleet.

Even so, Barbarossa sighed as he wondered if any of it would be worthwhile; if in fact the *Black Sun* even stood a chance against the opposition. Very few of the crew seemed to think so. Though they continued their duties with minimal protest, Barbarossa need only look in their eyes to see their hopelessness and their belief that they would, in fact, not be returning from Ephesus. Only their constant activity and focus on the off chance that they may, in fact, survive kept morale from falling any lower, which in itself was part of the reason Barbarossa had kept them busy, to begin with. Sentient minds, Leo, Terran and otherwise, had no time to despair when they were active and in full motion. He would have liked to think the Captain and First Officer, who remained dormant in sickbay, would have realized and done the same in his place.

As for Barbarossa, he had to admit even his morale was not as high as usual. Rather than performing his duties in the hope of one day acquiring the *Black Sun* to take before his Caliph in triumph, Barbarossa was now about to fight another personal jihad against the Terran Empire. Another war against an enemy many times his size, containing far more in the way of resources and manpower and headed by one of the best warriors and tacticians that Terra had ever produced. Twenty years ago he would have anticipated such a bout, but not today. Today he was wizened from the years, and knew that such battles, as glorious as the various media of his race and even those of Terra tended to portray them, were quite inevitable in their outcome. And that outcome seldom valued the gallant yet very lone "heroes".

The rogue Leo captain let out a sigh, again mentally recalling Hassan's line on faith equating to salvation. He could only hope that remained true here; that the salvation Aslan held for him indeed meant his and his compatriots', infidels they may be, survival if not triumph. Otherwise, all Barbarossa could hope for was to take as many Imperials with him before he, at last, rose to his awaited place at Aslan's side.

Interrupting his thoughts was the sound of the door swishing open, allowing another figure to enter into the observation deck. At first, Barbarossa was about to order the intruder away, but upon his sharp ears picking up the intruder's distinct footfalls, he decided to allow the newcomer in. After all, if there was anyone on the *Black Sun* that held the same thoughts and corresponding experiences as he, it was *her*.

"Trouble resting?" Boss inquired as she, already smoking her characteristic pipe, came to his side while holding her own gaze toward the streaking stars.

"No time for it," Barbarossa explained. "I'm due back on the bridge in an hour," he then cast a corner glance upon the ace. "And you?"

Smirking around her pipe, Boss elaborated. "I just came off a mockfight with my pilots. Thought I could use a breather."

With the explanations given, Boss looked toward the stars. "Do you usually stargaze at times like this? Or is this some Leo tradition I haven't heard of?"

Barbarossa allowed a smirk of his own to form before answering. "A personal habit of mine," he replied. "I like to look upon the stars before a coming battle."

Intrigued, Boss pressed further. "In case you don't survive to see to them after?"

"Yes, but not entirely," Barbarossa clarified. "Long ago, before my people embraced the will of Aslan, they believed the stars to be great kings of the past who, despite having departed the realm of the living, continue to watch over us and even guide us on occasion."

His eyes then narrowed further upon the stars. "Such belief has since transitioned into mythology," he continued to explain. "And yet, all the same, I can't help but feel there really is much wisdom to be had from the stars."

Intrigued, Boss asked. "And what are the stars telling you now?"

Pausing for a brief moment, as if literally trying to determine the answer to that question, Barbarossa let out a small laugh. "That I have gone completely mad. Taking part in another hopeless battle after *narrowly* surviving the last time."

Boss laughed. "Story of our lives Kapta," she let out. "You'd think, for all the brilliance the historians equate to us, we would learn the first time around."

"In my experience, madness and brilliance all too often coincide," Barbarossa retorted. "This time, however, I feel there is far too much of the former in us."

Letting out another soft chuckle at that retort, Boss allowed a brief pause to enter before speaking again. "Still, we may yet prevail," she said, taking her pipe out momentarily to exhale a cloud of smoke. "And if we do, we'll be stronger and wiser than we were before."

Barbarossa nodded in concurrence. "I've reached that conclusion as well," he replied as he waved some of the smoke away, so it didn't obscure the view. "What lies ahead of us is not a battleground, but a proving ground."

Stepping closer to the viewport, Barbarossa expounded. "A place in which many things will be put to the test. The capabilities of this ship, the skill of her captain, the mettle of her crew..."

"Whether or not we are strong enough to continue on," Boss again surmised.

Grimly, Barbarossa nodded. "As well as whether we are *brilliant* enough," he stated, placing his hands behind his back in thought. "All will be determined at Ephesus."

A frown crossed Boss' expression before she exclaimed. "Just like it was for Morganna Flint fifteen years ago."

The Leo inhaled a sharp breath before responding. "Indeed, all too certainly in fact."

A brief moment of silence filled the observation deck before Boss worked up the will to speak again and turned to look at the Leo. "You think we have any chance at all?" she inquired in a near whisper.

Glancing down at the ace, Barbarossa paused before answering. "Only Aslan and the stars before us know the answer to that question, Commander," he replied evenly, his voice now holding grave seriousness. "Only Aslan Himself and the stars before us."

He then looked back at the streaking lights. "And right now, neither seem interested in giving that answer."

Nodding solemnly at that explanation, Boss turned back to face the streaking stars, silence engulfing the observation deck.

"Truly," Braun spoke appreciatively as he gazed over his tankard. "There is nothing like cold grog after a hard day's work," he said before taking another drink of his beer.

Quietly yet solemnly concurring, Davis took a drink of his rum. As he did, he once more felt as though he were a condemned man, taking his last drink before his inevitable execution. And just like the many previous times that feeling had come up that evening, Davis forced it to the back of his mind and concentrated on savoring the alcohol. It helped he was one of the few on the ship who could afford to do so at that time.

Compared to the evening before the *Black Sun*'s arrival at Bonham, the lounge, at the present time, was an entirely different setting. Instead of the sound of music, whether from the jukebox or the Psirens and the sounds of laughter and banter accompanied by the clinking of tankards, the area was now in a state of near silence. No music played in the background, and a select number of lights were the only electrical systems active. Instead of the room being filled with celebrating pirates, only Davis, Braun and Lloyd, who Davis secretly believed had never left his station since day one, were present. And instead of the exuberance that naturally accompanied the partying atmosphere, there was only cold solemnity and a dreadfully silent observance toward the days ahead.

Or at least, that's what Davis would have expected the latter to be. Had his drinking partner not been the ever pleasant Maximilian Braun.

"This almost reminds of three hundred years ago, when I was working on the then-next generation Arc Engine," Braun explained, his right hand absently twisting the tankard around in its grip. "By the time I took my first break during that project, I had been active for almost an entire week."

"Sounds fascinating," Davis replied flatly, hoping that Braun would catch the hidden message under his tone. He really didn't want to hear any stories at that time. In fact, outside of the sound of intaking liquid, he didn't want to hear *anything* at that time.

Unfortunately, Braun didn't seem receptive of the hint. "Yes indeed," he said, his tone remaining upbeat. "By the time I decided to take a break and at last get a much-deserved drink, it was about 0413 on a Thursday and the only tavern that was open at that time was Milliways'."

"That's nice," Davis let out, feeling his patience drain even further.

"Not quite," Braun corrected, again failing to catch the helmsman's displeasure. "I personally always found it a shabby establishment, the kind you would find at the darker end of the universe," he clarified, a small look of disgust appearing over his face. "But even so, it served decent grog, and it was quite early in the morning, so..."

"Seriously!?" Davis finally let out, frustration at last reaching the surface.

Braun didn't quite know what to make of that response. "Well, I can't say I was happy about it either," he continued on evenly. "But as the old saying goes, beggars..."

"That's not what I mean!" Davis nearly shouted, all the while resisting the urge to bash his head onto the bar counter. He could not believe the man beside him, for all his brilliance, could be so obtuse to the atmosphere.

Now hyperventilating, Davis persisted. "Don't get me wrong, Professor, I'm sure it's *another* good story, just like the other *six* you told..."

Braun opened his mouth to reply, but Davis was unrelenting. "Haven't you been paying attention to what's been going on? We could all be dead in the next few days!"

Had the Professor still possessed his eyes, he would have blinked at the exclamation. "I am keenly aware of this, yes..." he spoke evenly as if he were observing a poor man losing his grip on sanity.

"And yet, you're still carrying on like business as usual!" Davis bellowed, flabbergasted. "Doesn't any of *this*..." he gestured around the empty lounge. "...have any meaning to you!?"

Again Braun would have blinked had he his eyes. After a brief moment, realization came to him and the Professor let out a chuckle. Much to Davis' exasperation.

"What!?" the helmsman demanded.

"Oh, nothing..." Braun declared amidst his laughter. "It's just that I find you to be a rather funny man Mr. Davis."

Davis appeared as though he were about to explode. "Funny!?"

"Yes," Braun commented, then gesturing over his body. "Look at me!" he exclaimed, retaining his amusement. "I'm over three hundred and fifty years old, and I only have forty percent of my original body left intact!"

Now it was Davis' turn to watch as though a man were losing his grip. Or so he initially believed.

"My beloved wife is long dead, as are my children, my grandchildren, and my great-grandchildren. And my descendants have long forgotten their relation to me!" Braun continued. "And though *that* part of my anatomy remains intact, it is *highly* doubtful I will ever procreate again, even if I did find another interested woman to do so with!"

Another bit of laughter. "Outside of this ship, I have no ties, no affiliations of any kind!" the engineer went on. "And though my mind remains ever willing to continue scientific endeavors, I would only be able to do so through this vessel as it journeys across the universe!"

He then finished. "And yet here you are," Braun stated, looking back at Davis with a grin. "A man one-fourteenth my own age and still quite the child compared to all I have seen and experienced, speaking to me as if death, whether it comes for me in this instance or not, is something to be feared!" he said, again laughing. "Something to be horrified by!"

Suddenly realizing what the Professor was getting at, and much more that he *hadn't* lost his grip on reality, Davis sullenly turned away, now feeling like the idiot certain members of the crew thought of him as. Quietly he passed his tankard to Lloyd, remaining passive throughout the exchange. The barkeep picked up the vessel and refilled it with rum.

Laughter dying down, Braun at last explained. "Yes, I am keenly aware that I may no longer *be* in the next few days," the engineer explained, also passing his tankard over for Lloyd to refill. "But that doesn't mean I should be dreading the prospect."

Taking back his tankard, Davis let out a sigh as he looked down at the liquid. "I take it you're not afraid of death?" he asked in a far calmer voice.

Braun took a moment to consider. "Three hundred years or so ago, I probably would have been. But now, I hardly concern myself with it."

He took back his own refilled tankard. "It has only been through my dedication to science and my eternal yearning for further knowledge, both for myself and the rest of the universe, that I have continued for this long. Thus, death would simply be a release for me. And perhaps a gateway to a whole new plane to explore..."

"As well as a means to reuniting with your wife and family," Davis surmised.

Braun's bloated smile only increased at the prospect. "Precisely."

Davis sniffed. "Well, I wish I could say I was the same Professor, but I'm not."

Then, taking a long, hard drink beforehand, Davis at last admitted. "I'm afraid of death."

"Oh?" Braun let out, now keenly interested. "And why is this so?"

Davis let out a laugh of his own, a far darker one than Braun had given. "That's the funny part of it, I don't have a reason. I'm just *completely* and *utterly afraid*."

Watching as Braun became further intrigued, the helmsman elaborated.

"It's not like I'm afraid of being judged for whatever transgressions I've committed. After all, as the good book says, 'all have sinned and fallen short of the glory of God.' And, on the assumption that they actually exist, I'm not overly concerned about my ending up in Heaven or Hell..."

A frown crossed his face. "I'm just afraid of death in itself," he exclaimed. "To the point that I've gone well out of my way to keep on living..."

As extreme anxiety began to manifest, Davis closed his eyes. "I *really* don't want to die."

A brief silence ensued as if the words remained hovering in midair. This time, the only sound that could be heard was the light background hum of the *Black Sun*'s engines.

And then, with seeming understanding, Braun nodded. "Is that why you did what you did on Sumatra III?" he asked, holding no accusation whatsoever.

Hearing that question, Davis opened his eyes and appeared as though he were restraining tears. "Yes," he admitted, a look of slight annoyance crossing his expression. "That's why I jumped the gun on Sumatra III. Along with many other things that ended up biting me in the ass."

"I see," Braun replied sympathetically, gazing down at the counter. "It's not an unheard of malady. Death, even without all the religious and philosophical banter behind it, has always been a subject of fear for our species. In fact, I don't think there's an existence or being in the universe that hasn't feared it at one time."

He then shrugged in thought. "Some just fear it far more than others."

"Yes," Davis sighed, his grip tightening around his tankard. "And in the next few days, I'm going to be closer to it than I've ever been."

"Indeed," Braun agreed, this time hopefully. "And yet, this isn't necessarily a bad thing," he encouraged, earning a side glance from

Davis. "You are, after all, our helmsman. The one in charge of guiding the flight of this ship."

Braun smiled knowingly. "What better position should there be for one who fears death?" he pointed out. "As that one would naturally guide this ship away from death?"

Blinking, Davis looked away in consideration, feeling renewed somewhat. "I have to admit, I never thought of it that way before."

Retaining his smile, Braun raised his tankard. "Perhaps it is presumptuous of me, but I think we yet retain hope."

A small smirk appearing on his own lips, Davis raised his tankard as well. Both took a drink before putting their cups down again. "You..." Davis spoke up once more as soon as he swallowed. "You're not going to tell anyone else, are you?"

Again Braun chuckled. "I see no reason to."

Nodding in appreciation, Davis eyed the bartender.

"Don't look at me," Lloyd retorted while casually cleaning another tankard. "I just serve the drinks."

Hearing that, Davis nodded his thanks to the bartender as well. And yet, right after, Davis felt his smirk die away as the prospect of facing his worst nightmare, even if it was still days away, remained a deep fixture in his mind...

---

She had been sitting there for well over an hour. Her terminal was active, the appropriate program had been brought up, and the keyboard was within her reach. However, as her eyes lingered upon the blinking cursor on the pure white field, her mind remained just as blank. Even as she inwardly clawed at herself to come up with appropriate words. Words that would not only be the first she wrote to their intended recipients in years but words that she knew all too well she may not have another opportunity to share.

Sighing in frustration, Anna leaned back against her chair and stared at the ceiling of her quarters. After spending a good portion of the day either on the bridge at her station or performing checks on the *Black Sun*'s various systems with the maintenance crews, she was well and truly exhausted in body and mind. In fact, a part of her felt she should be resting, in the lounge having a drink or finding some other means to relax before her next duty shift. Her body's lethargy only emphasized that temptation. However, as much as it chafed her inside, she knew that she couldn't relax just yet. Not until she wrote her damned letter to her much further damned family.

As she continued staring at the blinking cursor, Anna knew she wasn't suffering from simple writer's block. Her situation, just like the relationship with her family back home, was far more complicated than that. Helping even less was that the more she continued to stare at her unwritten letter and think of the words she wanted to send back, the more her body yearned for a cold tankard of grog. A nagging voice in her mind pointed out that the more alcohol she consumed, the better the likelihood she would find the words to write, and as a bonus, it would also dull the affiliated memories. She initially chose to ignore that voice, but as the minutes went by with each blink of her cursor, the more she reconsidered.

And then her door buzzer rang, snapping the pirate out of her trance. "Enter," she replied out of reflex, right before her mind caught up and chastised her for not checking to see who it was first. For all Anna knew, it could have been Davis with a bouquet in one hand and a bottle of spiked champagne in another.

Fortunately, that turned out to not be the case. Door shifting open, Gran casually accepted her invitation and entered into her compatriot's domain.

"I'm surprised," the Lyran commented. "I didn't expect you to still be awake after all this time."

Anna grimaced in turn. "To tell the truth, I wish I weren't," she said before her frown disappeared. "But some things just can't wait."

"Ah," Gran replied as she took a nearby seat. "So who's the message to?"

Anna turned in mild surprise.

Sighing, Gran clarified. "I can hear the activity of the terminal in front of you, just as I can hear your muscular structure continuously shifting your body's sitting position. What I *don't* hear, however, is the sound of typing keys or the electronic noises associated a processing computer, which means you're not inputting commands and the terminal itself remains inactive. And finally, there's your breathing pattern, which is a constant yet drawn rate, indicating a deep yet inconclusive thought process and passive frustration."

Hearing all this, Anna couldn't help but look on in shock. The Lyran naturally picked up on this as well.

"And now your eyelid muscles have constrained, indicating your eyes have just widened in astonishment," Gran continued with a smirk. "Do you want me to continue, or has the point of my being blind but *not* helpless finally reached you?"

Now closing her eyes in a glare, doing the exact opposite of what the Lyran just described, Anna then asked. "How do you know the program I have active now is a writing one?"

Gran naturally grinned. "Computers, like musical instruments, generate different sounds depending upon how they are utilized. That and you wouldn't be in such a worn state if you were looking up some random cortex page."

Anna shrugged. "Depends on the page. After all, I could have been reading the latest on the Bahram Boys' breakup..."

"Besides the fact I've never heard you play one of their songs, which lends credence that you hold actual musical taste, you never struck me as a follower of boybands," Gran interjected with her usual sarcasm.

"Now, are you going to tell me who that message is intended for, or do you want me to describe, with exact detail, what you are currently digesting?"

A brief moment of silence lapsed before Anna, letting out her own sigh, conceded. "It's for my family," she explained with some hesitance. "Back on Orpheus."

Gran's head tilted up in surprise. "Orpheus?" she queried. "The headquarters world of the Dreyfus Company?"

Anna let out a breath. "Yes, that Orpheus," she confirmed.

Gran was quick to note the disdain within her compatriot's voice. On that, she was tempted to ask if there was any connection between the Dreyfus Company and Anna's family but decided it would be inappropriate. Even so, there was still one thing she had to ask.

"I take it you're not on good terms with your family?"

Anna let out a short, derisive laugh. "I've *never* been on good terms with my family. Part of the reason I became a pirate was just to get away from them."

"So I've heard," Gran surmised, recalling the story of Anna's impromptu wedding and the Flints "kidnapping" her alongside the wedding cake. "And yet, here you are."

The operations officer nodded. "I may hate them as far as I can throw one of them in zero grav, but they're still my family, and they deserve to know I might not be coming home ever again. Not that I would anyway."

She then faced back to the Lyran. "What about you?" she asked. "You... *recite* a message to your family?"

Gran smiled at the choice of wording. "Still formulating it," she said. "And like you, they're not overly fond of my leaving home and taking employment offworld."

"Let me guess," Anna posited. "They wanted you to become a singer."

Gran let out a laugh. Her species were viewed as singers and musicians the way Leos were regarded as religious zealots, and Delphinians were perceived as quirky and overfriendly technophiles. It was the most associated, and therefore stereotyped, profession allotted to her people.

"No, much worse," Gran replied. "They wanted me to be a florist."

Anna looked on in confusion. "How does that work?" she exclaimed. "Do Lyran flowers generate sound as well?"

Pausing in her own confusion, Gran then realized the misconception. "Excuse me, I suppose a more proper term would be *cristalist*. My family owns a crystal shop back in Jugum," she clarified, referring to a prominent city on her home planet.

"That makes more sense, yes," Anna agreed. As an almost entirely sound-based society, Lyrans valued crystals and other acoustically oriented minerals the way Terrans valued flowers. "The way I've heard it, your people don't care much for plants."

"Not entirely true," Gran clarified. "We utilize them like everyone else, namely for sustenance. It's just we don't regard them as 'beautiful' or 'pleasing' to our senses."

"Right, because they don't oscillate the way metals, minerals and ceramics do," Anna understood, then moving back to the subject at hand. "I take it they wanted you to inherit the shop?"

Gran nodded. "My brother Donal and I, yes," she replied, frowning. "We come from a long line of cristalists, and that shop has been in the family for generations. So, as far as our parents were concerned, we were the next in line."

Anna couldn't help but feel sympathetic. "But you both had other ideas."

Again Gran nodded. "We both wanted to reach the stars. Something that Lyran cristalists are seldom called to do."

She faced down again. "As a result, we ran away from home when we came of age. He ended up joining the military, and I took up with a freighter in desperate need of a skilled communications officer. As far as I know, neither of us has been home since."

"I see," Anna responded, looking down as well. "Do they know of your *current* occupation?"

Gran seemed hesitant about that. "Not yet," she admitted. "I guess I have little choice now."

"What about you? How did your family drive you all the way out here?" she asked. "Beyond marrying you off to some deadbeat?"

As that question was presented, Anna again turned back to her blank page, her brows furrowing. "They wanted me to take up the family business as well," she explained, feeling her fist tighten at the memories. "Only not as an heir, but as a servant to the *real* heir, and the rest of my family by extension."

Inadvertently she glowered, causing Gran to wince from the intensity.

"My marriage was meant to seal that fate. To put me in my 'rightful' place, and yet ensure that I would continue towing the family line and cleaning up all the messes," she elaborated disdainfully. "All so that my parents and my siblings could continue to make more messes and *still* believe themselves as perfection incarnate."

Sighing, she looked up again. "So you can understand why I'm having trouble writing them, even at this time."

"Indeed," Gran returned, letting out a breath of air as the tension washed away. Again she was tempted to ask what connection Anna's family held to the Dreyfus Company; from the way Anna described them, the Reeds, assuming that was their real name, weren't a simple group of Terran commoners. In fact, they sounded a lot like a particular family that she had heard of in passing.

However, she refrained at the last minute. "But as you said, they're still your family," she offered in place on the desired inquiry. "And you don't know if you'll get another chance."

Closing her eyes, Anna nodded in confirmation. "Yes," she acknowledged, before looking back at her terminal screen yet again. Even then, the cursor continued to blink aimlessly, all while Anna still could not come up with a single word.

---

Executing a combination of five punches toward her invisible foes, Kaguya leaped and performed a flying spin kick, one that would have broken the jaw of any opponent she would have otherwise been facing. Upon landing, she dropped down and completed a foot sweep that would have taken away her opponents footing, then jumped up again to deliver a followup roundhouse that would have incapacitated those she missed. A pair of palm thrusts, followed by another kick, this one straight and solid, finalized the fight sequence.

Deep within the lower decks of the *Black Sun*, specifically in the cargo bay that she had been using as a training space for the ship's raider contingent, the young ninja continued to fight her imaginary opponents, her various movements as rapidly and efficiently executed as they were graceful to behold. Though it was after hours, and the other raiders had long retired for the evening after a whole day of training and preparation, Kaguya only felt anxiousness from within; a kind of restlessness that could not be sated by simple relaxation. As she always did with such feelings, she chose to fight. Or more precisely, fight opponents that only she could see and make contact with; opponents that existed solely in her mind.

Normally this measure was more than enough to calm her and allow her to retire for the evening. But not now; not this night. Though she hadn't been paying attention to the time, Kaguya knew that it had been some time since she had begun her shadow fight. Yet, despite the tremendous physical and spiritual energy that she had exerted, she did not feel the least bit exhausted. Quite the contrary, in fact, she was even more restless than before. She felt as if her body could actually move on its own without her mind to direct it.

But of course, her mind was just as active as her body, and she could do nothing as it played its own contrasting melody to her present dance. Like a steady trickle of ice water, the thoughts, memories, and emotions poured out of her soul, even as she executed each punch and kick. The images of the near-death Flint Brothers, the grinning face of Raphael Drake, the picture of the solitary world of Ephesus, the knowledge that the final battle was nigh... it all flowed through her as she fought the shadows, all the while threatening to overwhelm her. To overtake her and break her under their strain.

Thus, Kaguya was not only fighting the shadows around her but also fighting against those within as well. And unlike the former, those within could do actual damage to her being.

Then, suddenly sensing another presence nearby, Kaguya twisted around and, with the blade appearing in her hand, launched a kunai straight into a nearby corner of the bay, one that was cast in substantial darkness. Upon the sound of the kunai impacting against the metallic wall, Kaguya straightened and glared.

"You have great audacity to come before me at this time."

Casually stepping out of the shadows, Lorelei merely grinned in turn. "Do I?" she asked, sweetly and innocently.

That display only served to infuriate Kaguya further; she flicked another kunai into her hand. "Give me one reason," she growled venomously as she brought the blade up into view. "Why I shouldn't carry out my warning from before."

Despite the viciousness behind the tone, Lorelei remained undeterred. "I can give you three," she replied. "First, my death would only result in the destruction of this ship. Second, you still need me both to unlock Arcadia and to potentially support you and the others in the coming battle. And third..."

Her smile increased. "You would risk angering *them*."

Rage suddenly consuming her, Kaguya launched the kunai at the intruder; she followed up with two more. However, whether by her aim or by the psion's power, none of the blades hit their target, instead they flew past Lorelei's immobile form. All while the siren retained her smile, which now took on a gloating tone.

"You're the one who drew them there!" Kaguya shouted with great fury, her voice echoing around the bay. "You're the reason they almost died!"

Though she continued holding her grin, Lorelei momentarily appeared stung by the accusations. "Perhaps..." she admitted before regaining herself. "But even so, neither of them would forgive you."

Furious, Kaguya turned around to face away from the psion. Lest she really did lose control. "What do you want?"

Lorelei smile grew. At last progress. "A moment of your time," she began. "Specifically, I want to establish a more peaceful disposition between us."

Kaguya, while remaining with her back turned, scoffed at the idea. "I have yet to eviscerate you. As far as I'm concerned, that's the extent of *any* disposition between us."

"An extent that I find limited," Lorelei replied as she approached the ninja, appearing unaffected by her vehemence. "To be perfectly honest, I believe you and I had a bad start. In fact, I do not see any reason why we cannot have a more amiable relationship."

Again Kaguya scoffed. "Apart from you being a manipulative witch," she shot back. "Namely to those I care about."

"As opposed to being a potential executioner?" Lorelei countered. Though Kaguya remained with her back turned, the psion knew that her comment struck a blow. She let out a small chuckle. "If I really am as callous as you perceive me, then I have much greater reason to kill you than anything else."

She then smiled again. "After all, I cannot have you costing me my most valuable pawns."

That too struck a blow, compelling Kaguya to turn to face the psion, palpable anger in her eyes. Regardless, Lorelei retained her smile.

"But I'm not," she replied softly. "Despite what you may think of me, I do not see them as a simple means to my end any more than you see them as targets to assassinate."

Slowly, Lorelei began to walk around the ninja. "Have I not proven that I do actually care for their well being?" she asked as she walked, Kaguya's eyes tracking her throughout her motion. "Have I not gone out of my way to ensure their survival?"

"You said it yourself," Kaguya spat. "They are your most valuable pawns."

"Fair enough. But even so..." the psion exclaimed as she moved back to her original position behind Kaguya. "...I know that, deep down inside, you know that I am not their enemy. Nor yours."

Kaguya's fist only clenched further, something Lorelei did well to notice.

"And that's part of your hate for me," she continued. "Because, despite my entrancing them with my song, you know that it is not the rocks that I am leading their ship toward. That I wish for their fortune and survival as much as my own."

"You are not helping yourself," Kaguya let out in a low voice as a kunai appeared in her palm.

Lorelei again remained undeterred. "For all your disdain, you know that I am *not* an adversary," she stated perceptively. "Otherwise, you would not have given me a warning at all; you would have attempted to kill me from the very start."

"Perhaps not," Kaguya rejoined in a low tone. "But you're still a threat."

"So you believe," Lorelei replied. "Because I am 'leading' those two on as the *kitsune* you claim me to be?"

"Because you are a creature of misfortune," Kaguya shot back scathingly. "One whose hubris and trickery have only brought harm to others. And will only *continue* to do so."

Lorelei let out a small laugh at that claim. "Which brings me to the second factor behind your hatred," the psion then came up to face the kunoichi directly. "You're afraid of losing those two not to *my* influence, but rather that of whatever may lay ahead of us. If not Arcadia itself..."

The motion a blur, Kaguya extended her hand and pressed the kunai edge against Lorelei's throat. Still, the psion remained unfazed, much to Kaguya's growing anger.

"You are leading them to their destruction."

"Or their betterment. Something else you cannot help but feel I just might be doing."

The ninja pressed the edge of her blade harder; it would not take much more pressure to draw blood. "You're already having us face an entire Imperial armada," she hissed. "What else would you have us, have *them*, go against?"

"The universe itself, and beyond if necessary. Which *they* would do all too willingly. Not unlike that 'utterly gutsy shinobi' you idolize so much..."

*"Kono ana!"* Kaguya shouted, anger again rising to the surface.

Lorelei merely shrugged off the outburst. "All the same, however, I reiterate, despite everything that has happened, and whatever inclinations we may hold for each other, I do not see any true basis for us to be enemies."

Slowly, she reached up and grasped Kaguya's wrist. "You may not agree to the extent I'm willing to go to reach Arcadia, nor my utilizing the Flints toward it," she said as she slowly drew the ninja's blade away from her throat. "But you and I both hold high regard for them, and we both want to see them not only survive this ordeal and those that may yet follow but succeed and prosper in the end."

Her hand only tightened as she persisted. "And for that, we would both do *anything* to protect them. Both from threats on the outside..." the psion spoke, again knowingly. "...and threats from *within*."

Lorelei saw, for the briefest moment, the hatred within Kaguya's eyes waver. She inwardly celebrated; her words had indeed reached the Blue Dragon princess. Perhaps not enough to make the ninja *not* see her as an object of hate, but just enough to make her think.

Thus, Lorelei unclasped her hold on the ninja's wrist, allowing it to drop to its owner's side.

"Surely we can reach a greater common ground than that," she said. "Perhaps even become *nakama*."

Disgust welled up on Kaguya's face. *Not likely,* she thought as she withdrew the kunai.

Even so, the psion's words remained with her. When it came down to it, she knew that Lorelei cared for the Flints' wellbeing, just as she had seen the psion go out of her way to ensure their continuation, and she acknowledged Lorelei actually felt guilt toward the events on Bonham IV. For all accounts, Kaguya knew, from a purely objective standpoint, that there was no reason to hold onto her hostility. In fact, again being purely objective, the psion had proven herself to be a worthwhile ally, if not an actual *friend*.

However, as disciplined as she was, Kaguya knew that objectivity had its limitations. Specifically, it ended where her instincts began. It was as Lorelei had said; her disdain toward her wasn't about the psion having malevolent intentions toward the Flints, but rather because she had drawn them onto a path that was entirely clouded and full of danger and misfortune. She was leading them onward like the *kitsune* Kaguya had once claimed her to be. All through manipulating their hopes and desires, such that they followed willingly and unconditionally.

And it was due to that factor that they had reached the ultimate misfortune. The brothers faced a battle against a full Imperial fleet, led by one of the best commanders in all of Starfleet, at the very world where their mother had perished. All because of a "slight" miscalculation, as well as great hubris on the psion's part. No, she had not intended for such an event to take place, of that Kaguya was sure, but the fact remained that, as with the fate that eventually befell all *kitsune*, Lorelei's trickery and pride had caught up to her and those she led on. And now, whether they proved victorious or not, they would pay with their lives, with only the slightest hope in cheating the *shinigami*.

That, of course, was not dismissing the other subject the psion had brought up, a subject that had haunted Kaguya from the very beginning. Just how far was she willing to go to reach Arcadia? Would she be willing to put aside her dream for the sake of her supposed *nakama*, or...?

Kaguya forced aside that thought. Like it or not, they remained on course to Ephesus, just as they remained set to face Drake and his fleet. Nothing would change that, least of all Kaguya's hatred. Especially in the face of the psion's admittedly noble attempt to mend their differences.

Thus Kaguya had no choice but to relent. "I will consider your words, but not now," she stated, allowing her disdain to cool somewhat. "For the moment, I wish to be alone."

Nodding in understanding, Lorelei turned around and quietly proceeded toward the door.

As she watched her depart, however, Kaguya couldn't help but inquire once more. *How do I know this isn't another manipulation on your part,* she purposely thought with near accusation. *That you're not trying to entrance me into your song?*

Continuing on, Lorelei grinned slightly toward the inquiry. *How do you know you're not already,* she replied telepathically, before disappearing past the doorway.

Now alone once again, Kaguya let out a sigh before she went back to her fight with her shadows. As she pushed back all lingering thoughts and concentrated once more on her physical motions, a part of her couldn't help but wonder...

————————— —————————

With Apache having long retired for the evening, sickbay had transitioned into a strangely tranquil state. The lights were dimmed and a very present, very encompassing silence had settled into the area, with only the minute sounds of operating medical machinery, as well as the breathing of the still dormant Flint brothers, breaking the quietness. Combined with the number of Aquilan ceremonial masks and icons that had been placed around the compartment one could almost believe that again, with the exception of the Flints, only spirits actively dwelled within sickbay at this time. Spirits and the foreboding sense that accompanied all medically inclined facilities.

As for the Flints themselves, they too had made a great transition from their original states. With Apache having performed the proper surgeries and medical procedures on them, they were no longer as close to death as they had been three days ago, but neither had quite recovered from their wounds. They remained in dormant, yet otherwise stable conditions, with their bodies now placed in medical beds in the sickbay's main area. Long stripped of their clothing and personal articles, their bodies were swathed in blankets while breather masks covered their mouths. The scanners and computers of their respective beds continued to monitor and administrate their healing. Overall they were no longer in any danger, but there was still some time yet before either Jon or Alex could recover.

Knowing this, Kaiser, upon entering the sickbay, quietly moved through the facility, being sure not to touch or interact with any of the medical devices, whether technological or rudimentary, that were present. This was more than a little difficult for the Herculean given his body mass, but he remained careful all the same. After all, he dared not risk causing any additional harm to the brothers as they slept.

Once he reached the beds, Kaiser stood and gazed at the two Terran men that laid upon them. Though his physical eyes easily identified them as adult men, having long transitioned physically and mentally from their early years, the eye in Kaiser's mind only showed them as the children that they had once been. The two small and quite fragile Terran boys that Lady Flint had personally tasked him to watch over and protect. To the point that she had even stated that he was to look upon them as his own brethren.

*Do not think of them as your wards, but as your younger brothers,* Morganna had told him, her voice now reciting from his deepest memories. *Brothers that you are to love and look after as well as protect.*

Kaiser recalled the feeling of warmth from Morganna reaching out and laying her hand on his shoulder. *Those two are my greatest treasures, Kaiser, the dearest and most valued parts of my life,* she had told him, her eyes sparkling as a warm smile embraced her lips. *And from now on, with respect to your father and biological siblings, they shall be yours as well.*

That exchange caused the years to revert back into Kaiser's mind; memories that he both treasured and many times wished to forget. Besides their statuesque physiques, Herculeans were renowned throughout the galaxy for two additional facets; their long lives and their being universally family oriented. The first was self-explanatory given their impressive physical states, while the latter was due to the dynamics of their so-called society. Herculeans were a highly tribal race that was constantly at war within itself.

As a result, Herculeans valued large and extensive families above all else, as war and death were constants within Herculean culture.

In Kaiser's case, he was the eldest child of Golem, having been born well before the Herculean patriarch had become the infamous

"Stonebone" pirate. War and other tribal conflicts had been numerous throughout his early years, as was death taking members of his family. From his beloved mother to his various siblings, Kaiser had seen many of his own die during his childhood, only for many more to follow when he had reached adulthood. By the time his father had at last grown disillusioned with his tribe and race and made the monumental decision to take his family offworld and into the galaxy at large, only twelve of Kaiser's siblings were still alive. Twelve out of what had once been well over thirty.

The remembrance only caused Kaiser to cringe and his fists to tighten momentarily. As per tradition with the eldest child within a Herculean family, it had fallen to him to manage and look out for his various brothers and sisters. As numerous as they were, he had been close to all of them. He had known all their names, their likes and dislikes, hopes and dreams, just as he had known exactly how each and every one of them had perished. Their passing, in turn, never became easier to accept and move on from. In fact, for the longest time, Kaiser had felt that a little bit of himself had died each time one of his own was taken. Thus, by the time his father had at last left Hercules behind for good, Kaiser had felt as little more than a hollow shell, nearly devoid of all feeling and emotion beyond spite and anger, his own hopes and dreams long spent.

Little had he known at the time that hope would return to him, in the form of a young and quite beautiful Terran woman who had birthed two sons. At first, Kaiser had been apprehensive when his father had directed the family into Morganna Flint's employment, and that apprehension had grown when Lady Flint had assigned him as the "family bodyguard" to both herself and her children.

However, as the time passed, and as Kaiser continued to watch over her and those two boys, who had not been born into war and strife and who retained hopes and dreams for the future, the Herculean slowly began to feel himself return to his original "completed" state. That, at long last, Kaiser had gained a little of what he had lost with his brothers and sisters long ago. Just as, in the words of Morganna Flint, he had gained two more brothers, as vastly younger as they were, to look after.

A small, barely audible sigh escaped from his lips at that memory. Morganna Flint was long dead now and, upon her demise, he had again lost a part of himself, specifically his ability to speak. But even so, her children, the vastly younger brothers he had looked after, were still alive and before him. As if in validation, he quietly reached out and, as softly as he could given his hardened flesh, stroked their faces, one after the other. Just as he had done during their much younger years, upon his turning them in for their "bedtime".

Feeling their flesh against his own, Kaiser again inwardly remarked how completely different these two were from himself. Whereas his skin was rough and hard, theirs was soft and smooth to the touch. Whereas his skin radiated cold not unlike stone, theirs held a very present and very tangible heat that warmed his fingers. And while his body remained unblemished, again like polished stone, Kaiser could just depict the first of numerous scars along the brothers' forms, all illustrating years of hardship between the death of their mother and the present. Years they had endured without him by their side.

And now, it seemed that history was bound to repeat itself. Already heavily wounded, the Flints and their compatriots were now charging back to the very place they had lost their mother. The very place Kaiser had once again lost his family. Only this time, they were bound to lose their own lives along with those around them, Kaiser included.

Gritting his rock-like teeth together, Kaiser withdrew his hands, just as they began to clench into fists, his knuckles making distinct tightening noises as he did. No, he refused to believe that, to believe any of it. Yes, they were returning to Ephesus, the place they had lost so much, but this time it would be different. This time, Kaiser swore to himself, he would not lose his family again. The brothers, *his* brothers, no matter how fragile they were compared to him, would survive, as would their ship and their crew. And he would fight the entirety of the Terran

Empire, and the other Twelve Galactic Powers along with them, to ensure it.

For, alongside the rest of his family, they were the dearest and most valued parts of his life.

Thus, with a renewed sense of duty, if not hope, Kaiser took one last glance at the Flints, who continued to sleep under his gaze. And once more, in his mind's eye, he saw the children, the siblings, that he had protected and looked after so long ago. With that image imprinted into his mind, the Herculean let out a small, warm smile toward the pair, before turning around and discreetly making his exit.

The sickbay once again returned to its completely tranquil state.

# Chapter XXXII: Precipice

*He was no more than ten years old, only three years away from the treacherous beginnings of adulthood. A brilliant boy, many had remarked of his keen intellect, which, if expected given his lineage, was said to surpass most of his age and even some of the adults.*

*He was kind and courteous, sweet and innocent, deep minded and thoughtful, all the while possessing none of the darker experiences of life nor the marring traits that were inherent through those of greater age. This would likely change as he grew older and came to understand the chaotic and oft times merciless universe around him, but for the time being his young spirit roamed free and untainted.*

*That it was only eight more days until Christmas made him all the more exuberant. He had taken to running about the halls of his family estate with wild abandon, often leaping up and down in joy and anticipation over the celebrations. Unlike most his age, he cared little about the presents he would receive upon that day.*

*Though he enjoyed and cherished them like anyone else would, they were mere accessories toward the holiday's true meanings. Life and celebration, love and family, laughter and merriment... those were the things that he looked forward to the most, as the ancients of his race had done long before him. Alongside that, it was also one of the few days in which his mother, whom he loved dearly, and the rest of his "family" would not be working the "business" as they called it.*

*Thus, as his mind raced alongside his body, bringing about images of the magnificent celebrations that awaited him and his family only eight days away, he ran through the decorated halls of the estate like a comet – a description he had just thought of, much to his pride – in constant search for his wayward mother. He had much to talk to her about now, and it was almost lunchtime anyway. Even his baby brother, who was five years younger, was starting to get hungry.*

*During the last hour, he had been looking over the Apotheca, the Terran mass information database, on various subjects, namely Christmas based, both historical and modern, when he had stumbled over a story that he had never heard before. A story that entailed a strange, grouchy monster who, possessing a heart two sizes too small and a deep hatred toward all things Christmas, snuck into a neighboring town in the dark of night and stole all the townspeople's Christmas items, only to learn, at the very precipice of his actions, what the true spirit of Christmas really was. A story that spoke of hatred and isolation being turned into love and redemption, alongside acceptance that there was more to the world around one than what one may have initially believed.*

*Needless to say, he had loved the story so much that he just had to share it with his mother. Though he suspected that she had heard it, it was after all an old story, and she held her own deep interest in such things, that didn't stop him in the least. In fact, it only increased his desire to discuss it with her, as he was interested to hear her own explanations. Where it came from, who wrote it, what else it could have meant and many other subjects that held his interest and fascination.*

*Eventually, his search came to an end as his ears picked up the sound of her voice from a nearby room. Slowing down considerably, he quietly moved toward the room, only to hear additional voices coming from within. It wasn't hard to recognize those other voices; they were his mother's "officers" and subordinates, those who followed her and bore*

*the sigil of the gold dragon upon their own ships. That could only mean
that whatever was being discussed was of great importance toward the
"business". He frowned as he felt the first vestiges of disappointment.
There was no way he could wrestle his mother away from work when
such discussions were being held.*

*He supposed he could simply wait for her to finish before entering,
though that in itself could take hours depending upon what was
being discussed. He decided it was the best option and so made his
way toward the door regardless. It was then he noticed that the door,
through some apparent malfunction, had not closed all the way. It was
just barely open, revealing the inside of the room from the smallest
divide. Now even more curious, and completely contrasting his original
run, he quietly crept up to the door and, ensuring that he made the least
amount of noise possible, peaked inside.*

*He saw his mother standing before her officers, all dressed in the black
and gold clothes that were prevalent throughout both the "business"
and upon their homeworld. Whatever they were discussing seemed to
be of great importance; though he couldn't quite understand the words
being exchanged, he did understand the tones behind them.*

*While his mother remained calm and composed, if somewhat direct
and forceful, the other reactions were mixed between disbelief and
uncertainty. While his mother was quite adamant about the subject at
hand, some of the officers seemed to have great doubt toward her, with a
couple even questioning whether "it", whatever "it" was, was worth the
risk. Some claimed that "it" no longer existed; that "it" was just a myth
from ancient times, and that she was chasing after something nonexistent.
And then there was one who claimed that "it" was not meant to be found;
that "it" had been purposely lost and was to remain so.*

*Then, after a brief exchange, one of the officers spoke up and asked
just how she was going to "unlock" the item under discussion; that
apparently some had claimed that "it" was not only lost but also locked
away. With that question, he watched as his mother reached into her*

*coat pockets and withdrew a pair of peculiar looking objects. One of gold, and one of silver. Both shaped like keys to his eyes, though not the "modern" keys he was used to. Rather, keys that belonged to the stories that he read; keys that directly interacted and unlocked the boxes, or treasure chests, in question.*

*Upon seeing those keys, the officers all silenced, which was exactly what his mother had intended. The message given, she withdrew the keys back to her pockets, then stating that it would still be some time before they would be able to pursue "it", again whatever "it" was. However, when the time was right, and they were all prepared, she assured them, they would go on to the "promised land".*

*And when one of the officers asked what the "promised land" was, he watched as his mother, flashing a mysterious smile, began to describe a lone red planet orbiting an equally lone red star...*

## Flint Pirates umbra *Black Sun*
## Arcspace

Consciousness slowly returning to his mortal form, Jon's eye fluttered open, straining to adjust to the light. He could already tell that he was in the *Black Sun*'s sickbay; besides the fact it was the most logical place for him to be outside of before God and his final judgment, both the lighting, the smell, and the surrounding Aquilan masks and icons were all too familiar to him. It also helped that his body, while no longer in critical condition, had a sharp pain in the chest area that indicated he was, indeed, still alive. After all, the way Jon understood it, he would have either felt no pain or unending pain if he had passed onto whatever awaited him.

Sighing at the thought, he pulled back the blanket that covered him to inspect his injuries. Aside from having several additional scars on his torso, ones from being operated on recently, there didn't seem to be any other wounds. The pain in his chest, while somewhat aggravating, also wasn't as bad as it could have been. Thus, Jon could only conclude that not only was he still alive, but he was now healed of the wounds he had endured on Bonham. The wounds inflicted upon him by Raphael Drake.

A tinge of anger colored Jon's face at that name, all while his memory recalled the events that were entailed. After fifteen years, he had, at last, come face to face with the one who had cornered the *Morgan le Fay* at Ephesus; the one who was directly responsible for his mother's death. The result was just as spectacular as it was damning. Jon, in one of the very few times in his life, had lost control and attempted to kill Drake then and there, only to be repelled by the opposite Devilblade Wielder and eventually defeated in battle. The sudden intensification of the pain in his chest served to further remind him of his defeat, and Jon had a feeling that pain would remain with him for some time yet. As would the visage of Drake's mocking face.

Then he remembered that he hadn't fought Drake alone; he instinctively glanced to his side. There, he saw Alex lying on another medbed, still unconscious but otherwise appearing alive and unharmed. Seeing that, as well as confirming that his younger brother was indeed breathing, Jon let out a breath of air he hadn't realized he had been holding. Yes, they had been defeated, but both of the Flint brothers were still very much alive. And as long as they were alive, they would only continue on in spite of their present disgrace.

"About time you're conscious," a very familiar and very grumpy voice spoke up from the other side of the room. "You and your brother have been taking up space in my sickbay for a week now."

Sighing once more, Jon turned to see Apache saunter over to him, his face holding a cross expression. However, the elder Flint need only look into the Aquilan's eyes to see the doctor's relief toward his awakening.

"Any more and I would have woken you up myself," Apache firmly stated, his tone also belying his relief. "With or without utilizing certain kinds of sharp and pointy objects."

Jon could only nod in both acceptance and discreet thanks. "Clothes?"

Apache gestured his approval. "Go ahead, I suggest you try black and gold."

Though somewhat tempted to reply to that, Jon didn't feel like trading barbs with his doctor at this time. He merely got up from the bed and proceeded to reform his clothes. It was only at that time, much to his dismay, that he realized the strain on his body. He was forced to grit his teeth as he moved around.

"I suppose this is where you lecture me on what happened before?"

Apache pretended to be nonplussed. "Would never dream of it, Jonathan. I mean sure, you went off and picked a fight with a Starfleet Admiral of all people, in which you not only endangered yourself but your brother as well. And the only reason you would have *ever* done something so irresponsible would be because you invariably lost yourself to your rage and played right into said Admiral's hands."

He then fixed his patient with a hardened glare. "And then there's the fact that your actions put the whole crew in jeopardy, up to and including the part where Barbarossa had to risk the entire ship just to save your sorry carcass..."

After allowing a momentary pause for the words to sink in, the Aquilan then waved it all off.

"But no, I would never, *never* lecture you on such things," he spoke dryly. "Nor how much of a cretin you are, nor that if your mother were still alive, she would beat you senseless for acting so stupidly. Hell, I wouldn't even point that, had I not delivered you personally, I would question whether or not you were actually her child."

He then smiled sardonically. "That would all be beneath me."

"I'm sure it would," Jon replied just as dryly. That's when another thought came to mind, specifically around the final phase of the fight. "I should be dead Apache," he spoke in a dismayed voice. "As you said, I played right into his hands, and he didn't hesitate."

"Very true," Apache concurred.

Jon gestured at his chest. "So why am I still alive?"

Knowing precisely what Jon meant, Apache couldn't help but swallow before he proceeded over to a nearby vidscreen. A second later, the vidscreen activated, displaying an anatomical readout. "Take a look at your stomach and lungs," he instructed. "Do you notice anything in particular?"

Having just reformed his vest and belt, Jon glanced over the readout and quickly realized what Apache was hinting at; a set of highlighted areas around those very parts, specifically where Berith had pierced.

"What is it?"

Apache raised a talon as if wagging a finger. "That, Jonathan," he replied evenly, almost conspiringly, "is, or more accurately *was*, residue Devilblade energy."

Hearing that, Jon took a closer look at the screen, only to reel back in shock. "Was it doing what I think it's...?" he nearly gaped, eye widened.

"No, it didn't heal you," Apache replied reassuringly, knowing how much such a prospect terrified the elder Flint. "If it had, things would have turned out a lot differently, wouldn't they?"

Jon nodded, feeling immense relief. Though entirely possible, one *never* used a Devilblade to heal! To do so was to inevitably lead the one being healed into possession by the blade. Thus, amongst Devilblade Wielders, healing was considered the ultimate taboo, akin to trading one's soul for the devil's respite.

The thought only caused Jon inward revulsion; he would have rather died than allowed Astaroth or any other blade to heal and possess him. The same choice his mother before him had made.

"Instead," Apache continued, snapping Jon out of his thoughts. "The energy 'merely' sealed the wounds, keeping your organs from bleeding out and making them continue to function simultaneously," the Aquilan stated. "Just long enough until you were transported here, at which point the energy dissolved. Possibly to allow me room to operate."

Jon felt a perturbing feeling well up inside him. "And Alex?"

Apache shook his head. "He wasn't as grievously wounded as you, so Drake didn't apply the technique on him. However, if it did come to that point, I have little doubt he would have done the same."

The Aquilan then fixed his patient with a hard gaze. "I'm sure I don't have to tell you how fine and delicate such a procedure is, or how much control the Wielder would have to possess in order to execute it, especially in the middle of combat."

Jon looked up in mild surprise at the realization. "He spared me."

Apache nodded. "And he went well out of his way to do it," he stated. "To impale you and simultaneously seal the wound is not something that can be done so easily. Even for a Devilblade Wielder."

Jon frowned as the most likely explanation came to mind. "He did it because he can't afford to kill me just yet," he exclaimed in dismay. "Not until I lead him to Arcadia."

"Perhaps," Apache spoke in concurrence. Though it was the most likely explanation, the Aquilan couldn't help but wonder if there were additional reasons behind the Admiral's actions.

Jon also felt that there was more there, but decided not to contemplate it too deeply. He had things of greater importance to worry about at this time.

"Did Lorelei retrieve Aurea?"

Appearing more hesitant to answer this time, Apache eventually nodded. "Yes, she did," he said, before reaching out his right arm with Jon's eyepatch in his palm. "And with it in tow, the Circumgressus has identified Arcadia's resting place."

Nodding in gratitude, Jon took the eyepatch and quickly slipped it on. Now, sans his greatcoat, he was fully dressed. A condition that made him feel complete.

"What is it?"

This time, Apache did not answer straight away, with a measure of disturbance entering his eyes. Catching onto the latter, Jon pressed regardless.

"Apache!" he demanded.

Clicking his beak, Apache closed his eyes and at last relented.

"Ephesus," he answered solemnly. "According to the Circumgressus, Arcadia is on Ephesus."

All at once, Jon's world came to a halt as that single word seemingly echoed in his ears. Feeling a cold and underlying shock well up from inside of him, accompanied by a feeling of remorse, Jon solemnly closed his eye and let out a rush of air from his nostrils. It was an answer that he had almost expected, and yet it had caught him off guard all the same. For Arcadia to be at rest in the very place where so many lives, including his and his brother's and much of the *Black Sun*'s present crew, had been changed forever was as fitting as it was abhorrent. A place that held many ghosts, some of whom still walked among the living.

That's when Jon recalled the scene from before. The memory from eighteen years ago that frequently emerged within his mind's eye; the time in which he saw his mother speaking to her officers about the future expedition to Ephesus, with what he believed to be Aurea and Argentum in hand. As his shock gave way to wonder, Jon quietly moved away from the Aquilan, his gaze turning to the side of the room. Then, as his arms folded, he began to ponder.

"You don't really think that's a coincidence. Do you?"

Apache seemed confused. "I don't understand."

Taking a breath, Jon began to explain. "Three years before the first expedition to Ephesus, my mother held a secret meeting with her chief officers. At the time, I didn't understand what the meeting was about, but I think I do now."

"Oh?" Apache asked, now intrigued.

Jon continued. "During the meeting, she spoke of searching for something on Ephesus, something that had been hidden and locked away for ages, which only she had a lead on," he now spoke conspiringly. "Something that required two keys, one of gold and one of silver, to unlock."

He then fixed his gaze back on Apache. "I don't suppose she informed you of any of it, did she?"

Apache shook his head at the notion. "Why would she? I'm the family doctor, not a fleet commander," he said, before looking down in thought. "However, if you are suggesting what I think you are, then that puts many things into context."

"Yes?" Jon replied, now intrigued in turn.

Apache elaborated. "For the most part, no one within the Gold Dragon or the other clans understood why your mother had gone to Ephesus in the first place. The other Lords pressed her on it before the trip, but she never gave a definitive answer, and though it was suspected those closest to her were in the know, they wouldn't give any explanations either."

He stroked the bottom of his beak with an outstretched talon as he recalled. "Whatever the truth was, however, there was *something* there that she wanted. Something that seemed to draw her in..."

Again Jon frowned at the idea. Could that have been the true motive behind the expedition to Ephesus? Could his mother have been seeking Arcadia fifteen years ago? Again, it seemed the most likely explanation, but Jon wondered if there were additional reasons.

And there was also the question of *how*. How could his mother have even heard of Arcadia? As well, how could she have understood the Predecessor language well enough to read over Arcadia's unlocking process, namely in utilizing Aurea and Argentum for it? And how could she have pinpointed Arcadia's location without the aid of the Circumgressus, which Jon didn't recall her possessing at the time?

Amidst the various explanations that his mind came up with, one was prominent. An answer that belied another all too certain secret that Jon, and only Jon, was privy to, even in the modern time. A secret that he had kept to himself for fifteen years since that fateful day.

He decided, as with Drake's allowing him to live, there was no reason to dwell on the subject now, especially in front of Apache. Thus he moved on.

"Are we heading there now?" Jon asked.

Though Apache noted the quick change in subject, he decided it was best to dismiss it as well. "So I last heard," he replied. "We should be there in a few days time, give or take the usual obstructions and schedule slips."

Before Jon could reply, both suddenly heard a soft groan from nearby. They turned to see Alex, having seemingly just awakened, begin to stretch his arms.

"Morale is, naturally, quite low," Apache continued to explain as they watched the younger Flint sit up in his bed and let out a long yawn. "General consensus is that none of us will be coming back."

"I take it they all know what's chasing us?" Jon inquired. It was an obvious question, but he felt the need to ask it anyway.

"With how fast news travels around here?" Apache replied rhetorically. "Give it an hour, and we'll be hearing about Davis' latest round of digestion problems."

"Now there's an image I didn't need at this time," Alex moaned as he rubbed the back of his head. "What'd you do to him, Apache? Spike his drink?"

A smirk enclosed Apache's lips. "A little dosage of Fuchsium Eight," he replied assuredly. "The upstart owes me money from the last Rhinos-

Tigers game."

Alex laughed. "Well, I can't cast stones there," he replied, recalling what he did to Tom Ferret so long ago.

A moment later, Alex was fully awake and sitting upon the side of his bed, looking over to Jon and Apache expectedly. "So," he began, "what did I miss?"

Taking another breath to force back the apprehension, Jon began to explain everything. And following that, what they had to do once Alex was dressed.

---

Lorelei was on her way back to her quarters when she sensed a sudden surge of activity throughout the ship, with much of it centered around the lounge area. And if that were not apparent enough, she saw several crew members, clearly in a great hurry, rush past her toward that destination, all holding onto a mixture of shock and great anticipation to whatever it was that had just occurred.

For a moment, she stood and watched as more people moved around her, all heading toward the same place. Whatever had happened, she realized, was causing commotion throughout the ship, such that those who were close enough to the lounge had abandoned their duties to rush onto the scene. Needless to say, it wasn't hard to guess what that cause was, much to her own rising hope.

Picking up her pace, Lorelei moved down the deck toward the lounge, the zeal and fervor from the various gathered minds intensifying as she drew closer. After nearly running from corridor to corridor, she, at last, came to the lounge and entered through the set doors, barely waiting but a moment for them to open. Once inside, she saw that there was indeed a great gathering and accompanying commotion, all of it centered around the bar area. As she approached, that said gathering, upon taking notice of her, parted to allow her through.

There she saw a sight that she, in spite of all her power, hadn't expected to see for some time yet. Casually sitting upon the barstools, tankards of rum placed beside either of them, the Flint brothers looked outward and continued to address the surrounding crew, who were all too appreciative for their recovery. Standing closest to them were Kaguya, Anna, Davis, Gran, and Kaiser, who, while doing their part to keep the rest of the crew in order, all shone with visible relief.

Lorelei picked up on the various mental images of the transference. True to form, the Flints had merely entered the lounge, specifically during the off hours and casually made their way to the bar where they ordered drinks. The present crew noticed the entrance but had remained hesitant in approaching, however, upon the brothers' drink orders, had crossed the boundary with Kaguya even going as far as to almost tearfully embrace the pair once she realized they were alright.

Even Davis, who appeared to be quite sickly, was rather joyous over his captain and first officer having made their recovery. After all, as he and much of the other crewmen had surmised, they would especially need the two Devilblade Wielders in the coming fight. Not to mention Jon's knack for planning.

As she approached, a grin now encompassing her lips, Lorelei waited for the pair to notice her before speaking.

"Somehow, I knew I would find you two here after your recovery."

Casually taking a drink from his tankard, Alex smiled. "What can we say? Neither of us has had a decent drink in a week."

Taking his own drink, Jon observed the psion before speaking. "Your eyes are gleaming," he posited. "Are you that exhilarated to see us active once more?"

"Very much so," Lorelei replied just as nonchalantly. "With all that is happening, it would have been quite difficult to search for a new Captain and First Officer at this point."

"Oh?" Jon rejoined with a raised eyebrow. "You were set to replace us that quickly?"

"Only if necessary Captain. Only if necessary," she shot back, allowing her own warmth and relief to be seen in her gaze. Then, as a measure of remorse shifted into her eyes, she began to say. "I..."

"Don't worry about." Jon knew what she was going to say. "What happened before was more my fault than yours," he exclaimed, then grinned knowingly. "Besides, isn't it natural for every songstress to have at least one overzealous fan?"

Momentarily considering that point, Lorelei nodded. "I suppose that's one way of looking at it, yes," she admitted with a warm, appreciative smile. "Should I consider myself honored?"

"Only if you like insane stalkers," Davis replied dryly from the side, now looking quite sickly. "Does anyone remember what we had for lunch today?"

Sensing an opportunity, Alex, with an insidious smile, spoke in a sing-song tone. "Just the usual Davis, pizza with cream cheese, sea rat sausage, blue peppers..."

"Don't forget the white garlic and wine sauce," Anna chimed in, watching in bemusement as Davis turned an interesting shade of green.

Alex comically slapped his head. "How could I?" his smile grew larger as he watched Davis turn an even darker green. "And then there were the sides, futomaki with wasabi..."

Suddenly gagging violently, Davis covered his mouth before running toward the lounge door. The doors barely parted as he reached them, with Davis running through just as Barbarossa, Boss and Braun entered. The trio came to a point in the middle of the lounge before stopping completely, with Barbarossa in the center.

All at once the celebration ceased as the group took note of the harsh expression on the Leo's face, his eyes piercing straight through the crowd and into Jon's. Knowing what was about to happen, Jon silently rose from his stool and walked through the crowd, until he was facing the Leo. A brief silence ensued before Jon began to speak.

"My compliments Barbarossa," Jon stated evenly. "From what I understand, you ran this ship quite well while Alex and I were incapacitated." *And you didn't even so much as attempt to take* full *command, Kaiser's presence notwithstanding.*

Barbarossa caught the underlying message but chose to ignore it for the moment. "It was the least I could do," he replied with a measure of anger. "Considering your foolishness nearly cost us everything."

A cold swell quickly encompassed the lounge; even Lloyd froze in his motions, as the Leo continued.

"Do not misunderstand me, Captain," Barbarossa declared, purposely emphasizing Jon's position. "I sympathize with you and your desire to avenge your mother, but that is no excuse to give in to your rage as you did and lash out like an incipient cub," his voice grew more and more terrible as he went on. "You needlessly pitted yourself and your brother against an opponent that you had no bearing, no advantage over, and you did it out of anger. You did none of this when you fought me before, or any of the other times you took a direct hand. You were always in control, and you never, *never* let your emotions rule you."

The Leo then raised his arms out, gesturing to the surrounding crewmen. "And if that wasn't enough, your actions not only jeopardized yourself and your brother but your ship and crew as well," Barbarossa admonished, watching as Jon listened, as did Alex who came up beside his brother. "It is not just the two of you anymore; you're no longer two orphans floating between worlds, taking on random work as it comes by. You are a Captain now, and your ship is crewed by sentients that you have drawn in under your care. Under your command."

Then, almost daringly, Barbarossa stepped forward, until he was nearly face to face with Jon.

"Whatever actions you take now not only reflect on yourself but those you see around you. By your hand, you will either bring this crew to providence as you promised upon this ship's launch from Ryugu, or you will bring them to damnation."

Jon was quick enough to catch the 'will' in that statement. As in he hadn't damned them just yet.

"Because this is your first official captaincy, I can understand why none of this has settled in with you yet," Barbarossa stated. "After all, the best way one may learn is through direct experience."

He then brought up his right hand, baneclaw extending. "That being said, I will tell you now," he glowered. "This is the *only* time I, and this crew, will allow you to act so callously, so foolishly," he affirmed, bringing the tips of his claws directly in front of Jon's eye. "Should you ever do so again..."

He then folded his hand into a fist. "We will not be so forgiving," he avowed in a low growl.

Jon, slowly and cautiously, turned away from Barbarossa and surveyed the surrounding crew. And indeed, despite their retaining relief and sympathy toward him and Alex, he could see in their eyes that Barbarossa had spoken the truth. Some of the less sympathetic ones had even recalled whatever anger they had possessed initially, such that their own return gazes were more condemning.

Even Boss, who continued to stand beside Barbarossa, merely folded her arms as he looked toward her, giving off a glance that told him she was dissatisfied and expected better of him. And as for Braun, the engineer merely stood by without visible emotion, seemingly in wonder toward how Jon was going to take it all.

"And now," Barbarossa spoke as he stepped away from Jon and took a seat at the bar. A second later, Lloyd appeared with a tankard of Leo raki. The Kapta took a sip of before continuing. "We stand at the precipice Captain, moving toward what may be our final battlefield."

This time, he gazed at Jon challengingly. "What will you do at this time?" he posited. "Especially when it was by your hand that we have come this far?"

Knowing precisely what Barbarossa was inferring, Jon, without another word, brought his left hand up and tapped his wristcom, accessing the *Black Sun*'s whole intercom system.

With a slowly drawn breath, Jon started.

"All hands, this is Captain Flint," his voice sounding throughout the ship. "By now you have heard I and the First Officer have recovered from our wounds and are walking amongst you once more. Part of this message is to verify that fact."

He briefly paused before going on.

"The other part of this message is an apology," he stated, causing all heads to snap up in shock. "Because of my arrogance, we have now been thrust into a situation in which none of us may return. In approximately three days time, we will be on our final approach to Ephesus, where our original objective awaits...only to face an Imperial taskforce led by one of Terra's greatest Admirals, and perhaps additional elements along the way, before we can lay claim to our prize," he paused again. "One ship against the might of the Imperial Thirteenth Fleet."

Again Jon glanced around to see if the crew present were listening to his words, and was satisfied to know that they were.

"Perhaps it was inevitable from day one that we would face an adversary such as this, perhaps my actions on Bonham simply finalized our course," he said. "Whatever you decide for yourselves, we are set regardless, and as Captain of this ship, the responsibility of our fates rests with me, and me alone."

He then looked to Lorelei, who nodded for him to continue.

"And yet..." he said, momentarily trailing off in thought. "And yet, at the risk of embracing further arrogance on my part, I believe there is still hope for us."

Yet again the surrounding crew looked up, this time with inquiry.

"From the very first day, in which I and only a handful of you took this ship from one of the most secure installations ever conceived, we have fought on our own and yet accomplished the impossible," he affirmed, his voice rising with every word. "Three times before we have done battle against the Imperials, and three times we have emerged, even if by the barest factor, victorious."

He glanced around yet again.

"Some would equate this to the advanced capabilities of this ship, but I believe it is due to something far more," he declared. "I believe it is due to all of *you*. You men and women, harkened from different origins and different backgrounds, now gathered upon this very ship and performing your duties and ensuring our survival and fortune," he stated, again momentarily pausing. "I believe *you* to be the masters of this ship's fate. I believe *you* to be the *true* captains of this ship's soul."

With that, he took another breath.

"Thus, as we stand here on the precipice, looking upon the coming battlefield that will either be the result of your successes or the culmination of my mistakes, I can do no more than ask of you, the true power behind the *Black Sun*...Whatever awaits us at Ephesus... Whatever we may face upon that lone world... Will you follow me?" he spoke almost pleadingly. "Will you fight with me?"

Then, for perhaps the final time, he looked at the gathered crew. And for the first time since he had begun this journey, he could not read their eyes or their emotions.

"Again, it is still three days to Ephesus. If necessary, we can drop out of arc and signal any nearby ships to take on passengers. From there, you may go to whatever destination you deem fit."

His eye then narrowed. "However, if you too believe that there is still hope...that we may not only survive, but *win* the day that lies ahead... then give your signal."

Quietly Jon took in another breath, knowing that there was no turning back.

"I am standing by," he concluded, signing off.

Finished, Jon moved back toward the bar and sat down, quietly taking another drink from his tankard. Only silence prevailed, seemingly for time immeasurable, as those gathered awaited to see if a reply would actually be given. Some had even begun to take bets on it.

For his part, Jon felt anything was possible, but the probability of a supporting reply was unlikely. Yes, he and the crew had been through much together, but this time it was different; this time he had directly asked them to follow him into Armageddon. In that regard, he would not blame them if they wanted off the ship as soon as possible. Just as he knew he would continue, even if it would only be himself, Alex and Lorelei to command the *Black Sun* and unlock Arcadia.

Then, with the suddenness of a thunderclap, the sound of the intercom went off once more.

"This is the engineering crew," a voice spoke. "We are all with you, Captain Flint."

There was just enough time for amazement to dawn throughout the lounge as another comline sounded.

"This is the Hangar Deck, we stand ready!"

"This is Damage Control, we're with you all the way!"

"This is Sickbay," Apache spoke up grumpily. "I don't know or care if anyone wants my signal, but someone's got to be around to patch all you idiots up! I'm staying right where I am!"

"This is Buccaneer One. Assuming our Boss is with you, then the rest of us are ready to kick ass!"

"This is Lundgren, speaking for the Raiders. You've gotten us this far, and we're definitely not going home before one last score!"

From there, dozens more calls came in, all signaling that they were ready and willing to fight, regardless of the outcome. Once the last signal was given, Jon turned toward the present crew around him.

"And you?" he asked toward those beside him. "Are there any of you who wish to get off?"

Save for a few glances to their fellow crewmen to see if they did, in fact, wish to depart, none of the gathered moved or spoke. In turn, the officers, minus Davis and Apache, all gave their own indirect signals. Boss casually withdrew and lit her pipe, Barbarossa folded his arms and nodded in approval, Anna and Gran nodded as well, Braun was in another fight with his artificial arm and Kaiser and Kaguya both gave obvious glances. Even Alex, who Jon turned to on a whim, merely lifted his tankard and took a drink.

Jon then gazed at Lorelei, who also nodded while retaining her grin. A grin which informed Jon that, even now, she believed she made the right decision on Aurora.

Thus, with his answer received, Jon tapped his wristcom once more.

"You all have my gratitude," he said, before standing once more. "Thus..." he declared with an appreciative smile. "We set sail for the promised land."

With that given, Jon nodded toward Barbarossa, who turned back to the crew. "Return to your stations!" he barked, triggering the crew to disassemble. "We have three more days to prepare the ship! And they will be spent well!"

Upon that command and those that followed, the crew departed through the lounge door. Only this time they did not return to their duties with desperation and anxiety within them, but resolution and willingness. It was just as their captain had said; whatever awaited them at Ephesus, they would fight and fight to win all the same. Just as they had been doing to this point.

Silently watching the crew leave, Jon continued to drink from his tankard, all the while waiting for the last of them to depart. Once they were gone, and both he and Alex finished their drinks, he signaled to his brother and Lorelei, who nodded in turn. The trio rose from their seats and made their own departure, all three heading toward the bridge, where their own duties awaited.

------------------------

Letting out a yawn, Alex continued his trek through the *Black Sun*'s decks, observing the various crewmen at work. It was almost a mirror of his first time aboard the ship, back when she was the *U-7501* and still docked in Rochelle; no matter where he went, he found the crew diligently laboring in their preparing the ship for eventual action. The main difference between the two occasions, as far as Alex was concerned, was that he and the crew were now properly dressed in black and gold rather than masquerading around in Starfleet uniforms.

Of course, the change in uniform wasn't the only thing Alex noticed. Though he had been unconscious for the better part of the trip from Bonham IV, from what he understood talking with Anna and Kaguya, the entire demeanor of the crew had changed. Now, rather than feeling as though they were marching off to their deaths, the crew believed they may actually survive and be triumphant. The brothers' awakening, as well as Jon's speech two days ago, had revitalized their hopes. And though there was still a substantial sentiment amongst certain crewmen that they would, in fact, not return from Ephesus, they would at least give the Imps a hard fight before they were finished. Overall, the crew was ready and willing to go to war.

And as for Alex's own outlook, it really could go either way. Yes, Drake had a sizeable advantage over them, both on a personal level and in terms of resources and manpower. But as Jon had highlighted before, the *Black Sun* was no ordinary starship any more than her crewmembers were ordinary pirates. Braun and the rest of his team had specifically designed the *Black Sun* to operate on her own, and that included against entire enemy forces if necessary. And though she was largely untested in that area, as the most she had fought was against an enemy taskforce of roughly a dozen ships, and she had sunk the majority of them through the element of surprise, Alex had little doubt she would perform exemplary in the coming battle. Whether she was sunk in the end or not.

The crew was much the same. When they had left Rochelle, they were an individually experienced crew but still one that had been all too recently comprised. As a result, they had little to no familiarity or loyalty to one another. Now, while the loyalty portion was still debatable, the crew had served together for several battles as well as a fair amount of days in just running the ship. Now they could genuinely be called the crew of the *Black Sun* and the newest generation of Flint Pirates. In the coming battle, they would operate at full efficiency both on the ground and in space, and both the *Black Sun* and their chances of survival would be augmented by it. And what he saw now only emphasized that fact.

But would they, in fact, win in the end? That question could only be answered once the dust settled, and likely after many had perished.

Just then, as Alex moved down another corridor, he caught sight of a familiar face directing crewmen on a job. And though the owner of that face was now adorned in black and gold instead of Imperial grey, Alex was more than able to recognize him.

"Things progressing well, Chief?" the First Officer asked as he came up to the much older man.

Upon hearing the younger man's voice, the Chief smiled as he turned to face Alex. "About as well as they can be Commander," he replied dutifully, purposely repeating their last conversation word for word. "At this rate, we'll be ready for battle soon enough, assuming we don't break the poor girl in the meantime."

As if on cue, a sharp clang sounded across the deck, prompting Alex and the Chief to turn reflexively.

"One *still* can never tell with this bunch," the Chief said dryly.

"All too true," Alex agreed, before moving on. "And what do you think of our chances? Think we have a shot at the finish?"

The Chief's responding grin was wry. "Not a chance in Hell, no matter the circle," he replied. "We'll be lucky if we're not blown up on sight."

Alex eyed the Chief carefully. "I take it that's the general assessment?"

"Damn straight Commander. Only the more optimistically inclined think we have a chance, and still not a very good one," the Chief responded, grin maintained. "Still, doesn't stop us from trying, now does it?"

Alex smiled also. "No, it doesn't, Chief."

"Can't say I look forward to dying, even at my age," the older man stated. "But to be honest, going out in a blaze of glory doesn't sound so bad with you and the Captain at the head."

The younger Flint gleamed. "Leading you into battle?" he said half-jokingly. "Or being the first to fall?"

"Hah," the Chief let out a sharp laugh. "As much as I'd like to see you bastards go before me, chances are if anyone's going to survive this fight, it'll be you two, with or without your Devilblades."

"Your reassurance is touching," Alex replied just as dryly, before looking down in thought. "Still, it would be rather poetic. The Flint Brothers holding their final stand around their mother's gravesite."

"All the more reason for you two to survive," the Chief spoke, this time seriously. "And that's not just my opinion."

"Oh?"

The Chief frowned as he went on. "I wasn't kidding about before. Most of the crew believe they won't be coming back after this one. In fact, despite the Captain's earlier words, a few of them are even considering mutiny. Even so, there are a number of us that will see to it that the Flint bloodline doesn't end at Ephesus."

Alex raised an eyebrow. "Why?" he bluntly asked.

The Chief nodded understandingly at the question. "We all have different reasons. Some of us want to see at least one survive while the rest fall, others believe that you'll carry on our names and our memories once it's all over...

He then readopted his wry grin. "And then there are those of us who wish to see the spirit of Morganna Flint live on."

Suddenly at a loss of words, it was all Alex could do not to look away. "And you?" he asked, almost forcing the words out. "Do you have any particular reason?"

The Chief shrugged. "Let's just say I've had my day in the sun, and it would be a shame for you and your brother to miss out on yours. Besides, thanks to you two, I've had the most fun doing what I do since leaving Starfleet, so it's only fair that I give back."

Again Alex nodded. "I appreciate that," he replied softly. "Carry on."

"Yes sir," the Chief affirmed, allowing Alex to move past him. Before he could make it into a nearby turbolift however, the Chief spoke up again.

"Just one more thing Commander," he said, stopping the younger Flint in the middle of his tracks. "Has the Captain come up with a plan yet? Like he did at Rochelle?"

Alex stopped to consider. "If he has, he hasn't told me," he admitted, before allowing a renewed smile on his lips. "But knowing the Captain, it probably won't be long..."

---

Casually moving past the working crewmen, Kaguya continued her way toward her personal sanctum with minimal regard. She had just concluded the final training exercise with her raiders, and so was relatively exhausted from the endeavor, if not somewhat battered. The whole session had lasted over an hour, and much of it had been spent having the raiders fight her on multiple levels.

She had done her part to prepare them for the battle; from standard hand-to-hand combat and weapons to conventional and unconventional tactics, she had spent the time since Bonham training and honing them as best she could. For her part, she found herself strangely proud of her work. She believed that even one of the *Black Sun*'s raiders was worth at least a company of Imperial Marines. Whether or not they survived the coming battle would, not unlike the rest of the ship's crew, be due to their own efforts. But again, Kaguya had done all she could for them.

For now, however, the training was complete. As such, she had instructed the raiders to take whatever time was left and rest. Whether that entailed sleeping in their quarters, writing to their loved ones or having a drink or two in the lounge, she didn't care. She wanted them primed and healthy for the battle that was ahead, just as she intended to be once she returned to her own quarters. After her usual report to her father, that is.

That last thought irked even as her eyes came upon the dual doors that divided her quarters from the rest of the ship. She was loyal to her father and the Blue Dragon, yes, but that didn't mean she enjoyed what she did. Especially if any of her words caused her father to decide on a specific order. One that Kaguya was hesitant, to say the least, to carry out.

That discomfort remained with her even as she stepped up to the doorway. It conflicted with the relief she felt upon reaching her private space once more. And it continued to hold onto her as the door opened and allowed her inside. However, once the door closed behind her, that emotion was quickly replaced as she sensed another presence in the room. Freezing in her motions, Kaguya felt dread well up in her as her eyes came upon an all too familiar figure, leaning against the side wall.

"Retiring for the evening?" Jon inquired as he rested against the bulkhead, arms folded over his chest and eye gazing upon her expectedly. "Or were you going to report in first?"

Her fingers flexing back and forth, Kaguya could only close her eyes in resignation.

"How long have you known?"

"Since the moment Lord Fuma requested your posting," Jon replied as he straightened from the wall and moved toward her. "What, did you really think Alex and I were that blind? That we couldn't figure out what both your intentions were?"

He then spoke accusingly. "That you were placed here to spy on us, and strike us down if your Lord deemed fit?"

Dread intensifying, Kaguya found herself backing away from the imposing elder Flint, all the while resisting the urge to instinctively draw her ninjato. Not just because she was hesitant of hurting Jon, but also knowledgeable and weary of the complete opposite. All the while, she attempted to speak in turn but failed to even develop a single word within her mind, let alone utter it in the open.

Eventually, Kaguya felt her back press against the doorway whence she came, only this time the doors didn't open. All throughout she kept her eyes upon Jon's singular eye, which blazed with a terrible force of will. One that, in spite of all of her emotional control, made Kaguya feel a growing vestige of fear.

When Jon stopped his advance, he was face to face with her, his eye continuing to bore into hers with terrible intensity.

"Needless to say," Jon enunciated darkly, his voice now low and reverberating; Kaguya almost felt it like heat against her skin. "You and I have much to discuss, *imouto-chan*."

# Chapter XXXIII: Realm of the Lost

## Flint Pirates umbra *Black Sun*
## Ephesus System

All at once, the tunnel of flashing stars ended as the *Black Sun* reverted back to normal space. Upon doing so, an uncharacteristic silence embraced the bridge as the present crew gazed through the viewscreen, toward their destination. That silence, in turn, quickly spread throughout the rest of the ship as the remaining crew, despite not possessing the ability to actually see into space, knew all too well what lay before them.

Standing out against the backdrop of space like a blood ruby, the planet Ephesus shone with a crimson gleam that seemed almost ethereal. The sole planet of the titular Ephesus System, Ephesus was a largely desolate world. Its surface consisted of little more than a glistening red desert, not unlike the Terran world of Mars, with various mountains and rock formations spread about. Its composition was rather unremarkable. As far as the *Black Sun*'s sensors could tell, its crust contained nickel, calcium, aluminum, titanium and several more otherwise common ores, while its mantle was mostly comprised of magnesium and silicon, all ensuring that Ephesus held little in the way of valuable resources. And though it possessed an atmosphere and gravity rating that was roughly equal to Terra, a lack of fertile topsoil alongside the aforementioned lack of resources, as well as certain hazardous areas along the surface, had dissuaded any potential inhabitants, Terran or otherwise, from pursuing colonization. Overall, Ephesus was, by and large, nothing more than a great red rock in space.

Even so, one need only gaze upon Ephesus once to tell that, for all that it was lacking, there was something *different* about this world. Whether it was the aforementioned blood-red surface when cast against the light of its nearby star, or the magnificent rings that surrounded the planet much like Saturn's back in the Sol System, Ephesus held a strange and somehow alluring beauty about it. A beauty that seemed out of place when compared to the rest of the galaxy, almost as if Ephesus didn't actually belong where it was; that it had not always *been* amongst the present stars. Or perhaps even the mortal plane itself.

For Jon and Alex, however, the most crucial part of Ephesus wasn't its beauty or its mysteriousness, but rather its remembrance. It was at this very world that their mother, the Golden Queen, had made her last stand against an Imperial ambush. It was here that she had fought her greatest enemy and, to some degree, triumphed before succumbing to her wounds. And it was here that the Flints, cast into a shuttle and sent out into the depths of space with little more than the clothes on their backs, along with certain other provisions privy only to Jon, had begun their lives as orphans, forced to fend for themselves against an ever hostile galaxy.

It was here, above this lone planet that seemed to exist at the very ends of the galaxy, that one chapter of their lives had ended. And another had begun.

"We've entered orbit," Davis announced as he brought the *Black Sun* over the planet, just above the rings. His tone only emphasized the solemn vigil that had spread throughout the ship; no one dared show any sign of disrespect or improper behavior upon this sacred ground.

Especially if the stories regarding the spirits of the crew of the *Morgan le Fay* were in fact true.

"Sensor scan?" Jon questioned. He was half-tempted to lower his scope and look over the readout himself, but he held back.

Anna took a moment to go over her readings. "No abnormalities to report. Terrestrial conditions are all normal, and life scan shows only inhabitant lifeforms."

She then looked back at Jon. "No sign of any other ships," she said, knowing exactly what he was about to ask next. "Imperial or otherwise."

"Nothing on the communication bands either," Gran imparted. "Not even on the Enigma frequency."

"Looks like we beat them to the finish line," Alex commented, letting out a breath he didn't know he had been holding.

Jon nodded. It made sense. Even with Drake's authority within Starfleet, it would have taken him some time to assemble a sizeable taskforce, to say nothing of the head start the *Black Sun* held at Bonham. However, Jon knew that this was only a temporary relapse; at the very best it would be one or two days. They only had a few hours, both to find Arcadia's resting place and to set up a worthwhile defense around it.

Before he considered that however, another thought occurred to Jon. One that he almost didn't want to ask, but eventually relented.

"Debris?" he inquired, his voice little above a whisper.

The silence only grew more profound as that single word, despite its low volume, seemingly echoed around the bridge. Nodding sympathetically, Anna again addressed her scanners.

"Negative," she replied, feeling as though a vice were pressing against her heart. "I'm not picking up any sentient made metals, debris or otherwise, anywhere in the system."

Both Jon and Alex felt a tinge of anger well up inside of them.

"Either the *Morgan le Fay* was completely obliterated..." Alex spoke in a low fury.

"...or the Imperials cleared out her remnants after the battle," Jon surmised.

It was the ultimate insult as far as either was concerned; the Imperials hadn't even allowed their mother a gravesite. Even some of the other crewmen present, especially Kaiser, felt similar anger embrace them at that revelation.

As the bridge crew contemplated this discovery, the turbolift doors at the back of the bridge opened, allowing Lorelei to enter. Taking note of her presence, Jon dismissed his anger and focused on their primary purpose. Avenging his mother would come later; for the moment they needed to find what they were looking for.

Sensing the mood of the bridge crew, Lorelei quietly took to her post and began inputting her commands. A short moment later, a set of coordinates appeared on her screen.

"I've isolated the final set of coordinates," she spoke, her voice also holding a solemnity to it, but for a different reason than the rest of the crew. "Putting on viewscreen now."

Within a few seconds, a tactical readout of the planet appeared in the center of the viewscreen, with a gold-colored marker placed upon the planet's northern hemisphere, about halfway between the north pole and the equator.

Pausing an instant to memorize the exact coordinates, Jon looked to Anna again. "Deep scan," he commanded.

Anna quickly set to work, directing the *Black Sun*'s sensor array toward those exact coordinates. A moment later, she reviewed her readings and found herself taken back.

"What...?" she murmured in surprise.

"What is it?" Jon almost demanded.

Anna looked up. "Captain," she began evenly. "You need to see this."

Quickly the tacscreen magnified over the marked area, bringing up a full view of the planet's surface for the crew to see. And, upon the tactical display switching out for a real-time image, the crew looked on in bewilderment. Even Jon and Alex couldn't contain that emotion within themselves.

Beyond the red sands and the surrounding mountains, the bridge crew beheld what could only have been sentient made structures. They formed a great city that rose up from level ground, spanning several kilometers in all directions. And though there was an additional number of ruins and remnants along the surrounding terrain, it was evident that the city was the most prominent fixture. As well as that was where the marker was centered.

Sitting back in his seat, Jon found himself strangely drawn to the city, his eye scanning over it with inquiry. Possessing numerous dilapidated buildings and structures, all of which were placed around visible streets and within a line of boundary walls, Jon found it comparable to Ancient Terran city ruins. Yet, despite that comparison, Jon could tell it was all Predecessor design, as there were numerous fixtures that no modern culture would have implemented. The all too certain feeling that came over him only emphasized that fact.

"A city?" Alex gaped from the side, entirely mystified. "Indeed," Jon replied, narrowing his gaze.

"I don't understand," Davis spoke up from the helm. "Ephesus has been explored and evaluated for colonization before. Why hasn't anyone reported this?"

Anna went over the appropriate records. "He's right. There's no listing of these ruins within Imperial records or elsewhere. It's rather eerie."

Deciding that explanation could wait for another day, Jon instead focused back on the present. "Can you isolate the exact set of coordinates?"

"I'll try," Anna said, keying commands. As she did, the monitor magnified, zooming down upon a precise part of the city. A moment later, it centered upon a specific point and produced an accompanying gridline image, again prompting the crew to look on in astonishment.

Erected at the exact center of the city was a single structure. One that was as massive as a Terran skyscraper and possessing a heavily arched and slanted design, all the while holding numerous indentations and icons along its exterior. A single point that stood out amongst the rest of the city.

"A citadel?" Alex looked on aghast, as did the rest of the crew.

"No," Jon proclaimed as he gazed over the construct, even rising from his seat to step toward the screen as if enraptured by it. "A temple."

Feeling a sense of unease with his brother disposition, Alex couldn't help but ask. "How do you know?"

Without turning around, Jon answered in a near monotone. "I just do."

Lorelei also stood up and moved toward the screen. "I sense something within," she voiced, her gaze also remaining in place and appearing as distanced. "Something ancient... Something dormant..."

She then, at last, moved to stand beside Jon. "Something *powerful*."

Jon looked down, his eye closing as he considered those words.
For a time, it appeared to the crew that their captain was inwardly contemplating whether or not he would turn away or continue on.

Eventually, however, he raised his eye to gaze back at the screen. And this time, it burned with determination.

"Senior officers to the briefing room," he commanded as he turned away and moved off toward the turbolift.

Seconds later, the bridge officers all rose from their posts to join him. Braun, Boss, and Kaguya, upon receiving the word, made their way from the lower decks.

"My my," Braun let out as he observed the rotating holographic image of the city, which was being projected from the center of the table. "So, this is where it will all conclude."

"So we think," Davis quipped as he looked over the image, with some level of apprehension. "For all we know, this thing is the Predecessors' equivalent of a beachside resort and casino."

Alex rolled his eyes at the suggestion. "Considering the lack of beachfront, as well as the fact the Predecessors weren't economically oriented, I have strong doubts about that Davis," he retorted, as he also examined the holograph. "It is impressive, however..."

"Indeed," Barbarossa added. He studied the city a little more before nodding in approval. "It seems we will not be quite so vulnerable in the coming fight."

"My sentiments exactly," Jon replied as he leaned forward, surveying the cityscape. "We have the perfect fortress to mount a defense."

He tapped a switch, triggering the hologram to freeze in its rotation.

"Since ancient times, urban combat has been the most strenuous form of warfare for any invading army," he began. "Though the invaders can advance from virtually any angle, the defenders have far more in the way of ground and cover, granting them a decisive advantage. It is around these areas we will build our stratagem."

The captain then tapped another switch generating a series of markings around the temple, namely around the buildings on the summit and the sole gateway.

"The battle will be split into three stages," he explained. "The initial stage is, obviously, the ground."

He nodded toward the still image. "We will be dividing the raiders into two groups. The first, and obviously the larger group, will spread out around the city, specifically within the buildings and the streets.

From there, they will repel any Imperial incursion, using the cityscape to their benefit."

Jon then gestured toward the summit. "The second group will disperse across the higher towers to provide a combination of fire support and anti-air defense. From this vantage point, this group will be able to repel any ground armor or airborne assault vehicles that Drake may throw at us, as well as provide sniper protection for the first group."

"Is that really necessary?" Davis contested, a little unsure. "I mean, marines are one thing, but do you really think he'll send gunships and tanks in there?"

Jon fixed the helmsman a knowing look. "At Kurzis, the Imps utilized Condors to both forwardly deploy troops and to suppress us from the air. This time, I believe the Imperials are going to send even greater firepower."

He again gestured at the city layout. "Alongside, those streets are wide enough for tanks to move through. Drake would be a fool not to take advantage of them."

"What about orbital bombardment?" Anna queried. "Because if I were Drake, I would find that the most efficient route to take..."

"Too risky," Alex countered. "Until Drake has his hands on Arcadia, he can't afford to damage the temple." A flash of discomfort entered his expression. "Especially since we don't know how Arcadia, assuming it's really there, may react to hostile forces."

"And besides," Jon explained, once again knowingly, "his fleet is going to be too *preoccupied* during this period."

A series of hesitant nods acknowledged that comment. Jon continued to elaborate.

"We will be using every piece of weaponry we have on the ship for this. Everything from the standard beam pistols and rifles to anti-tank cannons and anti-air missile launchers will be utilized, with the latter especially being spread out around the summit. These, combined with the city's established defenses, should grant us the measures we need to repel Drake's ground forces."

With that, Jon again tapped a switch, from which the temple zoomed away to show the whole of Ephesus.

"The second stage, once more obviously, is the *Black Sun* launching concentrated attacks on the incoming fleet," he described, looking toward Alex specifically. "You will utilize a combination of umbra and battleship tactics, engaging targets in the open with the main guns when necessary and then cloaking and engaging with missiles and torpedoes when able."

"And my fighters?" Boss inquired.

"They'll play their usual role, yes."

Biting his lip, Alex couldn't help but feel discomfort toward his brother's words. Didn't Jon intend to bring him down to the surface as well?

Regardless, the elder Flint only explained further. "At the very least this will all dissuade the Imperials from advancing. At the very best, it will break their formation and eventually lead to their surrender, in which their ground forces will have no choice but to comply."

"That's rather optimistic," Davis grumbled.

"Which is why I said at the *very* best," Jon countered, before moving forward. "And that brings us to the *third* stage..."

"Drake himself," Barbarossa surmised.

"Indeed," Jon added. "Due to Drake's mastery over Berith, he will undoubtedly penetrate our defenses and reach the inner sanctum of the temple, regardless of any efforts on our part..."

He then looked toward Lorelei, who nodded at his unspoken inquiry. "Thus, I will deal with Drake personally," he concluded. "All while Lorelei focuses her efforts on Arcadia."

Barbarossa fixed Jon with a hard stare. "Are you prepared to deal with him *properly* this time?"

"I am," Jon affirmed, retaining his gaze against the Leo's. "Whatever the outcome, it will *not* be the same as Bonham."

Allowing a small smirk to form over those words as well as the fierceness behind Jon's eye, Barbarossa leaned back into his chair. It seemed the young captain was indeed prepared to face his worst enemy. Though the question remained whether he would triumph in the end.

For his part, Alex only felt further discomfort. What about him? Wasn't he going to fight Drake alongside Jon? Or did his brother intend for him to lead the raiders against the marine forces?

Coincidentally, the answer soon came.

"Obviously Kaguya will be leading the raiders," Jon stated, earning a nod from the present but silent kunoichi, as he regarded Barbarossa and Kaiser. "But I would like you two there to provide support as well."

Both the Leo and Herculean looked up in surprise.

"Oh?" Barbarossa let out.

"Yes," Jon confirmed. "Long ago, you made your name in the field, facing down an entire force of Imperial Marines singlehandedly. And now, you will do so once more."

Realizing the meaning behind that, Barbarossa's smirk became a full, feral smile, one that was emphasized as he raised his right baneclaw into view. With a growl, the Kapta accepted the assignment. "Captain, it will be my genuine honor."

Jon then looked toward Kaiser. Much to his surprise, Kaiser held a similarly bloodthirsty smile on his rock-like lips, which took Jon a moment to understand. Though Jon doubted any marines from the first Battle of Ephesus would be present, Kaiser would proceed as if they were. And he would avenge his queen the same way Jon intended to avenge his mother.

"Forgive me for interrupting this otherwise heartwarming moment," Davis spoke up sardonically. "But I'm a little confused. If you're going to be facing Drake, and Barbarossa is going to be supporting the raiders…" He then glanced over the rest of the table. "Who's going to be commanding up here?"

Jon took a breath, knowing what was about to follow. "The answer again should be obvious," he replied, this time looking toward Alex. "As we have a First Officer for that exact purpose."

A sudden measure of shock ensued as all eyes looked upon the younger Flint. For his part, Alex initially felt disbelief, but after taking a moment to realize the true meaning of that declaration, he became filled with dismay. His responding glance toward his brother was anything but pleasant.

Ignoring him, Jon turned toward Braun. "The weapons we will be employing on the surface, Professor, will they perform as you led me to believe?"

Braun nodded with all due seriousness. "I assure you they will, Captain. The raiders will be fully prepared against the coming assault."

"I hope so," Jon said, before rubbing his hands against his face. Despite all of his plans and preparations, he knew that the fight ahead was going to be momentous. And also despite his assurances, he knew a victorious outcome would be similar.

With that in mind, taking a breath, he perused his gathered crew once more.

"All I can say now is another passage from Ancient Terra. *Fortuna Audaces Iuvat.*"

Boss immediately understood. "Fortune favors the bold," she translated.

Jon nodded. "During ancient times, Fortuna was personified as an actual Goddess of Luck, and that phrase reflected upon her showing regard for those who took risks and gambits."

He looked around the table, observing the quiet determination amongst those gathered.

"Let's hope she at least takes notice of our efforts. Dismissed."

The officers all rose from their chairs, their respective duties now clear. In silence they exited the briefing room, one after the other, all the while Jon continued to sit and observe. Following along at the last, Barbarossa moved to exit but stopped, his head tilting down in thought.

"Something the matter, Barbarossa?"

Slowly, Barbarossa backed away from the doorway. "I did not wish to bring it up during your briefing, Captain, but...I have considered your strategy."

"I figured you had," Jon replied. "And what does the master think of it?"

Barbarossa wandered back to sit at the table and tapped the panel at his chair, bringing the city's holographic image back on display. "Your tactical arrangement is well thought out and organized, and you have ensured that your forces are adequately armed and provided multiple points to attack."

Barbarossa folded his arms. "Overall, your strategy is quite sound..."

"Indeed," Jon nodded, taking the explanation as a compliment.

"...if your objective is to hold out against a superior enemy," Barbarossa finished, then looking at Jon with peculiarity. "As opposed to defeating that enemy entirely."

Jon closed his eye, knowing what Barbarossa was referring to. "You said it yourself, we're facing a superior enemy. Their firepower and numbers are far greater than ours, and their chain of command is such that, even if I were able to kill Drake, their forces would only continue to fight."

He sighed. "Defeating them by ourselves would be impossible."

"Exactly," Barbarossa replied in acknowledgment. "So what we are holding out for?"

Jon pursed his lips as he considered his answer. "To tell the truth, I do not know. If I were a religious man like yourself, I would say we are holding out for a miracle."

Barbarossa arched an eyebrow. "A miracle?" he repeated. "As in Aslan, Jehovah or this *Fortuna* raining holy fire down upon our enemies?"

The Terran mulled over the reference. "While that would certainly be worthwhile and greatly appreciated, I was thinking of something more conventional."

As Barbarossa looked on, Jon elaborated. "Eons ago, there was a battle that took place in a land called Rorke's Drift. In defense of a local mission station, a group of just over one hundred fifty stood their ground against an aggressor force of approximately four thousand."

Jon noticed how Barbarossa leaned in to listen more closely. "For nearly two days the battle waged, in which the one hundred fifty, despite being lightly armed and possessing only the most basic defenses, held out against constant assault from the four thousand. Even when the four thousand closed in and took away the advantage of firearms, the one hundred fifty remained at their posts and battled at close-range. It soon reached the point where the aggressors had to crawl over the bodies of their fallen brethren in order to advance."

"Hmm," Barbarossa uttered, considering the story.

Jon continued. "Even so, while the one hundred fifty held against the tide, it could only be for a short while. Slowly but surely the four thousand advanced, eventually taking the northern wall, then the hospital and then the cattle housing. All the while, the defenders were forced back into a small bastion around a nearby storehouse."

Though intrigued, Barbarossa remembered that they were pressed for time. "When does the miracle take place?"

Jon explained further. "After hours of continuous battle, a brief pause ensued as the aggressors broke off their advance. Now only one hundred and forty-two defenders remained, with even fewer supplies and ammunition. And then, during the early morning, another regiment of aggressors appeared on the plains, and the aggressors were seemingly prepared to take the station at last."

"Seemingly?" Barbarossa repeated.

The captain clarified. "Despite their numbers, the aggressors did not attack," he said, looking on as surprise dawned on Barbarossa's face. "As history would later reveal, the new regiment had marched for six straight days to reach the field, during which they were unable to eat or rest properly. Alongside, several of their numbers remained wounded from previous conflicts."

He leaned back again. "In the end, the regiment withdrew almost as soon as they had arrived. Just in time for an allied force to appear and relieve the defenders."

"Interesting," Barbarossa replied. "But I fail to see the miracle."

Jon quickly realized that was the first time he had seen Barbarossa not understand the subject. "The miracle, Kapta, was the battle itself. A group of one hundred fifty held out against a larger group of four thousand just long enough for their adversaries to become fatigued and for reinforcements to arrive. Any alteration of that point, up to and including the enemy reinforcements being properly fed, rested, and in good health, would have directly affected the outcome."

He clasped his hands together. "That would be the kind of miracle I would bet on. That we hold out just long enough, that the conditions be set to our gain and that when the battle reaches its apex..." he spoke with utmost seriousness. "Fortune will favor us."

Barbarossa nodded, now understanding the message. He couldn't say he adhered to it, as he had always found such miracles to be fickle and inconsistent. Even so, outside Aslan's guidance and protection, it really was all they had to go on at this time.

Committed to their path, the two stood back up and exited the briefing room.

Following Barbarossa, Jon stepped out of the briefing room and was about to proceed to the hangar deck. Unfortunately, however, his path was blocked. Leaning against the side of the bulkhead, such that he could allow Barbarossa to pass, Alex stood by with his arms folded. Clearly awaiting his elder brother's arrival.

"We need to talk."

Jon immediately tried to head it off. "Now is not..."

"I insist," Alex countered before straightening and moving down the corridor. Inwardly sighing, Jon followed his brother. A few moments later, both entered the main cabin, with Alex coming to stand before Jon's desk.

"What in the First Circle are you thinking!?" Alex began as Jon moved around the desk and took his chair. "Are you really going to leave me behind at a time like this!?"

Resting his elbows and clasping his hands together, Jon fixed his brother a hard gaze. "Yes, as a matter of fact, I am," he replied evenly, attempting, despite the obvious futility, to assuage his brother's tension. "I need you more up here commanding the ship than I do down there."

Alex inwardly shivered, both at his brother's gaze and his words. Even so, he refused to back down.

"Please," he hissed, his anger apparent. "You know it's the exact opposite. You need me more on the planet, helping you fight Drake, more than you need me here. Just as you also know Barbarossa would be far better for the latter."

"That remains to be seen," Jon responded, once again evenly. "It's not like you're inexperienced in the field of command yourself..."

"Don't chastise me, brother," Alex pressed on. "You're keeping me here *on purpose*."

He leaned onto the desk before asking. "And I want to know *why*."

Again sighing, this time outwardly, Jon closed his eye. He really didn't want to bring the subject up. However, now that Alex had forced him to the point, he had no choice but to do precisely that.

"On Bonham IV," he again spoke evenly, though with an underlying tone of accusation. "You lost control and allowed Forneus to take possession," he said, before fixing a much fiercer gaze than before. "Didn't you?"

His prior anger instantly extinguished, Alex could almost feel the color drain from his skin toward the accusation.

"How did you know?" he managed to force out in little more than a hoarse whisper.

"I was unconscious," Jon answered, watching as his brother actually began to shake under his eye. "But not *unaware*."

With that having been declared, Alex could only close his eyes and lower his head solemnly. "Yes," he admitted, after a long and uncomfortably drawn pause. "I got desperate and lost the edge. And Forneus naturally took advantage..."

He then looked up once more. "But still," he continued, willing up whatever strength he had left. "That doesn't mean it will happen this time...!"

"It won't," Jon said as he rose up from his chair to meet his brother's gaze. "Because you're going be here, taking the *Black Sun* against the Imperial fleet."

Alex opened his mouth to respond, but Jon only went further.

"We lost against Drake the first time for several reasons, but the most prominent was we let our emotions get involved. And not just because of his part in our mother's death."

This time, the younger brother looked away slightly, knowing exactly what his elder meant. Jon continued.

"We can't afford that this time. We can't let Drake play on both of us, much less take one of us down to dishevel the other. Thus, the only viable option is for *one* of us to go in."

"And between the two of us," Alex surmised, much to his dismay. "I was the one who ended up possessed."

"Exactly," Jon agreed.

The younger Flint glowered at that knowledge. Rationally speaking, he knew Jon was making the correct decision. Between the two of them, he was the calmer and more objective one, and therefore the least likely to falter if something terrible happened, his prior actions on Bonham notwithstanding. However, that didn't mean Alex liked it, any more than he liked being left behind at such a crucial hour.

Sensing that precise emotion, Jon stepped around his desk. "That's the main part of it," he explained. "The other part is that I believe it is time for you to assume command."

When Alex looked up in confusion, Jon specified. "Up to this point, it's either been Barbarossa or me who has captained the *Black Sun* in battle. Whereas you've only held command outside of it."

"What does that have to do with...?" Alex began to question, only for Jon to raise his hand.

"The crew has seen what Barbarossa and I can do from that chair. You, however, remain a mystery to them. Some even think you're only the First Officer because you're my direct relation."

He then reassuringly grasped Alex's shoulders. "Suffice to say that is entirely incorrect. I didn't make you my second-in-command because you're my brother."

Again Alex opened his mouth to respond, only for Jon to go on. "I made you my second because, besides the fact you are the only one that I trust, you also hold the bearings of a commander. Outside myself or Barbarossa, you are the only one I would willingly leave the *Sun* to."

Jon then withdrew his hands. "The crew has yet to understand this, and much more look upon you as they do me..."

"Or Barbarossa," Alex again surmised.

Jon nodded. "Which is why you must show them. And the only way you can do that is through battle."

Another brief pause intervened as Alex mulled over his brother's words. Again rationally, he saw Jon's purpose and knew that it was the correct course of action, both regarding his holding command over the ship and the coming battle against Drake. And yet, just as before, he didn't like any of it in the least, particularly the idea of Jon facing Drake alone. Especially when it had taken the both of them merely to keep up with the Admiral the last time.

Even so, as Alex closed his eyes in resignation, he knew that there was no choice in the matter. Like it or not, Jon was the captain and, even worse, his arrangement held more in the way of sense than anything Alex would have preferred. Besides, as much as he didn't want to admit it, it really was time for him to take that center chair into a fight. To prove that he was indeed worthy of being the *Black Sun*'s First Officer.

"Very well," he acquiesced. "I will do as you command."

Nodding, Jon moved toward the doorway. However, just as he passed Alex, the younger Flint reached out and grabbed his shoulder.

"*Ad victoriam*, brother."

Jon smirked. Alex was quoting yet another ancient phrase; one that, as Jon recalled, had been used as a battle cry by a once triumphant empire. It was a fitting sign off.

"*Victoria et vita*, brother."

Jon proceeded out of the main cabin and headed toward the hangar bay. A few minutes later, Alex returned to the bridge.

———————————  ———————————

Fully loaded, the shuttles rose up and exited the *Black Sun*'s hangar bay, immediately proceeding toward the planet. Once well away from the ship, they shifted their courses and progressed into planetfall, their black and gold tinted hulls flaring with red heat against the surrounding atmosphere. Though a bumpy ride as per usual with reentry, the passengers paid it little mind. Besides the fact they were all rather callused to such travel, they were too concentrated on what lay ahead, with the majority either gaining as much rest as they could or contemplating their chances of survival. Jon, Lorelei, Kaguya, Barbarossa, and Kaiser were wisely among the former.

Eventually, the shuttles entered Ephesus' troposphere, where they continued through the abundant cloud cover toward the surface below. Once past the clouds, Ephesus' entire surface was revealed for all to see. And, not unlike Dante upon reaching Hell's gateway, many beheld what lay before them and, with their knowledge that this may be their final battlefield, despaired.

As had been verified from orbit, Ephesus was little more than a vast open desert. An utterly barren landscape of crimson, with a select number of mountains and rock formations spread about to prevent the land from being otherwise entirely flat. Cracks and crevasses were abundant, with some having developed into entire canyons; the only sign that there had once been water and fertility within this desolate land. Craters were also present, dotting the various edges of the landscape, seemingly adding to the desolation as well as indicating that past incidents had taken place upon Ephesus. Not a single form of fauna could be seen, nor any other sign of life; whatever form of inhabitance that had once existed here clearly disappeared long ago. All that remained now was a wasteland.

And then, after several more minutes of open flight, the group came upon *it*: their intended destination as well as the first sign that Ephesus held more than rock and barren soil. Spread out in the middle of a flatland, surrounded by various mountains and jutted rock in the distance, the Predecessor city stood out like a lone field of flowers upon tundra; an image that, despite it being far from its intended purpose, somehow inspired those who beheld it that all was not lost. Once again Jon recalled the image of Ancient Terran ruins as he studied the city's dilapidated exterior. Buildings of differing shapes and sizes surrounded the eponymous temple within the center. All with numerous markings, clearly of Predecessor design, visible along various areas.

Upon Jon's command, the shuttles descended to their specific landing points, which were divided from the highest towers to ground level. Once moored, the raiders immediately disembarked, with those having been placed on the towers directly advancing to their firing positions. Due to the towers' great heights, each of the fire teams held a wide view of the surrounding cityscape, granting them exceptional latitude for their longer range firearms. Alongside this, several automated turrets, ranging from beam guns to missile launchers, were also deployed to specific advantage points to provide additional fire. Whether they would hold out against the Imperial onslaught was anyone's guess, but nobody dismissed the validity of the captain's plan.

Those on the ground, meanwhile, rapidly spread out, with the majority taking up cover around or within any of the nearby ruins. Following their dispersal, Jon and his entourage, escorted by several additional raiders, exited and proceeded to the temple. Once they were a fair distance away, the shuttles took off once more; Jon had ordered them to return to the *Black Sun* after troop dispersal. They could not afford to risk their only means of returning to the ship in the coming battle, especially when Jon knew the Imperials would have stronger anti-air systems than his force.

Stepping in front of the temple's single arched entryway, Jon gazed upward, studying the massive construct that seemed to extend past the sky itself. "So..." he murmured, a strong wind causing his greatcoat to whip and wreathe around him. "This is what we fought all this time to reach."

Longcoat swaying in the same wind, Lorelei walked up beside him. "Indeed," she smiled, looking upon the temple in marvel. "I've waited a long time to stand here. To see this with my own eyes."

Jon closed his eye at her words. He knew better than to ask if it had all been worth it. "To think that this has stood here since the galaxy began..." he thought aloud, feeling some measure of marvel as well, if only toward the visible exterior. "'When the stars were but children and the planets were but seeds.'"

Lorelei smirked at the quote. "All to contain the greatest treasure of its creators."

Jon shook his head. "That remains to be seen. We still don't know for a fact if Arcadia's really in there."

"Oh?" Lorelei asked, eyebrow rising in curiosity. "After coming all this way and seeing so much, the great Captain Flint retains doubts?"

"I *always* retain doubts," he rejoined, before looking back at the structure. "I will say one thing, however..."

Again he tried to peer through the darkness, only to find... nothing. Even so, he knew there was more than what his eye beheld.

"*Something* is in there," he said. "Something that has been at rest for a long, long time."

Before Lorelei could reply, Kaguya moved up to them. "All units are in position," she reported.

"Very well," Jon replied, before nodding to Lorelei. "We will proceed from here."

Kaguya opened her mouth but quickly closed it. There was no point in asking Jon that question now.

"Understood," she acknowledged. *"Ganbatte kudasai."*

Jon bowed slightly. *"Anata mo,"* he answered.

Kaguya nodded in appreciation before turning away, but not before sparing one last scowl of warning and accompanying thoughts toward Lorelei. Message communicated, the raider commander walked back to her original position where she would continue to await the incoming Imperials.

Silently watching her leave, Jon again turned toward the entryway. And then, after a brief hesitation, he gave the command.

"Let's go."

He and Lorelei proceeded through the entrance, disappearing into the darkness not long after. All while the wind continued to run its course across the ever desolate cityscape...

# <u>Chapter XXXIV: Depths of the Unknown</u>

## Flint Pirates umbra *Black Sun*
## Ephesus System

Battlestations were now manned, as indicated by the darkened bridge, the red flashing of the surrounding alert lights and the now silenced klaxons. The ship, while remaining in Ephesus' orbit, was cloaked with all weapons armed and loaded, and ready to move into attack position. And finally the crew, each observing a cold silence as they continued to operate their posts, remained at standby, albeit a relatively uncomfortable standby, for combat. By all accounts, the *Black Sun* was ready for a fight.

For his part, Alex, now seated in the center chair, watched and waited for the first Imperial warship to appear on the viewscreen, all the while resisting the urge to stand up and pace. It was the waiting he hated the most, more so than the actual combat even. No matter how many times he had gone into battle, Alex could never get used to it; standing by for the fight to at last begin, all the while being forced to keep a look out for when the enemy made his or her first appearance.

He could not step off the bridge, nor so much as order a cup of tea from the galley. All he could do was remain in that damned chair and wait with the rest of the crew. His nerves were wracked from the intensity and anticipation.

Again Alex chafed at his position. He shouldn't have been there at all. Yes he understood Jon's logic, and yes he was the First Officer and therefore second in command, and especially yes he needed to show that he was indeed as capable of running the ship as either his brother or Barbarossa. But even so, these were not the right circumstances for it. Not when they were about to face a whole Imperial armada with Jon being left to face its Devilblade wielding commander alone. Had it been any other fight at any other time, Alex wouldn't have thought anything of it, but not now. Now he would give everything to trade places with Barbarossa, if only so that he could be at Jon's side fighting against Drake.

Unfortunately, however, it was what it was. Jon had placed him in charge, and the crew had accepted the fact. To go against it now would have undermined both, and Alex knew far better than to do that. As such, all he could do was remain in that chair and continue looking out at that viewscreen. Watching and waiting with those around him.

"Any indication of umbra presence?" he posited toward Gran.

After taking a moment to listen in, the Lyran shook her head. "Negative," she replied. "All channels remain clear."

Alex figured that was the case – Gran would have reported if she had detected something – but had to ask anyway. Anything and everything to relieve the tension, even a little bit of it.

"Maybe they decided to call it in ahead of time," Davis sardonically offered from the helm. He then looked on almost wistfully. "Wouldn't that be nice?"

A series of nods quickly went around the bridge.

"Very much so Davis," Alex agreed. "Though we all know that's not going to be the case."

"Yeah..." Davis grunted before purposely focusing back on his post. "About as likely as Emperor Lucian showing up to give us a pardon."

Alex had a response to that as well but decided to bite it back. There was too much going on, strange to imagine given the current inactivity, for him to be trading barbs. The cold silence quickly made a return as everyone went back to their posts and Alex returned to looking over the viewscreen.

Several more minutes passed with the younger Flint quickly becoming as inwardly anxious as he had been before. The accompanying boredom also didn't help much. In fact, Alex could almost feel himself alternate between unease toward the coming battle one moment and lack of stimulation toward his current situation the next. All while the viewscreen in front of him remained otherwise blank, with not so much as a comet appearing upon it in the last several moments.

Alex quickly shook his head of the thought. He was almost beginning to wish Drake would just hurry up and appear if only so they could get it over with. Just as he was beginning to wonder if this was all part of Drake's strategy, to withhold his fleet long enough to cause his adversaries discomfort.

"Any word from the Captain or Lorelei?"

Again an obvious question, as Alex and the rest would have likely heard or perhaps even *seen* if the pair had reached and unlocked Arcadia. However, Gran answered the question, regardless.

"Nothing more since the last transmission," she replied. "Same with Kaguya and the others."

Alex nodded grimly. The last transmission reported that the defenses were all manned and Jon and Lorelei had proceeded into the temple. That had been almost a half hour ago, but it might as well had been days given how events were progressing.

*Just what are they doing down there?* Alex couldn't help but think amidst the strain. He had already figured it would take time for Lorelei to reach the inner sanctum of the temple, and additional time to unlock and activate Arcadia. All enough for the Imperials to arrive in force. But now he found himself wishing she and his brother would *hurry the hell up*! The sooner they activated Arcadia, whether it was indeed a weapon or not, the closer they got to victory. Or so he wanted to think.

Thus, with little choice but to remain as he was, Alex let out a sigh and settled back into his chair. All the while continuing to wait for the enemy's inevitable arrival.

# Predecessor Temple
# Ephesus

The darkness was virtually unending. No matter what direction Jon looked, no matter what open area he shined the light from his wristcom toward, he could see essentially nothing, save for any solid wall he happened to pass. Had anyone else been in his current position, they would have easily been blinded, perhaps even instilled with fear at the darkness, but not Jon. He had been one with the darkness for fifteen years, therefore, despite his needing a light to see at the most efficient level, it did not bother him.

Lorelei, who notably did not utilize a light, seemed to be just as adjusted. In fact, as the pair continued through the current walkway they were in, Jon watched as the psion looked about at the surrounding walls, searching for anything out of the ordinary.

Recalling her disposition on the *Daedalus*, Jon kept a close guard on her, monitoring her reactions as they moved deeper and deeper into the temple. For the moment, however, the psion addressed her surroundings with her usual curiosity, glancing over the walls and constructs and pausing for a moment to analyze Predecessor script every now and then. Had she not been so focused on the true prize within the structure, Jon would have believed that the scholar would have been enjoying herself as she went about her work.

That wasn't to say that Jon wasn't paying close attention to their surroundings. Like the temple's exterior, the interior was entirely "alien" in design, possessing traits that Jon could equate to certain parts of Ancient Terran culture, but otherwise being almost wholly different from anything he had seen before. The corridor they were now in was massive, being wide enough in space to allow entire crowds to pass through and large enough for giants to move about as well. The walls, in turn, were elaborately structured and nuanced, while the passageways were arched toward the top, again not unlike that of a Terran cathedral. Once upon a time, there might have been color, as well as light, throughout, but now the corridors were blanked into a dull grey, with only their various indentations and scripts keeping them from being otherwise no different from stone.

*This is a tomb,* Jon thought as he continued to follow Lorelei through their current corridor, hoping that they reached their destination soon enough. While Jon was ambivalent toward the idea of ghosts and spirits haunting ancient structures, he did not like to remain in them for long. That and they had a schedule to keep.

"How much further?"

Pausing in her movement, Lorelei took a moment to glance through the darkness, scanning her surroundings with her telepathy.

"Still some distance yet," she answered. "If I'm reading correctly, our destination is at the very center of the temple, at the deepest level."

"That's not surprising," Jon said as he consulted his wristcom. As before, it failed to scan; something in the temple, possibly one of its components, was resistant to sensor waves. Thus, Jon had no choice but to follow the psion.

Coming across another set of Predecessor hieroglyphs, Jon was tempted to ask Lorelei for a translation, but chose not to. If they had been vital, the psion would have explained them already. Alongside, Jon suspected that, given the nature of the Predecessors' recordings, Lorelei had no idea what they meant. Whatever events they spoke of, whatever stories they told, were so far in the past that they predated virtually everything the two of them knew and understood. And even with all her brilliance and intellect, there was only so much the scholar could tell without being a direct witness.

"Oh?" Lorelei suddenly stopped to look down. "That's different."

Jon immediately saw what she was alluding to. At the end of the corridor was a single doorway, approximately the size of a building. Like the rest of the temple, the two sets of doors were elaborately and intricately designed, possessing lines and symbols that only the Predecessors themselves could have identified.

"Yes," Jon agreed as he shone his light across the doors. "That is different."

Without another word, Lorelei moved to the right wall, specifically to what appeared to be a control panel. After taking a moment to read the script, she then tapped precise symbols on the panel in an equally precise sequence.

The result was near instantaneous. The two doors began to open, slowly and steadily, generating a thunderous creaking that echoed across the corridor. Another burst of wind caused their coats to flicker as the doors screeched open. Both stood by and watched, all the while making sure they remained outside the door's swing.

And then the doors opened completely, revealing a whole new area to the intruders. An area that neither of them had expected.

Before them lay a great hall, which Jon assumed to be some sort of audience chamber. Massive in scope, such that he approximated it to a coliseum, the hall featured two audience areas on either side of a walkway, which led toward a single towering podium area. Additional towers and edifices were placed around key points of the outer regions, each taking a strange shape and form that Jon, and seemingly Lorelei, were unfamiliar with. Though they undoubtedly were meant to be statues depicting great heroic or spiritual figures or symbols, neither he nor she could understand nor comprehend their meaning. Even the mysterious sigil placed at the center, etched upon a giant tablet-shaped object that strangely hovered above the podium, was lost to them.

And yet that was not the most spectacular of what laid before them. Rather, it was not the center that drew their gaze, but instead, what was placed around the borders. Tremendous multicolored icons lined the walls, each depicting different patterns for all to look upon and wonder. These were the sole source of illumination within the chamber; though it was clear that they were not actual windows since they were located deep within the temple instead of along the outer walls. The light shone through them regardless, both revealing the chamber for all to see and to display the icons' various patterns for all to comprehend. Or so they were meant to, as one could imagine.

"Truly magnificent," Lorelei commented as she continued to gaze, her voice sounding distant.

Jon couldn't help but be transfixed as well. Specifically on the surrounding icons.

"Is that stained glass?"

Smiling at the question, Lorelei shook her head. "No, it is some sort of crystalline composite. Though the intended purpose is clearly similar."

That information triggered additional thought. Apparently, this was the Predecessor equivalent of a worship hall; a place where they could congregate en mass. But that was something that Jon found strangely unnerving.

*What had they worshipped? What could a civilization that had emerged approximately the same time as the galaxy itself possibly have revered? What could they have regarded as an existence more significant than their own?*

For a brief moment, Jon pondered the questions. It certainly couldn't have been any present-day object of worship. Even 'God', or at least the modern portrayals of Him, seemed unlikely in this place. Baseline concepts such as the universe, light or evolution seemed just as unseemly for a civilization so scientifically and technologically advanced. And yet...

"The Patriarch," Lorelei suddenly spoke up, watching in bemusement as Jon's head snapped toward her in surprise. "From what I understand, the Predecessors worshipped a being that they referred to, at least in today's common language, as the Patriarch."

Lorelei smiled knowingly. "That was what you were wondering about, yes?" she inquired. "What a civilization as advanced as the Predecessors could possibly see as a superior deity?"

Jon closed his eye. "The thought did cross my mind," he admitted, before looking ahead again. "I don't suppose you know who or what this Patriarch is?"

Lorelei shook her head. "Unfortunately, no. Like Arcadia, the Patriarch was never described in any great detail, so I imagine it, or perhaps Him, to be something the Predecessors universally knew and understood."

"I see," Jon replied, once more thinking. Patriarch. A most ancient word that descended from the Terran sub-language of Greek used to denote the founder and/or leader of a tribe or family. He imagined that this Patriarch was simply that; either the original founder of the Predecessors' civilization or a leader that the Predecessors held in higher regard.

*That would certainly explain many things,* Jon thought while withholding a sigh. As much as he would have liked to validate his hypothesis, there really was no way to do so now. They had a schedule to keep.

"We should go on."

Lorelei nodded. "We'll likely find a passageway to the lower levels around the podium."

"Very well then," Jon replied, straightening his coat as he did.

In silence the pair walked down the great walkway toward the podium, moving under both the shifting light of the icons above and the shadows of the edifices spread about.

# Predecessor Ruins
## Ephesus

The wind was picking up again, lifting her hair to sway slightly. With an almost surreal calm, Kaguya quietly sat, waiting for her enemy to come. Her eyes were closed, and her body was at ease. The kunoichi was using whatever few moments she had left to rest and gather her strength up for the coming fight. Despite that, however, she remained well aware of her environment, as well as quite ready to deal with attempts at intrusion should any occur. Such was her nature; she almost always held her defense, even in the most tranquil of situations and environments.

It had been well over an hour since they had touched down on Ephesus, and she and the rest of her raiders, as well as Barbarossa and Kaiser, had long since established their defenses within the city ruins. The layout of the city had been mapped and memorized by each of them, with the raiders spread about in key locations, either hidden in the ruined buildings or along the streets. Additional defenses, such as automated weapon mounts and traps, had been placed, while barricades had been formed from nearby shards. All the while the fire support teams remained on the towers above, keeping their respective sensory organs out for any incoming craft or sentients. As far as any of them, Kaguya included, were concerned, they were dug in and ready for the incoming storm. It just needed to arrive.

At the moment, Kaguya was sitting in what she assumed to have been a park, or the Predecessor equivalent of such. There was a central pedestal that held a long forgotten sculpture, while around it was what could have only been fields of plants or flowers at one time, but were now little more than patches of dirt. There were also a number of ruined benches, or so Kaguya believed, laid about as well, further lending credence to the hypothesis that this was a recreational area of some sort. And finally, there was an additional number of pedestals, all of which held objects of unrecognizable intrigue, the subjects of their representation long forgotten. A desolate garden, placed within a desolate city upon an equally desolate world.

Suddenly, Kaguya's eyes snapped opened and looked up. "Don't bother trying to hide," she exclaimed. "I've been keeping track of your presence for some time now."

Somewhat reluctantly, Barbarossa moved out into the open. "Most impressive. Very few are even capable of detecting my presence, let alone keeping track of it."

He put on an air of disappointment. "Perhaps my time amongst infidels has made me soft."

"Not at all," Kaguya replied evenly. "It was only when you were close by that I was able to detect you. Something not many could accomplish."

That seemed to satisfy the Leo.

Kaguya quickly moved back to the subject at hand. "What are you doing this far out of position, beast?"

Hearing the question, Barbarossa came to stand next to the still sitting

Kaguya. "Doing what all beasts do when confronted with an object of interest. I was observing you, Miss Fuma."

Kaguya peered up at the Leo. "I don't understand."

Barbarossa had no qualms answering. "The stench of fear is ever prevalent amid our band," he explained disdainfully. "Even upon the most hardened veterans amongst us, I could smell their fear, taste their lamentations. Though many attempt to shroud it, it is not enough to dissuade me."

A sneer crossed the Leo's eyes. "Even if these men and women are worthy of wearing the mantle of the Gold Dragon, a pirate, in the end, is simply a pirate," he growled. "Too obsessed with their own mortality, all the while willingly refusing a higher purpose."

He let out a soft growl. "For a proud warrior of Aslan such as myself, it is all repulsive. *They* are all repulsive."

"I can imagine," Kaguya replied dryly. "So what makes me so interesting by comparison?"

Barbarossa looked directly toward the woman, somewhat mystified. "Because you do not hold that stench," the Leo spoke evenly. "I smell neither fear nor anxiety upon you."

Kaguya closed eyes. "This will not be the first large scale battle I have fought," she explained. "Nor the first in which the odds were greatly stacked against my side."

"Oh?" Barbarossa exclaimed, strangely intrigued. "I was under the impression your kind fought under stealth and shadow, not in the open battlefield."

Kaguya nodded, understanding. "That is how I fight *primarily*. However, as the daughter of the Blue Dragon Lord, I have been trained to fight in the open as well, and, when necessary, actually do so."

She looked down at the dirt, remembering. "I have been trained to fight since I first learned how to walk. And I have been fighting and killing in the name of my clan since I first came of age."

Kaguya then looked up again. "So, what is one more battle?"

Barbarossa let off a smirk at that answer. "Indeed. One more battle would be nothing to a warrior like you."

Before he continued, however, the felinoid took a moment to sniff the air. "And yet, I'm picking up one trace scent upon you," he proclaimed. "Resolve."

He let off another fanged grin as Kaguya glared. "Almost as if you welcome the coming battle. Almost as if you welcome death..."

The Leo stopped upon a shuriken launching past his head. Mere millimeters away from contact.

"Say another word," she spoke in warning, three more shurikens fanning out in her hand. "And you will be dead long before the Imperials reach this place."

Barbarossa blinked, then smiled in a near apologetic fashion. "My apologies. As much as I would like to see you *try* to kill me, I did not intend any offense."

Hearing that assurance, Kaguya withdrew her throwing blades, her eyes boring into Barbarossa's own. And as he looked into the assassin's deep blue eyes, the Leo found himself quite satisfied with what he saw.

"I told you, I am merely observing you. Nothing more, nothing less."

"Observing me," Kaguya repeated. "As potential prey...Or as another predator?"

Barbarossa again smiled. "You catch on well, little princess. Amongst the *Black Sun*'s various officers, you are the only one that I have not directly interacted with. And yet, I have heard so much about your exploits."

Kaguya wasn't sure, but she thought she saw something flicker in the

Leo's eyes.

"With this brief moment before the battle," Barbarossa said. "I thought it would be the opportune time."

The kunoichi mulled over that explanation. Even though she didn't think it was a lie, a part of her felt there was more to Barbarossa's intentions than what he spoke.

The felinoid only seemed to detect that as well. "Now you are considering my words," he stated with clear approval. "Attempting to find any trace of deception."

"Among other things," Kaguya indicated, before rising from her seat, so that she could face her 'comrade' directly. "What is it you're really after beast?"

Barbarossa let off a fanged smile. "As I said, to see if the great Dragon Princess really is a fellow predator," he replied, seeing no point in trying to hide it. "As well as a threat."

Disturbance quickly welled up within Kaguya toward that explanation.

"For your next attempt to take over the *Black Sun*?" she asked, recalling how Barbarossa became part of the crew in the first place.

"That is one scenario, yes," Barbarossa replied, seemingly picking up on the disturbance as well. "But far from the only one in which we would be adversaries."

The Leo seemed to consider for a moment. "For example, let's say I were to wage jihad against your clan," he said, stroking his chin. "Or perhaps make an attempt on your father's life..."

With that statement, Barbarossa could sense a shift in the ninja's demeanor. Despite not making any forward movements, she was quite ready to fully draw her sword and attack. Even so, Kaguya managed to keep that instinct in check, something that Barbarossa found himself approving.

"Would you indeed be a threat to my agenda as I have been led to believe?" Barbarossa continued on regardless. "Or would you simply be another victim of mine?"

Kaguya said nothing, instead steadied herself in preparation of drawing her sword. All the while keeping her fierce blue eyes centered upon Barbarossa's red.

A slight purr emerged from Barbarossa's lips. "You should see yourself as you are now. I have never seen such a fierce gaze from a Terran woman."

This time, Kaguya did reply. "I'm not just *any* Terran woman. I am Fuma Kaguya of the Blue Dragon," she snarled. "And if that name alone does not establish me as a threat to you..."

Her glare only intensified as she declared. "Then what you see before you now certainly will."

Upon that declaration, silence reigned as the wind once swirled. For time seemingly eternal, the two warriors held their gaze, as if waiting for the other to falter first. All the while Kaguya kept her right hand steady and ready to draw her sword, just as Barbarossa held his then-retracted baneclaws close.

Eventually, however, the apparent duel did end with Barbarossa closing his eyes. "Yes," he said. "You indeed live up to your legend, Dragon Princess."

When he opened his eyes again, they glowed with anticipation. "And should the time come," he stated. "You will be a most worthy opponent."

Before Kaguya could reply, her ears picked up a comline from one of the raiders.

"Echo Three to Alfa One, come in."

Without thinking, Kaguya answered. "Alfa One here."

"Alfa, be warned we've lost contact with Lima One," Echo Three announced. "Repeat, we've lost contact with Lima One. Do you have a visual from your position?"

Kaguya again glared at Barbarossa. Lima One was his callsign.

"Affirmative, I have visual of Lima One. He appears to be returning to his original position."

A brief pause before the reply. "Acknowledged Alfa One," Echo Three responded, then signed off.

With that, Kaguya returned to the matter at hand. "This is where you get out of my sight," she declared. "And return to your post."

Though Barbarossa was the Second Officer, Kaguya, as Raider Commander, held ultimate authority when on the ground. Barbarossa had no choice but to comply with her orders, which he had no apparent qualms doing.

"Very well then," the Leo replied, before slowly backing away. "Let us both survive this battle and meet again, Princess."

Silently, Barbarossa disappeared back into the shadows from whence he came. Still, Kaguya waited until he was entirely out of her range of detection before she returned to her original seat. And even then, she remained ready to attack at the slightest provocation.

# Predecessor Temple
# Ephesus

It hadn't taken long to find the passageway, much to Jon and Lorelei's appreciation. In fact, the corridor in question had actually been a lift, strategically placed as a seal behind the main area's podium. After identification, it took only a moment for Lorelei to activate, from which the lift began its descent to the lower levels of the temple. A long and overly drawn descent as far as Jon was concerned, but still progress all the same.

As he waited for the lift to reach its end, Jon, knowing that they were drawing close to the source, again looked toward Lorelei. As with before, the psion seemed relatively unaffected by her surroundings; the hood of her coat was down, and she didn't seem to be exhibiting any kind of emotion beyond her usual curiosity.

For the moment, however, since there was nothing for her to study on that lift, she had her eyes closed and her arms crossed. Clearly, she was waiting for the descent to end as well, but from Jon's point of view, it seemed to be more than simply to reach the anticipated destination. Specifically, the closer they moved to the source, the more Lorelei could *feel* it.

Eventually, however, the lift did indeed reach its end, bringing Jon and Lorelei into an area that, not unlike the preceding center, caused them to look around in awe. Deep underground and almost as large as the hall above, the cavern was vast and shaped like an amphitheater, being circular in design with a series of steps leading down toward an epicenter. Like the rest of the building above, the walls and treads were all in faded gray, while additional numbers of stained glass-like icons, albeit much smaller than those in the above space, were also placed around the outlining walls, encircling the entire area.

Once again, Jon looked upon the various patterns of the icons but was unable to decipher them. However, upon studying each of them, he experienced that strange sense of familiarity he felt previously. All the while, Lorelei observed them in equal wonder, a small smile crossing her lips as she momentarily regarded them with intrigue.

And then, at long last, their eyes drew upon the center. There, at the end of the steps, was an enormous opening, one the size of a meteor crater, that descended into a complete void. No matter how far Jon or Lorelei gazed into it, they could not see the bottom, only absolute darkness. Darkness that, Jon disturbingly felt, really was looking back upon them.

Carefully the pair proceeded down the stairs toward the center, their eyes never leaving the void. Only when they reached the very edge of the chasm did they stop, their respective boots mere millimeters away from the emptiness.

"Is...?" Jon began to murmur, his eye probing the palpable darkness with bewilderment. "Is this it?"

"Yes," Lorelei confirmed. "This is where the ancient power lies."

Jon noted that Lorelei didn't explicitly say it was Arcadia.

"For eons, it has slept, long since the age of its creators," the psion murmured as she continued to gaze downward. "Dormant and forgotten. Waiting to be awoken once more."

Slowly, she raised her hand outward, as if to actually touch the invisible force.

"Do you feel it, Captain?" she asked, almost mesmerized. "Do you behold it?"

Silence was the pirate's response as his eye held to the darkness, his gaze seemingly descending into it as far as it could reach. Then, progressing slowly enough that Jon just barely realized it was all happening, the pirate captain watched as strange images began to take shape from within the darkness. Visions that initially began as simple lights and patterns, but then, like the icons that surrounded them now, took on great depth and complexity.

Suddenly, the visions emerged from the abyss seemingly grafting themselves into his mind. Visions that he could not comprehend, but still recognized as holding to terrible prophecy. Chaos and destruction of the utmost magnitude, with each image more nightmarish than the last. And once more before he realized it, Jon was at the center of it all, watching as a bewildered observer, too entrapped to feel even vestiges of terror.

The sky shattered as lightning erupted, and the earth quaked with unending thunder. Starships and far stranger craft rained fire upon one another and the surface of countless worlds, reducing all that existed upon them into smoldering ruin. Beings of various shapes and sizes, identifiable only as blank and colorless silhouettes, fought each other using equally diverse weapons and powers to destroy one another with vengeful fury. Infinite voices, each calling out in anguish or rage, echoed through the galaxy, such that even the void itself trembled with their power. All cumulated into a great maelstrom of destruction, one that ostensibly engulfed the entire galaxy in fire.

And then, abruptly, it ended. Jon was once again only viewing the darkness below. No more shapes took form, no more visions emerged. And where the roars and screams had once been infinite, there was only silence. All except for the voice beside him.

"Captain?" Lorelei repeated, her face now one of concern. From her perspective, it seemed her compatriot was transfixed, his single eye gazing toward something that lay beyond the abyss.

Hearing her voice, Jon blinked his eye once and then narrowed it. "All I behold," he stated with finality. "Is darkness."

Blinking her own eyes, Lorelei decided to proceed. "Well," she said. "Then let us bring about the light."

Purposefully, she held her arm outward over a precise part of the floor. A moment later, a single tile rose up and levitated before her, its smooth and featureless surface then reforming into a peculiar configuration: two slots, obviously keyholes, on either side of a single colorless orb, all with various Predecessor script inscribed around.

Hand still outstretched, Lorelei looked toward a pouch on the right side of her belt, which, acting without aid, opened allowing Aurea and Argentum to float out. Seemingly resonating, the two keys momentarily circled in the air before slowly and carefully descending and inserting themselves into the keyholes. Aurea in the right slot and Argentum in the left.

Feeling a sudden surge of energy around him, Jon looked down to see an elaborate network of energy lines begin to pulsate through the floor, moving from the edges of the room and down into the opening. The surrounding stained glass icons began to glow, their colors and imagery becoming all the more illuminated and vibrant as additional energy lines throbbed around them. And then, at last, both Jon and Lorelei watched as the initially colorless orb began to glow, taking on a fire-like radiance as energy lines, emanating from the keyholes, flowed directly into it.

Slowly, Lorelei withdrew her arm in order to undo her glove and reveal her right hand.

"It will likely take time to gather the appropriate amount of energy," she warned as she placed her glove in her coat pocket. "I do not know how long the process will take."

"Or what will happen when it is completed," Jon surmised.

"This is what I pursued from the beginning Captain. This is why I had the *Black Sun* created, why I took you and your brother into my service on Aurora."

She then cast her usual smile. "It's only proper that we see this through to the end. Regardless of what may happen."

For a time, Jon only stared at the psion, searching for any sign of hesitance on her part. However, upon finding none, he closed his eye and took a step back, giving Lorelei room to work.

"Do as you must," he said simply. "I will hold the ground until it is done."

Giving one last nod of gratitude, Lorelei returned to the floating console, her amethyst eyes gazing upon the orb. Then, without any further pause, she closed her own eyes and reached her hand out, placing it onto the orb's crystalline surface.

Upon that action, the energy outpouring intensified.

## Flint Pirates umbra *Black Sun*
## Ephesus System

"Picking up an energy surge emanating from the planet," Anna reported as she looked over her monitor. "Looks like it's begun."

Alex nodded. At the very least that part of the trip was on track.

"Continue to..."

Anna's monitor beeped before he could finish. With trepidation, Anna looked it over.

"Incoming arc signatures, bearing one-nine-two mark zero-three-nine!" she announced, causing all heads to snap around. "They're Imperial!"

Alex's hands tightened around the chair's armrests. "How many?" he asked.

"Approximately thirty ships, likely more," Anna replied, her voice apprehensive.

The younger Flint closed his eyes. He had expected Drake to personally lead the charge, but that didn't mean he had been looking forward to it. Any more than he had the rest of the battle.

"ETA?"

"Ten minutes."

Alex nodded at the information. "Move to intercept," he commanded. "Standby to attack."

Upon the First Officer's order, Davis brought the still cloaked *Black Sun* around and moved her at her best speed toward the exit area of the Imperial armada. Minutes later, once she reached an appropriate position, Davis brought the ship to a slower, more stable velocity. From that vantage point, she would automatically be facing the enemy fleet once it emerged from arc.

The bridge once more fell to silence as the crew waited for the first emergence. Whereas before they had merely anticipated the Imperial taskforce 's arrival, now they knew for a fact it would come in the next few minutes. As a result, an even greater degree of anxiousness emerged within the bridge crew. All eyes never left the viewscreen.

However, none of them were as anxious as Alex. Though the younger Flint did well to keep it concealed, there was no way he could keep it from affecting his inner being. This would be the first time he would command the *Sun* during combat, and thus his mind became wracked with self-awareness and borderline doubt while the rest of his body responded in kind. Was he up to it? Could he really command the ship as well as Jon or Barbarossa? What would happen if it turned out he wasn't sufficient to the task?

"One minute to reversion!" Anna announced as she continued to monitor the enemy fleet's approach.

Swallowing, Alex knew, regardless of whatever doubts he had, there was no turning back now. Like it or not, he was in command, and the crew, despite not knowing what to make of him at this time, were looking to him for guidance and authority. Therefore, he inwardly forced all of his doubts back, focusing instead on the imminent battle, but not before closing his eyes to give a silent prayer.

*Mom, if you're out there... Please be with us!*

"Ten seconds to reversion!" Anna pronounced. "Nine... Eight... Seven... Six... Five... Four... Three... Two... One...!"

At that, the bridge crew watched as the armada emerged from arc. One after another, the grey warships appeared over Ephesus, each bearing the Imperial Crest somewhere upon their hulls. Their cannons were already fully charged, their projectile tubes were already loaded, and within seconds the armada assumed an attack formation and began to advance toward the planet. All while smaller craft, from fighters to transport shuttles, started to launch from their respective motherships.

Now with the fleet fully emerged in front of him, Alex could only take one final breath. Somewhere in the back of his mind, he recalled a line spoken amongst Imperial umbramen.

"There are only two types of ships," he murmured under his breath. "Umbras… and targets."

With that thought in mind, he lowered the command scope and peered in, selecting the nearest targets for a torpedo attack.

Hopefully, the *Subjugator* would be amongst them, in which case he just might be able to end this early...

"Enemy weapons targeting!" Anna suddenly shouted in warning.

Before Alex could shout a responding 'What!?', a number of the Imperial ships suddenly turned their respective beam cannon turrets about and fired at once, sending golden beams toward the *Sun*'s position. And not only were the beams on track, but one or two of them even managed to strike, causing resulting explosions across the umbra's hull.

"Evasive maneuvers!" Alex called out before he realized it, all the while Davis worked the helm to bring the ship out of the firefight. "Decloak and return fire!"

A moment later, the *Black Sun* materialized in space, her shields immediately raising and her own beam cannons firing back at the aggressors. An unlucky *Dauntless*-class destroyer was caught in the line, her form instantly obliterating upon the crimson beam shots striking home, while another ship, a *Judicator*-class cruiser, took considerable damage to her stern. However, the Imperials were far from intimidated, with a number of ships breaking off from the main formation to pursue the now retreating umbra, raining beam and projectile fire upon her as she sped away.

"How in the First Circle did they do that!?" Davis hollered as he struggled to keep the ship on course. "We were cloaked for god's sake!"

Contrarily it wasn't hard for Alex to realize the answer. "Psions," he muttered in rising frustration. "They're using psions."

A cold wave quickly eclipsed the bridge, even as it shook from the incoming weapons fire. It was the only logical explanation. Psionic Terrans were far from unheard of, and Starfleet had an open policy toward their recruitment. And though the majority of them endeavored to become Warlocks, more than a fair number, namely those whose powers were too weak to use in a weaponized fashion, had chosen to join other Starfleet branches.

As a result, Drake now had the perfect countermeasure to the *Sun*'s cloaking system. Whether there were psions aboard each ship or only aboard the taskforce flagship or another designated control ship, the fact was they could track the sentient minds aboard the *Sun*, which could not be cloaked with the rest of the ship. And given that the Imperial fleet had responded quickly, Alex realized, the psions in question were directly tied to the tactical stations.

*Well,* Alex thought as the ship rumbled again from beam shots striking her stern shields. *Looks like we're going to be following your strategy after all Jon.*

With that in mind, Alex began making adjustments upon the scope's controls.

"Davis, I'm giving you control of the cloaking system!" he shouted to the helmsman. "Engage it when you see an opportunity.

Otherwise, we're fighting the old fashioned way!"

Another rumble as more weapons hit. "All ahead full!" Alex bellowed amidst the rocking.

"Aye sir!" Davis immediately replied, watching as the new switch materialized on his console. By now, in spite of his nature, the helmsman was too focused on his post to be afraid, his professionalism and will to survive overriding whatever cowardice he possessed. The same was true for the rest of the crew.

With that, the *Black Sun* twisted back around to face her pursuers, bringing her bow cannons and projectile launchers to bear.

Moments later, her beam cannons rang with crimson fire while torpedoes and missiles exited their respective tubes, striking down the various warships and opening a hole for the umbra to slip through, thereby allowing her to, once again, advance at best speed upon the enemy fleet...

# Chapter XXXV: Into the Fire

## Predecessor Ruins
## Ephesus

All at once, the telltale sounds of sub-arc engines filled the air, alerting the raiders that the Imperials had, at long last, reached them. Though they had been forewarned ten minutes ago when Gran made the call from the *Black Sun*, it was only at this point that the pirates appreciated that the battle had begun. That feeling lingered when their anti-air batteries and fire support units began to fire, launching crimson shots into the sky and shooting several of the approaching shuttles and transport craft out of the air before they could advance, only for the supporting air units to return that fire with their own beam and projectile weapons. Two of the automated batteries and one of the raider fire support units were instantly obliterated in the counterattack, forcing the others to deviate between attacking the transports and the assault units. As a result, a number of transports slipped through the defenses.

Soon, the first transport units dropped down both within and around the ruins, deploying their troops and armor in rapid succession before lifting away. Dozens upon dozens of marines cabled down from the ships as they swooped in while armored vehicles, namely tanks, were also dropped in midflight. They landed either in the vast desert or the open streets of the ruined city. And though some were picked off in mid-drop, the majority managed to make it to ground level. Their response fire, especially from the tanks, forced the raiders to either fallback or take whatever cover they could. Additional shelling from the air, namely Shrike and Vulture gunships and the ubiquitous Condor, only furthered the Imperials advance, such that they were not even hindered by the city's natural obstacles.

However, the defenders ensured the fight was not entirely one-sided. Having sensed the Imperials' approach even before she and her ground forces had received the warning from the *Black Sun*, Kaguya was well on the move, sprinting through the city streets with her ninjato already drawn. Immediately she ran toward a marine team as it touched down, advancing through their formation at a speed too fast for them to react, cutting them down one after another. Even when one barely managed to raise his rifle just as he was falling from his initial wound, it was all too easy for Kaguya to twist around and send a kunai into the marine's throat, finishing him off for good. From there, she snapped a grenade off one of the corpses and threw it straight up into the still present Condor, whose pilot had made the mistake of remaining to launch an attack against her. A second later, the assault shuttle was rocked by the explosion; its ruined form spun out of control before crashing into a nearby building.

Kaguya just barely had enough time to take another grenade off one of the corpses before additional beams flew at her. During her initial attack, another marine force had advanced onto her position and was beginning its assault. Forced to leap backward, she used her ninjato blade to deflect the incoming fire. The ninja then went into another dead run, dropping behind an obstruction, then quickly moving to another, larger one. By that point, the marines had dispersed in an attempt to envelop her, all the while continuing to fire upon her position. The raider commander responded by throwing two more kunai, both impaling the heads of two marines, who instantly fell. Never still, she darted out of her cover once more, beam fire trailing her as she ran at her attackers.

Suddenly, she twisted around and leaped into the air, landing a solid kick into one marine's faceplate. Now knocked on the ground, Kaguya wasted no time in finishing the soldier by impaling him with her ninjato, then redrawing it to stab another marine, who was attempting to spear her through the back. A third attacker moved in for the kill. The Dragon Princess swung her ninjato around and catapulted the second marine forward as a flying shield, both deflecting the third's fire and distracting him long enough for her to leap back into action. As the Imp moved aside to avoid the impromptu shield, Kaguya landed next to him then sprung upward in a spin, beheading the third marine in one slash.

A stray beam soared past her cheek. At first, she attempted to respond with another kunai strike, but following another beam shot that she barely evaded, Kaguya opted to duck and charge straight at the offending marine. With her advance, the Imp pulled a grenade and threw it at her. Kaguya instantly inverted her ninjato, bringing the dull side about, and swatted the grenade in midair, reversing its course. The resulting explosion dispatched the attacker, but his comrades were quick to storm the position, pouring beam fire at the charging ninja and forcing her to retreat.

With a series of back handsprings, Kaguya moved out of the line of fire and back into nearby cover, but not before dispatching another Imp with a well-placed shuriken. Simultaneously, a Vulture's rocket attack from overhead resulted in a series of nearby explosions, momentarily obstructing her hearing. Knowing that her attackers' hearing was also impeded, the kunoichi chose to advance, sprinting to the left and into a set of building ruins. No beam fire trailed her this time, indicating that the marines hadn't seen her switch places. This was quickly verified when she peered out; the marines were indeed still focused on her previous location. Now having abandoned their own cover they were redeploying to surround it.

Quietly, Kaguya waited until the Imps were in the position she wanted before striking. Charging from the building, she redrew her ninjato and went into another sprint, cutting into the marines as she ran. So fast did she move that, even with enhanced optics, the marines barely made out their aggressor beyond a blur and complimenting series of glinting silver arcs. Once the last soldier was dispatched, the Dragon Princess ended her dash, her boots practically skidding to a halt. And then, with no small amount of flourish, she slashed her ninjato to the side. Only with the end of the distinct cutting sound did the marines, who had seemingly frozen upon their being struck, fall over dead.

A moment later, Kaguya picked up a new sound, precisely that of caterpillar treads and the shattering of a set of ruins. Realizing the danger, Kaguya raced away from the area, just as a Decurion medium tank emerged from a nearby crumbling building. Within seconds its main cannon discharged a golden beam straight into a nearby tower, taking out one of the raiders' anti-air units in the process. Continuing its advance, the Decurion's turret rotated, firing off several more shots at different angles, before a nearby raider successfully launched an AT rocket, obliterating the tank. Said raider was quickly gunned down by a passing Vulture's beam vulcan.

Taking a moment to catch her breath, Kaguya listened intently as the battle continued around her. She could tell that the raiders, having initially been pushed back, had regained their initiative. The sound of gunfire and explosions had intensified over the last few minutes, and the comm., which she had only now deigned to listen in on, was filled with calls from her troops striking back against enemy positions. Even better, the Imperials were already blundering into the traps that had been previously set; more than a few calls reported of enemy troops triggering a tripline explosive or tanks moving over previously hidden mines. And then there were those who ended up crossing into the firing zone of automated defense turrets. What had initially begun as an Imperial advance was now, slowly – *too* slowly in Kaguya's opinion – transitioning into a far more even battle.

*But how long will it last?* Kaguya wondered almost grievously. Yes, the battle had just begun, and to hold the line was indeed the whole objective. To hold the Imperials back just long enough until the fight at last shifted and the pirates gained the offensive. But would it actually happen? Could the raiders fulfill that objective, despite all that was occurring now? Kaguya had no way of knowing for sure, but she definitely had her doubts.

The raider commander momentarily closed her eyes. Though she had stated to Barbarossa earlier that she was no stranger to battle, a part of her couldn't help but feel that, perhaps, this one would be different. That, indeed, this may very well be her last fight...

Suddenly, she picked up a new sound, that of another Decurion tank moving by the building she was using as cover. Kaguya's eyes flashed with understanding; this tank was not only unaware of her presence but also well within her reach.

Moving up to the second story, the kunoichi ducked beside a nearby wall and looked out. Sure enough, the Decurion was proceeding slowly down the street, its cannon and secondary weapons firing at different points, destroying distant targets and keeping any nearby raider teams from advancing. And as Kaguya surmised, none of those weapons were turning toward her position.

As such, when the tank moved right under her, Kaguya, her ninjato redrawn and angled to impale, dropped down from the building onto the Decurion. Immediately she pierced her blade through its shield and armor, killing the driver and forcing the tank to halt. An instant later, she withdrew her ninjato and bayonetted another section, killing the secondary gunner as well. Suddenly, the turret hatched opened and another tanker, likely the commander/main gunner, emerged. Seeing Kaguya, he attempted to shoot, but Kaguya was quicker, dispatching the enemy soldier with a shuriken.

Jumping onto the top of the turret, the ninja produced the second grenade that she had taken from the dead Imp, activated it, and dropped it in.

Though she had been tempted to capture the tank upon killing the crew, she didn't know how to operate it, and she doubted any of her raiders would have been able to as well. Besides, using an enemy vehicle was a good way of being taken out by friendly fire. Thus, upon hearing the distinct 'clang' of the grenade landing on the floor, Kaguya leaped off the tank and into the distance. One loud boom later, and the Decurion was little more than flying shards and a burning hulk.

With that completed, Kaguya slashed her ninjato about and ran down the street, looking for more enemies to kill. The explosions and gunfire continued to sound around her as the raiders held the line against their aggressors.

# Predecessor Temple
# Ephesus

It hadn't taken much for Jon to learn that the Imperials had just arrived. Even as deep below ground as he was now, the rumbling was practically constant, with rocks and debris occasionally falling from the ceiling. For a fleeting moment he wondered if it would become so intense that it would result in the collapse of the whole roof, but after further consideration decided that the chamber was deep enough to protect them. Alongside, he doubted the Predecessors hadn't considered *that* possibility when they created the space.

With his usual calm, he moved to another part of the space, all the while holding his watch over Lorelei. Though she appeared dormant since she first placed her hand on the orb, Jon knew that it was taking all of her focus, as well as her power, to break the final seal. The energy lines continually flowing into the opening were the only indication that the process was on-going. Whatever it was that lay within the darkness, hopefully, would soon be released.

A significant rumble erupted, jolting additional dust and falling fragments from the ceiling. The vibration was so strong Jon had to steady his footing, albeit marginally. He could tell, even from this depth, that the Imperials were stepping up their assault with each passing moment. What he could not tell, however, was how the battle was proceeding. Yes, the fact there was still rumbling indicated that there was still fighting, but which side was dominating the fight? Were his raiders holding the line, or were the Imperials already in the process of breaking through to the temple?

Sneering, he shook his head of such thoughts. Like it or not, there really was nothing he could do about it. As much as a part of him yearned to be there, to directly lead the raiders against the Imperial advance, he was neither in a position to do so nor was it his role in this battle. Whereas theirs was to hold the line against the smaller pieces, his was to confront the enemy king. As such, all he could do was trust that the raiders would hold out regardless, though Kaguya, Barbarossa, and Kaiser being amongst their number gave some reassurance. 'Some' being the keyword of course.

Forcing that thought away, Jon continued to pace, his eye moving away from Lorelei and toward the ground under him. The energy lines seemed to have sped up over the last few minutes, but not by much. It appeared that, whatever Lorelei was doing, it would indeed take some time before completion. Jon naturally grimaced at that thought; the process could take anywhere from minutes to hours, perhaps even days, and the Imperials would only continue their assault throughout.

That, of course, led to the other problem he had to face. What was *really* lying at the bottom – if there was indeed a bottom – of that opening? At this point, Jon was willing to utilize any advantage he could gain against the Imperials, but would it be something along that line? Could it indeed be a weapon of great destructive power, or would it simply be an item of archeological value and nothing else? Or even worse, was it something that, once brought back into activity, would turn against both the Imperials and his forces? Perhaps even possessing its own sentience and accompanying hostility?

All worthwhile questions, yet they could only be answered through the process being completed. Until then, the Flint Pirates would have to make do with what they already had available while hoping against hope that, whatever laid in that abyss, it would not be something else for them to contend with. Jon especially didn't appreciate the possibility of fighting a long lost Predecessor superweapon.

Fortunately, that was not amongst his list of worries at the moment. With the two battles ongoing in orbit and on the surface, as well as the one he would soon face, he already had enough issues to capture his attention. That in itself brought another thought to Jon's mind; where was Drake? The most logical answer was that the Admiral was still aboard his flagship, directing the battles at hand until they reached a point where his troops could fight without his leadership. If that were the case, then the Flint Pirates were holding their own, as the Admiral was forced to delay his entry until his initial objectives were assured.

Strangely, Jon found himself both appreciating and disdaining that theory at the same time. On the one hand, it meant that the good Admiral already faced difficulties, thereby allowing Jon, and by extension Lorelei, a brief moment of calm. On the other, a part of Jon, the part that seriously hated waiting, was all too anxious to get the fight started. Both so he could have his rematch, and the potential of at last avenging his mother, and that he wouldn't have to continue this near helpless inactivity.

Another set of violent rumbling only accentuated his thought. Jon closed his eye as he again forced back that line of contemplation. Just as it was with the fighting on the surface, he would fulfill his role to watch over Lorelei and stand by until Drake made his sudden and all too likely theatrical appearance. Stand by within that tomb, long buried and until recently forgotten, all while its creators' last remaining treasure was slowly but surely brought back to the light.

With that resolve, Jon moved to another part of the chamber and quietly sat down on one of the steps. Once he managed to make himself comfortable, he then resigned to wait and watch.

# Flint Pirates umbra *Black Sun*
# Ephesus System

With another surge of crimson, the *Black Sun*'s bow dorsal cannon fired off a single beam striking a nearby *Ravager*-class cruiser. With its shields already battered, the strike was more than enough to decimate the cruiser's defenses, penetrate the starboard side of the hull, and exit the portside. Seconds later, the cruiser's entire structure buckled from the strain and energy flux, resulting in the *Ravager* detonating in an enormous explosion.

Momentarily feeling elated at the cruiser's destruction, Alex only became dismayed to see that, from the glare of the explosion, two *Harbingers* emerged and began firing off a spray of missiles. Fortunately, Davis noticed their approach as well and, without Alex having to order him, engaged the cloak and increased thrust, bringing the *Black Sun* out of the firing line. However, it wasn't long before the destroyers, as well as other imperial ships, switched to their beam cannons and began raining fire toward the *Black Sun*'s new position, forcing Davis to disengage the cloak and bring the shields back online. Alex, still operating from the captain's scope, returned fire.

"Another *Ravager* – off our stern!" Anna warned as she continued to monitor the sensors. By now her voice was strained from all the readings she had been forced to declare. "And a *Vindicator*-class battlecruiser moving against our starboard side!"

"Goddammit, they just keep coming!" Davis growled from the helm. He was forced to put the ship back into another evasive pattern to avoid another spray of missiles. Fortunately, those that he was unable to evade were quickly picked off by the *Black Sun*'s phalanx emplacements.

Alex cringed as he returned fire with the *Black Sun*'s beam cannons, as well as throwing in a few missiles of his own. It was one of the few times Davis was right about something. Alex wished he was dead wrong. There were Imperial ships everywhere; whether he looked into the command scope or the viewscreen, Alex's eyes saw nothing but grey hulls moving about space like great leviathans, their gun turrets continuously trained upon the *Black Sun*. A virtual school of grey sharks attempting to prey upon a lone black orca.

The younger Flint grimaced as the *Vindicator* open fired its main guns, scoring hits across the *Black Sun*'s starboard side and causing the entire ship to rumble from the shock. At Anna's last count, they had been engaged with thirty ships within the Imperial ranks, several of which he had quickly dispatched. But that number had increased within the last few minutes as more and more Imperial warships entered the system. Drake had devised his strategy well in that regard. Keep a number of the Imperial fleet within outlying space, such that for every ship the *Black Sun* destroyed, two would enter the system to replace it.

*Possibly the most efficient way to overwhelm us,* Alex thought as he continued to fight, waiting for a firing solution to form upon the *Vindicator. He knows he can't take us out all at once, so he's going to wear us down first.*

When the scope beeped indicating a target lock, he launched a single torpedo at the *Vindicator*. He watched as the torpedo twisted through space toward the battlecruiser; the warship attempting to shoot it down with its main cannons and missiles. However, the torpedo's shielding held. It struck the *Vindicator,* smashing into its bow shields, almost breaking them upon impact. Alex followed up with a barrage from his own cannons, breaking the shields entirely and turning the battlecruiser into fiery remnants. Only its stern quarter remained mostly intact.

Alex rapidly fired off another torpedo toward the incoming *Ravager* which had moved in so close it had no time to respond. He suspected that the enemy captain hadn't realized the umbra held another loaded and readied torpedo. Regardless the result was the same, with the torpedo plowing through the cruiser's shields and burying itself right into the bow. The resulting explosion obliterated the *Ravager*.

Holding himself steady from the resulting shockwave, Alex just managed to see three more destroyers – two *Dauntless* and one *Interceptor*-class – firing torpedoes of their own.

"Left full rudder!"

"Left full rudder aye!" Davis affirmed as he brought the ship about, resisting the urge to bite his lip. Upon the torpedoes approach, he re-engaged the cloak and sent the umbra into a steep bank, causing the projectiles to suddenly lose their target. The warheads passed by the *Black Sun*'s stern without harm, though one had come agonizingly close to hitting an aft beam cannon.

"Don't decloak!" Alex ordered as he reangled the beam cannons, setting them upon each of the three destroyers. The defensive left turn had presented the *Black Sun*'s broadside to the enemy vessels. A second later, Alex fired, scoring hits on all three Imp ships, obliterating them before they could aim their own beam cannons accurately. Swiftly, he took out another *Harbinger*, which had blindly moved into the kill zone, before allowing Davis to drop the cloak. Alex continued firing at Imp targets, even while the ship was in the process of rematerializing.

Despite the odds, the battle was not entirely one-sided. While Drake had been meticulous in his plans as expected, Alex had come to realize that the Flint Pirates possessed a few advantages of their own. And not just with the *Black Sun*'s capabilities.

The first advantage was regarding the enemy psions. While they were indeed directing their fleet's tactical firepower, Alex quickly recognized that they were acting as spotters rather than gunners; they were only feeding targeting data to the warships rather than directly operating their weapons. As such, upon the *Black Sun* cloaking, there was a brief lag when the psions had to estimate the *Black Sun*'s position and then feed the resultant data to the actual gunners. A truly miniscule window in time, but one Alex found he could easily exploit by striking down enemy vessels before they could properly return fire, forcing the *Black Sun* to decloak. This also meant the enemy weapons were not entirely accurate, even when the *Black Sun* was in the open.

The second advantage was, ironically, in regard to numbers. The Imperials numbered anywhere from the tens to the hundreds, and yet all of their energy was being directed toward sinking a single, smaller target. As a result, Davis was free to maneuver the *Black Sun* in any way he wanted, while the Imperials were forced to coordinate and move more elaborately lest they collide or fire upon one another. The *Black Sun*'s superior mobility, as well as her cloak, only emphasized this advantage that much more.

However, as indicated by an additional set of golden beams striking the *Black Sun*'s shields, those advantages only held up so much. When it came down to it, Alex thought as the ship again shook around him, the Imperials' superior firepower and numbers gave them a far greater edge, especially in the long run. All he and the rest of the crew could hope for was, like those on the surface, to last long enough for a miracle to happen. Such as Arcadia turning out to indeed be a weapon.

"Multiple torpedo launches detected!" Anna suddenly alerted from her post. "Origin unknown!"

Alex grimaced, knowing all too well what it meant. *I was wondering when they'd show up,* he thought with more annoyance than anger.

"Gran!"

"Listening in now!" Gran affirmed from the comm. station. A few moments later, she followed up. "Enigma signals identified! Triangulating coordinates!"

The resultant coordinates soon filtered into Alex's scope, highlighting another wolfpack of enemy umbras. Alex's eyes narrowed at the data. Just like at Kurzis, the umbras were kept on the outskirts of the system, from which they would be used to bombard the *Black Sun* with torpedoes and missiles. All while the *Black Sun* was held up fighting the conventional warships.

"Damn you, Drake," Alex snarled under his breath, before barking orders once more. "Evasive maneuvers! Unmask beam cannons!"

"Wouldn't it be better to cloak!?" Davis called out just as another beam shot struck, causing the *Black Sun* to shake once again.

"Standby!" Alex replied. He suspected that was part of the reason behind the umbra attack; to get them to cloak and leave them open to bombardment from the other warships. Of course, with the torpedoes closing in and the *Black Sun* maneuvering as she was, they were in position to bombard her anyway. Especially when her own weapons were focused on the enemy torpedoes.

Even so, there was no other choice to be had. Coming about, the *Black Sun*'s beam cannons swiveled around and began firing at the incoming torpedoes, while her broadside missile launchers and phalanx providing additional if only delaying force. One after another the torpedoes were struck by the weapons, with some managing to deflect with their shielding while others were immediately obliterated. However, the rate of destruction was far too slow. More than a handful of torpedoes managed to break through the *Black Sun*'s defensive fire.

Grimacing, Alex again knew that there was no choice to be had.

"Cloak. Now!"

Without hesitation, Davis again engaged the cloak. While the *Black Sun* flickered from existence, he brought the ship to full speed. As with before, the torpedoes, their guidance and target now lost, shot aimlessly through space, narrowly missing the umbra's cloaked form as it moved away from their line. This time none of their numbers even came close.

However, the Imperials had not only anticipated that outcome but also prepared for it. While the *Black Sun* had been preoccupied shooting down the enemy torpedo barrage, a number of ships had moved closer and into ideal firing positions. This, combined with the gunners predicting the *Black Sun*'s simple evasion without the aid of their psion spotters, allowed the ships to fire their beam cannons on target almost instantly.

Struck from numerous vectors, the *Black Sun* shook as beams raked across her hull. Though her armor did well to withstand much of the damage, it couldn't prevent it entirely. Scars and breaches began to emerge around different areas of the hull, while secondary damage became a near constant. Only when Davis managed to disengage the cloak, in turn allowing the shields to automatically reengage, was the assault fully deflected, with the now thoroughly battered *Black Sun* charging through the fire.

Alex grimaced as the last of the shockwaves died away, allowing the bridge to return to a relatively stable point. He had known exactly what would happen the moment the *Black Sun* cloaked, but once more was not in a position to do anything about it.

"Damage report!" he shouted as he returned fire with the main cannons.

"Hull breaches in Decks Five, Seven and Ten!" Anna shouted in return. "Moebius is engaged in those areas!"

Alex took that report with minor solace. It could have been *a lot* worse.

"Move us deeper in!" he commanded just as the Imps began firing again. "The umbras won't fire if their own ships are in the way!"

Following that command, Davis brought the *Black Sun* around and moved her further into the Imperial formation, drawing even closer to the individual ships. Though this made the *Black Sun* more vulnerable to the visible ships' firepower, it accomplished exactly what Alex intended and kept the umbras from gaining a straight target lock on her. As well, it even had the advantage of surprising a few of the Imperial commanders, who had not expected the umbra to come charging into their midst. The bonus was realized when the *Black Sun*'s cannons struck multiple Imperial ships, damaging or destroying them outright.

However, the *Black Sun* remained even more within reach of the Imperial guns all the same, and the surrounding ships were quick to capitalize on that opportunity. More gold beams struck the *Black Sun*'s shields, while Alex struggled to return fire against the aggressors. By now the pirate ship was so close to the enemy that Alex was using her phalanx against the Imperial warships, and vice versa. An additional number of rival vessels were obliterated as a result, with the singular fire of the cannons and the overwhelmingly rapid fire of the phalanx working in tandem.

All at once, a pair of *Fury*-class frigates, which had moved to run on the umbra from different vectors, were obliterated, one being struck by beam cannon fire while the other buckled to a sheer wall of phalanx fire. Another pair of ships, a *Malevolent*-class cruiser and another *Harbinger* respectively, attempted to move against the umbra in their place, but by that time the *Black Sun*'s missile tubes had been replenished, and Alex was quick to fire off a spray against either ship. As a result, both Imperial warships broke off their assault, being forced to gun down the approaching missiles, thereby allowing the *Black Sun* to turn around and bring her beam cannons to bear. The *Harbinger* was quickly destroyed, while the *Malevolent* was struck in her bridge tower, rendering her brainless. The rest of the cruiser was promptly obliterated by a follow-up cannon shot.

Alex was just about to breathe a sigh of relief when he saw another ship move against him, a *Thunderer*-class battleship. Before he could give the order to evade, the massive warships' bow mounted triple beam cannons open fired, sending triplet beam shots into the *Black Sun*'s port shields. Such was the power of the cannons that the *Black Sun* rocked against the fire.

"Shields down to sixty-seven percent!" the tactical operator standing in for Barbarossa announced.

Inwardly snarling, Alex returned cannon fire upon the Imperial battleship. However, unlike the destroyers and cruisers he had killed to that point, the mighty battleship's shields easily held against the *Black Sun*'s cannon fire. In turn, the *Thunderer* fired a second salvo, as well as a compliment of torpedoes and missiles.

"Evade! All power to main drive!" Alex shouted to Davis, who was already gunning the *Black Sun*'s arc engine.

With a blast of crimson from the main thruster, the *Black Sun* nearly reached its maximum sub-arc speed in a matter of seconds, all the while her cannons and phalanx worked to strike down the incoming torpedoes and missiles. The umbra managed to rocket away, just as the great battleship crossed into her previous position.

Tensely, Alex waited until a firing solution formed on the *Superior* before triggering tubes one and two. Immediately, two torpedoes shot out of the *Black Sun*'s bow, then twisted around and moved against the enemy battleship. The *Thunderer* was already throwing up a storm of phalanx fire while attempting to bring her own cannons to bear. Unfortunately for the Imperials, the torpedoes easily bored through the phalanx fire and plowed straight into the battleship's port shields, which barely held against the dual impact.

However, that was more than enough for Alex. With the battleship's shields weakened, it only took a few more shots from the umbra's stern beam cannons to break through the defenses and rip into the port side. Unrelenting, Alex maintained fire as the *Thunderer* completed its pass. Suddenly the battleship was rocked by an enormous explosion that instantly left her powerless. And though her scorched and darkened hull remained intact, it now floated aimlessly in the void, entirely out of the battle.

Suddenly, Anna spoke up again. "I'm picking up multiple signals incoming at arc speed!" she warned. "All small craft!"

Alex inwardly cursed. Like the umbras, he was also wondering when *they* would show up. If he had to guess, Drake had kept his carriers, which lacked the firepower necessary to take part in the direct battle, in outlying space so they could launch their fighters and bombers away from the melee. As well as being able to keep supplying said fighters and bombers in a continuous and consistent stream.

*He's definitely trying to wear us down,* Alex thought, sneering as the ship shook once more from enemy beam cannon fire. *And doing a damn good job of it!*

The sensors quickly beeped again. "Enemy warships now launching fighters!" Anna announced, just as Alex's scope picked up the designated smallcraft emerging from their motherships. And though he wasn't detecting any bombers coming out with them, the younger Flint knew that they would not be far behind.

"Launch Corsairs!" Alex commanded as he made adjustments to the weapon systems for anti-air defense. "Standby for enemy bomber attack!"

Taking a short, collected breath, Boss lifted her Corsair from the deck and slowly moved it toward the launch area. Once in position and authorization from the control deck was received, the veteran gunned her thrusters and fired out of the *Black Sun*'s underbelly port, launching into the battlefield at instant combat velocity. She was followed shortly after by the other twenty-three fighters that made up Corsair and Buccaneer Squadrons.

Sensors quickly highlighting enemy positions throughout the surrounding space, Boss didn't like what she saw, in either her displays or through her canopy. It seemed like the entire sector was now filled with Imperial warships of various types, ranging from the smaller frigates to the enormous battleships, all while fighters and bombers began to add their own numbers to the battle. Even worse, her sensors were picking up multiple craft moving in from arc speed – to say nothing of additional warships that might have been coming in alongside them – further augmenting the Imperial ranks. All against her own meager group of twenty-four.

*At least we won't have any shortage of targets,* Boss thought banefully as she continued to look out over all that was before her. As she had instructed before launch, the squadrons broke up into individual elements, two fighters each, and moved to engage at will, sweeping the immediate space around the *Black Sun*. With Corsair Two by her side, Boss once again gunned her thrusters as she found her first set of victims, a flight of Mustangs that had already changed their vectors to intercept her and her wingman. A costly mistake.

Quickly entering range, Boss and her wingman both let loose their vulcans, striking down two of the Mustangs as both groups intersected. Swiftly, she and Corsair Two broke up and turned against the remaining pair, with Boss trailing her selected target. The enemy Mustang immediately entered evasive maneuvers, but Boss held to it all the same, then firing her vulcans once the target indicator lit up. The Mustang was instantly torn apart by the beam spray, with Boss flying her Corsair directly through the explosion. A minute later, her wingman had also dispatched his target and moved to rejoin her.

Additional enemy fighters soon appeared on their scopes. Boss' warning indicator lit up with a buzz; she was being targeted. Sneering, she brought her Corsair toward the incoming formation, gunning down a pair of Warhawks as she passed, and then taking out a third that had been trying to get a bead on her. A fourth attempted to take a potshot at her rear as well, but Boss, without slowing her velocity, easily flipped her fighter around and shot the Imp down before reorienting her bird back on its initial vector. Despite her efforts, however, several more of the enemy craft managed to pass through her fourth kill's remnants and tail her, firing their own vulcans and missiles in sequence.

Letting out a silent curse, Boss immediately put her fighter into evasion, maneuvering around the vulcan fire while the missiles and Mustangs continued their pursuit. Suddenly, she dove toward a passing *Harbinger*, whose phalanx emplacements lit up upon her approach, precisely what Boss intended. She put her thrusters back to full power and shot through the beam fire. Several of the pursuing fighters and missiles ended up getting shot down by their comrades. Switching to her beam cannons, Boss made a pass over the topside of the destroyer, hammering through the ship's shields, taking out the Imp's beam cannon emplacements before delivering a follow-up shot into the bridge tower for good measure. After that, she turned her fighter around and fired several more shots into the *Harbinger's* arc engine, generating a chain reaction that obliterated the entire ship while Boss flew away, a contingent of fighters in pursuit.

Eventually Corsair Two caught up to her and began picking off the pursuing fighters one after the other, forcing the survivors to break off and evade. Now entirely free from opposition for the moment, Boss angled Corsair One toward a nearby *Ravager*, which had already fired a swarm of missiles toward her advance. Easily blazing passed the projectiles with a combination of maneuvering and vulcan fire, she charged the cruiser, firing her beam cannons. Unlike the *Harbinger*, the *Ravager*'s shields initially held, but after a few concentrated shots, they collapsed, allowing Boss to rake the ship's starboard side. A fiery explosion ripped across the hull, leaving an open gash along the cruiser's side while lights flickered across its form.

"Finish her Two!" she commanded to her wingman. Following his leader, Corsair Two unleashed his own cannon fire into the gash. Moments later, just as Corsair Two broke off his attack, a deflagration broke the cruiser into two, with the now burning bow and stern sections floating away at different angles.

Suddenly, as the afterglow of the explosion began to fade, Boss' sensors beeped in warning; several additional craft were starting to drop out of arcspace. However, instead of further fighters or bombers, the incoming objects were something far worse.

*Son of a bitch!* Boss mentally called out as her sensors identified the incoming objects as torpedoes, all converging from multiple vectors. Initially, she thought it was impossible. Though interstellar missiles and torpedoes had been experimented on profusely by the Starfleet Science Corps and other entities, there had never been any resulting production model.

But then Boss remembered a crucial fact. Imperial bombers, so long as they were arc booster compatible, *were* capable of arc speed itself and could very easily launch their payloads from arcspace. After that, it was only a matter of timing the shot. Without their own arc engine, the torpedoes were incapable of continually "arcing" spacetime around themselves and would eventually decelerate to sub-light speed, thereby allowing them to come into contact with objects in realspace.

"Buccaneer One to Corsair One, are you seeing what I'm seeing!?" Buccaneer One called out in near horror.

Before Boss could answer, she picked up an additional complement of torpedoes appearing in the system. The enemy umbras had apparently decided to add their own numbers to the attack.

"Burn in hell, Drake," Boss hissed under her breath. She knew right away that this was one of the Admiral's tactics. "Corsair One to all fighters! Intercept all incoming torpedoes! Repeat, focus on the torpedoes! Don't let a single one hit our ship!"

Upon their leader's command, the Corsairs broke off and moved toward the intercept points. Moments later, the torpedoes dropped out of arc speed. Upon their reversion to realspace, their systems activated – they had launched unpowered – and their preprogrammed guidance systems instantly isolated and targeted the *Black Sun*. With their drive systems engaged they flew at high speed toward the umbra.

Ignoring the fighters that were attempting to pursue her, Boss moved against the first set of torpedoes, which were streaking toward the *Black Sun* from "above". Once in range, she fired several timed bursts, striking a number of the torpedoes and generating a multitude of explosions. Corsair Two, as well as Three and Four, also added their shots, destroying additional projectiles.

Unfortunately, however, there were just too many torpedoes for the fighters alone to intercept. A large number of them managed to break through. Upon their approach, the *Black Sun*'s beam cannons and phalanx went all out, filling the space around her with continuous beam fire. This had the effect of destroying several more torpedoes, but the rate of destruction just wasn't enough. At the last possible moment, the *Black Sun* redirected all available power to her shields.

Still evading Imp fighters, Boss could only watch as three of the torpedoes slammed into the *Black Sun*'s shields from different vectors, the glare of their explosions forcing her to shield her eyes. Much worse, one of the torpedoes managed to break through the ship's defenses, nearly penetrating her armor before detonating. As a result, the *Black Sun* rocked to starboard, with a large cluster of flame erupting from her port side.

"Goddamn it," Boss hissed. The ship was still intact but, given all the damage she had withstood, how much more of a pounding could the vessel take?

The surrounding Imp ships seemed to have the same idea as a number of them turned toward the now stricken *Black Sun*, obviously to make a direct assault upon her. Even worse, more were deploying their own bombers for further torpedo attacks.

Gritting her teeth in aggression, Boss brought her Corsair around with the rest of her fighters and moved to intercept the encroaching craft.

# Predecessor Ruins
# Ephesus

With a bellowing roar, Barbarossa charged through the field as the marines continued their assault. Unlike the raiders that were behind him, providing fire support with their own beam weapons, the Kapta had no issue moving in the open, nor even maneuvering around the fire. His armor was made of the most durable alloy his race had ever procured, and its shielding easily weathered the Terran beams. Thus, when he reached the optimum range for attack, Barbarossa leaped into the air, attaining a height that no Terran infidel could ever hope to match, and landed inside the marine ranks with a thundering metallic boom. Without hesitation, he brandished his baneclaws and began his offensive, slashing down the combatants that were within his reach. Unlike his armament, the Imp shield and armor was quite susceptible to his claws.

None of the shocked Imps, who still could not believe a Leo was fighting alongside the raiders, dared engage the beast at close-range. The marines only response was continuing their beam fire. However, Barbarossa easily withstood their assault and tore through their ranks, either slashing down any marines within reach or firing back with his own beam weapons, striking them down from a distance. A great juggernaut, he was unstoppable; a previously chained beast once again let loose to rend his former captors, his eternal adversaries. None of their numbers, no matter how great or powerful, would stand before him and his rage.

Lacerating a nearby marine, Barbarossa rapidly spun and fired a two shot burst from his right baneclaw into another pair. Death was immediate. Without hesitation, he leaped into the air again and kicked his greaved foot into the head of another, knocking him down to the ground. A follow-up kick into his prey's chest shattered it upon contact. He twisted about and gunned down a marine sniper, before proceeding into a run and tackling another Imp, sending him smashing into a stone column, then finishing him with a point-blank shot to the head. Hoisting up the corpse, he launched it into a marine team that was attempting to sneak behind him. The impact sent the offenders through a courtyard wall. The Leo finished them off with multiple beam bursts.

Before Barbarossa could select another target, his ears picked up the sound of rubble being pulverized under caterpillar tracks. Turning to his left he spotted a tank, specifically a Princeps light tank, moving down the street, its main gun training toward him while additional marines prowled about its flanks. Raiders immediately began evasive maneuvers, with one even calling for an anti-tank missile to be dropped in the area. Barbarossa would have none of it; he was not about to cower before a "light" tank. Thus, letting out another deafening roar, he charged straight toward his newfound target.

The Imperials open fired instantly, with the Princeps letting loose its main and secondary guns while the marines supported with their beam rifles. As with before, Barbarossa charged through it all, his shields deflecting the incoming beams with ease, though he did make it a point to dodge the tank's cannon. This he had no problem doing, easily banking around and narrowly avoiding each of the Princeps' beam cannon shots, with an agility that should not have been possible for a creature his size. All while he picked off several of the marines with responding beam shots of his own.

Such was the fury of his advance that the Imperials were instantly horrified, realizing all too quickly that this was no mere Leo they were facing. Judiciously, the Princeps' driver put the tank in reverse, its treads screeching across the ground as the tank retreated, simultaneously throwing up a wall of gunfire. Additional cover fire was provided by the flanking marines. Even so, Barbarossa continued his pursuit, cutting through the marine ranks with ease while charging after the tank. This time he didn't even bother evading the main cannon, whose aim had become so erratic that it was striking everything *but* the incoming Leo.

Letting out another roar, Barbarossa vaulted into the air once again and landed directly on the tanks shielded turret. Immediately after impact, he reached down, his claws readily bypassing the shield, and ripped open the hatch. He then reached further and pulled the tank commander out as well. The hapless Terran attempted to draw his pistol, but Barbarossa simply threw him into the side of a nearby building, letting the impact kill him. Continuing his assault, he extended his baneclaws into the opening and triggered both of his beam guns, killing the other two crewmembers and striking several vital systems. Finished, he leaped away and allowed the tank to explode on its own volition.

"Damn," one of the raiders proclaimed, just as the group managed to catch up to the Kapta.

Suddenly, Barbarossa picked up another sound, that of sub-arc thrusters. "Take cover!" he commanded.

Just then, a Vulture came charging down, triggering a swarm of rockets as it passed. Explosions rocked the ground around Barbarossa and the raiders. The Leo was forced to dive behind the remnants of a once massive edifice. As proud as he was, he knew when it was best to take cover. Once the assault had passed, he fired a few shots at the Imperial craft, but the gunship had gained altitude and moved out of his reach.

Sneering at the retreating craft, Barbarossa, quickly looked for the raiders. Much to his regret, the Vulture's assault had been effective;

the raiders that had been supporting him were now dead, their remains scattered across the area.

———————————————————— ————————————————————

Despite his disdain for Terrans, Barbarossa found himself letting out a snarl. He normally didn't think much about the deaths of infidels, but these raiders had been a part of his crew, and much more, they had fought *with* him. However, he knew he couldn't let himself get distracted by their deaths lest it affect his performance. Death was a constant in battle, and unless his ears were fooling him, this one was no different.

*No, it's not different at all,* Barbarossa thought as he heard the unending cries of beings, both Imperial and pirate, being struck down by one means or another. He couldn't even tell which side was winning. He assumed that the battle was evenly matched at this point, with both the Imperial offense and the raiders' defense effectively holding against one another. Barbarossa knew that wouldn't last, especially given his own experience with the Imperials.

A sudden beam shot to the back only reminded him that he was, in fact, in the middle of said battlefield. Glowering in hate, Barbarossa turned to see another squad of marines advancing toward his position, their beam rifles firing as they moved. Brandishing his baneclaws and bellowing another deafening roar, the warrior charged his enemies once more, determined to continue the fight.

# Predecessor Temple
# Ephesus

It seemed as though a full hour had passed since the battle had begun. The tremors had grown in intensity and frequency while the flow of energy into the darkness had gradually increased in speed, to the point that Jon, still sitting silently and in relative passivity, could feel it throughout his body. Even so, he remained where he was, at watch but in an ironic peace as if he were in the center of a storm's eye. A complete, tranquil peace amid violence and carnage.

And then, that peace ended.

Leaping to his feet, Jon twisted around with Astaroth in hand, just in time to clash its blade against Drake's advancing Berith. His eye now filled with hate toward the Admiral's grinning expression, Jon quickly reeled back to parry any follow-up attack. However, before he could reconnect, a golden flash erupted between them, with Drake's smile being the last sight Jon beheld before everything turned to gold, and then white.

An instant later, the white faded away, revealing to Jon his current surroundings. He was no longer in the underground chamber; now he was back within the main hall, standing atop a magnificent, towering pedestal that overlooked the podium area, the hovering tablet only a short distance from his position. Jon also noted that the hall had changed from when he and Lorelei first entered it. The space was now luminescent, with energy lines pulsing across the walls and ground as had happened in the chamber below. The crystalline panels shimmered brilliantly, as did the tablet at the center.

It was now apparent to Jon that the temple wasn't solely a place of worship, but also an immense energy conduit for whatever lay below.

"So, this is where we stand."

Drake's voice alerted Jon to the Admiral's presence on the pedestal opposite of his. The son of the Golden Queen's only response was a dispassionate glare.

"The keys have been entered, the final lock has been undone," Drake went on dramatically. "And the prize is within reach."

He then declared challengingly. "All that remains is to see which of us lays hands upon it!"

A brief pause intervened before Jon responded.

"You know that's not why I am here."

Drake sniffed, appearing almost disappointed. "Of course," he replied sardonically. "You're here to avenge your beloved mother..."

"No," Jon interrupted Drake midsentence, taking minor pleasure in the Admiral's surprise. "Don't think the mistake on Bonham will be repeated."

"Then..." Drake queried, still contemptuous but intrigued. "Why are you here, Jonathan Flint?"

"To fulfill a certain arrangement I made not too long ago," Jon answered as memories, from the beginning at Aurora and to the last at Bonham, flowed through his mind. Memories that held more sway over him than he thought possible, much less cared to admit.

"To see her through to Arcadia."

With that declaration, Jon gazed upon his adversary with calm determination.

"And since you're the one standing in her way, *our* way, I will strike you down all the same, Raphael Drake."

Drake eyed the young pirate momentarily. It was as if a different man stood before him; not the vengeful youth he had found on Bonham, but a man who was driven by a clear and concise purpose and objective. A warrior who would fight his enemies to the end, and yet would retain himself throughout the battle in order to gain the victory.

*A worthy opponent at long last.*

With that thought, Drake again flashed a smile – not one of cruelty, but one of anticipation – before drawing up his fist, placing it against his heart and then extending it forward, executing the Imperial salute. And though he was slightly caught off guard by the gesture, Jon, despite his own standings, respectfully reflected it.

Following that exchange, both combatants brought their swords about once more and leaped into the air. The entirety of the temple echoed with the clashing of their blades.

# Chapter XXXVI: Maelstrom

## Flint Pirates umbra *Black Sun*
## Ephesus System

"Report!" Alex demanded as he continued to look through the scope. Technically he could have brought up the data he wanted through said scope, but he was too focused on shooting back at the Imperials for that.

"Shields are back online!" the tactical operator responded as he looked over his display anxiously. "Hull regeneration remains in progress!"

"Helm is back online as well!" Davis reported as he took back control, maneuvering the ship around the oncoming fire while presenting the *Black Sun*'s guns a better angle of attack. The process, however, used more energy than Davis had anticipated. *Those parts of the ship must still be under regeneration,* he stewed.

Before Alex could shout a reply, his eye caught sight of a lone Thunderbolt moving into an attack run. A second later, the bomber was picked off by a passing Corsair, but not before the bulky, oversized craft released both of its torpedoes, which immediately sped toward the

*Black Sun*'s bridge tower. Cursing, Alex could only destroy one of the torpedoes with a cannon shot before the second slammed headlong into the umbra's bow shield, its detonation obstructing the viewscreen and blinding the bridge occupants.

Initially shielding his eyes from the glare, Alex waited a few seconds before opening them, allowing his vision to adjust. As he did, he saw an additional number of Thunderbolts, alongside a pair of *Warrior*-class frigates, moving in to engage.

"Hard to port!"

Immediately, Davis brought the *Sun* into a hard turn, one that presented her bow to the oncoming craft, while her cannons and phalanx filled the surrounding space with crimson beam fire. A number of the bombers were successfully obliterated, as was one of the frigates, but the Imperials continued to close in all the same. Fortunately, a flight of Corsairs had just taken notice of the advance and quickly dove in, shooting down the remaining bombardment with their missiles and then striking against the frigate with their beam cannons. An additional compliment of missile spray from the *Sun* eventually caused the frigate to erupt into a sea of fire. Ship rumbling from the shockwave, Alex was again forced to grasp onto the scope handles to remain grounded.

*We're not getting anywhere like this,* he thought disparagingly, just as an additional number of Imperial ships moved to engage. Moments later, another field of golden beam fire rained down upon the *Black Sun*, slamming into her shields with great force. *We're only picking them off one after another, barely holding out!*

Even so, as Davis brought the *Sun* about so that Alex could direct her bow weapons to return fire, the first officer could only wonder, what else could they do? Surely there was some type of strategy that they could use to even the odds or at least allow them to fight offensively rather than merely keeping the Imps at bay. And yet, no matter how much Alex forced his head around it, he couldn't come up with anything. *We're but one ship fighting against an entire armada!*

"Imperial arc signatures incoming!" Anna announced as her sensor display flashed in warning. "Twelve ships, plus additional smallcraft!"

Alex bit back a livid curse. This would be the third set of reinforcements since the battle had initiated, and they were coming in more frequently. Again, Drake had planned this out well, keeping the bulk of his forces in reserve and having them gradually enter in, slowly overwhelming the *Black Sun* and her crew with strain and fatigue. As much as he hated to admit it, Alex was beginning to see how his mother, herself a master tactician, had been outdone fifteen years ago.

At the very least they were, in fact, holding their own. Despite the vast numbers against them, the *Black Sun*'s cannons and torpedoes continued to strike down enemy ships in all reachable vectors while her phalanx and missiles did the same against the fighters and bombers. Several of the former were blasted out of space from a spray of phalanx fire while a single torpedo bore into the bow of a *Nemesis*-class cruiser, breaking her apart before she could cause any serious harm to the pirate ship. Another group of bombers attempted to move in for a torpedo attack, but a burst of missiles forced them to abandon the run, with a large number of their group being struck down before they could evade.

And then there were the Corsairs, which, despite taking damage themselves, remained prominently in the fight and in support of their mothership. The fighters of Buccaneer Squadron remained close to the *Black Sun*, providing a defensive screen against the enemy ships that were attempting to move in. Those of Corsair Squadron continued their own assault on the enemy formations, obliterating numerous Imperial smallcraft while adding their own fire against the capital ships. As a result, bogeys were being shot down en masse, while the Imperial warships struggled to keep the cannon-armed Corsairs from entering firing range, only to end up being damaged themselves.

Even so, despite the pirates' valiant efforts, the Imperials were far from defeated and only continued their assault as evidenced when the twelve newer ships, spearheaded by a pair of *Aggressor*-class battlecruisers and supported by numerous arc booster equipped fighters and bombers, entered into the system. Moments later, the capital ships' main guns set upon the *Black Sun* and fired their first volleys, while the fighters and bombers jettisoned their arc boosters and charged into the fight, with the former moving against the Corsairs and the latter making their torpedo runs on the umbra.

*Damn it!* Alex inwardly cursed as he saw the first squadron of Thunderbolts enter into range. They wasted no time in launching their payloads. A spray of twenty-four torpedoes was now streaming toward the *Sun* at full speed.

"Continue evasive maneuvers!"

"Already on it!" Davis shouted as he accelerated the ship in an attempt to maneuver around the torpedoes. Or at least buy enough time for Alex to shoot them down.

Taking his own cue, Alex redirected whatever unmasked phalanx were available toward the incoming projectiles, launching bursts of red energy directly at them. Though the beam cannons could destroy the torpedoes faster, it would put them on the complete defensive, something that would only embolden the Imperials further.

To Alex's surprise, the phalanx by themselves, albeit in concentrated shots, were sufficient to pierce through the torpedoes' shielding detonating several of them in a chain of explosions. However, it wasn't long before the second squadron entered into range and launched their torpedoes, followed by the third, adding additional numbers to the initial attack. From that, it became as before, with the rate of destruction greatly lagging behind the enemy advance. Even the addition of missile fire, the *Sun*'s missile tubes having just reloaded, could only do so much against the Imperial attack.

Alex ground his teeth as he saw several torpedoes were closing in. Only then did he release the beam cannons from attacking the capital ships and have them target the incoming torpedoes, adding their own beam shots to the phalanx and striking down additional numbers.

Unfortunately, it wasn't enough, three torpedoes managed to slip through the screen.

"All hands brace for impact!" he shouted before once again bringing all available power to the port shields.

The first two hit, slamming into the shields and, with their combined power, breaking them. The third torpedo blasted its way into the *Sun*'s midships, encasing itself into its armor before detonating.

The bridge rocked violently as the lights and monitors flickered in and out from the resulting power fluctuation, all the while klaxons sounded in the background. From the still extended scope, Alex watched as damage reports mounted from all over the ship, with a great mass of red now encompassing the *Sun*'s schematic. Yes, they had survived, but now the ship was nearly dead in space, with the majority of the port side weapons offline and the shields burst open. The only point of solace was that the arc engine remained intact, thereby allowing Moebius to engage and regenerate the damage.

Needless to say, it didn't take long for the enemy ships to take advantage of the situation, as an even greater volume of beam fire now rained down upon the *Sun*. Alex again grasped the handles of the scope as the violent shaking only increased.

"Bring us about!" he ordered to Davis as he shot back with his available weapons. "Redirect all available power to shields and weapons!"

Suddenly, Gran's head shot up again. "I'm picking up activity on the Imperial channels!" she called out in warning. "I think they're setting up for another arcspace torpedo run!"

Alex bit back a curse word. "How long!?" he demanded.

"Approximately fifteen minutes!" Gran answered. "Bombers are en route as we speak!"

"Multiple torpedo launches detected!" Anna suddenly sounded from her post. "Incoming from vectors outside of the melee!"

Taking a breath, Alex watched as the torpedoes appeared on his scope. It was evident that the torpedoes had been launched from the still present enemy umbras, given that there were no signals detected from their origin points. Even worse, an additional number of ships were also launching torpedoes to further increase the quantity, just as the Thunderbolts had done before.

*They're going to hold us down until the main assault arrives from Arcspace,* Alex thought as he watched the incoming projectiles and the advancing warships. It was the only thing the present Imperials could do at this point. As damaged as the *Black Sun* was, she was still intact and the longer she remained so, the more she regenerated. As such, the Imperials could only hope to take her out with an overwhelming attack, likely one made up of hundreds of torpedoes coming in from arc speed, in all vectors, and timed as to revert only at the least possible distance. With that firepower, the *Sun*'s destruction would be one of the most spectacular to ever be seen.

The younger Flint could only glower at his knowledge of this, and much more, his inability to come up with a decent counter-strategy. How could he? He was not Jon or Barbarossa; his areas of expertise laid in science, not in the art of war. Yes, he could come up with tactics and strategies when needed, but none of them compared to what his brother or the legendary warrior of the Third Leo War could do. And the result spoke of itself; a crippled ship barely holding on against a vastly superior enemy force, with destruction imminent.

And yet, as painful as it was, Alex pushed back that feeling of inferiority. "All power to main drive!" he ordered as he concentrated on the battle. Now was not the time to come down on himself, no matter how out of place he felt.

*I am the son of the Golden Queen, damn it! I will give you thrice-damned Imperial bastards a fight to be remembered.*

Thus, as Davis worked the *Black Sun* into another turn, Alex began redirecting whatever weapons he had available against the incoming torpedoes while making sure to focus all functioning beam cannons on the enemy warships. If nothing else, they would keep their present enemies at bay for that much longer.

# Predecessor Ruins
# Ephesus

The beam fire only intensified as Kaiser continued his run through the gauntlet, either returning fire and striking down the attacking marines or moving in close enough to pummel them with his massive fists. Unlike the majority of the raiders, namely those who were in the firefight beside him, he wore no armor nor retained any personal shielding, being totally bare on his torso and only wearing his usual garb on his hips and legs. Protective clothing had never been a facet of the Herculean race, whose stone-like skin was more than enough to weather but the strongest of weapons. In fact, to go into battle with the very least amount of garb possible was considered a sign of ultimate pride.

Alongside this, Herculeans very rarely fought their battles from cover. No, only under the most strenuous circumstances did any of his own kind hide behind some sort of barrier for protection. They fought in the open, and they fought with unrelenting force, all in the very fashion that their Terran namesake alluded to. And that was precisely how Kaiser fought his present opponents, whose miniscule attacks made very little progress in actually harming him. As far as he was concerned, they might as well had been throwing pebbles.

Taking aim with his massive Blunderbuss B-60 pistol, Kaiser let loose a single beam into a distant marine, punching a fist-sized hole through his chest plate and out the back. Just as that newly formed corpse fell, the pirate turned around and fired another shot at a marine's head, which was obliterated entirely, and then struck yet another through the chest before *that* body fell. Just to the right, a fellow marine moved to throw a grenade; Kaiser responded by launching himself forward and performing a lariat, smashing his outstretched arm into the marine's faceplate. With the Imp completely stunned, the giant grasped onto its body, activated the grenade that was still clutched in its hand, and threw it up at the top of a nearby ruin, where two more marines had set themselves up to provide fire support. The resulting explosion added three more kills to Kaiser's ever-growing tally and destroyed the ruin entirely.

However, it didn't take long for more Imperials to appear as a pair of Condors dropped from the air, allowing marines to cable down from their holds while providing covering fire with their onboard weapons. Kaiser glowered as they descended. Whether they had been present since the battle began or were reinforcements from orbit, it seemed as though the Imps were coming out in a continuous stream. All while the raiders' own numbers dwindled and their defenses depleted with each passing minute. Entire sectors of the battleground had to be abandoned as the Imperials gradually made their way toward the temple.

Redrawing his Blunderbuss, Kaiser fired several beams at the Condors as they took off, managing to do enough damage to one that it caught fire and spiraled out of control before crashing in the distance. Undaunted, he charged at the new group of combatants, wading through their fire before leaping into the air and executing a dropkick on the nearest opponent, breaking him or her in one hit. He jumped up again and spun, backfisting another marine with enough force as to send it flying into one of its comrades, before finishing both with another Blunderbuss shot. And when a sniper attempted to fire at him from behind, Kaiser's gigantic arm snapped out and ensnared the hapless Imp by the head, dragging his entire form into the Herculean's hold. Without pause, Kaiser lifted the marine overhead and then slammed it into the ground, leaving a slight indentation upon impact.

By that point, the marines, sans those that had initially been picked apart by the raiders, had retreated to whatever cover they could find. Undeterred, Kaiser, again drew his Blunderbuss and fired several shots into the marines' locations, his gun's power effortlessly penetrating the rubble and striking whatever Imp that tried to hide. Several were felled, with additional numbers choosing to abandon their cover entirely only to be subsequently gunned down by the raiders.

Kaiser turned his sights upon whom he believed to be the squad commander. The officer was currently ducking behind a nearby edifice. Rather than shoot him, the Herculean bent down and charged forward, slamming through the structure, shattering it upon impact and effectively tackling the marine. Though dazed, the Imperial managed to stagger back to his feet and, upon seeing his rifle was smashed, moved to draw his dagger. His actions were not fast enough. Kaiser grasped the Imps arm, whipped the marine around and send him airborne into another nearby group. The entire platoon was quickly taken out by a grenade.

Whirling to find another target, Kaiser spotted a marine squad advancing on his position with daggers drawn, having apparently realized that their rifles could not penetrate his skin. Others in the distance were bringing about heavier weapons, namely beam and rocket launchers. Even worse, larger marine complements were moving into the area, with some targeting him while the others went against the raiders that provided backup.

Gritting his teeth in an almost violent snarl, Kaiser reholstered his pistol and charged at the oncoming squad, knocking several Imps to the ground before fisting his hands together and hammering away several more. A few of the marines managed to strike out with their blades and cut through his skin, but in spite of the wounds, the damage was not enough to slow him down Impervious to the sting of the cuts, Kaiser quickdrew his pistol once more and fired off several shots, striking some of the distant, launcher wielding marines, before concentrating on the surrounding Imps.

The remaining marines opened fire with the heavy artillery. Their beam and rocket launchers, having been designed to destroy armored and shielded vehicles, had more than enough power to do serious harm to the massive pirate. Knowing this, Kaiser backfisted another marine's head and returned fire while moving out of the site line. With the beam and rocket fire intensifying, Herculean pride notwithstanding, Kaiser quickly ran into a nearby ruin, smashing through the front wall just before an explosion caused it to collapse around him.

This actually had a beneficial effect; despite the miniscule aggravation of dislodging himself from the rubble, the resultant dust cloud made for an effective smokescreen. Knowing that it wouldn't be long before the marines recommenced their fire if only to confirm that he was dead, Kaiser took a moment to catch his breath. The abundant dust and particulate in the air were no more obstructive to him than natural air, though he hoped it was just the opposite with the marines' sensors.

Pausing within the seconds of calm, Kaiser closed his eyes and allowed his ears to decipher the myriad of sounds around him. Amidst the unending bursts of gunfire, calls to attack or retreat and the screaming of those wounded, he eventually picked up on what he had been anticipating. Marines entering the ruins, moving ever cautiously. As he had half-expected, the suspended particles in the dust cloud had both blinded their sensors and obstructed the fire support teams. Thus the advance team moving in was effectively blind. However, as the wind began to pick up, it wouldn't be long before the cloud dissipated. The time to strike was nigh.

Taking one last drawn and growingly labored breath, Kaiser quietly redrew his Blunderbuss and crept toward the advancing unit. Moments later, the sounds of additional gunfire, explosions, and breaking objects quickly emanated from the cloud. All of which instantly merged with the rest of the battle.

# Predecessor Temple
# Ephesus

With as much force as he could muster, Jon swung Astaroth downward, forcing Drake to jump back as the obsidian blade split the temple floor. A wave of dark energy emanated from the damage. Without hesitation, the pirate captain vaulted after the admiral, unleashing a flurry of attacks, both physical and energy based, that kept Drake on the defensive. Undeterred, Drake swept Berith around generating an extended energy blade, which Jon just managed to evade by flipping high into the air and landing a short distance away. The elder Flint rushed to renew his attack, but Drake was prepared, firing a series of golden energy bolts at the pirate's head, forcing Jon to raise a protective black shield. Spinning, Drake teleported away to another part of the temple, and upon dropping his shield, Jon surged in pursuit.

Clashing swords even before landing, the combatants continued to trade blows with one another, switching from offensive to defensive and back again in split-second intervals. Feet barely touching the temple floor, Drake hurled a point-blank energy wave at Jon, forcing him to duck and evade. After exchanging an additional number of slashes and parries, Jon pivoted to the side, dove out of range and launched an energy wave of his own at the Admiral. Drake deflected the onslaught with Berith's blade, channeling the destructive energy into a nearby column. The pillar exploded into shards.

"Running away already?" Drake taunted, teleporting directly behind Jon. Prepared, the pirate kicked out with a spinning power attack that caught the Admiral off guard and sent him airborne, crashing into an artifact, a fair distance to the side. Drake was quick on the rebound and wasted no time in launching himself back at Jon, their blades colliding again with a thunderous echo.

"You're certainly doing better," Drake goaded, his grin ever present, as he thrust Berith's blade against Astaroth. Such was the force between the two that both blades started to emit gold and black sparks from the contact point. "What caused this change, I wonder?"

"Enlightenment," Jon glowered back, using his left arm to power-punch Drake in the stomach, breaking the clash between them. Abruptly, he smashed Astaroth's hilt across the Imperial's face, knocking him off his feet. Just as he lunged to impale him, however, Drake recovered and parried the blow with Berith, then kicked Jon away. With a backflip, the Admiral was on his feet, wiping the blood from his nose.

The two Wielders moved at each other once more, slashing at one another with their respective blades while either evading or deflecting the other's attacks. Even Jon's surprise sweep kick was easily dodged when Drake jumped upward. While still in midair, the Imperial hurled a golden power roller at the pirate's position. Raising Asteroth as a shield, the attack was readily absorbed.

Instantly, a series of black holes formed around Drake, from which the energy Asteroth had just drawn in shot out in a succession of surging golden arcs. However, anticipating the counterattack, Drake generated a full dome shield around himself to deflect the fire, then expanded it outward at high speed to obliterate the holes. Though unsuccessful, the strike provided enough of a window for Jon to move in. He again swept Astaroth overhead with a downward chop, which Drake only avoided by teleporting to the left. Astaroth's impact with the temple structure, however, triggered a sizeable black shockwave, forcing Drake to vault several more meters away and generate a countering wave to deflect the energy. The colliding shockwaves showered the area with gold and black energy bands that destroyed all they impacted. Unflinching, Drake shaped Berith into its spear form, twisted around and flung it at the pirate, who deftly evaded it and the resultant aftershocks.

Reforming Berith, Drake teleported to Jon's left side in an attempt to impale the pirate. Instantly, Jon swung his left hand around, darkness swirling about the palm, and repulsed Drake, sending him flying toward a stone podium. Before impact, however, Drake disappeared, materializing a second later overhead of Jon. With Berith's blade aimed downward, he plunged. Jon dove sideways, using Astaroth to absorb the resultant energy burst and debris as the Admiral's sword struck the ground. Again the pirate opened a black hole and fired out the captive energy and material in a concentrated beam at his adversary's head, which Drake again deflected with Berith's blade before launching eight golden orbs to home in on Jon. The elder Flint bolted upward to evade.

Leaping up after him, the two combatants again exchanged sword blows midair, the resultant sparks showering the floor below, burning portions of the area upon impact. Jon eventually gained the upper hand and slammed Drake toward the side wall. However, only slightly fazed, Drake flipped around and, landing feet first on the wall, teleporting away once more just as Jon followed up his attack with a black swell, obliterating that portion of the structure. An instant later, the Admiral rematerialized behind Jon and hurled another golden orb, only for it to be absorbed by a quickly formed black field across Jon's back. Sneering, Drake dematerialized yet again just as Jon redirected the golden energy. It flew aimlessly into a nearby edifice; more wreckage littered the temple floor. This time Jon knew where the Imperial was going to reform and swept Astaroth at his right, only to be parried by the expectant Drake.

"I must admit I haven't had this much fun in a long time," Drake declared jovially as Astaroth and Berith's blades vibrated against one another, sparks again igniting between them. "I'm grateful to you, Jonathan."

Sneering at the usage of his first name, Jon hammered Drake back, only for the Admiral to disappear once more. Drake rematerialized at the top of a nearby pedestal.

"That being said, you're still a long way from actually defeating me," he proclaimed, as Jon released a black energy bolt toward his location. Drake teleported away only to reappear on another pedestal. "Let alone killing me."

A black hole quietly formed behind Drake; a split second later Jon charged out with Astaroth aimed to impale.

"As are you!" the pirate avowed.

Drake spun away and vanished a split second before Astaroth could make contact, but Jon was satisfied that the message was given. Drake reappeared at ground level and generated a golden wave, which Jon deftly evaded before descending to the temple floor. Without hesitation, both Wielders charged at one another yet again, their blades slamming into the other with a tremendous clang.

More parries, more lunges, and the following ripostes; passing seconds with black and gold energy bursts from the colliding Devilblades destroying anything they impacted. Amidst the violent clashing of their blades, Jon glared once more at Drake's grinning expression. Suddenly, the pirate captain feigned right, broke the contact and executed a power attack, catching his opponent in the stomach. Drake immediately disappeared.

"Running away, Raphael?" Jon taunted.

Drake, now standing on what could be construed as a seating area, countering with another elongated energy blade sweep that compelled Jon to vault to a distant dais. Drake immediately continued his offensive, firing multiple sprays of energy bolts, forcing Jon to defend by generating black holes to absorb the projectiles.

Undaunted, the elder Flint executed an aerial leap, hurling toward Drake at high velocity. Just before impact, the Admiral redirected the momentum of the attempted blow, sending Jon flying back across the vast area toward an elevated platform. Instantly Drake vanished, this time reappearing behind Jon just before he landed.

Rather than attempt to strike him with Berith again, however, Drake quickly extended his left hand and dropped down to the floor, his palm hitting the platform in a hammer-like motion. Though Jon didn't see the movement, he did feel the coming onslaught 's energy and swiftly dove off the platform just as a series of golden beams rained down from above. His previous location was now a blackened hole, its edges littered with rubble. In free-fall, Jon rotated mid-air, forming a spinning black vortex around him. Though Drake naturally teleported away before he could be drawn in, a multitude of debris was captured regardless. Upon completing the spin, Jon landed on the chamber floor and formed a large black hole high overhead. The ensnared debris, having now been broken down into razor-sharp shards, were violently expelled from the void, aimed toward the Admiral.

Now in an effective reverse of his initial bolt attack, Drake was forced to teleport at faster rates, disappearing and rematerializing rapidly as the weaponized shards fell around him, impacting and obliterating the adjacent structures. A few shards struck their target, slashing portions of the Admiral's uniform, stains of red declaring their success. As embarrassing as it was to personally admit, he hadn't expected that vortex maneuver nor the resulting scattershot; the elder Flint really was a creative opponent. That being said, however, he was still far from defeated, which he emphasized with his next teleportation, reappearing directly in his opponent's face.

Though initially caught off guard by the Admiral's point-blank resurgence, Jon nonetheless was quick to react, parring with Astaroth. However, Drake responded just as quickly, knocking the sword away with Berith's blade, and grabbing Jon's left arm. With a malicious snarl, the Admiral drove Berith's blade directly into Jon's torso.

Leering at his apparent victory, especially as blood began to flow out of his opponent's mouth, Drake started to comment on how disappointed he was. Before he could utter a single word, however, his leer changed to an astonished gape as Jon's mouth suddenly turned up into a grin, and black energy began to emanate from the pirate's "body".

Realizing all too fast what was about to happen, Drake teleported away just as "Jon" turned completely black, then reshaped "himself" into a black hole that drew in its surroundings for a few seconds before dissipating. At that, the real Jon quickly emerged from another black hole, this time at Drake's right. Though caught by surprise, Drake managed to bring up his defense, parrying Jon's attack with a quick over the shoulder deflection. The Imperial flashed a complimenting smirk before deflecting Jon's blade and counterattacking with a spin slash, again forcing Jon back.

The exchange escalated further as both combatants moved down the temple grounds, eventually leaping up into one of the audience areas. It then transitioned into a running battle, in which both Jon and Drake tore through the section, hurdling and slashing at one another as they went, moving around whatever obstacles they encountered, whatever ruins they created while continuing their battle. For a period both matched each other's blows evenly until Drake caught Jon in an upward slash, sending his momentarily dazed adversary airborne.

Teleporting above the 'flying' pirate, Drake brought his left leg down into Jon's back, and kicked him in the opposite direction, sending him careening back down to the temple floor. Rapidly gathering an aura of golden energy around himself, the Admiral positioned Berith to impale and descended at extreme speed. Only at the last moment did Jon manage to flip out of the way, and then jump again to avoid the resulting shockwave. Reversing his travel, the pirate raced back to spear the admiral, but Drake teleported away before Asteroth could connect.

"As I said," Drake taunted upon his reforming next to his opponent, clashing Berith's blade against Astaroth's while matching his grin to Jon's glare yet again. "A long way off."

Sneering in response, Jon repelled Berith's blade catching the Imperial off-guard with a black wave attack from behind. Drake flipped away before extensive damage could occur and then soared upward. Jon leaped after him, with both blades striking each other soon after.

---

With the twin reticules flashing red to indicate a target lock, Boss pushed down on her trigger. A moment later, two of her missiles launched out from its wing hardpoint, shooting across space and striking the pair of Tempest bombers she had been tracking, obliterating them in two great explosions. Flying through the resultant fire, she instinctively opened her mouth to check on Corsair Two's status, noticing that he was not on her wing. Only then did she remember that he had been shot down by a wayward missile not too long ago; one of the seven that had been lost up to this point.

*We're not getting anywhere like this*, she thought as she flew at her next target, a *Fury*-class frigate. Immediately detecting her approach, the

*Fury* began to fire off her phalanx emplacements toward the Corsair, complimented by a spray of missile fire. In response, Boss executed a barrel roll and banked from right to left, narrowly evading the phalanx fire while using her vulcans to shoot down the missiles. She knew that if she dodged them at that range, they would simply turn around and continue seeking her. Mid-roll, she let loose her beam cannons into the frigate's shields, firing until they at last collapsed. Quickly Boss fired into the ship's main hull, taking out the two top mounted beam cannon turrets in the process, and then discharged another burst into the bridge.

Much to the ace's surprise, the *Fury* remained intact, albeit on fire, drifting and without her command structure. A phalanx burst suddenly slammed into the Corsair's tail as she passed over the stern; though her shields easily deflected it, the burst still shook her fighter, and her with it, to the core. Glowering, Boss moved to swing around to finish the frigate, only for her threat indicator to sound; a pair of Mustangs were racing toward her. With little choice, she abandoned her attack on the stricken warship and shot out into space, with the Imperial fighters in hot pursuit.

Boss could tell that the Mustang pilots were a bit more skilled than the others; not only did they keep up with her maneuvers, but they also kept up their vulcan and missile fire, holding her on the defensive as they gave chase. Even when she flew over the top of a *Ravager*-class cruiser, which was exchanging fire with the *Sun*, the Mustangs maintained their pursuit, flying straight through the beam and missile fire without even deviating slightly. And when she attempted to flip her Corsair around to shoot back, the Mustangs intensified their fire, forcing her to maintain her flight path.

*Good to see that there are still some worthwhile Imperial pilots,* Boss dryly thought as she banked and rolled around additional beam fire. Though her shields remained functional, they were weakened and would likely buckle under strain. The Mustang pilots were obviously aware of this from their crafts' sensor scans, and so maintained the pressure, keeping the fleeing Corsair boxed in between them. And though Boss did well in evading most of their fire, some of the golden beams managed to make it through, wearing down her shields even more.

147

Eventually, she found her opportunity. Coming across the burning hulk of a *Malevolent*, escape pods still launching from her hull, Boss put her Corsair into a dive over the destroyer's port side, intending to loop around the wreckage. As anticipated, the Mustangs gave chase, following her into the loop around the cruiser's underbelly and then up to its starboard side. However, once she emerged from the loop, Boss put her thrusters to full power and shot up over the stricken ship's hull, then flipped around and keyed in her missiles. Moments later, the Mustangs emerged from the loop as well, at which point Boss gained immediate locks on both fighters and quickly fired off a pair of missiles. The Mustang pilots were dead before they realized what had just happened.

After enjoying a moment of satisfaction toward her work, Boss flipped her Corsair back around and returned to the battle. As she half-expected, an additional group of Imperial ships, this time numbering five, arrived in the system; three *Harbingers* and two *Ravagers*. No sooner had they emerged from arcspace than their fighters and bombers launched out from their respective bays, with the former advancing quickly toward her fighters while the latter aimed toward the *Sun*. Sneering at their arrival, Boss brought her Corsair around and moved toward the newcomers, firing her vulcans in sequence as they shot by. Two Mustangs and a Cobra were instantly obliterated, while the rest scattered around her like leaves in the wind, moving out of her sight line before dividing up to pursue their respective targets.

Boss' threat indicator quickly sounded off as several fighters attempted to target her, but she ignored it, maneuvering around their fire with ease. Instead, she pursued the bombers, who were already beginning their torpedo runs on the *Sun*. Boss subconsciously grit her teeth; with another arcspace torpedo attack coming in, the *Sun* couldn't afford to take additional damage. Especially when she was still battling it out with the surrounding capital ships.

"Corsairs Seven and Ten, follow me. We're going after the bombers," she commanded as she moved in. "Everyone else, engage at your discretion."

Thus wading her way through the escorting fighters, Boss and her compatriots made their own run at the bombers. To the Imperial pilots' credit, the bombers remained in formation even as the three pirates swept over them with their vulcans, obliterating several with the initial pass. Rapidly, Boss and her subordinates looped around and took out several more bombers in the second pass. Despite the losses and the fact their escorts were unable to protect them, the bombers maintained their formation and continued on toward their target.

*This isn't good,* Boss thought as the bombers pressed on, regardless of their dwindling numbers. She knew her adversaries weren't just fanatical; Imperial bomber pilots were explicitly trained to focus on their targets, never completely breaking off until their torpedoes were launched. Making the situation even worse was that this group knew how vital they were; that their attack would be the crippling blow, the one that would leave the *Sun* open for the final strike. They could and would not afford to break away, even with enemy fighters gunning for them.

And then, Boss was reminded that the bombers were not entirely without help. Just as she was about to mount her next run, her threat indicator again sounded, alerting her that she was now under missile lock. And much worse, rather than it being only one or two missiles tracking her, there were dozens of them streaking at her from a distance.

"Where did they come from!?" Corsair Ten sounded off as he and Corsair Seven both abandoned their own attack runs, going into evasion as the missiles flew in around them. "No way those came off the fighters!"

It didn't take much for Boss to answer that question. "Goddamn umbras," she muttered in disdain before going into a sharp turn, then twisting around and using her vulcans to shoot down several of the oncoming projectiles. She momentarily forgot that umbras could safely fire missiles under cloak.

Gunning her thrusters, Boss launched her fighter away, narrowly evading several of the missiles while turning around and shooting down an additional amount. Unfortunately, over a dozen missiles were tracking her, and she could only barely keep ahead of them. Her subordinates had similar difficulties. As a result, the remaining bombers reached their firing range and launched their torpedoes, only then banking away and retreating.

Once again sneering, Boss knew what she had to do. Barrel rolling around another passing missile, she re-angled her Corsair toward the torpedoes and began shooting them down, one after the other, with her beam cannons. Moments later, the *Sun* added its own power to her defense, launching phalanx and missile fire at the oncoming projectiles and destroying an additional number. However, several torpedoes still managed to shoot through the net, forcing Boss to continue her pursuit.

Switching back over to her missiles, Boss quickly brought her fighter in line with the remaining torpedoes, her target reticules gradually locking onto each for a spray attack. Seconds later, the last reticule flashed red, and Boss began to press down on the trigger. Which was precisely when the world exploded around her.

Her fighter was violently struck and thrown off of its course. Alarms and red light blaring in her ears and eyes, Boss fought to maintain control. Already she realized what had happened. One of the missiles she thought she had evaded had gotten close and proximity detonated. Already weathered and only marginally regenerated, her shields had instantly collapsed, allowing the shockwave and shrapnel to impact her Corsair, substantially damaging its structure and its internals. Had she been piloting a Mustang or any other fighter, Boss knew she would have been killed.

Reorienting her fighter toward the torpedoes, Boss switched back to her beam cannons and attempted to fire a snapshot. However, just as she pulled down on the trigger, a new diagnostic window appeared on her display. Her weapons were offline, the force of the explosion having damaged and incapacitated her central power systems.

*No!* Boss' mind let out in horror, knowing all too well what was about to happen. Her damage control systems were already active and were attempting to repair or marginalize said damage. They would take several minutes to complete the work, whereas the torpedoes were only seconds away from their target. And if that wasn't bad enough, her still active sensors picked up a pair of Cobras moving toward her direction, their weapon systems already tracking her.

Thus, with her gut clenched and her teeth gnashed, Boss had no choice but to abandon her run, bringing her fighter up and away as the Cobras gave chase. An instant later, the torpedoes met their target.

## Flint Pirates umbra *Black Sun*
## Ephesus System

Struck along her starboard side, the *Black Sun* instantly pitched to starboard, nearly throwing the bridge crew out of their respective chairs. Again the ship rumbled as her shields buckled, lights and monitors flickered while klaxons sounded in the background. Instantly, the damage reports began to mount.

"We lost shields again!" the tactical operator proclaimed hurriedly as he read over the console. "More hull breaches along decks ten and eleven! Cloaking system is offline!"

"Engine power down by sixty percent!" Davis yelled as he struggled to keep the ship on course. "I can barely keep her moving, let alone maneuvering!"

"Status of Moebius!?" Alex called out as he also struggled to return fire. Thankfully the weapon systems were still active, though much of their power had also been lost. Even worse, several of the phalanx and missile tubes had been taken out in the last barrage.

"It's active, but the damage is mounting too fast!" the tactical operator reported, just as the *Black Sun* was struck by another weapon discharge, causing the bridge to rumble yet again. "She won't last much longer!"

Amidst another set of rumbling, Anna just managed to peer at her display as it beeped in warning. "Picking up multiple signals coming in from arcspace!" Anna hurriedly warned, drawing all attention to her. "It's the torpedo wave!"

Ignoring the next set of rumbling and refusing the urge to swallow, Alex asked. "How many and how much longer!?"

Upon calculating the numbers, Anna felt her body run cold as she responded. "Over seventy," she let out in a short breath. "Time to emergence two minutes and seventeen seconds."

"Repairs to shields and main engines will take over five minutes," the tactical operator could only add, with equal cold coursing through his own body, his voice an eerie calm as he leaned back in his chair. "We're dead, sir."

At that, the bridge quickly turned silent as the crew all held that same realization, they were doomed. As strong as the *Sun* was, there was no way she could withstand over seventy torpedoes, especially with her shields down and her weapons nearly diminished. Just as they also knew she could not outmaneuver the wave with her engine power severely hampered. In the end, the Imperials had succeeded in their mission; they had laid the *Sun* open, virtually immobile and defenseless. All that remained was the finishing blow.

It was as surreal as it was inevitable, such that even as the *Sun* continued to rock from the surrounding attacks, the bridge crew barely felt it or heard the klaxons still sounding in the background. In fact, it seemed as though time itself had slowed down, each passing second felt like hours in the making while those present spent the moments shifting between their lives to this point and attempting to find a means of survival. Unfortunately, no one could think of a solution for the latter, further compounding the hopelessness.

Gritting his teeth, Alex could only look down and grimace. He had failed. In just over two minutes, the *Black Sun* would be destroyed because he failed to measure up to his brother or Barbarossa. Yes, he had done all he could and even managed to put up a good fight against a vastly superior Imperial fleet, but in the end, he still failed to measure up. And now they would all pay because he made a poor captain.

*"I didn't make you my second-in-command because you're my brother,"* Jon's words echoed from the depths of his memory. *"I made you my second because, besides the fact you are the only one that I trust, you also hold the bearings of a commander..."*

The memory then completed with, *"Outside myself or Barbarossa, you are the only one I would willingly leave the* Sun *to."*

*Damn you, Jon,* Alex glowered inwardly, hands tightening around the armrests of his chair. Though Jon had meant those words to be of reassurance, they now only burned in Alex's mind, punctuating the depth of his failure. *You knew I was out of my league; that I wasn't nearly as versed in that art of war stuff as you. And yet you still left me with the ship expecting me to do as you or Barbarossa would.*

More than anything Alex wished his brother was on the bridge right then. Not just to reassume command, but so Alex could slug him hard across the face.

*What in the Eighth Circle were you thinking!?* Alex scowled. *I'm not like you! I don't know nearly as much about tactics and strategies as you do! I'm a scientist! My expertise lies in the dynamics of an asteroid or the energy signature of an arc engine, not...!*

Then, with a sudden surge of realization, Alex's eyes widened in near shock. "Well... damn!" he murmured under his breath, feeling but the slightest ray of hope begin to well in him. Could it really work? As far as he could tell, nobody up to that point had ever conceived such a maneuver, let alone attempted it. But that didn't mean it was impossible, did it? Especially for one such as him?

Had he the time, he would have liked to consult Braun, but Alex knew he didn't have nanoseconds to waste. The torpedo wave would drop out of arcspace in one minute and thirty-six seconds, and he still had to make the necessary preparations. He reached back for the scope and began to enter in commands.

"Helm," he ordered, snapping Davis back to the moment. "Bring us toward our nearest target, all available speed!"

Without thinking, Davis worked. "Aye!" he let out as he entered the proper headings. He then inwardly prayed that, whatever Alex was contemplating, it wasn't going to be a clichéd final ram attack.

Hastily, as he continued his work, specifically on the dorsal bow turret, Alex looked over and saw the target Davis had selected, a lone *Vindicator*-class battlecruiser. Again he grit his teeth; the *Vindicator* would be a tough target to weather down, but it would have to do.

"Weapons, focus everything we have on that battlecruiser!" he commanded to the tactical operator, just as the ship rumbled again. "But do not, I repeat, do not use the number one cannon!"

The ship rumbled once more as Alex completed his orders. Seeing no obvious choice, the tactical operator instantly complied. "Aye sir!" he called out, readjusting the fire controls and the Moebius. A part of him wondered why Alex was sharing fire control; up to that point the First Officer had been handling the weapons himself, and the command scope was still extended in front of him. However, the officer knew better than to question his acting captain.

Coming about at a fraction of her standard speed, the *Black Sun* brought her bow toward the distant *Vindicator*, which had already taken notice of her approach. Turrets immediately shifting toward the stricken umbra, a shower of golden fire quickly erupted from the battlecruiser and those ships nearest to her, all angled toward the black and gold pirate ship. In response, the *Black Sun* returned fire with her own available weapons, but only utilized her underside bow cannon; the top mounted one remained inactive.

Shifting his gaze between the *Sun*'s advance and what displayed in his scope, Alex continued to work over the diagnostics of the top bow cannon, ignoring the rumbling from enemy weapons strikes. It was complicated work, especially with Alex having to utilize the scope controls to accomplish it, but the younger Flint remained focused even as the ship shook around him. Not even the indicator that hull integrity had fallen below seventy-five percent deviated him from his task.

"Status of enemy shields?"

"At sixty percent," the tactical operator reported. "We're throwing everything we have at them, save the number one cannon!"

"Inform me when we've broken through!" Alex responded as he continued his work, all the while double-checking his progress. He needed the numbers to be exact.

Still guiding the ship on her heading, Davis exchanged a subtle glance to Anna. Neither of them could even guess what Alex was planning, but they definitely hoped he knew what he was doing. At the very least it was better fighting to the last until the torpedo wave came out of arcspace. And much more, ramming the *Vindicator* in one final attack as the visos tended to have stricken ships do was better than waiting to die.

Suddenly, as the *Black Sun*'s latest torpedo shot struck the *Vindicator*, an alert went off on the tactical display. "Enemy shields have collapsed!" the tactical operator shouted.

"Target her arc engine!" Alex ordered as he continued, having reached the final stages of his work. "I want her immobilized!"

Hearing that, the tactical operator took direct control of the underside cannon and fired off several shots at the *Vindicator*. As luck would have it, the *Vindicator* had begun to turn away from the *Black Sun*, apparently to give herself a smaller targeting profile in lieu of her shields. This presented her stern, namely her arc engine, directly toward the charging umbra, allowing the singular beam cannon to fire several shots into it. Seconds later, explosions rocked the engine, and the glow of its main thruster flickered out. The battlecruiser began to drift as a result.

"Got it!" the tactical operator reported. "Enemy arc engine is offline!"

"Torpedo wave approaching!" Anna sounded off. "Reversion in twenty-five seconds!"

Again gritting his teeth, Alex just managed to make the final modifications to the number one cannon, as indicated when his display flashed. With that complete, he tapped the trigger.

The topside cannon fired a single crimson beam directly into the drifting *Vindicator*. However, unlike the other beams that had been fired, this one neither penetrated the hull nor exploded on contact. Rather, it seemed to scatter just as it struck, before the energy residue vanished entirely.

"Reversion in twenty seconds!" Anna sounded off again, in spite of her confusion at what had just occurred.

His task complete, Alex retracted the scope and looked toward Davis. "New course one eight zero mark two nine seven!" he commanded. "Three-second burn, and then full shutdown!"

Now Davis was especially confused. He got what Alex meant; having the main drive at full power for three seconds, from which the ship would continue moving via inertia upon shutdown of main power. However, he couldn't figure out how that would help them evade the torpedoes, which would home in on them regardless.

Even so, he quickly entered the command into the helm. "New course one eight zero mark two nine seven!" he repeated. "Three-second burn...*now!*"

With that declaration, the *Black Sun* turned away and went to full acceleration for precisely three seconds, after which the crimson glow of her main thruster faded out of sight. However, the proper effect had been established, as the now inactive warship launched through space, her acceleration maintained through zero resistance, distancing herself from the still drifting *Vindicator*.

"Reversion in ten seconds!" Anna continued as she watched the *Vindicator* become smaller and smaller in the viewscreen. Whatever was about to happen, she hoped with retained breath that it worked, as did the rest of the bridge. "Nine... Eight... Seven... Six... Five... Four... Three... Two... One...!"

Swallowing hard, she looked up at the viewscreen. "Here they come!"

An instant later, the torpedo wave reverted back to realspace. Not long after, their previously depowered systems went active, from which they identified their target and engaged their sub-arc propulsion systems. With a collective flash of gold, the torpedoes reangled themselves and shot across space toward their quarry.

That's when something occurred that several of the bridge crew, whether they believed in the supernatural or not, equated to a miracle. Rather than home in on the *Sun*, the torpedoes, flying over, under and around the still fleeing umbra without ever altering their course, launched themselves toward the *Vindicator*, which continued to drift unshielded.

Upon their approach, the battlecruiser's gunnery officer, realizing all too late what was happening, retargeted the ship's weapons toward the approaching projectiles. However, unlike the *Sun*'s weapons, the battlecruiser's phalanx and missiles could not hope to penetrate the torpedoes' shielding, all while her main cannons could only destroy a limited amount before impact. The torpedo wave closed in, virtually unhindered.

Soon enough, the mass of warheads struck the *Vindicator* and detonated, completely obliterating the battlecruiser in an explosion of far greater magnitude than any that had occurred to that point. Such was its power that the resultant shockwave struck the still depowered *Black Sun* and sent her throttling through the void, causing additional damage. Fires and secondary explosions erupted throughout the ship while crewmen were tossed about, damage control teams struggled to access the destruction while the Moebius System was strained even further in its regeneration.

On the bridge, Alex, having knocked his head against the back of his chair, struggled to look up at the viewscreen, which was now flickering with static. Despite the interference, he caught sight of the detonation's afterglow, causing him to smirk in triumph.

*I'll be damned,* he thought with smug satisfaction. *That actually worked.*

"Okay," Davis breathed upon the realization that he was, in fact, still alive. "What in the Seventh Circle just happened!?" he demanded while the other bridge crew members looked to the First Officer with similar inquiry.

Alex's smirk only grew. "I modified the number one beam cannon in a precise way," he explained. "Specifically to fire a beam whose composition matched this ship's energy signature, and one that would scatter and 'coat' the target's hull upon impact."

"Which, upon the disengaging of our main power, would read on the torpedoes' sensors as their target," Anna summarized, also smirking with evident approval.

Alex nodded. "Like moving a bullseye."

Suddenly, the ship rocked again as beams struck her hull. The Imperials, seemingly recovered from their collective shock, were not about to let them go.

"Reengage main drive!" Alex commanded as he lowered the scope. "Keep us in evasive maneuvers until the shields are brought back up!"

Thus, with a surge of newfound confidence and determination, Alex began selecting his targets and returning fire. It might not be much, but he had at last found his equilibrium.

"We're through letting these thrice-damned bastards have their way!"

# Predecessor Ruins
# Ephesus

Dropping down from the upper atmosphere and through whatever remaining anti-air fire there was, the Condors' aft compartments quickly opened up, allowing their marine squads to cable out and descend to the ground below. Seconds later, the marines touched down and disengaged their cables from their transports. The wires retracted nearly instantly into their armor. The Condors took to the skies once again, from there they would continue providing support while the marines moved out and advanced.

Monitoring them from her hiding point, Kaguya frowned as she watched the marines progress. They were the latest round of reinforcements, which never appeared to be in short supply. Whether they were part of the forces that had previously arrived on the planet or were part of a new contingent that had come in from arcspace, the Imperials held a steady stream of reserves to send in against the raiders. A stream that was in no way diminishing, no matter how many Kaguya and the others killed. All while her raiders were rapidly losing ground and overall defensive capability, with no available reinforcements for support.

*A segmented assault,* Kaguya thought as she continued observing the marines, just as another Condor roared overhead. It made sense; Drake would have realized from the beginning that the raiders would be dug in and prepared to face any direct attack, no matter how large the numbers. As such, the only solution was to divide his forces into individual groups and have them gradually advance. Instead of one great attack, they would come in waves, each wearing down the raiders' fortifications in concentrated and highly precise assaults until they, at last, reached the breaking point. It was a very slow way to fight, but against a well-fortified enemy with superior weapons, it was an ideal strategy. One that left Kaguya and her compatriots with little more than borrowed time.

Pushing back the very thought, Kaguya quickly flicked a set of kunai into her hand and quietly peered over the obstruction she was hiding behind. As expected, the marines had yet to detect her, even with the advanced sensors that were placed in their helmets; her tacsuit, which was made of special absorbent materials, prevented discovery. With that verified, Kaguya quickly launched her kunai, the throwing blades immediately sailing into the bodies of three marines. Only then did the marines realize they were under attack but were unable to respond fast enough as Kaguya slew another two in the follow-up assault; five marines were already dead before the first beam rifle shots were fired.

Knowing that the obstruction wouldn't protect her, Kaguya darted out and moved to another relic, one that would obscure her profile more effectively. By that point the marines had scattered and were seeking shelter of their own, all while maintaining their fire against her. Fortunately, Kaguya's hearing was sharp enough that she could detect when any of the marines moved from their cover to strike. She struck first with a shuriken throw; several more marines were taken out this way.

Suddenly, Kaguya heard the distinct sound of metal impacting near her position; one of the marines had thrown a grenade. Knowing that she had no time to disarm it, she immediately abandoned her location in favor of another site, one that would both shroud her from the marines and shield her from the explosion. However, just as she managed to move out, the grenade, having apparently been set to a shortened countdown, detonated in a great flash. Before Kaguya realized it, her body was picked up by the shockwave and thrown across the field, all while pieces of shrapnel struck her.

Moments later, she found herself sprawled facedown on the ground. She was very much alive that much she knew. There was no way she would feel such pain, especially from her now dislocated right shoulder, had she been dead.

Once the ringing in her ears subsided, Kaguya was able to hear the marines approaching ever cautiously to inspect her 'corpse'. Knowing that her right arm was useless for the time being, Kaguya quietly had a kunai appear in her left hand, which was fortunately arrayed outside the approaching marines' view. From there, she waited calmly and patiently, with her breathing and heartbeat under fierce control. In her current position, she had to time her attack perfectly, and in such a way that she wouldn't be killed after the initial strike.

Only when the marines' footfalls made specific sounds, indicating distance and position, did Kaguya at last roll to face up, immediately sending her kunai straight into the Imp on her left.

Faltering from shock as his comrade gurgled on his own blood, the Imp on her right was in the process of raising his rifle when Kaguya flipped back to her feet. In a blur of momentum, she produced another kunai and spun, both to dodge the marine beam rifle shot and to gain enough force to slash him across his torso, killing him instantly.

Other Imperials were quick to follow, training their rifles on her and firing, but by then it was too late. Moving around their beam shots while ignoring the pain of her swaying right arm, Kaguya closed the distance to the marines and, without ever slowing down, cut them apart with her reversed blade. As before, she aimed for the torso or the neck; she knew her opponents would be instantly killed the moment her kunai crossed their flesh.

Only the last marine managed to put up a decent fight. He was able to fire a shot that clipped Kaguya across her left hip, causing her to grit her teeth at the resultant burn. Before he could trigger another shot, however, the Dragon Princess leaped and flipped, landing right behind him. She impaled him straight through the back. Only then did his corpse fall, the improvised dagger left in it.

Now within a newfound calm, Kaguya paused for the briefest of moments, allowing herself to breathe more heavily as she regained control. For that period, she heard nothing but the sound of her own breathing; not even the constant gunfire or explosions or screams reached her ears throughout that short span. She was almost completely depleted, both in body and spirit. She didn't know how much longer she could keep on fighting like this, especially against additional groups of fresh reserves. Even so, she had no choice but to continue; the alternative was no more an option to her than it had been for Jon or Alex.

Resigned, she quietly moved out of the open and to the cover of untouched ruins. There she inspected her damaged right arm. It hung limply at her side; she didn't have to remove the sleeve to know there was a large amount of bruising at her shoulder. Fortunately, none of her other wounds were severe; just an assortment of small blemishes that would heal on their own, all while her internal organs remained relatively unaffected.

Thus, inwardly grimacing at the thought, Kaguya knew what she had to do next. Angling her shoulder toward a nearby wall, Kaguya closed her eyes and momentarily prepared herself, right before throwing her shoulder against the ruin. Newfound pain surged through her body as she felt her shoulder pop back into place. Kaguya resisted the urge to scream lest she draw unwanted attention to her location. Once the pain subsided, she flexed and raised her arm, rotating the shoulder to ensure it was functioning correctly.

With one final slow breath, she turned and, deliberately ignoring her body's trauma and the growing temptation to rest, returned to the battle.

# Predecessor Temple
# Ephesus

Landing back on the ground, the pain in his left side caused Jon to nearly stumble as his hand moved to his newest wound. Upon withdrawing the hand, he saw a large amount of blood smattered on the black glove. He sneered down at the image; just one more scar on his body, and it wasn't even the first from this battle.

"Come now," Drake spoke as he materialized before Jon, greatcoat billowing as he reappeared. "You've been doing quite well up to this point. Surely this isn't all you can manage."

Glaring back, Jon raised his bloody glove and slung a black wave at Drake. The black wave was naturally deflected by Drake's golden energy shield, but it didn't matter. The response had been given, though Drake wasn't finished talking.

"In fact, I should say you're doing better than well," Drake stated. "Even better than my expectations."

When Jon looked on with an inquiring eye, Drake elaborated. "Even now, as weathered as your forces are, they continue to hold out," he explained, tapping the side of his head to indicate his comlink. "The *Black Sun* is almost done in, and your ground forces are dwindling by the minute, yet they have done well to last this long against an obviously superior force."

Jon let out in a baneful laugh. "If your forces are so superior, how come they have yet to beat us?"

"All in good time," Drake retorted with a wagging finger. "And that's not to say you were entirely outmatched. Not when you left your brother, a man of unquestioned brilliance, to command the *Black Sun*, or the legendary Barbarossa to command your ground forces."

Drake actually laughed amusedly at the latter mention. "I must say that last one caught me by complete surprise. After all, who would have guessed the Caliphate's best warrior and commander would end up playing house cat to 'infidel' Terrans? And renegades at that?"

Hearing that, it was Jon's turn to smirk dominantly. And in spite of the compliment, it wasn't for the reason Drake suspected.

The Admiral went on, regardless. "That being said, you have my full compliments," Drake continued. "In the short time that was given to you, you have put together one of the finest crews I have ever seen. Possibly the best pirate crew independent of the Clans."

Niceties extended, Drake reformed Berith in his right hand. "Unfortunately, however, that time is about to pass," he said, pointing the blade at Jon. "And you are about to die."

Jon responded by bringing Astaroth's blade up to match, all the while ignoring the pain in his side. "Not going to spare me again?" Jon quipped. "Like you did on Bonham?"

"I spared your life on Bonham because I owed a favor," he answered evenly. "That favor has since been repaid."

*Could it be...?* Jon thought, before pushing the question out of his mind; he couldn't afford any distraction. Instead, he focused his gaze on the Admiral. "Well then," he said. "To quote a certain adage, 'Today is a good day to die...'"

With that, he lunged forward while Drake raised Berith to parry. However, at the very last second, Jon shifted his movement to Drake's left, where he passed the Admiral entirely, Astaroth appearing as a black energy trail as he went. A split-second later,

Jon ended his assault directly behind his opponent, his legs crouched and his blade at his side. "But the day is far from over."

Reaching up to his cheek, specifically where Astaroth had left its mark, Drake withdrew his hand and saw that there really was blood, a lot of blood. Smirking with minute approval, Drake casually observed his bloodstained fingers. "Indeed," he said quietly, before flicking it off of his glove, letting it splatter across the ground next to him.

Angered at his wounded face, Drake whirled around and unleashed a golden wave at the pirate, who spun about and used the motion to absorb the wave out of the air. Undaunted, Jon relaunched himself toward his opponent. A second later, both blades collided once more emitting a thunderous black and gold shockwave which sped outward, encompassing the chamber. Destruction was everywhere.

# Chapter XXXVII: Hope's End

It was the strangest feeling. A feeling that, amidst all that she had felt and encountered throughout her lifespan, she could not compare with any previous experience; a feeling that she could only describe in the most abstract of terms. It was the feeling of a vast ocean being centered and focused into one particular point. It was the feeling of an enormous light encompassing and shining into a great abyss. It was the feeling of newfound warmth overcoming an ancient cold. It was the feeling of life returning to a forgotten dead.

It was the feeling of a tremendous unstoppable force of energy, drawn from every conceivable point, being driven into the darkest of abysses. From which it disappeared into the depths, seemingly as fast and as spontaneous as it had emerged.

For what had seemed like hours, she had stood there, her hand fixed against the crystalline orb while the energy pooled and flowed around her into the pit. Initially, it had only been equivalent to a trickle, but now, upon its continuous build up, it surged like a raging river, such that she thought she could be swept off her feet any moment. A viable torrent of energy, whose make and composition even she could not identify, shifting around the entirety of the temple and being focused into the single point before her. All with such force and power that it

made the chaos she felt above – within the temple, around the ruined
city and amongst the stars themselves – feel tranquil by comparison.

And she indeed felt that chaos, in spite of the energy around her. From
the various weapons fire to the battle cries of the still able combatants
to the last vestige thoughts of the dying, she felt every last part of the
surface battle as she would a distant melody. As far as she could tell,
the pirates were continuing to hold their own against the Imperials; her
supporters continued to hold their own against their aggressors, her ship
continued to wage war against the opposing armada, and *he* continued
to fight against his destined opponent. Death was abundant throughout
while damage and destruction were dealt to both the aggressors and the
defenders, but the battle continued on all the same. For how long was
another matter, though, much to her emerging discomfort, it didn't look
like her supporters would hold out for much longer.

Even so, she kept herself focused on completing her task while ignoring
all that occurred above her. It was all she could do. She had come quite
far, and sacrificed so much, in order to reach this very place, this very
point; to turn away now would possibly forfeit her efforts. As such,
there was no choice for her; no alternative but to see it through to the
end, no matter how many perished above her. After all, it was what *he*
would have wanted her to do. That she was positive.

Thus, she continued, focusing her mind and her spirit onto the very
point that the energy around her convened; into the very depths of
the darkness before her. Strangely, in spite of the vast scope of that
darkness, she felt no fear, no hesitance toward it. Instead, she embraced
it, submerged herself within it, such that she dove through its depths
rather than fell. Throughout that time, outside the currents of energy
that continued to flow around, she beheld nothing within; no matter,
sentience and certainly no light. Just an endless scope of darkness, with
which the energy currents bled into before disappearing entirely. A
complete and utter abyss.

Confusion quickly entered her, even as she moved deeper and deeper.

How could such a void, one that seemingly surpassed the vastness of space itself, even exist? And much more, why would those who came before her and all others build such an edifice? Surely there was something that lay underneath it, something that the energy around her was drawn to. And yet, for all her prodding, for all that she dove into the depths and expanded her senses, she still beheld nothing. Nothing beyond the raindrops of energy that fell around her. Nothing beyond the darkness.

No, she refused to believe that. Everything she had analyzed, every relic and artifact she had studied from those who preceded her had led to this very place, this very darkness. And though her knowledge, as extensive as it was, of those predecessors remained limited, she knew that they would not have created a wasteful space, much less focused such power into it. There had to be a purpose in mind for all of it; a purpose that laid within the depths beyond all manner of reach. For without such purpose, nothing that had come to pass would have mattered, much less been brought into existence by the very creators of this place.

She pressed on, moving further and further into the void, keeping her special senses extended throughout. The chaos above felt even more distant now; she could still feel it, alongside the disappearing sentience of those dead or dying, but now it barely registered to her. She could not even see the light from which she had first come; the darkness and the void fully encompassed her perception by this time. Only the sparse light provided by the continuous flow of energy separated the darkness from her.

Continuing on, another thought occurred to her. Could the darkness hold a purpose in itself? Specifically, could it actually be there as a form of defense? As a form of dissuasion against intruders, making them believe that there was, in fact, nothing within the well? It was quite possible as well as the most logical explanation; the creators of this setting were said to have been granted great physical and spiritual power, so they would naturally have crafted such a defense against any unwanted intruders.

However, that in itself led to another question: what exactly had they defended their creation against? Yes, other races had gradually come into being as time went on, but even if they had emerged within *their* presence, surely none of their kind could compare to *theirs*. Or perhaps they had created the void in order to dissuade any future races, namely those that had come long after they had gone? Or just the opposite, perhaps this was a test to measure the worth of those that indeed dove into the darkness, to see if they could truly reach what it was that laid underneath?

She sighed as she pressed on. So many unanswered questions and she hadn't even reached whatever it was that laid below. That being said, however, she was sure, more than ever now, that there was indeed something within the dark. Something that had laid dormant for eons, and was now in the process of being reawakened. She need only proceed onward to reach it; to extend her own power to the ultimate level in order to at last gain what she sought. Perhaps only then would her questions be answered, her ignorance resolved.

And so, as her physical being remained on the surface, she delved further into the dark, all the while keeping alert to her surroundings. After all, even within the deepest darkness, the barest flicker of light may yet be...

# Predecessor Temple
# Ephesus

From his new position atop a tall obelisk, Drake generated a vertical energy wave that flew out at high speed, forcing Jon to roll to the side to evade. Drake moved to follow up with a second, but Jon brought up his left hand and formed a black hole in front of him, absorbing the oncoming energy. Immediately, three black holes formed around Drake and dispelled three smaller waves at the admiral, who instantly teleported away. Upon impact with the now vacant obelisk, the waves initiated a small explosion that echoed across the temple. More debris littered the chamber floor.

The pirate's frustration grew; this had become Drake's standard response, attack and then teleport away. A veritable cat and mouse game. Part of Jon wanted to finish the fight face to face, but the less frustrated part knew that the Admiral would take that as a sign of weakness and exploit it accordingly. Not that it would have done their field of battle any better. As more debris fell from above, Jon could only hope that the entire temple didn't collapse on top of them before the battle was through. That would have been most inconvenient.

Parrying with Astaroth, Jon deflected another one of Drake's energy augmented slashes, then countered with his own. Before his strike could connect, however, the admiral teleported into the distance...again.

A near instant later, Drake reformed behind Jon, but not as the pirate had predicted. Rather than appearing right behind the elder Flint, Drake had maintained his distance, thereby keeping out of Jon's reach when he twisted around to attack. Realizing this a split second too late, Jon attempted to launch another black wave, but Drake was faster, slashing Berith about and generating a subsonic shockwave that lifted Jon off of his feet and sent him flying into one of the temple walls. He hit with a hard crash and slid to the floor. Pain radiated throughout his body, yet Jon was ready as Drake reappeared in front of him. Lurching away, the elder Flint narrowly avoiding the Imp's attempt to impale him. Jon opened his left hand to launch a black ball, but Drake kicked him across the face before he could initiate his attack and teleported yet again. The Admiral rematerialized at Jon's right and tried to finish off his opponent, but this time Jon was faster, opening a black hole on the ground which he "fell" into before Drake's blade could touch him.

A second later, another black hole opened up overhead; Jon fell through with Astaroth set to impale. Drake naturally teleported away, but reappeared a second later, hovering in mid-air over what appeared to be an ancient art form. From that distance he launched another subsonic shockwave, once more sending the elder Flint flying. This time, Drake teleported along the pirate's trajectory, momentarily 'soaring' in a parallel path and slashing Berith across the pirate's back. Jon let out an angered cry of pain; he twisted around, striking back, but the admiral had already vanished in a golden flash before Astaroth's blade could connect. Reorienting himself before impact, Jon's boots struck a hard surface. Instantly, Drake reappeared at Jon's left side and slammed the end of Berith's hilt against the pirate's face, causing him to reel back in additional pain and shock. The admiral dematerialized immediately.

"You're slowing down Jonathan," Drake taunted from his new position while Jon bent and spat out a fair amount of blood. "Not a good sign."

"Silence," Jon growled in turn before impaling Astaroth's blade into the ground, triggering a black pillar to rise exactly where Drake was standing. This forced Drake to teleport before the pillar could absorb him. He appeared at Jon's right side and sprang forward, once again set to impale. Before his blade could connect, however, Jon had another black pillar rise, this time over where he was crouching, forcing the admiral to halt his advance and teleport away before he was drawn in.

And the chase continued. Drake teleported multiple times; black pillars erupted wherever he reappeared. Upon the fifth teleportation, however, a different attack occurred. Still formed, two pillars swept across the ground to where Drake had materialized, forcing him to teleport yet again. In pursuit, both pillars danced across the temple grounds, continuously advancing upon Drake as he rapidly teleported about, narrowly avoiding being drawn into either. It was only when Drake reformed atop of a nearby pedestal that the pillars at last diminished, though he was forced to teleport again when a sixth pillar formed where he had once been.

Reappearing on the podium, Drake at first opened his mouth to taunt Jon again, but was forced to refrain when the pirate, moving through a newly formed black hole, sought to strike Drake from behind. So close was he that Drake, knowing that he wouldn't be able to teleport in time, spun around and parried the pirate's obsidian blade. After that, both reengaged their sword duel, exchanging slashes and parries while dancing across the platform, launching their respective energy wave attacks upon there being an opening. All the while, Jon made sure to keep up the pressure, keep Drake from regaining the advantage.

Despite the pirate captain's persistence Drake did eventually manage to teleport away, but only a slight distance. At that, Jon raised his hand; a multitude of black holes formed overhead, or so Drake assumed at first. Rather than grow into full black holes; however, they appeared as little more than black specks that hung high in the air, filling the chamber. It took only a second for Drake to realize precisely why thereby allowing him some room to evade as they suddenly began to fall as black rain.

Immediately knowing that Jon had only filled the surrounding vicinity of the temple with Astaroth's energy, but not understanding just how far the field reached, Drake was forced to teleport even faster, moving from one area of the temple to another to avoid the black raindrops while also searching for open space. Begrudgingly admitting this was a well-founded tactic, Drake felt several of the raindrops brush against him as he teleported, instilling a sharp, cold pain within the admiral before he dematerialized. That pain remained with him as he kept teleporting. At last, he found a clear location.

No sooner than he regenerated into the area clear of 'black rain' did Jon emerge from another black hole to the side. Both immediately clashed swords yet again, while Jon smirked at the series of newfound cuts across the admiral's clothes and features.

"Now who's slowing down?" Jon shot back.

Drake flashed his own smirk. "Don't let it go to your head," the Admiral snapped before launching another shockwave, which sent Jon sailing back into the distance. Only his disappearance into a spontaneously generated black hole saved him from slamming against a piece of debris. A moment later, another black hole appeared at Drake's left; Jon charged out to strike, only to be parried by Berith once more. "It will take *far* more than that to defeat me."

"So you keep reminding me," Jon retorted as Astaroth and Berith crashed together, energy bands flashing between them once more.

The elder Flint forced both blades upward to break the parry, thereby allowing him enough time and space to smash his left fist against the Admiral's cheek. The connection sounding with a dull 'thwack', Drake could only look on stunned as Jon pivoted and executed a spin kick, one that smashed into the Admiral's chest. Feeling more surprise than pain, Drake stumbled back in near shock as Jon followed up with another black wave attack. It was only then Drake managed to teleport away, gaining yet one more field of distance from the pirate.

Once reformed, Drake unleashed another golden wave, which Jon diminished with a defending slash. Just as he recovered, Drake then teleported beside Jon but did not attack, instead allowing the pirate to take another slash at him before teleporting behind him once more. From there, Drake slashed at Jon's back yet again, causing him to flinch from the pain.

"The question that remains unanswered, however," Drake commented as Jon twisted around to slash at his neck, only for his blade to be parried. "Is how much longer will *you* last?"

Drake teleported away once again, with Jon dashing after him once he reformed. The Admiral naturally took advantage of his opponent's charge to teleport behind him once more, where he released another energy wave. And this time, when Jon lifted his sword to deflect, the wave exploded to create a shockwave, throwing the pirate across the floor yet again. "To say nothing of your ship and crew."

Ignoring the comment, Jon launched himself back to his feet and fired off a black wave in return. Drake, of course, simply teleported away before the wave could connect.

## Flint Pirates umbra *Black Sun*
## Ephesus System

"How much longer!?" Alex called out as the *Black Sun* was again struck, causing her to shake violently once more.

"Nearly complete!" Gran responded as she worked feverishly at her console, typing commands into her keyboard as the ship shook again. "There's only a few more adjustments to make!"

"Better hurry up!" Davis shouted amidst the chaos, keeping the helm steady in spite of the enemy barrage. "I'm not sure how much longer I can keep ahead like this!"

"Steady!" Alex shouted back as he gripped the arms of his chair yet again. A part of him wished he had kept the command scope extended – he had retracted it in order to "rest" from manning the guns for so long – if only to give him a more stable anchor to hold onto.

"Maintain stern fire!"

"Aye!" the tactical operator replied as he returned the Imperial fire with the stern beam cannons, keeping the pursuing warships at bay. It was the first time in the battle he had been allowed to take control of the weapon systems, and he would be damned if he didn't make the most of it.

Feeling the return fire strike the ship, Alex again held himself down as the bridge quaked around him. Thankfully they had managed to get the shields back online, though they were now only at marginal power and would likely buckle again in another few minutes. At least, that would be the case if Alex's plan didn't work. He inwardly hoped and prayed to the heavens that didn't happen.

Focused on the viewscreen, the younger Flint watched as the remaining Imperial warships chased the "retreating" *Black Sun* across space, bringing whatever weapons they had to bear against her form. The *Sun* naturally returned fire, as did the Corsairs that flew alongside her, doing damage to the Imperials in kind. And in spite of her damage and depleted energy, her weapons remained formidable enough to break through the shields of several of the pursuing ships and either impair or outright obliterate them at once. As such, several of the pursuers were enveloped in flame, but this did nothing to hinder those remaining.

Alex subconsciously bit his lip. Though the tactic did little beyond keeping some distance between the Imperials and the *Sun*, especially since their arc engine was still not at full operational capacity, it at least bought some time for his plan to be implemented. And as a side effect, it also bottlenecked the Imperials into a tighter formation than they had been using. Their ships were now almost entirely narrowed toward a single point. That would prove advantageous once his plan was executed.

Of course, whether or not Alex and the rest of the *Black Sun* would last long enough for Gran to finish her work was another matter.

Though a large portion of the earlier damage had been addressed by the Ambrosia System, the umbra remained severely damaged and almost crippled, all but limping away from her enemies. Her arc engine was now functioning at less than forty percent of its standard capacity, while much of the power distribution system remained impaired. As a result, offensive and defensive power were significantly reduced, while the Ambrosia System strained itself in its function. All while the rate of destruction remained a constant factor, as indicated by one of the pursuing destroyers firing her missiles into the *Sun*'s stern. The umbra quaked even more.

*We're definitely on our last legs,* Alex thought amidst the shaking, again gripping the arms of his chair; he had done it so much he was beginning to wonder how his hands retained feeling and blood flow. All the same, however, his eyes never left the viewscreen or the Imperial ships therein.

"Gran!"

"Just a little longer...!" Gran replied as she steeled herself and retained her focus. She knew she was the only one capable of properly instituting Alex's plan; to make it so that it accomplished its desired effect without doing damage to the *Sun* or the Corsairs alongside. As such, the Lyran could not afford to deviate from her work, even when it appeared death would reach out to her and those around her at any possible second. The latter feeling was far from unique to her.

At the helm, it took every bit of Davis' physical energy, as well as every bit of focus on performing his duties, to keep him from yellowing in his pants. Anna, who was far more stoic than the helmsman could ever hope to be, could also sense the impending doom, as did the tactical operator that was sitting in for Barbarossa. Unless Alex's plan worked soon, he knew they would all be dead in the next few minutes. The fact it was a very unorthodox plan that none of them, save for Gran, really understood helped even less.

*Come on baby,* Alex thought as he looked around the bridge as if he were speaking a prayer. Though he didn't know what viso it had originated from, he had heard more than one ship captain quote that line when under fire, such that it held a reputation for luck. *Hold together...*

Suddenly, Gran's console beeped an indication. "It's ready!" she shouted to the rest of the bridge. "Standing by for broadcast!"

Taking a deep breath, Alex focused on the viewscreen. "Circle us around!" he commanded. "Set up for forward barrage on my mark!"

"Forward barrage aye!" the tactical operator reported as he began implementing commands. In a matter of seconds, the *Black Sun*'s remaining missile and torpedo tubes were loaded, and her beam weapons were fully charged. At the same time, firing solutions were established on the various enemy ships. "Ready to fire at your command!"

"Coming to course one-six-seven mark nine-two-zero!" Davis shouted as he guided the ship into a left bank, as sharp as he could manage it with her current speed. "We'll be facing them down in less than a minute!"

Gritting his teeth together, Alex kept watch of the Imperial warships on the viewscreen. Having noticed the *Sun*'s abrupt course change, the majority were now attempting to match her turn, though a few stragglers were going into evasive maneuvers. Whether it was to avoid collision with their comrades, or the attack they knew was coming, Alex didn't know. Either way, however, none of it would matter in the next few seconds, when the *Sun* was halfway through her turn.

Waiting, Alex recalled another quote. One that had supposedly originated from Ancient Terra. "The audience is listening," he murmured to himself, right before giving the awaited command.

"Broadcast!"

In response, Gran, after disengaging her audio set, tapped the specific key. A moment later, the *Sun*'s communication array sent out a precise signal; a burst transmission that was aimed directly at the enemy fleet. One that, in spite of all the defensive safeguards the Imperial ships implemented with their own comm. systems, they would not be able to ignore.

The effect was nearly instantaneous. Mere seconds after the broadcast was made, the ships began to move wildly off of their original courses, their grey hulls shifting uncontrollably in different vectors. What was once an orderly attack formation quickly degenerated into chaos as the various warships accelerated or decelerated, ascended or descended or turned in construed and random angles. Some, namely the few remaining fighters and bombers, even ended up colliding with their comrades, while others fired their weapons just as wildly as they moved, causing additional damage.

His own ship now fully turned about, Alex took a moment to feel pride in his work. The Black Note was a huge success. Essentially a grandiose audio distortion, the "note" took the form of a burst signal that overloaded shipwide communication systems via oscillation, both against the standard arrays and the ship hulls themselves. As a result, the Imperial ships were now completely overcome with unending audio feedback, with their comm. lines not only jammed but their crews straining against the constant overbearing 'hum', which was far too powerful for their auditory senses. All while their ships flew wildly about, as those in respective control were too overwhelmed with pain to maintain their posts.

*Of course, it hadn't been without risk,* Alex thought as he watched the disarray continue to unfold. *Had the frequencies been off by even a point, the Imperials would have remained unaffected...or we might have been the ones with bleeding ears.*

In that regard, Alex would be sure to properly reward Gran later; as well versed in the sciences as he was, only she could have made the precise audio calculations. However, they had to survive and win first.

"Fire!"

With that, the *Black Sun* let loose her bow weapons. Torpedoes launched from all six bow tubes while missiles erupted from their side VLS, all supplemented by the crimson fire of the two bow cannons as well as those of the Corsairs'. The effect was almost as instantaneous as the bomb itself, with ship after ship being obliterated from the continuous stream, their shields buckling and their hulls erupting in flame one after the other. And this time, no return fire came, thereby allowing the *Sun* to proceed through the now displaced formation with complete ease, in turn bringing her aft weapons back to bear as well.

Minutes later, all that remained of the Imperial armada were flaming debris, with only a few mostly intact hulls here and there. As the *Sun* moved past the remnants, the bridge crew looked upon the debris with almost visible relief. It seemed that their fortune hadn't run out after all.

Despite that feeling, Alex knew it wasn't over. After taking another moment, this time to catch his breath, he looked back at Gran. "Those umbras are still out there," he breathed, exhaustion starting to catch up to him. "Track them and..."

Suddenly, Anna's sensor display lit up again. "No..." she breathed, this time in horror. "Picking up additional Imperial arc signatures! All warship grade!"

No sooner had Anna made that announcement than those very ships emerged from arcspace, opening fire as soon as they reverted. Once again, the *Black Sun* was buffeted by beam and projectiles, with Davis struggling to put the ship into evasion.

Alex seethed, he should have known. "How many!?"

"Fourteen present, many more still coming in...!" Anna reported, before looking up with dread. "The lead ship is the *Subjugator*!"

Closing his eyes to force back the weariness and frustration, even as the ship quaked around him, Alex instantly understood the message. This was it; the Imps' final push. There could be no other explanation for Drake's flagship to emerge at this point when it hadn't even taken part in the initial assault.

Everything else was pretty obvious, especially as Alex lowered the command scope and studied the sensor readings. The Imps were focusing every ship they had, including carriers, on this assault wave, as well as fighters and bombers. All while the *Black Sun* remained as damaged as she was, with her own fighter contingent depleted and no hope of Ambrosia regenerating even the most vital systems in time.

Taking another, more drawn breath, Alex did all he could to steel himself in that instance. Right before he focused everyone back into the fight.

"Bring us about, all ahead full!"

# Predecessor Ruins
# Ephesus

The resounding roar of sub-arc engines instantly alerted Barbarossa that another pair of Vultures had entered the battle. Inwardly cursing as he knew what was about to happen, the Leo went into a dash as the first micromissiles began raining down from above, generating a set of explosions around the Kapta. He just managed to evade the resulting debris. Moments later, one of the few remaining automated anti-air batteries opened fire, downing a passing Vulture, only for the gunship's wingman to destroy the ground force with a beam vulcan fire, right before ascending and moving away. From there, the Condors descended, laying down additional rocket fire across the landscape before dropping down and allowing their marines to cable their way to the ground.

Once again Barbarossa inwardly cursed. He had lost count of the waves of Imperial troops now; they seemed to be coming in at every moment and from every direction while his side's numbers dwindled. Even so, he was not about to give up. Leaping out from his cover, he quickly opened fire upon the still descending marines, shooting out several of them before they even touched the ground. However, he was not able to get them all. The remainder, who retained nominal numbers, were just as quick to return fire the moment they dropped down and retracted their cables. Without hesitating, Barbarossa re-extended his baneclaws and charged into the fray, all the while beams continued to slam against his armor. By this point, his shielding had been completely depleted, and his once immaculate armor was heavily blemished from the constant fire. But it still held to its purpose and kept the Imperials from harming the mighty Leo as he moved against them.

Once he reached close quarters, Barbarossa went to work, slashing at the first two marines that he was able to reach, laying one open across the chest and swatting the other into the surrounding rubble. By sheer fortune, the second, upon surviving the impact, raised his weapon and fired a shot at Barbarossa's right side, just grazing him across the cheek. The Leo twisted around and finish the Imp with a single beam shot of his own. With the latter dispatched, Barbarossa turned back around and slashed another marine across the faceplate, leaving massive gashes in the skull-shaped device as red blood began to pour out. He was quick to finish this marine as well, stabbing him with both sets of claws, one after the other, and then throwing the resultant corpse aside.

A burst of beam fire across his back alerted him that several of the marines had moved in, and much more had taken cover behind the ruins' debris. Barbarossa started to twist to return their fire, but before he could turn, he felt a sudden surge of pain smash through his right hip. He let out an anguished roar. As much as his armor held against the beam fire, it could only limit the force of their impact. The continuous physical shock had bruised and battered Barbarossa underneath. Even so, the Kapta refused to let that slow him down. He quickly shot back with his baneclaw guns while darting out of the line of fire, taking down several of the covering marines in the process. However, he couldn't ignore the marines that remained near him, and so alternated between firing his guns at those in the distance and using his claws against those in close proximity.

It wasn't long before another beam found its way into a wounded area, causing another round of pain to run through Barbarossa. He knew what that meant; the exhaustion was catching up to him, and he was slowing down as a result. And much worse, the damned Terran infidels were coming to realize that fact and were coordinating against him more efficiently.

Fuming at that thought, Barbarossa let out another defiant roar and leaped at the marine nearest to him. He dug his claws straight into the man's torso. The marine weakly attempted to raise his beam rifle, but Barbarossa was quicker, impaling his middle claws directly between the twin eye sensors on the marine's faceplate. He then withdrew the claw and whirled around, firing another set of beams into two more marines. They were instantly eliminated. A third marine, upon watching his comrades fall, immediately withdrew a grenade and threw it at the Leo. Barbarossa pivoted around and kicked the grenade away. It exploded harmlessly in the distance. That marine was dispatched just as quickly.

Suddenly, Barbarossa's ears picked up the sounds of sub-arc engines again; the Vultures had returned. Sure enough, his eyes caught sight of two of the assault craft descending, and this time they were aiming for him directly. Letting loose a beam spray at their approach, which the nimble gunships easily evaded, Barbarossa went into another dash as both crafts fired their chin- mounted beam vulcans. Beams scraped across the ground as the Leo ran. As worn as Barbarossa was, and knowing that the gunships' weapons were much stronger than any handheld arms, the warrior understood he could not take any chances with these two. He focused on evasion, moving from cover to cover, while seizing any possible opportunity to return fire, even managing to clip one of the gunships before being forced to dive into a ruined building.

No sooner had he entered the ruin did the Vultures launch their micromissiles, instantly demolishing the edifice. Fortunately, Barbarossa, anticipating their strategy, ran toward an opening on the opposite side, leaping out of it just as the missiles slammed into the relic. That being said, however, he was unable to evade the resultant shockwave, nor the spray of debris that followed. He was catapulted out across the ground as shards slammed into him. And though his armor continued to hold up, the sheer force of their impact was enough to throw the Leo onto his stomach, while his head was streaked with cuts and bruises.

His ears ringing, pain welling across his body and the scent of his own blood mixing in with the stench of the dust and debris, Barbarossa knew he was near his end. No, he was not about to give up, especially not against Imperial scum, but he could not deny that his body was worn and exhausted. It would not take much longer before it, at last, gave out on him, or worse, some random infidel gained a lucky shot and managed to take him out. And that was assuming he was able to survive those damned Vultures, which, despite his momentarily inhibited hearing, he knew were still hovering close by. And, he was certain, were about to fire their vulcans to make sure he was dead.

However, as he waited for the beam shots, at which point he planned to leap up and fire back, a curious thing occurred. As the ringing died away from his ears, he caught an altogether different noise. Instead of vulcans chattering, he heard the sound of a massive beam blast launching from the ground and slamming into one of the Vultures, followed by the gunship, now on fire, whirling out of control and crashing into the distance.

As the second Vulture turned to face the new attacker, it presented its left side to the Leo. Acting instinctively, Barbarossa reemerged from the rubble and fired his baneclaw guns striking the cockpit. An enormous explosion demolished the entire front of the gunship, while the back half felt to the ground and crashed, exploding as well.

With that enemy slain, Barbarossa turned to look at the one who intervened on his behalf. As he half-expected, a beaten and battered Kaiser trudged through the resultant dust cloud and into the open, his immense Blunderbuss pistol slung over his shoulders. Noting the Leo's gaze, the Herculean simply nodded in acknowledgment. No words were needed.

However, before either of them could exit the field, Barbarossa's ears picked out several new sounds, specifically the roar of a great engine, coupled with the rumble of crunching earth below it. Both of which were far more intense than anything Barbarossa or Kaiser had fought to this point.

"No..." Barbarossa whispered in growing horror. Though it was the first time he had heard such sounds, he knew exactly what was about to appear.

A second later, a vast juggernaut burst through the ruins of a nearby building, the rubble pulverized beneath its caterpillar treads and its top turret turning to face the Leo and the Herculean. And then, with a mighty bellow, its main cannon fired.

---

Her footsteps light and her profile discreet, Kaguya continued down the street as best as she could, fully alert for additional enemies. Though there were none present around her, at least as far as she could tell, she knew that the battle was long from over. The gunfire in the background was enough of an indication, to say nothing of the grinding of tank treads and the sounds of sub-arc drives flying overhead. For the time being, however, there were no Imps within her reach, allowing her some measure of peace as she kept moving. To stop and rest now would only invite further temptation to sleep, something that she especially could not afford to do.

That being said, however, she couldn't deny that her body, wounds aside, was heavily strained. Merely walking down the street, at least in an efficient manner that didn't require hobbling, was taking a toll on her.

Though her legs weren't quite ready to give out on her, they still felt weighted and heavy, just the process of lifting them to take a step took great control and effort on her part. Her arms were not much better; again wounds aside, her limbs felt limp and almost numb, while her hands felt raw from continuously drawing and gripping her sword. All combined with the battering and bruising across her torso, alongside the nicks and cuts on her head, and one could only wonder how Kaguya could move, let alone travel, in such a state. The kunoichi herself suspected that, if she had been a lesser woman, she would have been dead a long time ago.

Eventually, she decided on an internal compromise. While she refused to sit down, again lest her body give out entirely, she did allow herself to stop and lean against a wall, nearly staggering as she moved up to it and pressed her back against it. Now standing still and in a far more stable position, Kaguya focused on catching her breath and allowing her body to regenerate some energy. Coincidentally, a cool breeze began to blow across her location, which against her head, provided further refreshment and relaxation. She even allowed herself to close her eyes to focus on it. If nothing else, it was a nice distraction from the continuing gunfire and explosions in the distance, as well as more positive reassurance that she was, in fact, still alive. Alive, if only for a little while longer.

However, that relaxation did not last, as Kaguya detected approaching footsteps. Acting instinctively, she pushed herself off the wall and quietly advanced toward the sounds' sources, her hands ready to draw her ninjato or a shuriken at a moment's notice. As exhausted as she was, she could still fight. One need only look toward the myriad bloodstains across her face to see that.

Fortunately, it turned out force would be unnecessary. A second later, the sources revealed themselves and Kaguya was relieved to see that they were all dressed in black and gold garb and armor. Some of the raiders nearly jumped upon seeing her but were quick enough to recognize her. And much more, not raise their weapons upon contact.

"My god ma'am," the apparent squad leader spoke in relief, at least as much as his burly accent would allow. "You nearly scared what little shit we had left out of us."

Kaguya nodded in acknowledgment; vulgarity aside, the feeling was almost mutual. She then looked over the other six that were with him. "How many of us are left?"

The squad leader shrugged. "Unknown, but not too many, I reckon," he answered. "Last I heard, most have withdrawn to the sectors outlying the temple, though a few brave idiots remained to hinder the Imps more."

Again Kaguya nodded as she took in the information. By those words and the state of the raiders in front of her, she could tell that they were on their last legs. "Any word from the *Sun*?" she asked.

The squad leader shook his head. "Not a peep," he replied. "If she's still there, then she's neck deep in Imps right now."

"Just like us," one of the other squad members griped cynically, earning nods of agreement from the other five. Kaguya didn't blame them in the least.

"Very well," Kaguya exhaled. She knew the *Black Sun* was still up there fighting; otherwise, additional Imperial forces would be emerging from the sky. Alongside, she knew how tenacious Alex could be, especially in a fight.

"Contact those who are left and tell them to withdraw to the temple grounds."

Hearing that order, the squad leader looked toward one of the others, who immediately began to relay the command.

Kaguya continued further. "Our enemies are as nearly depleted as we are," she stated. "If we can just hold them back for a bit..."

A sudden flash ran over Kaguya's body as she felt an all too certain feeling – an all too certain feeling that ran through her head – causing her to trail off. Suddenly upright and very much alert, Kaguya turned away from the raiders as her eyes tracked the surroundings. All while her hand drifted toward the hilt of her ninjato.

"Ma'am?" the squad leader queried, all the while he and the others raised their weapons. Whatever was happening, it could not be good.

Eyes moving about while her ears and other senses remained open, Kaguya attempted to pinpoint the source of her discomfort. She knew it was out there somewhere, watching and probing them. There could be no other explanation, given what she felt running through her mind.

And then, without warning, she felt a spike within her head, alongside the glint of a humanoid profile emerging from a nearby hiding place. "Take cover!" she shouted as she darted away.

No more than a second later, two beam shots fired from that position, instantly striking two of the raiders in the head, killing them before they could comprehend the situation. A third was then struck down before he could reach cover, followed by a fourth before he could duck into said cover. All four were killed with single shots, and all were precisely aimed.

"Sniper!?" one of the surviving raiders called out to the others as he huddled behind the rubble.

"No," Kaguya called back from her side. "Something far worse..."

The squad leader, who was close enough to overhear it, paled at the realization. "A Warlock!"

From that, the third surviving raider attempted to peer out from the building wall he had ducked behind. One shot later, his body also fell to the ground, a newly formed hole burned between his eyes.

"Goddammit, there's no way we can take on one of those!" the other raider called out as he fired his beam rifle wildly. As if to emphasize that point, a following shot struck the beam rifle right out of his hand, causing the man to let out a horrified curse.

Again Kaguya closed her eyes, but this time for an entirely different reason. Unlike the two beside her, she knew what they were really facing. As she had told Lorelei not too long ago, she had hunted and battled psions before. And much more importantly, she had *killed* psions before.

Her body calm and her mind open, she could feel the psionic waves reach into her, attempting to both read her thoughts and dishevel her at the same time. Being highly trained and disciplined in both their craft and physical combat, the Warlock was more effective at this than most. Only Kaguya's strong mental fortitude, as well as her mental concealment, kept the psion from scanning too deeply into her. However, she allowed him all the same, all so that she could 'feel' the waves and from there trace them back to their source.

Ah, she found what she was looking for, crouching atop a nearby building. And though she could not read the offenders mind in turn, she could tell from its positioning, as well as the caution behind his shots, that her target was holding in a sniper's pose, waiting for her or the two others to so much as peer out from their hiding places. Just as she could also tell that caution was from scanning her, and realizing just how much of a threat she was despite being a 'mundane'.

And there was even more than that. Amidst the telepathy she felt from the psion near her, Kaguya also felt more enter her ever receptive mind. While the one upon the building was certainly the closest to her position, the waves she felt coming from that point were but one within a whole tide. A tide that was now coursing throughout the battlefield originating from multiple points of contact that were moving in through the city. Like a pod of Ryuguan dolphins using their natural acoustic capabilities to hunt.

*A team,* Kaguya realized as she felt the distant waves, frowning as she mentally calculated the numbers. *Split into individual units across different sectors.*

Suddenly, the Warlock began firing again, his beams aimed precisely at Kaguya's position. The kunoichi inwardly smirked; as she had intended, the Warlock realized just how true of a threat she was. To him and his comrades.

"Commander!" the squad leader yelled, attempting to peer out to return fire.

"Stay back!" Kaguya glowered, her eyes now fierce with determination and virulence while her exhaustion was all but forgotten. "He's mine."

"Are you insane!?" the other raider called out from his position. "He'll pick up on everything you do before you do it!"

Now Kaguya flashed an actual smirk, even as the beams continued to rain around her. "He can keep up with my mind," she replied as she prepared herself. *"But not my body."*

With that declaration, Kaguya, at last, emerged from her cover and darted directly through the street, sword already drawn. The Warlock, aware of her approach, abandoned his earlier sniper pose and adopted a more open one. He fired beams in rapid succession, all aimed toward the approaching assassin. However, much to the Warlock's surprise, he found that none of his shots were connecting. Though he could read her mind like any other 'mundane', the female pirate was moving far too fast for him to aim accurately. Every time he so much as gained a bead on her, she would shift her approach and move out of his target line.

Traveling as fast as her tired legs could propel her, Kaguya zigzagged across the street, narrowly evading both the beam shots as they impacted the ground around her and the flying debris. The Warlock was a crack shot, a fact he had proven by killing five of her men in mere seconds, but he had the same fundamental weakness that nearly all psions possessed, overreliance on their telepathy. Yes, he could read her mind and track her movements, but that only mattered so much; he still needed to adjust his aim with his hands, still needed to pull the trigger with his finger. So long as that remained, there would always be a lag between what he "read" and his response.

The Warlock seemed to realize that too, and so quickly switched tactics. While keeping his rifle trained, he focused his telekinesis on the surrounding rubble, causing them to lift up from the ground. Again his assailant's speed kept him from focusing his powers on her, but stone and earth were naturally inert. Once levitated, he then launched them forward at high speed, turning them into effective projectiles that rained down across the apparent ninja's path, supplementing his beam fire. He even fractured some of the shards even further, turning them into spray shots that fell upon his target like a meteor shower.

However, in spite of his focus, the Warlock saw that none of his shots, whether beam or projectile, were connecting. Quite the contrary, Kaguya evaded the flying shards as deftly as she did the beams, flipping and twisting around them with outright elegance. The closest one of the shards came to actually striking her was grazing her left cheek, inflicting a new cut but failing to do any further damage. And much worse, when she got close enough, she actually jumped on some of the flying stones, using them as steps to move through the air and eventually reach the building's roof. Upon landing on the very last stone, Kaguya raised her ninjato and leaped into the air at the Warlock, poised to strike.

Only a quick reaction on the Warlock's part saved him. As Kaguya leaped, he dropped his rifle and reached his hands out, effectively halting her in mid-flight. Feeling some momentary satisfaction at finally catching his target, he then pushed his hands outward, throwing the ninja across the air at high velocity. A few more seconds and she would be little more than a splatter across a nearby wall. Or so he thought.

Just as Kaguya began to feel the repulsion, she flicked a kunai into her left hand and launched it out, instantly striking the Warlock's exposed throat. Now gurgling on his own blood, the Warlock lost his telekinetic grip on her, thereby allowing Kaguya to perform a midair flip and drop back onto the street, where she crouched and skidded on her boots to a full stop. Seconds later, the Warlock was dead, and Kaguya no longer felt his psionic "presence" within her mind.

Now calm again, the two remaining raiders could only look on aghast as they watched their leader do the impossible. For her part, Kaguya ignored their glances and instead focused back on catching her breath. She would need it for what was to come.

"Fall back to the temple grounds," she ordered to the pair. "Do not wait for me."

Hearing their orders, the pair quickly withdrew and moved back down the street without any further words. After seeing what their leader had just done, they knew better than to question her, let alone worry about her.

Once they were gone, Kaguya again felt the strain begin to creep up on her, but she pushed it back. She could no longer allow herself to feel exhausted, no matter how weakened and barely functioning her body was. She now had higher profile targets to kill; targets that, upon picking up the death of their comrade and her presence, abandoned their advance toward the temple and began to converge toward her location. Clearly, they were intent on killing her first and foremost.

Thus, focusing her mind back on the psionic waves as they emanated, she resheathed her ninjato and ran further into the battleground.

## Flint Pirates umbra *Black Sun*
## Ephesus System

"Hull integrity down to fifty-three percent!" the tactical operator shouted as another set of beams slammed into the *Sun*'s port side. Besides the standard shaking, the additional damage also spawned power fluctuations, evident by the flashing bridge lights and monitors. "Shields are non-responsive!"

"Forget the shields! Concentrate regeneration on the hull!" Alex ordered as he targeted another *Ravager* and fired with the topside bow cannon. The underside bow cannon, as well as the topside stern cannon, had been destroyed not too long ago. "And see if you can get cannons two and three back online!"

"I'm trying!" the tactical operator called as he entered commands. Unfortunately, this proved to be quite tricky as his monitor kept flickering, the power fluctuations becoming more and more frequent.

Just then, another shot slammed into the *Sun*'s bow. Fortunately, aside from bludgeoning the blade tip, the bow remained mostly intact. In turn, Alex fired a missile spray toward the offender, another *Harbinger*, which had moved in too close to evade. The missiles pierced the destroyer's bow shield and spread themselves across her hull, triggering a multitude of explosions. The destroyer was quickly obliterated, adding its debris to the surrounding space.

Even so, there were many more where it came from, as three more destroyers moved in from their comrade's vector, firing their own beam cannons at the *Black Sun*. Rocked by the sudden burst of energy as the lights dimmed even longer than they had before, Alex grit his teeth and returned fire, striking one of the destroyers on the bow but failing to destroy it. The stricken warship simply moved out of the way as the two other destroyers, joined by a *Ravager*, kept up the assault.

That was when the *Black Sun* was struck from behind by a much more powerful weapon, the ship outright lurched. Just then, an *Imperator*-class battleship made its presence known off of the umbra's stern, right before it launched a second barrage of beam fire, complimented by a spray of missiles. Alex sneered at this as he focused what few beam phalanx remained to intercept the missiles. Fortuitously, the battleship had moved into one of the *Sun*'s sensor blind spots, which were another casualty of her damaged state.

In response, Alex fired back with the underside stern cannon, but unlike the lesser ships present, the battleship withstood most of the blasts. However, the continuous rapid firing, in spite of the cannon's depleted energy, did manage to drain enough of the Imperial ship's shields, thereby allowing Alex to launch a torpedo shot. The outcome was much like it had been with the previous destroyer, only the battleship attempted to turn to port to reveal her phalanx. The torpedo closed the distance before it could complete said turn.

As he watched the afterglow of the explosion, Alex's mind reeled to come up with another plan. His ship was taking more and more damage by the minute, and what little energy they had left was spent picking off one enemy after another, all the while the Imperials maintained their numbers. He needed a strategy, and yet he didn't know what he could do given his dwindling resources. Unless Braun had a nuclear weapon stashed somewhere aboard, he could not come up with any fresh ideas, while those he already had couldn't be implemented.

*Come on Alex, think!* he mentally bellowed at himself as he fired more beam cannon shots, this time at an approaching *Fury* that was sweeping by for a high-speed strike. Unfortunately, no answer came, not even as Alex managed to obliterate the frigate before it could fire its own weapons. *Think of something! Anything!*

His rambling was interrupted by another sound. Not that of the ship rumbling, but rather of Anna's monitor beeping in warning. Followed by Anna calling out in near horror. "Additional arc signatures incoming!"

A newfound sickly feeling overcoming him and the rest of the bridge, Alex closed his eyes as if he were stung. Just how many ships did Drake bring with him to this battle? Was the whole Thirteenth Fleet out there, waiting to move in for the kill?

"How many and how long!?"

After several attempts to gain those readings, Anna shook her head in frustration. "I can't tell! Long-range sensors are highly depleted! It could be anywhere from a small taskforce to a whole fleet!"

Again the *Sun* rocked as more beams struck her side. A second later, Davis shouted in warning as he looked over the indicated damage, "I lost the helm again! And unless Moebius kicks in, I don't think I can get it back!"

Another rumble. "Hull integrity now forty-four percent!" the tactical operator also alerted. "We've lost the number one cannon!"

Sneering once more, Alex retracted the command scope. There was almost no point in manning the guns anymore. "Prepare to...!" he started to order only to trail off.

Though the viewscreen was filled with static and interference, Alex just managed to catch sight of a pair of Mustangs flying toward the *Sun*, specifically the bridge tower.

"Redirect all available anti-air fire!" he shouted to the tactical operator.

One more rumble, right before the operator banefully shook his head. "Weapons are offline!" he shouted, the inevitability clear in his voice.

Biting back a curse, Alex knew it was too late to clear the bridge. As such, he could only do one more thing. "Brace for impact!" he called out, right before closing his eyes.

Seconds later, the two Mustangs launched at the bridge and let loose their guns. Several explosions followed.

# Chapter XXXVIII: Despair's Beginning

## Predecessor Temple
## Ephesus

Black and gold energy flaring between them in blazing sparks, the duel between pirate and Imperial continued throughout the temple's main chamber. Surging forward, Jon fashioned a series of black waves in varying arcs as he slashed Astaroth about, forcing Drake to move back, deflecting the offensive with golden parries as he retreated. The Admiral swung Berith up to clash against Jon's sword, holding the obsidian blade immobile for a brief moment, before deflecting it to the side and moving to counterattack. Jon naturally moved to defend. However, the Admiral lept into the air and spun rapidly to generate a vortex to deflect Jon's retaliating slash. Successful, he landed behind the pirate and reached to inflict another laceration into Jon's back. Undaunted, Jon executed a sudden spin attack of his own, duplication being fair play, and generated a black field that poured toward the Imperial. Drake teleported before the blade's energy could connect with his flesh.

He didn't move far this time, allowing Jon to reengage as soon as he reformed. The pirate swung Astaroth down in a formidable diagonal power slash, forming a black crescent that was meant to cleave the Admiral in half. Unfortunately for Jon, Drake foresaw the attack. Holding Berith up with both hands he again deflected the strike, then pivoted and lunged, aiming at Jon's stomach. Jon jumped back, avoiding Drake's blade, and launched another black wave to counter. Drake shifted to the left to evade, then immediately proceeded on the offensive, exchanging several slashes and parries with Jon before unleashing a golden wave of his own. Reaching out with his left hand, the elder Flint absorbed all the incoming energy into a black hole. A moment later, several black eddies opened up around Drake, forcing the Admiral to teleport yet again before the smaller but more numerous golden waves fell upon him.

"That's the extent of your arsenal, strike and run for cover?" Jon sneered frustratingly in response, then leaped to the right to evade as Drake reformed behind him and attempted to bayonet his back. A black energy ball flew at Drake, who batted it away before advancing yet again. Another section of the temple exploded, and shards rained about the combatants.

Even now, while they again exchanged strikes and parries with flashes and bands of energy flying about creating further destruction, Drake maintained his smug disposition, as if he were in complete control over the battle. Much worse, Jon knew his opponent wasn't too far off in that belief. His ground forces, or whatever remained of them, had to be in full retreat now, while the *Black Sun* had to be on her last legs. Too much time had passed for there to be any other conclusions, and Jon knew full well, for all the advantages his ship and crew retained, they could only hold up for so long against Drake's superior resources.

And that was not dismissing their present duel of course. Jon hated to admit it, but Drake really was the superior Wielder. Not nearly as good as his mother, but more than enough that Jon was merely keeping up with him as opposed to dominating, let alone working his way toward triumph. Even the fact that Drake was teleporting far less now hardly mattered; the Admiral maintained the edge, either deflecting or evading every attack Jon made while executing powerful attacks of his own. And though Jon had managed to inflict damage as the fight went on, it was quite obvious that Drake had inflicted more in return.

Reforming in the distance, Drake launched a scattershot, forcing Jon to form a black shield to consume the energy. Undeterred, Drake immediately fired a second array of shots at a subsonic velocity, which pierced the darkness before they could be absorbed. Thrown back with their impact, Jon flinched as more wounds appeared on his person. Without hesitation, the pirate flipped around midair and countered with dual-energy rollers. Drake teleported away to avoid the collision. Just as Jon's boots touched the ground, the Admiral reformed at Jon's left. With Berith re-extended into an elongated golden energy blade, he sliced at the pirate, who barely managed to bring up Astaroth in defense. Despite that, Jon lacked the strength to withstand the blades full force, and so was knocked away yet again.

Drake teleported once more, this time reforming right behind Jon as he flew through the air. Anticipating the move, Jon, twisted around and swung at Drake's neck, only for the strike to be deflected when the latter raised Berith to guard. The resultant clash rang throughout the temple, as Jon's piercing sapphire eye met Drake's own self-confident, gleaming glacial and crimson eyes. A second later, Drake forced more energy into Berith and swatted Jon away for the second time, sending him crashing into a nearby wall. The resultant impact also sounded throughout the temple.

Much to Jon's credit, he managed to land on his feet after the crash. However, he was only able to remain standing for a brief moment. Slowly he collapsed onto his left knee while breathing in and out in rapid succession. A line of blood now emanated from the side of Jon's forehead as well; one more to add to the number spread across his body. He subconsciously lifted his left hand up to wipe it away, all the while Astaroth disappeared from his right. He was far from done, but his body still had its limits.

Drake, for his part, merely stood by and silently observed Jon as he attempted to right himself, only to fall back onto his knee. The Admiral had been true in his words before; the eldest son of the Golden Queen had surpassed his expectations and given him a good fight, one that had pushed him to the brink several times as well. However, such things eventually came to their end, and Drake had much more experience as both a Wielder and a commander than his opponent. The duel would conclude as such; the pirate, like his crew around him, would fight to the bitter end but would do little more than delay Drake's inevitable victory.

As Drake pondered this, his comlink sounded off in his ear. "*Subjugator* to Admiral Drake."

Blinking at the call, the flag officer answered. "Drake here."

"Admiral, we've succeeded on our end," the captain of the *Subjugator* replied. "The *Black Sun* is finished."

Drake shifted his gaze toward Jon, who, despite his defiance, closed his eye and tilted his head in anguish. Drake smiled; he didn't know how, but the good Captain Flint knew exactly what had just happened.

"Disabled or destroyed?"

"Disabled, as per your order," the captain informed dutifully. "The fleet awaits your command."

Smile growing even larger, Drake felt an all too familiar satisfaction begin to weigh in on him. The battle was technically still going on, but that was now a triviality. Without their ship, the Flint Pirates' ground forces no longer had any hope of winning.

"Standby *Subjugator*," he ordered before signing off momentarily.

Slowly, he began to walk, almost casually, to where Jon was kneeling. Visibly angered at his approach, Jon raised his left hand and launched a black shot at the Admiral's head. Drake merely caught the energy with his left hand and crushed it under his grip. Once he reached the pirate, the Admiral then used that very same hand to grasp Jon's neck and lift him in the air.

"It's over Jonathan," Drake proclaimed victoriously to his captive, who struggled to release himself from the Imps hold. "You put up great resistance, resistance indeed worthy of praise, but in the end just that. *Mere resistance!*"

With one final assault, Drake threw the pirate captain across the temple grounds, where he fell to the floor. And this time Jon didn't manage land on his feet.

Drake walked toward him again, kneeling beside his limp form. "Your ship is all but destroyed. Your ground forces, despite being in retreat, have nowhere to go. And you have reached the end of your strength," he declared as Jon struggled to lift himself off the ground. "All that remains is for me to finish you and give the final order."

Despite his struggles and his hampered breathing, Jon raised his head up to glare back at the Admiral. Drake merely grinned. Even to the bitter end, his opponent retained both pride and spirit. Strangely, that pleased him.

"However, I see no reason for that," Drake countered. "Not when we can still reach a mutual arrangement."

Berith dissipating from his hand, the Admiral reached into his pocket and withdrew a cloth, and began, with apparent care, to wipe the blood from Jon's forehead. "My original offer still stands," he said, dismissing Jon's miniscule attempts to resist. "Accept it, and I promise to spare both your ship and your remaining crew any further harm..."

Jon pulled his head back and, in a display that Drake had failed to foresee, spat blood tinted saliva onto the Admiral's face. Sighing, the Admiral withdrew the cloth and meticulously wiped the blood from his face, right before throwing the handkerchief away, as if it were a piece of refuse. Seething, he again grabbed Jon by the throat and threw him across the temple. This time with much greater power, such that Jon landed further into the distance.

Drake then teleported and reformed where the pirate landed. "It appears you are not quite finished *resisting*," he stated, his face betraying the barest signs of fervor, as he kicked Jon across the ground, Berith reforming in his grip. "Very well, then. Have at you, boy."

With that call, the Admiral charged forward as Jon flipped himself back up, Astaroth rematerializing his hand. A renewed clash of metalized energy quickly rang out.

## Flint Pirates umbra *Black Sun*
## Ephesus System

It was the throbbing he felt first, as he slowly started to realize that he was, in fact, still alive, Alex dazedly blinked his eyes open and attempted to focus, all the while, his head pounded like a drum. The *Sun*'s bridge, of what little he could see of it given his blurred sight, seemed to rock as he attempted to stand, at which point he realized his ears were ringing along with his throbbing head. He felt nauseated and totally off balance as if he had spent the prior evening wildly intoxicated, while his body seemed to ache and convulse in virtually every area. However, for all accounts and purposes, Alexander Flint was still very much alive. A fact he appreciated.

From there, he merely waited until both his sight and his hearing were gradually restored to him, which took the better part of a minute. As this progressed, his eyes adjusted to the now darkened bridge while the ringing in his ears gave way to the sounds around him. Sparks dropped down from the damaged ceiling as lights flickered wildly against the dark. The sounds of malfunctioning equipment and alarming voices were overwhelming, as was the smell of smoke and burnt metal. The viewscreen and the smaller displays were nothing more than a jumble of static and color, while sounds of coughing and wheezing filled the air, itself indicating that Alex was not the only survivor.

Once he felt he had regained enough of himself to do so, he looked over toward the others. Much to his relief, he saw that they were all still alive, though significantly wounded. Gran, who had to be "ringing" much harder than he was, had stripped off her headset and was bent over her console, trembling in pain but attempting to reorient herself. Anna was turned away from her own station, her right hand held her hat while her left was against her temple. Blood flowed between her fingers. Davis was wiping his sleeve over his eyes in an attempt to clear particulate from them, while the tactical operator, whose name Alex did not recall, was coughing from the smoke. The remaining crewmen were in similar states and dispositions; cuts and bruising were a near constant. Even so, they were all alive.

Alex tapped the comm. system of his chair, not even bothering to check if it was still working. "Available medical teams to the bridge," he commanded, before placing a hand onto his own head; his head was still throbbing. "Status report."

"Dead in the water," Davis banefully replied looked over his console. "Auxiliary power is online, and shields are back up, but I don't know how long either will last."

Swallowing as he fought to concentrate over the throb, Alex could only ask the inevitable question. "Moebius?"

Davis shook his head. "Gone, like almost everything else," he said as he got up from his chair, wiping the sweat off his face. "As I said, we're dead in the water."

Alex fumed. *Bastards finally got us,* he thought before turning to Gran. "Can you raise Corsair One?"

Gran, who by now had recovered somewhat, nodded and tapped a few keys. "Our transceiver was damaged during the last strike, but I think I can," she confirmed with some hope. "It will be audio only."

"Good enough," Alex returned as he stood up. It was the only way he could stem off nausea.

A moment later, Boss' voice sounded from the background static.

"Corsair One to *Black Sun*, requesting sitrep," she called out, her voice professionally calm.

Swallowing again, Alex tapped his link. "We're still here Corsair One. Bruised and beaten, but still here," he replied. "How are things on the outside?"

A brief pause intervened before Boss answered. "Unclear *Black Sun*. The Imps are still present and targeting you, but..."

"But?" Alex repeated almost demandingly.

"...They're holding position." Boss finished. "If I had to guess, I'd say they were ordered to stand down. At least for the moment."

It was then another key realization graced Alex's consciousness; the *Black Sun* was no longer pitching or shaking. And that would only be possible if the Imps had stopped firing on them.

*What in the First Circle happened?* Alex thought in wonder. Had something occurred on the surface? Or were the Imps merely taking a break?

"Recommend we form a defensive screen around you," Boss suggested. "Just in case they start shooting again."

Though he knew Boss wouldn't see it, Alex shook his head, and immediately regretted the action. "Negative Corsair One. If they start firing again, you'll simply be caught in the crossfire. Take your fighters to the far side of the planet and standby."

Another brief pause. "Acknowledged," was the reluctant reply. The comline was terminated.

Resigned, Alex tapped the intercom circuit. "Bridge to Engineering, are you still with us, Professor?"

"As much as I can be," Braun's exhausted voice replied through the static, much to Alex's continued relief. "I cannot say the same for several others."

Alex retained his focus. "What's the situation with Moebius? Can it be brought back online?"

Another brief pause as the engineer looked over whatever console was near him. "I cannot say..."

"That's not the answer I want Professor," Alex stated with calm directness. "Can it be brought back online or not?"

Pursing his lips, Braun responded. "Possibly," he stated evenly. "But it will take some time, and even more for it to regenerate the ship."

Alex reflexively nodded before he remembered the pain moving his head caused. Even if they did get Moebius back online, the ship was so damaged it would likely take months for her to regenerate completely, perhaps even longer since it would be functioning on auxiliary power. All while the present Imperials could start firing again at any moment.

All the same, however, it was their only option as well as their only hope. The *Black Sun* was simply far too damaged, as well as too complex, to repair the old-fashioned way. And if nothing else, it still presented them a fighting chance, no matter how slight.

"Do whatever you have to do," Alex commanded. "Bridge out."

With that, Alex signed off, just as the turbolift doors opened and Apache and several others moved onto the bridge.

## Predecessor Ruins
## Ephesus

Letting out a frustrated growl, Barbarossa leaped and rolled to the side as the tank fired its main cannon. Though he managed to evade the blast itself, the resultant shockwave from the golden beam's impact was enough to lift the Leo into the air and send him flying, landing several meters away. Seeing his teammate's plight, Kaiser immediately stepped up and fired off several shots from his Blunderbuss into the armored beast, but none of the strikes proved particularly damaging. He too was forced to evade when the tank's secondary weapons targeted him, firing several bursts of much smaller beams than the main cannon, but powerful enough that the already wounded Herculean dare not risk being hit.

Fortunately, it didn't take long for Barbarossa to recover. Leaping to his feet, he let loose with his baneclaws against the tank's sponsons, only to be forced back into evasion when the enemy returned fire. It was all Barbarossa and Kaiser could do to move about the field, evading whatever shots were fired at them and taking whatever cover they could manage. All while the tank continued to roar across the ground virtually unabated.

However, while eluding the tank's weapons, both the Kapta and the Herculean maintained their barrage, which, in spite of all preconceptions, was actually doing damage. Little by little, the Leo could see that his miniscule baneclaw shots and the much larger ones from Kaiser's pistol were actually chipping away at the tank's shields, doing far more destruction than any standard small arms could hope for against such an opponent. That being said, the pair remained naturally outgunned, though the tank's occupants seemed to realize that they were not quite as invincible as they initially believed.

Ducking behind a nearby piece of debris, Barbarossa took a moment to catch his breath while keeping an eye on their latest enemy. He had heard many stories about this type of vehicle from Leo ground forces but never had he, a space commander, held the displeasure of encountering one for himself. At the time he had balked at such tales, believing them to be mere exaggerations told by his planetside comrades, a vain attempt at impressing those who manned constructs that held far greater size and firepower. However, now that he was the one on the ground, ducking away as the panzer roamed about, Barbarossa fully understood his brethrens' apprehension.

One of the most potent ground weapons within the Imperial arsenal, the Centurion heavy tank was a sight to be genuinely dreaded. At just over thirteen meters in length, six meters in height and over three hundred tons in weight, it was the biggest heavy tank ever made by Terran hands; only the gigantic "super tanks", which were virtually land faring warships, dwarfed the behemoth. Its massive turret mounted beam cannon was one of the most powerful weapons ever installed on a ground vehicle. It could destroy anything from enemy tanks to armored basins in singular shots, while its secondary weapons could decimate entire enemy ranks in minor sweeps. And despite the apparent damage Barbarossa and Kaiser's weapons were inflicting, the Centurion was so heavily shielded and armored that it could literally wade through enemy formations on its own and break through the lines with little more than scratches against its storm grey hull. A genuine monster given metallic form.

Barbarossa's mind raced for an appropriate strategy. He knew that standard anti-tank tactics could not be utilized; as far as he knew, neither he nor Kaiser held any dedicated anti-tank weaponry, while air support was very much an impossibility. And though their respective enhanced beam weapons held enough power to at least chip away at the shields and armor, the rate of damage was nowhere enough to keep the beast from overrunning them. Even so, they did have some elements playing toward their favor, namely that there were two of them against one, with the Centurion's size and bulk limiting its mobility within the present field. And then there was the simple fact it was such a large target that it was not only impossible to miss, but likely had a design flaw or two that could be exploited. Barbarossa never put the latter past Terran technology.

His ears picking up the sound of the turret swiveling back to his position, Barbarossa quickly abandoned his cover just as the main cannon fired. Again he was launched into the air, from which he tumbled and rolled onto the ground. Reorienting himself, he returned fire. More shots were blasted into the tank's shields, but the Centurion was quick to respond with its smaller guns, forcing Barbarossa back into defensive action. Knowing that his armor's shielding had been wholly depleted, the Leo dared not allow a single one of the tank's shots strike him. Racing toward the tank's rear, Barbarossa attempted to move against the one area that lacked any weapons, but before he could reach his goal, the Centurion managed to outturn him ensuring that its right sponson guns were keeping track.

Meanwhile, Kaiser continued to perform his own assault on the tank's opposite side, firing shot after shot while maneuvering through the return fire and taking whatever cover he could. The tank's shields withstood the attack, but Kaiser knew that, given the enhanced nature of his and Barbarossa's weapons, they would not hold up forever. Eventually, the shields would be depleted enough that the shots would actually break through. Whether or not they would be able to accomplish the same against the tank's armor was another matter, but for the time being, it was all they could do.

On the other hand, Kaiser supposed, he could at least damage the treads. Though as per standard for Terran tanks, the Centurion would just retract them and switch to hovercraft mode at that point. Undeterred, he continued his attack run, inflicting even more damage to the tank's left while the side weapons attempted to keep track of him.

The Herculean knew that once the shields were depleted enough, or when another opportunity presented itself, he and Barbarossa would have to act quickly and destroy the tank before it could regain its defenses. But the question remained: how could they do it? Surely they need do more than merely work to deplete its shields and armor. That would take hours if not days at the rate they were going; time that neither he nor his comrade in arms had. They needed something that would work much faster, but for all of his experience, Kaiser could not come up with anything worthwhile. All they could do currently was continue to harass and antagonize the behemoth.

Having considered that however, Kaiser decided that harassing and antagonizing weren't necessarily impotent actions; they were known to work wonders against much larger opponents. Following that line, Kaiser noted a piece of exceptionally large debris not too far from his position. A smirk emerged upon his lips. It was time for him to live up to his race's Terran designation.

Running as fast as he could, Kaiser ducked behind the debris as the Centurion's guns raked fire over his previous position, its turret turned away from him for the moment. He reholstered his Blunderbuss and stretched his hands around the rubble, digging his fingers through the surface. Grunting, the security officer, slowly yet progressively, lifted the piece off the ground and over his head, appearing very much like another Terran mythological figure in the process, though Kaiser couldn't remember his name. A second later, just as the tank began to swing its turret toward him, Kaiser aimed and launched the debris into the air.

The impromptu boulder worked as much as he thought it would. The tank's shielding naturally deflected it, causing the debris to break into dozens of shards upon impact. However, besides applying further pressure against the tank's defenses, the boulder's impact also kicked up a substantial dust cloud around the behemoth, the particles of which were dense enough to obscure the panzer's sensors. The tank's guns halted their fire, its turret turning aimlessly through the cloud as it attempted to gain a target.

Knowing that he had very little time, especially as the tank drove forward to move out of the cloud, Barbarossa leaped upward, landing directly above the tank's right tread covering. Once he felt his feet balanced atop the tank's shielding, he aimed his claws toward the turret, at the location he expected the commander to be. He fired point blank in rapid salvos. Within moments the Centurion's shielding buckled, allowing the shots to penetrate and burn several holes into the tank's turret, as well as obliterate the Imperial sigil upon its side. However, the attack did not reach its intended target in time. The tank's turret swung around, using the cannon barrel to swat Barbarossa off of its side propelling him to ground level. The Leo did not move. Slowly, the tank turned, its driver intent on crushing the 'pirate scum.'

It never reached its quarry. Kaiser ran in front of the panzer and wedged another large piece of debris directly between the Centurion 's treads, forming an impromptu wall. Immediately, he pressed with all of his strength against the blockage, actually managing to thwart the tank's advancement long enough for Barbarossa, initially stunned from the impact, to recover and roll out of the way. Kaiser then redrew his Blunderbuss and fired several shots through the piece of debris and into the tank's forward armor, before being forced to bolt. Only at that point was the Centurion able to demolish the obstacle and move forward once more.

Breathing heavily, Barbarossa nodded his thanks toward the Herculean. "Now I understand why they call you Stonewall," he stated in outright appreciation. Kaiser merely nodded his acknowledgment before the pair were forced to separate again as the Centurion's turret, seemingly conveying its crew's anger at being "wounded", rotated to face them. Another cannon blast rang out, the shockwave obliterating several more ruins in its wake, but failing to strike either the Leo or the Herculean as they darted in separate directions.

---

They were all around her now; it no longer mattered to run. Even if she could outdistance them, they would continue to track her with little obstruction. The ruins and the debris failed to hinder them in any way, instead providing the majority of their number cover as they continued their assault. As such, it was all that she could do to attack them in turn, dashing and evading their barrage while closing the gap and striking them down. Just as she had always done against her prey, whether they were psionic or non.

With beam fire raining down on her from multiple vectors, Kaguya performed several back handsprings to evade, then, while executing a backflip, launched three kunai at the associated vectors. Just as she landed, she felt two telepathic "presences" disappear from her mind; her third shot was either off target, or her mark had managed to duck in time. Either way, she had no time to pause as a pair of Warlocks stepped out into the open, firing their beam rifles at her in tandem. She quickly went into a dead run, zigzagging from left to right, narrowly evading each shot with timed precision while decreasing the distance. Telepathy aside, the Warlocks naturally had better aim than their Marine brethren, such that a few shots came close to striking Kaguya on the side. Even so, she remained faster.

Eventually, she was within range, executing an upward slash that cleaved through the first Warlock before he could counter. However, when she pivoted to strike the second, the Warlock telekinetically sidestepped the assault. Outstretching his hand, he projected a shockwave. Fortunately, Kaguya anticipating the attack, spun and countered with a third slash, which immediately dispelled the wave. She dove forward and, catching the retreating psion entirely off guard, slashed him across the torso, cutting him in half. Two more telepathic presences vanished from her mind, right as the halves fell to the ground.

Feeling the remaining presences intensify with anger and frustration, Kaguya momentarily shuddered just as more beam shots rained from all around. Initially striking one more Imp down with a shuriken, she then went back into evasion, flipping and dodging each shot with careful precision while making sure to stay ahead of her opposition. This resulted in another Warlock moving out into the open, beam pistol drawn and aimed at her head. Just catching the glint of the pistol stock, Kaguya dodged the initial burst and deflected the rest with her ninjato before moving to strike. However, the Warlock, much to her own surprise, actually parried the blow with a telekinetic barrier from his hand, and then followed up with another shot that Kaguya narrowly evaded, yet was forced back. Even the follow-up shuriken attack was effectively evaded, while the second was deflected entirely with another barrier.

It was only when Kaguya feigned, moving to strike at the head while planning to move against the torso, did the Warlock finally lose his advantage. Though the Warlock naturally saw it coming, thus allowing him to dodge the feign and the real attack, Kaguya kept up her momentum, spinning rapidly and elaborately in her offensive, thus preventing the Warlock from mounting a proper defense. From there, it was only a matter of time before one of her attacks landed, striking the psion on the side, with the sudden pain and disorientation leaving the

Warlock completely open. She then proceeded to behead the Imperial, thereby causing another presence to vanish from her thoughts.

Satisfied, she finished her "dance" by flicking her left arm out and launching two more kunais simultaneously, one striking a Warlock peeking out from the top of a nearby ruin and the other hitting another Imp doing the same from within. Another two presences vanished as a result, though there were still more around her, as best shown by the intensified fire. Even worse, several of the Warlocks were now bringing their telekinesis to bare, lifting surrounding debris and launching them against her at high speed. Knowing that she couldn't dodge them all, Kaguya was forced to employ her ninjato blade to deflect or redirect several of the weaponized fragments, all the while continuing to move elaborately about and counterattack where she could. Even the feeling of one projectile grazing her arm at such velocity that it drew blood could not hinder her, though it did cause her to wince in pain momentarily.

That's when something curious occurred. Just as she evaded a large piece of what looked to be a bench, Kaguya caught sight of no more than four Warlocks abandoning their respective covers and leaping into the air, directly above her. Responding through instinct, she dove to the side and rolled just as the four landed. Feeling the ground shake under her, Kaguya, upon reorienting herself, realized that the group had impaled the spot where she had been with some kind of blade. Recognizing they had missed their target, the Warlocks, recomposed themselves toward her, allowing Kaguya to catch a better sight of their weapons. Each Imps each held a standard issue dagger in hand, but with their powers focused on the weapons, the blades were shrouded in pure psionic energy. Psi-blades.

She didn't have time to be surprised, however, as the Warlocks immediately moved against her, slashing at her, one after the other, with their respective blades. It was all she could do to scrabble back and deflect their strokes, all the while evading the support fire that came from their comrades. Executing a line of parries, Kaguya attempted to counter by launching a shuriken at one of the aggressors, but the psion managed to evade before continuing his attack. She then tried a sweep against another Warlock, but he immediately levitated off the ground and then soared backward just as Kaguya performed a follow-up kick. The other three attempted to press the advantage, swiftly thrusting their psi-blades at the Dragon Princess; but Kaguya remained faster, and so parried all strikes before counterattacking once more. And this time she managed to connect, with her blade just grazing her target's facemask, inflicting a prominent scar on the right side.

Seemingly angered by the strike, the Warlock extended his left hand and launched a surge of psionic lightning directly at Kaguya. This time she was unable to dodge. Sustaining a direct hit, Kaguya was flung through the air and slammed against a nearby wall as electricity coursed through her body. Her mind reeled at the sheer pain and anguish. Unfortunately for the Imps, that wasn't enough to stop her. She recovered fast enough to throw herself aside as two of the Warlocks charged, impaling their blades into the wall. The seconds it took the Warlocks to free their daggers allowed Kaguya to launch a kunai directly into one of the Warlocks, piercing his skull and killing him instantly. Another presence vanished. His partner was quicker to react, withdrawing his blade and attacking in the blink of an eye, but the ninja was fast enough to deflect the blow with her ninjato.

Unrelenting, the Warlock pressed the offensive, forcing Kaguya to continue moving backward while defending against his strikes. Even worse, Kaguya could feel herself slowing down, having not fully recovered from the lightning. When she attempted to parry and hit at the Warlock's neck, the psion was quite able to evade the blow and counter with his own, forcing Kaguya back on the defense. The strikes, parries, and thrusts continued; however, it wasn't long before the Warlock made a miniscule mistake. Bringing his blade around, he surged forward to impale Kaguya through the chest, but the ninja had anticipated the maneuver and acted faster. She not only evaded the blow entirely but struck at the psion's right side, plunging her ninjato deep. Now critically wounded, the Warlock could do little more than psionically throw Kaguya into another wall before bleeding out. One more presence to the line.

Fortunately, the dying psion's telekinesis lost its power midway through the throw, and so the impact didn't increase Kaguya's injuries. No more than a second later, she was mobile yet again, evading another barrage of beam fire from the supporting Warlocks. She even managed to elude another lightning attack from one of the remaining blade-wielding Warlocks near her, dodging to the left just as the lightning erupted from his hand. Turning, she moved at her best speed and slashed the psion across the torso, starting at the heart and progressing through to the lower right hip. Another presence faded from her mind, while another intensified. Forewarned, Kaguya spun around and deflected a strike from the remaining blade-wielding Warlock, the one with the scar across his facemask.

Immediately Kaguya sensed this Imp was different from the others. Not only was his "presence" stronger in her mind than most of the others, an indication he held greater power, but that "presence" was honed and controlled as well, indicating greater experience.

Not the squad leader perhaps, but definitely one of the more battle-hardened members of this particular team. Kaguya deflected the next few slashes, feeling her mind and vision darken and waver. Only out of sheer reflex was she able to deflect the blows while simultaneously fighting against the telepathic assault. In turn, she exploited any opening she could, moving to slash or launch a kunai out despite her disposition, but the Warlock was more than capable of deflecting or evading these offensives. The Dragon Princess was starting to lose her speed and form.

Focusing her thoughts on defeat, Kaguya momentarily slumped allowing the Warlock to maneuver for the final blow. As he moved to strike, the ninja immediately surged forward, forcing the Imp's blade up and away, then rapidly spun and kicked the Imp in the torso. In spite of his foresight, the Warlock was too slow to evade the assault and sailed backward into a large fragment pile. Infuriated at the deception, the Imp launched another blast of lighting, but Kaguya deflected it using her ninjato blade as a medium. Simultaneously, the Warlock perpetrated a telepathic attack, one that was meant to affect Kaguya's equilibrium. As she held the lightning at bay, Kaguya felt her balance shift while a headache and nausea manifested, threatening to topple her and leave her vulnerable. With sheer concentration and willpower, she ignored the new pain and forced the lightning aside before bringing her ninjato down against the Warlock. Unfortunately, the Imp managed to flip away while another one of his comrades took a potshot at her, forcing her to leap back as well.

Seconds after she landed, the scarred Warlock charged her once more, slashing at her torso, forcing Kaguya to jump back yet again. The Warlock followed up his assault by generating a shockwave, sending the kunoichi to the ground. Only by quickly rolling out of the way did she evade the Warlock's attempt to impale, and the following shots from his supporters. Further angered, the Warlock persisted, launching another lightning attack and another shockwave. Kaguya narrowly avoided both. Leaping high, she moved to strike the psion's head. Again her strike was telepathically slowed, with the Warlock easily parrying the blow and then slashing at Kaguya's right shoulder, inciting the ninja to let out a cry of pain.

The psion, seemingly emboldened by this wounding, quickly moved in for the killing stroke. In spite of the pain, the ninja deflected it, and then parried the following blows as well. She countered with a shuriken throw but winced as the Imp redirected the weapon's trajectory. The assault intensified. Kaguya could feel her concentration wavier and sight darken as her adversary pressed on. In an attempt to cloud her judgment, he let her feel his anger. She was only barely managing to hold him back, mentally and physically, now. She knew that if the fight continued much longer, another one of his strikes would connect, and she doubted that one would only be a graze.

And then, an opportunity presented itself. The psion moved to cleave the impudent ninja's head in half. Rather than deflect the blow entirely, Kaguya angled her sword up while simultaneously moving to her right, allowing her to redirect the psi blade's path so that it fell well away from where she was standing. Immediately, she reoriented her ninjato and smashed the hilt into the left camera eye of the Warlock's facemask, shattering it and breaking the psion's concentration. The telepathy now lifted, Kaguya, no longer sickened and disheveled, executed a slash that struck against the Warlock's chest, cutting him deeply. At last, that presence was eliminated as well, much to her inward satisfaction.

The remaining Warlocks retained their vigilance and stepped up their attacks. Additional beam fire rained down from the ruins while another three Imps moved out into the open with their psi-blades drawn. Mentally resolved, Kaguya resumed her dance.

# Predecessor Temple
# Ephesus

With a hard clang of blades, Drake struck out with an energy surge. Although Jon was able to deflect most of the force, he still ended up flying some distance back from the impact. Countering with a black wave before he even touched a hard surface, Jon launched himself back towards the Admiral, but Drake simply teleported away to evade the assault. The game was still "cat and mouse" with Drake striking and immediately teleporting away. This time the Admiral reappeared at Jon's side as the latter touched the ground again. He initiated an energy groundswell that Jon attempted to absorb with another black hole but failed. Again, the pirate sailed back an additional distance.

Drake remained relentless as he teleported again to where Jon had fallen and set to impale his quarry. Only a timely deflection with Astaroth's physical blade prevented the blow and allowed Jon to roll out of the way. Immediately reorienting himself, he exchanged several more slashes with the Admiral while biting back the pain and exhaustion. Drake might have outclassed him as a Wielder, and Jon might currently be in a poor physical state, but the pirate was not about to let his adversary win so easily. The Imperial seemed to understand this determination and delighted in his enemy's resolve. He held nothing back while pressing his assault on Jon, keeping the pirate on the defensive as they continued their battle about the temple grounds.

Attempting to retake the initiative, Jon broke away from the present engagement, knocked Drake's blade to the side, lept into the air and fired a scattershot of black energy pellets in the Imp's direction. Drake deflected the shots using an energy shield; however, one 'pellet' grazed the Admiral's left thigh. The wound immediately turned black. Angered, the Imperial quickly pursued the pirate, and the two combatants reassumed their duel midair as they moved to the far end of the temple. Upon landing, Jon attempted an energy assisted sweep kick to take away Drake's footing, but the Admiral jumped away. Jon then followed up with another black wave attack, this one executed much faster than previously, but Drake managed to bifurcate it with a parry, both halves sailing past, impacting and obliterating a distant temple artifact. However, when Drake retaliated with a golden energy blast at point blank range, Jon managed to absorb it and launch it back, but this too was simply evaded.

Jon started to generate additional black portals, but Drake quickly reinitiated his offensive, forcing the pirate back on the defense. The dance resumed with Jon just narrowly managing to keep his opponent at bay. All the while, Drake maintained his assault and pressed forward, refusing to allow his opponent any further respite.

Knocking Drake's blade aside, Jon wasted no time in smashing his left fist against the Admiral's cheek and landing a roundhouse kick in his stomach, causing the Admiral to stumble. However, Drake recovered quickly and deflected Jon's follow up strike, knocking his sword away and then thrusting forward in a fencer's form, grazing Jon's left hip in retaliation. Ignoring the sting, Jon spun around and aimed his slash at Drake's chest, but the Admiral nimbly jumped back and lightly deflected the strike with Berith's blade tip. Without hesitation the Imperial sprang forward, slashing at Jon in turn. Only a timely parry kept the Admiral from flaying Jon's chest open, just as a spontaneously established energy barrier kept Jon's follow up wave attack from hitting home.

Flying back several additional meters, Drake generated a power swell that would have cleaved Jon's upper torso had the pirate captain not plunged downward to the temple floor. Avoiding the following golden energy bolts now emanating from the surrounding terrazzo, the pirate leaped back and implemented a downward black maw; the Admiral teleported away to evade. Jon deflected another charge attack from his opponent and then twisted around to return the strike, only for Drake to deflect the blow with Berith's reverse side. Knocking the obsidian blade away, Drake was successful in slicing open Jon's arm with Berith's sawteeth, causing Jon to wince at the pain but otherwise maintain his form. He retaliated by slashing at Drake's stomach, but the admiral deflected this attack as well.

Recovering quickly, Jon spun around, feigned a thrust, then and moved to cut into Drake's neck, specifically against the carotid artery. Moving faster than the Admiral could defend, Jon initially believed he would at last strike the killing blow. But then, just as Asteroth's black blade was about to penetrate the skin on Drake's neck, Jon felt his arms suddenly halt in motion mere millimeters away. Dumbfounded, he pulled his sword back and attempted to strike at the opposite side of the neck, but again he stopped short of his efforts, his arms virtually freezing up before the edge could reach.

It was then Jon noticed Drake's prominent grin, as well as Berith having disappeared from his hand, which was now faced palm out toward Jon's chest. It wasn't hard to realize what had just happened. Much to Jon's dread, the Admiral had formed a barrier around him, evidenced by the golden outline around his arms and body, and frozen his physical motion before contact. In that regard, the Admiral hadn't slowed down and opened himself up, he had simply allowed Jon to work in close and near the killing point in order to establish the perfect defense. And Jon, in his haste to strike, had failed to realize it.

Jon struggled to break free of the barrier, but soon found his efforts to be in vain; he was too wounded and depleted of energy. His grin viciously enlarging, Drake slowly forced Jon's arms outward while levitating him in the air. Once he compelled his opponent into the position he wanted, Drake then sent him flying to the side of the temple, slamming him against the nearby wall with a hard crash. As the now dazed pirate attempted to regain himself, Drake gestured with his hand yet again, a pair of golden binders encased Jon's arms and legs. The elder Flint now hung in a crucifix position.

Unrelenting, Jon continued his struggle, attempting to draw energy from Astaroth to break free of the binders. However, just as he managed to gather enough strength, Drake materialized in front of him and proceeded to pull his head forward then smash it back against the wall. Astaroth's energy dissipated, as did Jon's sight and consciousness.

Breathing heavily from the strain, Drake, for the briefest of moments, considered finishing the elder Flint then and there. The pirate had repeatedly refused his offer for an alliance, even when it clearly would have benefitted them both. As well, with Arcadia now in the process of being resurrected, there truly was no further need for Jonathan Flint's services, nor those of his crew. And finally, alongside all of that, the little upstart had become an irritating thorn in the Admiral's side, much to his growing furor.

Ultimately, however, as he calmed himself, Drake decided that, with Jon as he was now, there was no need to rush to that point. Not when he still had his uses, alongside his remaining crew.

With that in mind, Drake brought up his left hand and pulled back the sleeve, revealing his wristcom. "Drake to *Subjugator*..."

## Flint Pirates umbra *Black Sun*
## Ephesus System

Suddenly feeling new sounds reach out to her, Gran quickly grasped her headset. "Alex, we're getting a signal from the *Subjugator*..."

As the younger Flint turned to face her, Gran hesitantly elaborated. "They claim Admiral Drake wishes to speak to you directly."

Suddenly feeling the gazes of all those present, Alex slowly rose from his seat and stepped forward. There could only be one reason Drake was calling for him now just as there could only be one reason why he was *able* to call him now.

Swallowing hard at that last thought, Alex knew all too well that he wasn't in a position to refuse. "Put him onscreen," he replied in a near whisper. "And broadcast shipwide."

A moment later, the static dissipated to reveal the Admiral's grinning face. Alongside the image of a bound, profoundly wounded and currently unconscious Jon in the background.

"A pleasure to meet you again Alexander," Drake greeted with apparent amiableness. "Kindly order your forces to stand down and surrender."

# Chapter XXXIX: To the Last...

She felt it. Even as deep into the darkness as she had journeyed, as far from the light above as she had come, she felt it strike her like a thunderbolt, causing her to pause in her descent. For the first time since she had delved within the void, she turned around and "gazed" back to the surface, a feeling of cold realization running through her mind as she verified the truth. There was no mistaking it. *He* had been defeated.

Alarm and anxiety ran through her as the images crystallized within her mind. Bound and incapacitated, held down in the most vulnerable of states. Blood dripping from several of his newly acquired wounds while his body remained strained and exhausted. Jubilation from his opponent, who believed with assuredness that he had won. And the shock and horror of those who remained above, who could only take in with utter helplessness that their commander, and their cause, had been overcome.

Reacting instantly, she turned back toward the surface and started to ascend. Yes, he had been defeated, but for the moment, he was still alive. There was still time; she could still save him.

However, before she could make any considerable way, she halted in her progress as her rationality returned. As fast as she could move in this state, she was still a long way from the surface, and it would take considerable time for her to retrace her steps and return to her physical body. In fact, she surmised that she was well past the halfway point in her descent, such that she was closer to the bottom now than she was to the top. Even if she moved as fast as she could in her ascent, she would be unable to reach him in time. His opponent was sure to finish him at any given moment, and she would not be there to prevent it.

Alongside, she remembered her cause, the reason they had traveled to this world to fight a much more powerful enemy to begin with. Though the battle was ongoing, she could not deny its current state. Their ship laid crippled and ruined in orbit while the few stragglers that remained of the ground forces continued to hold out, but with no hope of victory to be found. Many had perished through the course of the battle, fighting an enemy that held both greater resources and the will to use them. Many had died so that she could do what she was doing now. So that she could indeed break through the darkness and reach what laid underneath.

And yet she found herself struggling with that rationality, such that it caused her pain within. Yes, she remained close to her goal, and yes, much had been sacrificed so that she could reach it. But did he have to be one of them? One of the many instruments that she had used and depleted in order to come it this far? Did she have to expend him as well, even if it meant obtaining what she sought?

Him, the one who had unexpectedly entered into her quest and her life in spite of her precognition. The one she, throughout her search, considered perhaps the most fascinating being in all the universe, such that she had gone well out of her way for both his sake and to keep him within her influence.

The one she had selected to see her through to the end.

That last thought stung her even more than the images had; she almost wept. Yes, she had selected him to see her through, and that was precisely what he was doing. He and those who followed him had fought a devastating battle so that she could reach this very point and time so that she could indeed complete her own task. He would not wish her to turn back now, not when she was near the bottom. No matter how much she desired to save him, he would have wanted her to continue. He would have insisted she finish what they had started, even if it meant leaving him behind.

Thus, with immense agony, she turned back around and continued her descent, moving even further through the darkness as she pursued her goal. More than once, she was tempted to turn back as she had before, and more than once, she forced herself to maintain, to continue on in spite of all that was happening above. All while the increasing separation from him amplified her distress.

Even so, she persevered, with the end steadily growing closer and closer in her perception...

## Flint Pirates umbra *Black Sun*
## Ephesus System

"Kindly order your forces to stand down and surrender," Drake casually demanded, the words hanging in the air in a spectral manner.

Resisting the urge to swallow at the image, Alex forced himself to answer. "What are the terms?" he rejoined, ignoring the dubious glances from the bridge crew.

Drake's reply was a short, derisive laugh. "There are no terms, Alexander," he replied sharply. "Your surrender will be unconditional, or I will have you blown to the stars."

Alex inhaled slowly. That meant the Admiral's past offer to Jon, the one about making them privateers and all, was no longer valid. Not that Alex would have accepted it anyway; at the moment he was just buying as much time as he could get.

"Can't say we're disposed toward that action," Alex responded with similar casualness. "After all, if our surrender is without condition, how do we know you won't kill us all the moment we allow you to board our ship?"

"You don't," Drake stated in turn. "The only concern you should have is whether or not I remain in a good mood."

Alex let out a short laugh of his own.

Ire dawned over Drake's expression. "You've lost Alexander," he spoke with receding patience. "Your ship can no longer fight, your ground forces are being wiped out as we speak, and your Captain is left completely to my mercy. And the *only* reason you're alive now is that you and your brother may still be useful."

The emphasis on Jon and Alex was not lost to the bridge crew. They could see that the Admiral viewed them as nothing more than rabble, and would likely deal with them as such. Just as they knew that the crime of piracy remained punishable by death.

"So I say again," Drake repeated in a tone that left no room for argument. "Surrender, or die."

This time Alex did swallow. Like it or not, he was not in a position to counter the Admiral's demands. Fortunately, he still had one more card to play. "Give us some time to consider..." he countered, doing his best to feign hesitance.

Drake again laughed, this time with evident amusement. "So you can try and get your Moebius System back online?" the Admiral replied knowingly. "Very well, I will grant you twenty minutes to 'consider', and not a second more. Keep in mind, however, as you 'consider' more and more of your raiders are being slaughtered by my marines. I suggest you 'consider' quickly."

With that, Drake's image vanished, and the viewscreen returned to it's original static, effectively leaving the bridge crew to muse over what they had just heard.

# Predecessor Ruins
# Ephesus

The Centurion's main cannon bellowed yet again, obliterating the structure Barbarossa had been using for cover. Fortunately, upon seeing the tank's turret shift, the Leo had foreseen the attack and had exited the ruin before it was incinerated. The downside was he was in the open again, and the Centurion's secondary weapons were already targeting him. Letting out a roar of defiance, Barbarossa fired back as he ran, evading the returning beam fire while scrambling to search for some new form of protection.

Suddenly, rubble the size of a small building flew through the air and smashed against the Centurion. The impact, despite being absorbed by the tank's armor, actually forced the behemoth to tilt ever so slightly. Kaiser, who now held as many apparent wounds as his comrade, made his appearance known once again, quick drawing his Blunderbuss and firing several shots into the tank's right side. The main turret immediately swung toward him. Barbarossa, seeing an opening, made a mad dash toward the panzer and fired his own weapons into the front. More holes were struck into the tank's armor as a result, but none proved particularly damaging.

By the time the reprisal fire had come, Barbarossa had again ducked behind a piece of wreckage, allowing himself some moment of respite. He was now wholly ragged and exhausted, just barely managing to keep ahead of the tank. Nonetheless, their efforts had proven far from fruitless. Though it still functioned, substantial damage now graced the Centurion's chassis, its once immaculate storm grey body was now charred and broken in several places. It shields were completely drained, a result of its main power apparatus being damaged, while several of its secondary systems, including its hover drive, were rendered inoperable. Even so, the beast remained an insufferable credit to Imperial engineering; not only was it still able to function, but its weapons remained at full power. That latter fact was especially evident when Barbarossa again felt the blast of its main cannon as it obliterated the space he had just vacated; his instinct and reflexes overriding his exhaustion as he ran.

Barbarossa inwardly swore as the secondary weapons lit up once more, kicking up shrapnel from virtually every vector. His armor, while quite worn by now, deflected most of it, but Barbarossa could not keep the smaller fragments from striking his face, stinging his skin and inflicting new wounds. At the beginning of the battle, they had been little more than annoyances, but now, as wounded and exhausted as he was, each one felt like a life-threatening injury. There was not much time left, he knew. They had to kill this thing once and for all, while they still could.

Thus, with as much muster as he could bring about, he again swung his baneclaws around and open fired, raking additional scars into the Centurion's armor before he dove for another piece of cover. This time he didn't remain but took a few seconds to breathe before moving again and repeating the process. As he expected, the tank was concentrating mostly on him, its crew remaining intent on killing the famous Leo commander and scoring some fame of their own. This allowed Kaiser, who had caught onto the Leo's battle plan without any verbal exchange, to move against the opposite side of the tank, effectively flanking it with his much larger beam weapon. Virtually unhindered as the left sponson mounted gun had been taken out not too long ago, the Herculean fired several times into the massive treads, attempting to take advantage of the Centurion's inability to switch to its hover system.

Smoke soon began to rise from the treads as the tank's speed decreased, but not before its left side secondary turret swung around and fired. Kaiser managed to evade the first shot, but the second clipped his right shoulder and sent him flying back several meters. Tragically, the Herculean ended up landing amidst a heap of battle sharpened rubble. With the force of the impact, the shards had little issue puncturing his otherwise rock hard skin and embedding themselves into his back. The giant grit his teeth at the excruciating pain but managed to maintain what little focus he had left and labor back to his feet. With darkened blood coursing out from his massive back, the pirate continued his run, firing his Blunderbuss, albeit with somewhat less accuracy, into the tank as he evaded the secondary turret. After a couple of shots, the left tread, at last, gave way, thereby completely immobilizing the tank.

Upon the Centurion crew's realization that their ride could no longer move, they immediately stepped up its fire, launching several beam salvos at the Herculean as he made his advance. And though Kaiser remained agile, the exhaustion and the rapid blood loss slowed him down. One of the beams struck its target and sent the giant flying once more. He again landed in wreckage, this time within the fragments of a partially destroyed building. And though he struggled to get back up and return fire, he could only manage to lift up his pistol and fire a stray shot that nicked the Centurion's main turret. Several responding cannon beams later, the remaining building remnants collapsed on top of the Herculean, burying him completely.

While he didn't see precisely what had occurred, Barbarossa knew all the same. An infidel Kaiser may be, may *have* been, nevertheless, the Herculean had fought valiantly beside him. He would be damned before he let his comrade's efforts go to waste.

With his prey now completely immobile and open, Barbarossa charged, evading another blast from the main cannon as he did, and again he leaped to the top of the tank's hull. Within seconds, his clawed greaves made a thunderous clang as they landed against the tank's armored surface, the physical reverberations threatened to knock him out straight away. Even so, Barbarossa forced himself on, focused every bit of strength he had left and turned his weapons upon the open hull. Alternating between firing his beam guns and using his claws to rip off pieces of the armor, he proceeded to fire into the exposed interior. Within moments fire and smoke began to emerge from the insides of the tank, all the while panicked voices of those within became louder.

So depleted and focused was he on this task, the Leo failed to notice the top hatch on the turret open up, revealing the tank commander.

The Imp drew his beam pistol and fired several shots directly into the pirate's back. The physical shock and pain of the wounds caused the Leo to collapse momentarily; only by concentrating on his sheer fury did Barbarossa remain conscious. He reached around with his left arm and fired a burst into the commander's chest. The Imp fell back into the turret, no return fire was made. Enraged beyond feeling pain, Barbarossa continued his onslaught, savagely ripping armor plates or firing his guns over and over again, triggering more fire and smoke.

And then, without warning, Barbarossa's entire world was set ablaze. Before he even realized it, the Leo was lifted into the air as the Centurion underneath him exploded, propelling him across the battlefield at an even higher velocity than Kaiser had been forced to endure. He flew through several obstacles before crashing back first against another piece of rubble. By the time Barbarossa's senses and comprehension caught up with him, he found himself crumpled against the side of a since destroyed wall, his eyes staring back at the now flame engulfed ruins of the tank.

With his vision beginning to blur and the scent of his own blood filling his nostrils, the Leo could do nothing more than let off a satisfied smile at his handiwork. It had taken every last portion of strength he had left, but he had won all the same. His final opponent was defeated and laid in equal ruin as those around him. He and Kaiser with him were victorious.

As the wind kicked up across the desolate landscape, Barbarossa could feel his sight begin to dim. This, it seemed, would be his last fight after all. For some reason, however, as his consciousness slowly drained away, the Leo felt a strange sense of calm at that prospect. Though he was well away from his homeworld and his family, both of which he had not seen for a long time and missed dearly, he was at complete peace with his fate. If this world – this lone, forgotten world – was to serve as his gravestone, then so be it. He would embrace it all the same.

The small portion of his mind that remained active seemed to consider the reasons behind that. It was unlikely that this battle would be sung back on his homeworld, nor even remembered well outside his own family, and that was assuming they ever managed to hear of it. Even so, he had still fought and triumphed in both Aslan's name, as well as his Caliph's. And to die fighting and triumphing in their names was far from the worst way of departing this mortal realm.

*No*, he felt a sudden voice from within say, accompanied by an equally strange sense of pride. *It was not in* their *name that you fought and gained victory for this day.*

A spark of confusion welled within the Leo as the fading part of his consciousness tried to understand that message. In the end, he decided it didn't matter. Whatever it was, it seemed to be all the answer he needed.

Just as it was the last thing he 'heard' before the darkness at last faded in.

––––––––––––––   ––––––––––––––

Another telekinetic wave struck her, lifting her off the ground and flinging her to the side. Rolling out to reorient herself, her body becoming increasingly slow from the physical strain, Kaguya nonetheless remained conscious and active enough to evade as one of the Warlocks launched at her, setting his psi-blade to impale. Flipping back to her feet, she twirled her ninjato around and parried the follow-up slash, and all that came after. She eventually gained the offensive, striking the Warlock against the shoulder and inflicting a deep enough wound to draw blood, but just before she could finish him, two others moved at her from the opposite side, forcing her to defend once more.

Only five remained now, as she estimated from the telepathic presences she felt. Three were in the open, attacking her directly, while two remained in buildings on either side of the street, acting in the support role. The latter were not to be dismissed out of hand, as one peered out and took a shot at her, grazing her right shoulder. Reflexively, she drew a kunai and launched it toward the origin point, but by then the sniper had moved on to another vantage point. She would have attacked him further, but she was forced to twist around to deflect another psi-blade attack, all while the other three moved against her from different angles. Kaguya managed to deflect their strikes as well, but at the cost of much of her remaining strength. One of the Warlocks took decisive advantage of this, performing a power slash that sent Kaguya flying back into one of the nearby ruins.

Ignoring the pain generated within her body upon impact, Kaguya forced herself back to her feet in time to deflect another blade attack,. Pivoting, she twisted around and smashed her left palm into the Warlock's faceplate. Though the blow would do no harm to her armored opponent, it had been spontaneous enough to dishevel the Warlock and actually knock him off balance, thereby allowing her to slash at his chest. Unfortunately, her blow was too light; the Warlock managed to telekinetically pull himself back at the last second. Kaguya only cut him with her ninjato's tip. She attempted to correct this by following up with a shuriken throw, but this time the Warlock foresaw the attack and deflected it with a psi shield, right before rebounding off the ruined wall and moving to attack again.

Gritting her teeth as the Warlock's psi-blade slammed against her ninjato once more, Kaguya did all she could to hold him in place. Slowly but surely, she could feel her remaining strength slip away. She could barely keep the Warlock's blade away from her face. Suddenly, her ears picked up a distinctive sound; specifically that of cracks emerging across the ceiling. Instantly realizing what was about to happen, she broke the clash and, mimicking the Warlock's earlier move, leaped back while quick-drawing a shuriken and launching it at the Imp. The star-shaped blade pierced the Warlock's throat, a second after which the ceiling collapsed, burying the now critically wounded psion underneath. Seconds later, one more presence was gone, four to go.

Unfortunately, this did not hinder the Warlock that had initiated the cave in, who leaped down before her. As Kaguya moved to strike him, she was again telekinetically lifted and thrown, this time back onto the street. Landing on the ground, the kunoichi momentarily watched as two of the Warlocks leaped into the air, psi-blades set to impale her from dual angles. Somersaulting backward, then slashing her sword out and around, she managed to cut one of the Warlocks in the thigh. Though it wasn't deep enough to sever the leg altogether, it managed to lacerate muscle and tendon and cause the psion to fall to his knees as pain welled. Acting fast, Kaguya brought her ninjato down on the Imp's head, but his comrade was faster, deflecting her strike and launching a surge of lightning at her chest. Again she somersaulted out of the way, just regaining her feet when the fourth Warlock, the one that had been providing support, moved to engage.

Suddenly, a surge of pain swept through her body as she felt a beam slam into her back. That last Warlock managed to take a crack shot at her, hitting close to her left shoulder. And much worse, the beam had struck deep; she felt the strength drain away from her arm. Channeling her pain into anger, she spun around in time to parry the next psi-blade attack. With her left arm now useless, she focused all of her energy into her right and eventually overwhelmed the psion, forcing his psi-blade to waver. She took that as an opportunity to bring her ninjato around and slash, beheading the Warlock in a swift strike. Another presence vanished, leaving only three.

The sniper wasn't done yet, as several more shots were launched at her, forcing her to leap back several times. Her body was too strained to pull any further elaborate maneuvers. Even worse, the other two psi-blade wielding Warlocks, obviously sensing her strain, pressed the advantage, both moving at her like a pair of Lupians against wounded prey. Kaguya knew she couldn't beat them one at a time or in the long run. As she moved back, deflecting their blows with great effort, she could feel her body begin to fail her. Her steps became uncoordinated while her deflections were executed sloppily, all while the Warlocks retained both their strength and their precision. Even when she dropped down and completed a sweep kick, both psions easily evaded it, not even using their telekinesis to aid their respective jumps.

It was then that the second shot slammed into her back. She lurched forward while another silent cry of pain escaped her lips. For a seeming eternity, she felt the darkness enclose her while sight dwindled and her body numbed. Only by sheer force of will did she manage to keep herself from blacking out, as well as active enough to deflect the next psi-blade attacks. Unfortunately, she couldn't do the same for the psi lightning attack that followed them. Again, she flew back across the ground, unconsciousness nearly claiming her. Again, she forced it away and focused, concentrating on defending herself.

Much worse, the Warlocks weren't just attacking her physically now. Thanks to her exhaustion, Kaguya's mind was now wide open to their telepathy, and though they couldn't overwhelm her will at once, they could indeed drain it. With each passing parry and evasion, Kaguya felt her consciousness become hampered with strain and an emphasized temptation to let go. Various images flashed as she fought on, ranging from those of people she cared about to others that she had encountered over her lifetime. All different faces with different backgrounds, but all of them telling her to let go, that she had succeeded in her mission, that there was no further reason for her to continue fighting or suffering. Simply give in to the strain and let her body fall. She had done far more than enough in this battle. Peace had been earned.

Initially, the voices accompanying those images spoke to her as individuals, but as the fight continued on, and she felt more of her conscious give way, they started speaking out as one. One continuous voice emphasizing her pain, draining her will to fight on, and telling her to simply stand down and let her body rest. That she need not continue to do this, need not continue to fight. That the Flint Pirates would and could continue without her, that she could rest while they finished the battle in her place. And though she attempted to resist, Kaguya felt the voices impinge on her will, such that she now only offered a token defense against the Warlocks, who in turn only made lesser, prodding attacks to nudge her about. Like it or not, she was winding down, her mind giving in to the temptation to sleep while her body began to succumb to its wounds and exhaustion. Little by little, Fuma Kaguya felt herself give way to the night, to her need to rest and relieve the strain. All while the Warlocks, now having her completely at their control, quietly moved to finish her.

Thus, it was all or nothing for her now.

*Kuroi Taiyou-ryu...* the Dragon Princess purposely thought as she focused every last bit of her will and strength into her sword.

*...Majogari!*

With one last burst of lightning speed, Kaguya leaped back up and performed a full spin-slash, beheading both Warlocks in a single strike. So fast and spontaneous were her actions that the Warlocks, despite having foreseen it, were unable to react in time. The very last image their physical eyes would detect was the flash of her ninjato blade moving in an arc, at such a speed that it appeared as little more than a trail of silver. However, for the briefest of moments, both Warlocks thought they also saw a glint of blue emerge as well.

At the end of her spin, Kaguya, simultaneously isolating the location of the last Warlock presence, let go of her sword and let it fly blade first. In that instant, the final psion, moving out into the open to take a finishing shot at her, was impaled through the head. The final telepathic presence vanished just as quickly, well before the Warlock's body fell backward against the rooftop of the ruin he had used for cover.

Now breathing in pained gasps, Kaguya remained in that position for several more minutes as the adrenaline, slowly, began to ebb. With no more enemies around her, she let go of everything, allowing her right arm to fall to her side and her body to collapse on the ground. She didn't know how wounded she was, but she could sense that she was critically drawn. Perhaps...perhaps even fatally, considering that she could no longer feel her body.

As a slight breeze brushed over her form, which was growing ever still by the moment, Kaguya wondered if this was indeed her last hour. When she ultimately closed her eyes, would it be for the last time? Up to this point, she had been so focused on fighting and killing that she hadn't even considered it; too focused on surviving and completing her mission to allow such thoughts to intrude upon her. But now, as wounded and depleted as she was, as much as she had bled and overextended herself, she had no choice but to wonder. To focus upon what may very well be her last thoughts.

It wasn't like she believed that it wouldn't happen to her; she was a warrior and knew full well that any battle she took part in could be her last. In fact, a part of her had actually welcomed the prospect – as much as she had been hesitant – for reasons that no longer mattered. In that regard, she had fought with honor and dedication, as a scion of the Blue Dragon and the Fuma clan would have done. Surely that was enough to satisfy her as she drifted away, allowing her spirit to rise up and join her beloved mother in the afterlife. Both her clan and her family would remember her but still, continue on without her. Kazama would see to that once he took the throne.

And yet, somehow, she found herself feeling a certain amount of regret. A strange, panging remorse that she would die here and now, that she could not live her life for just a little bit longer. All while an emotion she could not identify, a feeling of yearning that was as foreign to her as Aurigans on Terra, began to take hold. A sentiment that, with her very last ounce of strength, triggered her right hand to raise back up.

Little by little, her hand lifted up. Slowly, shakily and with great effort, it rose from the ground and extended itself, seemingly with a will of its own, toward the ever darkening sky, its fingers splayed as if to grasp and unseen object. There, for a fleeting moment, Kaguya pictured the *Black Sun* still in orbit, fighting the good fight against the Imperial fleet as she had done just now. All under the command of the son of her father's mortal enemy, whose image burned itself into her fading sight as a defiant flame against the encroaching twilight.

That image would remain with her as Kaguya felt her strength give out, and her hand fall back beside her. Darkness prevailed thereafter.

# Predecessor Temple
# Ephesus

The time was drawing down, as Drake could hear from his wristcom's chronometer setting. Casually standing by one of the pillars, not far from where he had pinned the elder Flint, the Admiral waited patiently as the minutes passed, each one a step toward his long-anticipated victory. Minutes from his acquisition of one of the galaxy's priceless treasures, in the Empire's name of course, as well as several new resources to utilize in future ventures. Such was his anticipation that he was tempted to end the interval early, but he managed to resist. Whether regarding life or death, he was a man of his word. He merely need wait a little longer.

To say this was a hard run victory would have been a masterpiece of understatement. He had been truthful to young Jonathan before; he and his band of brigands had put up a worthwhile fight, far more than even Drake had believed them capable of. Granted, whereas he held the advantage in overall quantity, they had the advantage in overall quality. Their mothership was perhaps the most advanced ship in the universe at this point, while their ship crew and raiders were men and women of great skill and experience. Such factors were only emphasized by the Imperials' delay in arrival, allowing their ground forces to dig in and fortify themselves in one of the most ideal fields. Had Drake not taken the precautions he had with his quantity, namely in carefully assembling and deploying his forces, the so-called reborn Flint Pirates just may have triumphed through their quality. That was, after all, what the good Captain Jonathan Flint seemed to have been relying on.

And as for the elder Flint, Drake had to admit that he too, as he had previously claimed, had surpassed his expectations. Not only was he a capable leader and strategist, but when he had full control of himself, he actually proved to be a skilled combatant. In that regard, Drake couldn't help but feel some remorse over his failure in swaying the pirate captain to his side. He would have preferred the captain had accepted his offer and become a privateer in Imperial (his) service. Alas, Drake would have to do things the hard way now. Both Jonathan and his brother would have to be *coerced* into taking his offer while they endured the hellish rigors of Dis. And though Drake had little doubt that the brothers time within the Empire's primary and most infamous prison world would make them more receptive, it was a measure he could have done without.

*After all...* Drake mused to himself. *The best pawns are those who rally to one's service willingly, not those who must be* persuaded.

It was at that point that another thought occurred to Drake. Though he had effectively won the battle and Arcadia, his acquisition of the Flints and the *Black Sun* depended entirely upon the younger Alexander giving out the final order to stand down. And as Drake had learned fifteen years ago in this very place, opponents on the verge of defeat were not the same as those thoroughly defeated. They just may choose to fight to the end over surrendering. Morganna Flint had done precisely that, even quoting a famous Ancient Terran sea captain who made a similar stand against a superior force. Surely the younger son wouldn't follow his mother's ruinous example, choosing an act of senseless defiance over a more rational course of action...

Drake actually shook his head at that thought. No, he had learned from his mistakes fifteen years ago, as grievous as they had been. Back then, he had possessed no leverage over the Golden Queen, no means of coercing her into seeing that she had more reason to surrender to him than to fight a pointless battle. Even his call to consider the lives of her crew aboard the *Morgan le Fay* had fallen onto deaf ears, as her crew were more than willing to stand by her and fight with her to the end as opposed to seeing her suffer some perceived indignity. At least, all but one had been anyway.

Here in the present, Drake had far more than simple leverage; he had the entire winning hand. With the elder Flint bound to his ever depleting mercy and the raiders being picked off by his forces one at a time, Alexander really had no choice but to comply lest he see both his brother and his loyal crewmen slaughtered. At best, Drake estimated, the younger Flint would put on an air of indifference to their fates, perhaps even claim he despised his brother and never cared for any of those fighting on the ground simply to conceal the obvious truth. In essence, another delaying tactic to buy just a little more time to repair the *Black Sun*'s Moebius System and at least get her weapon and propulsion systems back online, which Drake would not fall for.

No, even if they could get Moebius back online, which Drake highly doubted at this point, he would not allow any further breathing room. Twenty minutes was as much as his thoroughly tried patience would permit. And though the younger brother may do exactly as he predicted or attempt another form of delay, Alexander simply did not have the emotional control that his brother retained. Drake need only apply his advantage, as well as his force of will, in the smallest of increments and the younger Flint would capitulate.

Of course, that still left the question of what he did with *her* after all was done. In truth, Drake didn't quite know yet. On the one hand, from what he saw on Bonham IV, she cared for dear Jonathan as much as his brother did and just may capitulate herself, thereby adding another prize to the Admiral's triumph, if Captain Flint's life were to be threatened any further. On the other hand, Drake did not quite know if that care and concern were legitimate. For all he knew, she may have been using her charm to manipulate him into compliance and would treat his impending death accordingly.

If the latter were true, Drake would have to deal with her himself, and he was already well and truly exhausted from the fight with Jonathan. Even more, he had seen the remains of the Warlock team that had been sent to hold her in place on Bonham IV. Drake knew that above all else, in spite of any charm and amiableness she projected, she was not to be underestimated. Perhaps he could attempt to make an arrangement with her instead, as he should have the moment he discovered her existence (yet another past mistake to learn from). She certainly did not have inhibitions making a deal with two pirates who, at the time, had not even possessed their own ship. Drake doubted she would not make one with him if approached, so long as they could reach common ground.

Either way, Drake was not worried in the least. In fact, elation flowed through his being. The Second Battle of Ephesus was over and, though it had cost him much, he had won again. All that remained was to secure that victory, and the rest would fall into place...

## Flint Pirates umbra *Black Sun*
## Ephesus System

Through the smoke and haze, Alex and his compatriots could only stand by and wait in silence as time wound down. Not a single word had been spoken on the bridge since Drake had terminated his message. Complete silence hung throughout the air as the gathered crew sat or stood by, awaiting the guillotine's inevitable fall. Only the flickering light of the static-filled viewscreen broke the stillness of the setting, with some continuing to gaze upon it as if expecting Drake to break his timetable earlier than expected.

What they saw, however, through the blinking light and black, was the line of Imperial ships holding stationary some distance from their starboard side, their respective beam cannons all trained toward their position.

Alex could not remember the last time he had felt so powerless, so helpless. Even when the battle had begun, he had held some idea of what to do and how to act, as well as corresponding options to choose from. Now, however, he could do nothing; nothing but wait and hope that Braun succeeded in restoring the Moebius System, and in turn regenerate the ship to fighting capacity before Drake could respond. A hope that, in turn, dwindled with each passing minute, Braun's continuing communications silence indicating that he remained nowhere close to completing his task. The feeling alone threatened to overwhelm Alex's mental barriers and cause him to breakdown, but that wasn't the hardest element he had to endure.

The hardest, he found, was glancing over the faces of the crew. Despite whatever front they attempted to convey, Alex could see in their eyes that they held no hope whatsoever. They knew they were effectively dead; knew that Drake's interests only lay with the Flint Brothers and not those around them. Whether Alex agreed to Drake's terms or not, they would be killed. The question was whether it would be under the waiting guns of the aforementioned warships or through the traditional way of executing pirates. A question that, again short of a miracle, they knew would soon be answered.

Every so often, Alex would open his mouth to reply to their wordless stares, but each time the words would die in his mouth, and he was forced to turn away lest tears begin to emerge. What could he say to them now? Could he reinforce their hopes? He couldn't even do that for himself. Could he apologize to them for what he and Jon had dragged them into? A part of him wanted to, perhaps even yearned to, but upon looking deeper into those eyes, he saw that none held accusation toward him. They had known from the beginning what they were signing up for, and that their fortunes could take an ill-turn at any time. That in itself made their lifeless stares even more difficult for Alex to endure.

Sighing, Alex retook his seat and stared at the viewscreen, where the Imperial warships remained amidst the static. Glaring at them with palpable hatred, a part of the younger Flint wondered if his mother had seen a similar image fifteen years ago, wondered if she had felt the same as he was feeling now. He could not remember. He had been quite young then and had been knocked unconscious during the last portions of the battle. What he did know, as Jon had relayed to him sometime later, was that Morganna Flint had not given up the fight. Even when the *Morgan le Fay* had been crippled and boarded, and she grievously wounded, she remained and fought the Imperial boarders so that her crew, as well as Jon and Alex, could reach the escape craft. To the end, she had remained fierce.

Visualizing the image of his mother fighting through squads of Imperial

Marines while slowly bringing her sons to the last shuttle, Alex silently prayed that he would have her spirit when the time came. That whatever happened in the next few minutes, he would live up to his mother's image. Just as so many had claimed him to already be doing.

A shrill beeping noise from Gran's console caused him to flinch. "Incoming hail from the *Subjugator*," she reported in near monotone. "It's time."

Rather than reply to her, Alex tapped the comm. switch on his chair arm. "Bridge to Engineering," he started, his breath almost hitching in his throat. "Status report."

A brief pause before Braun's reply came. "Moebius remains offline."

Slowly and solemnly, Alex closed his eyes as the reply sunk in. There was nothing left now. "How much longer?"

Another pause. "Alex," Braun grimly answered. "I'm not even sure it *can* be repaired."

Gran raised her head up again. "The *Subjugator* is insisting that we answer."

Exhaling a breath he did not know he had been holding and taking in another, Alex slowly nodded.

Drake's image soon reappeared. "Your time is up, Alexander," he started. "What is your answer?"

Taking another breath, Alex slowly began to speak. "My answer?" he responded as if it were something to ponder. "My answer..."

Drake started to react, but Alex spoke first. "My answer," he began, somewhat nervously. "Is one that has been uttered by many a sentient in my position, especially when facing beings such as yourself."

Then, fully resolving himself, Alex's eyes bore into Drake's as he shouted. "Go. To. Hell!"

Initially blinking, having been caught off guard somewhat, Drake let off another amused chuckle. "A commendable response," he rejoined, acting as though he had been told a clever joke. "But I would prefer we move past the formalities and..."

"It's no 'formality'," Alex interrupted sharply, again resolving himself. "I, no, *we* refuse to surrender."

With that statement, the amiableness disappeared from Drake's face completely. In its place were the first vestiges of darkness.

"You cannot possibly be serious," he declared in a dangerously subdued tone. "You are not in a position to fight on..."

"We know," Alex answered in turn. "And we still refuse."

"Do you have any idea what fate awaits you if you continue this charade?" Drake pressed on, the darkness growing even further across his expression. "Let's be rational about this, Alexander..."

This time, Alex responded with a cruel laugh. "If you knew anything about me, Admiral, you would know I'm anything *but* 'rational'. Whatever happens now, we stand together as the Flint Pirates."

Again he looked across the bridge, but this time he no longer saw despair in the eyes that looked back at him. This time he saw the very same thing he found in himself, resolution toward what was to come, acceptance of their shared fate. Indeed, whatever happened, they would remain to the end as they had first begun. The heirs of Morganna Flint's legacy.

"And if that's too much for you to understand," Alex continued, now fully assured and at peace. "Then, *you* can always surrender in our place."

The darkness quickly reached Drake's eyes, along with visible disbelief. "Don't do this," he spoke in a near rasp, almost out of pleading desperation. "Don't throw yourself away for..."

"Shut up!" Alex barked, his fists now trembling at his sides as he momentarily looked down. "My mother didn't give in to you!"

Then, upon looking back up with unflinching resolve, the younger Flint declared with full force. *"I sure as hell won't!"*

# Predecessor Temple
# Ephesus

Drake, for the first time in perhaps years, could only stand aghast in disbelief. Once again, he had been scornfully rejected. Against all reason and rationality, his opponent had chosen a pointless suicide over the Admiral's magnanimous offer. And for the life of him Drake, for all of his intellect, could not understand, could not reason why his present adversary had made this decision. Didn't he realize he and his band had been beaten? Was Alexander so intent on defiance that he was willing to die a meaningless death? What sort of madness was he looking upon now, as he glared at the face on his wristcom? Especially as he slowly realized that was the same face he had looked into fifteen years ago?

Feeling an unfamiliar anger rise through him, Drake seethed with visible fury. No, he would *not* be denied, outright refusing the merest prospect. Alexander Flint, apparently suffering from the same delusional thinking as his mother fifteen years ago, did not understand the position he was in, did not understand that he had been defeated and that his only option now was to surrender and capitulate. The Admiral would have to reinforce that fact a little further. Only then would the younger brother give into reason.

Drake's ears picked up the sound of a slight groan; Jonathan was apparently beginning to reawaken. Instantly knowing what he had to do, the Admiral stormed over to where Jon remained bound and grasped his neck once again.

As Jon struggled to breathe, Drake forced his wristcom into the pirate's face. "Tell him," he growled as Jon struggled against his grip. "Tell him to stand down."

Drake loosened his hold enough to permit Jon, who continued to struggle against him, to talk. Seemingly only when Drake tightened his grip again, indirectly threatening to cut off Jon's air supply permanently, did the elder brother begin to speak. "Alex..."

## Flint Pirates umbra *Black Sun*
## Ephesus System

Without even realizing it, Alex slowly stood up from the captain's chair, gazing at his brother's strained image with emotions he could not recognize. "Jon...?"

## Predecessor Temple
## Ephesus

Feeling Drake's grip tighten slightly, as if to remind him of his own position, Jon slowly whispered into the wristcom. *"To the last..."*

## Flint Pirates umbra *Black Sun*
## Ephesus System

With that single phrase, Alex felt the world come crashing down around him. Knowing its background and its significance all too well, Alex felt his eyes instantly water while his legs nearly gave way.

*"To the last..."* he repeated in a murmur, looking down for a moment to regain control. Fighting back the urge to breakdown then and there, he slowly forced his head back up, so that he could look back into his brother's eye. And with that gaze, Alex brought forth the full power of his will.

*"We..."* both brothers spoke simultaneously, their voices merging as one through the comm. line. *"...grapple with thee!"*

## Predecessor Temple
## Ephesus

Single eye glaring back into Drake's now utterly astonished mismatched pair, conveying all the hatred he and his brother felt toward him and his cause, Jon continued to speak alongside Alex's voice.

*"From hell's heart..."* Jon hissed, even now maintaining the struggle against Drake's hand. *"...we stab at thee!"*

With each of those classic words uttered, Drake came to realize the ultimate truth. That the Flints would never yield to him.

*"For hate's sake..."* Jon breathed, Alex's voice adding strength to his brother's near rasp, *"...we spit our...last breath...at thee!"*

Overcome in his rage, Drake instantly withdrew his hand from Jon's neck and reformed Berith. With one swift thrust, he stabbed Jon directly through stomach, finishing him off once and for all. And this time, feeling his blade cut into the pirate's flesh, Drake knew that it wasn't another projection.

Terminating his link to the *Black Sun*, Drake switched his comm. line back to his fleet. "All ships, this is Admiral Drake!" he roared into his wristcom. "Open fire on my mark!"

An astonished voice, one belonging to the *Subjugator*'s captain, quickly spoke up. "Say again, Admiral...?"

"I said open fire!" Drake shouted back with pure, undeniable rancor. "I want the *Black Sun* destroyed!"

He then bellowed with even greater force. *"NOW!"*

## Flint Pirates umbra *Black Sun*
## Ephesus System

The command given, the Imperial warships fired their weapons, launching multiple beams and projectiles toward the stricken *Black Sun*. In a matter of seconds, the wounded umbra was encompassed by golden beam fire, missiles, and torpedoes, her obsidian form entirely shrouded in vibrant flame. Only by virtue of her still raised shields was she not destroyed in the initial barrage. But as everyone aboard her knew, it was only a matter of time before the shields were depleted.

Through the vibration and the sounding klaxons, Alex, upon settling back into the captain's chair, felt that strange peace continue to embrace him. Whatever fear and anger he had possessed before were now replaced with muted acceptance. He and his crew had fought one of the hardest battles in history, and though they had been beaten down, they would leave the universe unconquered, just as his mother had done before. That thought alone made Alex feel an equally strange warmth in his heart, feeling that he had indeed followed in his mother's footsteps. He and Jon had lived up to and honored the name Flint, in spite of its short lifespan. For that, they were mighty.

Opening his eyes to peer out one last time, Alex glanced over to the others present. Much to his relief, he saw that, with the exception of Davis, they too had accepted their fate, choosing instead to remain as their ship was whittled to nothingness, pirates, and spacers to the end. None of them glanced toward him now; instead, they had all closed their eyes and tilted their heads, as if in silent vigil. If Alex didn't know any better, he thought he heard some of them whispering a prayer, heedless of the destruction that would soon be upon them. In an ironic sort of way, that made Alex feel more accepting of what was soon to come. The thought that, in spite of what was about to happen, those around him retained their faith in something greater.

Davis, however, was an entirely different story. The helmsman was violently shaking in his chair, his body jumping each time a solid hit struck the *Black Sun*'s shields while muffled whimpers were espoused every few seconds. At first, Alex wanted to shake his head in shame, but then he realized something more. Davis remained where he was, not so much as attempting to run off the bridge or let out a scream of horror. Having realized that, Alex could not find it in himself to condemn the terrified helmsman. Ever since Sumatra, he had figured Davis was not one who could stomach his fate, no matter where it led him. Yet here he was, forcing himself down and holding to his post, trying to go out with some level of dignity even when he was scared beyond all measure. If anything, Alex now felt a newfound respect for the man, something he was glad he would never have to admit to.

As Davis' shaking grew more and more frantic, Alex began to rise from his chair. He didn't know what he could do for him, but if he could make it over to him, he would at least try. Much to his surprise, he didn't have to do anything. Just as Alex began to stand, Anna's right hand extended from her side and slowly covered Davis' left. Taken off guard by this display, Davis looked over to the operations officer in complete surprise, only to see that her head remained tilted and her eyes remained closed. Even so, that was more than enough for Davis. He momentarily broke contact so he could turn his hand over and clasp onto Anna's, who in turn intertwined her fingers with his. From there, Davis, while still retaining his fear, calmed down considerably.

*I'll be damned,* Alex thought as he felt a smile emerge from his lips, before closing his eyes again and tilting his own head. It was then that he felt perhaps his only regret: Kaguya. Even in the end, he never got to tell her how he really felt, nor did he have a chance to live his life beside her. However, that didn't bother Alex as much as he thought it would. With all that was going on, he had a feeling he would see her on the other side as well. And whether they ended up in Heaven, Hell, or some other form of afterlife, Alex knew as long as she and Jon were with him, then they would find a way to make it all work.

In fact, that led Alex to wonder about another thought. Would... would he and Jon see their mother again? Would she be there to meet them when they arrived, ready and willing to bring them upon new adventures in their new realm? The mere thought caused fresh, warm tears to trail down from Alex's now closed eyes. After so long, after having endured so much, they would, at last, see her, embrace her once more. If that was to be true, then Alex swore a silent oath, this time, whatever stood before them, they would never be apart again. This time, they would be a family, forever and ever.

Amidst the shock and quaking, Alex's ears picked up an alert sound from the tactical console. He didn't need to open his eyes to read it, he already knew, the shields were about to fail. Taking one last deep breath solely because he could, Alex quietly awaited his fate with the others. He only hoped that it would be quick, just as it would be spectacular.

That's when he picked up another sound, this time from Gran's station. One that, against all of his expectations, he thought he would never hear again.

*"You have grown strong, my students."*

## Imperial *Superior*-class battleship *Subjugator* Ephesus System

Standing upon his bridge, watching as his ship's main cannons continued to rain fire upon their target, the Captain of the *Subjugator* could not help but feel amazement toward the enemy ship. Even now, as broken and beaten as she was, the *Black Sun* continued to hold out against her attackers, taking one last stand against the Imperial fleet. In that regard, the Captain also felt a bit of remorse for having to destroy her. The Empire could undoubtedly have used such a vessel in its service, but Admiral Drake's orders were clear.

*She won't be long now,* the Captain thought as he watched the bombardment continue. Slowly but undeniably, the *Black Sun*'s shields were nearing the shattering point. Just a few more shots and...

"All stations," a new voice spoke up, shifting the captain's attention along with the rest of the bridge. "Sensors hold new contacts incoming from arcspace! Multiple new contacts!"

"What?" the Captain let out in surprise as he retook his seat. Did the Admiral have another fleet in reserve? If so, why were they coming in now? "Can you verify their IFF?"

"Checking now sir," the operations officer replied as he ran through the data. "It's..."

Suddenly, his eyes lit up in pure shock. "Oh my god...!"

Before the Captain could inquire further, the bridge viewscreen became filled with newly emerging warships. One by one, the newcomers dropped out of arcspace in fleet formation, advancing at high speed toward the Imperials. All bearing a single, commonplace emblem.

That of a serpentine blue dragon.

"What...?" the XO could only gape in full shock and confusion as the clearly identified enemy armada advanced further upon them. "What is this...?"

Before the Captain could address his own confusion, the viewscreen flashed, projecting an unmistakable image. One that struck pure terror into the *Subjugator*'s crew, as well as the crews of the remaining Imperial ships.

"Imperial forces, this is Lord Fuma Kotaro of the Blue Dragon," the image spoke with unrelenting force. "*Black Sun* and her crew are under our protection."

The image's eyes then narrowed, as if to gaze upon those before him with manifest contempt. "Withdraw, or be destroyed."

# Chapter XL: Ascending Light

## Predecessor Temple
## Ephesus

"Impossible!" Drake breathed as deathly cold shock consumed him. Though he considered himself a man entirely used to unexpected turns in combat, this was surreal, altogether incomprehensible to him. The Blue Dragon Clan appearing *here*? Armed and ready to fight on behalf of the descendants of their most hated adversary? And under the direct command of Lord Fuma himself? Such an event should have been beyond the realm of possibility, and yet here it was, staring Drake directly in the face.

And for the life of him, Drake could not understand it. What sort of influence did the Flints possess over Lord Fuma? Surely it had to have been substantial in order to draw the Blue Dragon Lord into aiding them personally, and yet, for all their power, the brothers could not have possibly held anything that Lord Fuma needed nor did not already possess. Granted, there was the possibility that the Blue Dragon had appeared here with the intention of taking the *Black Sun* for themselves, but that did not explain how they had known of her presence in Ephesus to begin with, nor did it explain their apparent interest in her crew. And there were very few other explanations besides those, none of which Drake could rationalize. How could any of them be even remotely possible?

"How...!?" Drake continued to breathe, feeling his body tighten with convulsion as his mind rambled on for an explanation. "How can this be happening...!?"

*"Very simple actually,"* an all too familiar voice suddenly spoke up from behind. Shock dying away and being replaced with newfound alarm, Drake closed his eyes and, with great reluctance, slowly turned back to face Jonathan Flint's "corpse".

Still fully alive and breathing, Jon casually had Astaroth's black energy absorb the bindings from his hands and legs, allowing him to step out from his confinement. As he did this, the "fatal" gash in his torso and the "life's blood" that stained his vest slowly faded into black energy as well, leaving Jon untouched of any critical wounds. Clearly, Drake realized, to his frustration, his opponent had projected a shroud around his torso upon the finishing attack, both protecting his body and causing Drake to "feel" flesh being cut.

That's when Drake had another damning realization: Astaroth. When Devilblade Wielders are killed, their physical bodies, should there be any trace of them, are consumed by their Devilblade's energy in a sordid pyre, upon the completion of which the blade would reappear in its inert stone form. Not only had the pirate's body *not* been consumed after he had "died", but Astaroth hadn't reverted back to its dormant form, thereby indicating that its Wielder was in fact still alive. And Drake, much to his self-admonishment, had been too focused on his rage to realize it. However, that wasn't what concerned Drake at present.

"How?" Drake demanded, a fierce edge now within his voice.

Jon, as wounded as he remained, held no reluctance toward answering.

"I believed Lord Fuma would hold interest in the events occurring here," he explained as he took each step forward. "Just as I believed you would, due to his relationship with my mother, assume him to be my enemy and therefore not hold surveillance over him."

He then added, knowingly. "As you had my regular allies."

That only made Drake further confused. Not because his opponent was aware of his surveillance over his traditional allies, any lower rung cadet would have seen through that. Rather, just how the Blue Dragon Lord could possibly be amongst their number.

"He was your mother's most bitter adversary," the Admiral managed to let out in his bewilderment.

"It's precisely that ignorance I was counting on," Jon stated in turn, before facing Drake again. "You are a brilliant and cunning tactician and commander Admiral, but as with most beings of your ilk, sentient relationships are beyond you."

The pirate captain elaborated. "Yes, my mother and Lord Fuma were enemies long ago, but that wasn't the extent of their relationship. It was deeper and far more complicated than just that; something that, for all of your intellect, you will *never* understand."

He then came to stand directly in front of Drake. "And as for Alex and I, it's just as complex. Suffice to say Lord Fuma is not our direct ally, nor a being we can simply call upon for aid," he continued. "Yet he is still a man of honor and principle, and he would *never* leave us alone and isolated."

Seething anger beginning to reemerge over him, Drake began to realize even more. "Ryugu," he growled in clear spite, as his previously open question had at last been answered. "That was where you went after Rochelle. Where you refitted the *U-7501*."

And then one more realization came to him. One that caused all manner of cold to run through the Admiral's veins. "And the raider who fought beside you on Kurzis...!"

"The Dragon Princess herself," Jon confirmed, inwardly taking no small amount of pleasure in seeing the Admiral's expression. "All this time the answers have been directly in front of you, so close that you need only have looked down to see them. But, in your arrogance and your belief that you already understood *everything*, you never considered that need."

Jon's eye now looked directly into Drake's set, just as he had done before. Only this time, instead of simple defiance, that single blue eye held triumph.

"And for that," the elder Flint stated with visible cruelty. "You have lost, Raphael."

Drake, through his growing rage, did not fail to see the irony in those four words, nor did he deny their truth. He did not know the composition of the Blue Dragon fleet, but he knew all too well that his forces were not ready to fight them. Too many ships and troops had been lost fighting the *Black Sun* and her raider force. The Admiral possessed no further reinforcements or contingencies to utilize, while those already on the field were either too damaged or too exhausted to put up sufficient resistance. All while the Blue Dragon fleet was in whole form, their ships untouched and their raiders – and Drake knew they held raiders – were fresh and ready for battle. The conclusion, as much as Drake wished it otherwise, was inevitable.

It was the cruelest form of irony, even more so than what his opponent had just spoken to him. He was now in the exact position he had spent the battle forcing the Flints and their entourage into, while they and their apparent Blue Dragon allies now held his former seat. And, just as Jonathan was visibly doing now, they were looking down upon him from that very same height of superiority.

"And now, I extend to you the same courtesy you extended to my brother," Jon said as Astaroth reappeared in his grip. He then pointed its blade toward Drake. "Surrender, willingly and unconditionally, or die."

Glaring back, Drake took a few steps to his right, with Jon continuing to point Astaroth at him. He then stopped, without looking up, and proclaimed. "And I give you the same response that he gave me," he glowered, hands tightening with intensity as Berith reformed. "To hell with you!"

Upon that declaration, the Admiral brought his blade down once more.

## Blue Dragon *Nagato*-class battleship *Ryujin* Ephesus System

Standing upon the bridge of his flagship, hands clasped behind his back, Lord Fuma gazed over the viewscreen with visible interest and appreciation. Before him lay a field of devastation. Debris and remnants scattered as far as his eyes could see, each having once been part of an Imperial warship or smallcraft. Ship hulls, from frigates to battleships, were laid about as a line of metal corpses, while the broken forms of fighters and bombers could be depicted as virtual grey pinpricks against the backdrop of space. And every now and then his eyes would fall upon that of an actual Terran body, or whatever remained, floating aimlessly toward Ephesus' distant gravity well. An epic battleground, even if it had been centered around a single entity.

In the distance, through the remains of the Imperial armada, he could just depict that single entity, which hung against Ephesus' form as a black star against a crimson sky. Her hull was beaten and battered across every quarter, her once immaculate black and gold form now burned and blemished with damage and breaches. Her arc engine was inactive, what few weapons she possessed were completely disabled, and only the barest amount of power was coursing through her internals. And yet through it all, Fuma could see the Golden Roger still beaming from the side of her bridge tower, the emblem somehow having escaped any damage whatsoever. This caused a small smile to creep upon the Lord's face, as he found it a perfect allegory toward the *Black Sun*'s present state. Beaten, but unconquered.

*Indeed you have fought well,* Lord Fuma thought as he held his gaze over the stricken vessel. He did not know whether she would sail again, nor did he know just how much of her crew remained aboard her or on the surface. What he did know however was that, by all that had transpired here, she and her crew had proven their worth.

"My Lord," the *Ryujin*'s tactical officer alerted. "The Imperials are moving back into attack formation."

Fuma's eyes swept toward the Imperial ships, which, as stated, were now reforming their lines against his fleet. For obvious reasons, the Blue Dragon Lord was hardly surprised. They had come too far to be forced back now, even if it meant fighting a Clan.

"All ships," Fuma began as the *Ryujin*'s captain stepped forward, awaiting his command. *"Advance."*

Nodding in acknowledgment, the captain began relaying orders to the rest of the bridge crew. Moments later, the Blue Dragon fleet ignited their main drive systems and surged onward, launching toward the renewed battlefield.

---

It was all Boss could do to look on in utter silence at the Blue Dragon fleet's sudden appearance. Even from her current position at the far side of the planet, she could make out the distinctive black and blue shapes as they converged upon the Imperial ships. The latter having noticeably halted their barrage and were now reforming into an attack formation.

"Are you seeing this Lead?" one of the few remaining pilots from Buccaneer Squadron sounded off with approaching incredulousness. "Are you seeing...?"

Boss didn't initially respond, *couldn't* initially respond as she was too focused on fighting the tears back. Though she wasn't an overly emotional person in the least, even she could not keep from feeling elated with what laid before her. Just when all hope had been lost, when she had ordered a final charge in the *Black Sun*'s withering defense, salvation had at last come. And it came in the form of a blue dragon, who would protect its charge and devour its enemies. Needless to say, it took quite a bit of effort for Boss to regain herself. But regain herself she did, focusing her bleary eyes onto the scene before her. Their time was now.

"All fighters, move in and reengage," she commanded, her voice filled with renewed determination. *"Charge!"*

Upon that command, the Corsairs' main thrusters went to full burn, propelling the fighters toward the battleground with vigilance. As they closed in, Boss could depict additional fighters and bombers taking off from the various clan ships as well, with the majority launching from the twin carriers *Soryu* and *Hiryu*. In response to this, the remaining Imperial ships began relaunching their own smallcraft, but Boss knew that their numbers were not going to match up. Too many of the Imps had already been shot down, as she and her remaining pilots could attest to.

Moments later, the first shots were fired as the Blue Dragon battleships entered into range, lancing beams toward the Imperial ships. A whole swathe of grey was obliterated as the *Subjugator* and her compatriots returned fire. The Imps attacks were impacting but otherwise failing to break the Blue Dragons' fully energized shielding. Fighters of all shapes and sizes converged and moved upon one another, both sides attempting to open a hole in the other's formation for their respective bombers. All while the larger ships continued to exchange fire.

## Flint Pirates umbra *Black Sun*
## Ephesus System

"Is...?" Davis murmured as he and the rest of the bridge crew watched the viewscreen, hope slowly beginning to return to their eyes. "Is this really happening...?" Silence was the only response, yet the answer was quite apparent.

Retaining his calm, Alex watched as two Mustangs flew by the bridge, pursued by a pair of Blue Dragon Zeros. A few seconds later, both Mustangs were cut down by the pirate fighters' vulcan fire, the two clan fighters breaking ranks to avoid the debris. Alex caught sight of another two fighters, a Zero and one of the Corsairs, moving against another group, their vulcans already raining blue and red beams into the Imperial formation. A second later, a much larger set of blue beams eclipsed the viewscreen as two *Shinano*-class battlecruisers moved toward the *Black Sun*'s position, forcing away any Imperial ships still lingering around the stricken umbra.

Feeling the same resurgence of hope as the rest of the bridge crew, Alex allowed himself to slouch in his chair, the sheer emotion threatening to break him down then and there. It had all happened so fast, just as he had accepted all had been lost, and death was inevitable, he had in no way been prepared for their apparent salvation. Thus, it took every bit of effort for him to force back his tears and remain as he was; to remain as the objective and unwavering commander of the *Black Sun* for a little longer.

*My god...* Alex thought amidst his warring emotions, doing all he could to keep composed. Despite his efforts, however, he could not stop himself from tilting his head down and allowing the barest amount of tears to move from his eyes. *We did it. We actually did it.*

He was so focused on his emotions that he barely heard Gran's voice. "We're receiving a hail from the *Ryujin*," she announced. "They're inquiring of our status."

Blinking back the tears, Alex lifted his head back up. "Alive and feeling victorious," he answered, before glancing around the bridge and remembering the *Sun*'s present state. "Though we are very much in need of their assistance."

Gran quickly relayed the message. "*Ryujin* replies with their understanding, and will gladly provide that assistance when all is said and done. Until then, we are to stand by and let them take care of the rest."

Another pair of Zeros shot by the viewscreen, emphasizing the point. "No need to tell us twice," Davis quipped as he leaned back into his chair. No longer was he terrified or bewildered, just exhausted. It felt as if he had just learned how to breathe again.

The rest of the bridge seemed to heed to that advice, as they all moved to relax at their various posts. Only Gran continued to work at her station, maintaining her communications with the Blue Dragon ships and sending them data. This confused her fellow crewmen at first until they remembered that the enemy umbras were still out there. With that thought in mind, they let her go about her task while they began to rest.

Alex was among the latter, he gradually felt himself slump in his chair while keeping watch over the viewscreen. Only then did he feel his own exhaustion along with a strong temptation to fall asleep where he was. And this time he gave in, leaning back against the headrest and slowly closing his eyes.

"We won," he murmured, with no small amount of satisfaction as his mind began to darken. All that remained was for Jon and Lorelei to fulfill their ends, to which Alex had no doubt they would. Especially Jon, who Alex knew was still alive and still fighting. Just as he knew that his brother would, in the end, defeat Drake.

"We won," he repeated, again letting the satisfaction move over him. It had cost them much and brought them closer to death than he had wished, but in the end, they had triumphed. They had survived. They had, indeed, won.

*We won,* Alex thought for one last time, a small smile forming on his lips. Only then did he succumb to his exhaustion and fall to sleep.

# Predecessor Ruins
## Ephesus

Feeling consciousness embrace her once more, Kaguya blinked her weary eyes open, focusing on a pair of silhouettes standing above her. Acting instinctively, she, while still in the process of fully awakening, lashed her hand out and grasped the throat of the one nearest to her, from which she attempted to apply a choke hold.

Only the dozen arms that extended and held her back kept her from successfully executing it, all while the voice of the second silhouette began to register in her mind.

"*Ojou-sama*, it's alright!" the silhouette spoke calmingly, just as Kaguya's eyes adjusted and began to depict the black and cobalt armor she was wearing. "We're not your enemy!"

Blinking again, Kaguya, upon seeing the group around her were Blue Dragon raiders, quit applying pressure with her hand but did not release her grip. A Shinzan assault shuttle flew overhead, from which additional raiders cabled down and moved into the ruins. She could depict the distant sounds of Haru gunships providing close-air support. The shadow of one such gunship passed over her form.

Realizing she was not in danger, Kaguya released her grip on the raider's neck and started to rise. One raider moved to support her, but she signaled him away, instead choosing to stand on her own. After a brief moment to regain her balance, she eventually succeeded. "My sword," she commanded.

Another raider moved into the open, holding her ninjato in his hand. Using her still working right arm, Kaguya gratefully took the sword and gazed over it. After momentarily remarking how well it had served her in this battle, she twirled it around and resheathed it. As exhausted as she was, she was still a warrior first and foremost.

"*Ojou-sama*, we've come under the command of your father," the first raider spoke up again, just as another explosion sounded off in the distance. "We're here to relieve you and your comrades in this battle."

As if to emphasize that point, another Shinzan descended from above, landing a short distance away from where Kaguya and the Blue Dragon raiders were standing. "We've already established a safe zone," the raider pressed. "This will take you there."

Despite the temptation to get on the shuttle then and there, Kaguya remained where she was. Another shadow from a passing Haru cast over her.

"What are your exact orders?"

"*Ojou-sama?*" the raider questioned in apparent confusion, which those around her also shared.

Hesitantly, Kaguya clarified. "What are my father's exact orders," she spoke, a dangerous edge approaching her tone. "Regarding the Flint Pirates?"

Suddenly realizing what she meant, the raider nodded in understanding. "Our orders are to hunt down any remaining Imperials," she said, before glancing back at the Shinzan. "And to retrieve and render aid to all surviving Flints."

"Commander!" a voice shouted out from the shuttle, whose side door had slid open to reveal several individuals inside its passenger compartment. Kaguya quickly recognized them as raiders from the *Black Sun*.

Taking a sharp breath of relief, Kaguya at last acquiesced. "Very well," she replied. "I will go, then."

Bowing in acknowledgment, the raider sounded off a command to two of her subordinates before she and the other raiders began to mobilize. Those two, in turn, moved to escort Kaguya to the shuttle. They gently guided her in. Once she was clear, the hatch closed and the Shinzan ascended back into the sky, a pair of Harus moving to provide escort.

Looking out from the armored porthole, Kaguya cast one last glance over the ruins as they grew more and more distant. What had once been a tranquil and strangely majestic setting was now a battleground, with craters, burns, and debris littered about while the sight of burning vehicles and corpses were commonplace. Most, to her inner pride, were Imperial affiliated, but every now and then she caught sight of one of her own raiders lying across the ground, reminding her of the great sacrifice that had been made. Sorrow for those lost battled with elation at the victory.

Sighing, Kaguya continued to look over the field until the Shinzan moved past the boundary line, coincidentally just as additional Blue Dragon transports became visible from overhead. The battle was still going on, but her part, as well as that of her comrades from the *Sun*, was now over. All that was required of her was to rest and allow her father and her clan to finish it.

Even so, as she laid her head back against her seat, feeling the first vestiges of peace begin to embrace her senses, she couldn't help but wonder what was occurring now. Had Jon at last defeated Drake in their inevitable confrontation? Had Lorelei found what she sought from within? Was Alex still alive? Kaguya had no way of verifying anything, but she had a feeling she would learn soon enough. And when she did, things would be very, very different.

For now, all she could do was close her eyes once more.

———————————————

She could feel it. Though she could not "see" it even with her special senses, she could somehow "feel" it lying within the darkness before her, all while the energy lines converged on its specific point. A small measure of relief entered her upon that realization. At long last, she had reached the end of her descent. At long last, deep within the most bottomless abyss imaginable, she had found the treasure she had long sought.

For a time, she attempted to focus her senses onto that very point, attempted to see what precisely the energy flowing from above was converging on. However, for all of her power, she could not pierce the darkness around it. Actually, that wasn't quite true she realized; her senses could pierce through the void, but no matter how deeply she extended them, they could not reach whatever it was that laid within. For all the darkness that lay around her, this one felt thicker and with greater intensity, almost as if it were infinite. To focus her senses, to even look upon it, was futile.

She only found this intriguing. Were its creators so intent on keeping it dormant that they, even at the bottom of this great abyss, placed one last defensive measure in an effort to keep their creation completely safeguarded? Or perhaps it was meant to be a final warning, a final notice for any and all trespassers to return to where they came before the worst could occur?

*"Whatever Arcadia is, it's not something to take lightly... In fact, I can't help but wonder if it is something that should even be found at all."*

Her friend's words rang within her like a distant bell, as if to remind her that, perhaps, she could still go too far. A brief pause occurred as she contemplated this wisdom. Perhaps what she sought was indeed not meant to be found or brought back to activity. Perhaps she should indeed return to her physical form while she still had the chance. Perhaps the consequences of her actions could prove even direr than they have already.

However, she forced away the thought and the inclination to turn back. As she had concluded before, she had come too far now, and too much had been sacrificed for her to reach this point. Thus, whatever it was she had found and would soon revive, she would see her efforts through to the end. Regardless of her fate and those upon the surface.

With that in mind, she knew what she had to do next. Though she did not know where the information came from, she knew exactly how she was to proceed. Clearing her mind of any lingering hesitation, she again focused her power, this time concentrating on "force" rather than "sight", and turned it upon the darkness before her. As she did this, the "rain" of energy increased substantially like an accelerated heartbeat, flowing much faster and at a higher rate than before. All convening upon what lay under the darkness.

She found this satisfying in a strange way. Though it would still take a bit more time to focus the entirety of energy into that one place, the fact remained it was actually happening. The process had at last begun, and what she sought would soon be brought back into the light.

She could only hope, as she focused all of herself upon her task, that it would not be to her regret...

# Predecessor Temple
# Ephesus

With rage induced power, Drake leaped into the air and brought Berith into an overhead chop, smashing the ground Jon had previously been occupying. Quick to respond, Jon rolled to the side and slashed Astaroth out, sending another black groundswell at Drake. The Admiral raised his hand to generate a shield to deflected the energy. This allowed Jon time to spin back and slash at his opponent's chest, but Drake was fast enough to parry with Berith's physical blade. Both exchanged additional cuts and parries before Drake, managing to catch Jon off guard, extended his left hand back out and launched a shockwave, sending the pirate sailing back. The Admiral then leaped after him, intending to impale Jon, but the pirate captain managed to repel the blow in mid-flight and then land safely.

Even so, Drake remained relentless in his fury. *This turn in circumstance cannot be, this is* my *victory,* he raged as he continued his offensive, striking hammer blow after hammer blow against Astaroth's blade. *I am superior!*

At this point, whatever finesse the Admiral had possessed before was now completely overrun by his rage, and Jon found himself once more barely managing to defend against the power in his opponent's attacks. Fortunately, this was balanced by the Admiral's own defense becoming more open, which Jon ruthlessly exploited. Upon the last hammer blow, Jon dodged the strike by sidestepping to the right, followed with a slash into Drake's side.

Blood sprayed out, striking the pirate captain's arm. The pain of the wound managed to disorient Drake, but before Jon could deliver a finishing blow, the Admiral spun and caught Jon across the chest. More blood flowed but down his own right side. The Admiral then attempted to fire a gold energy shot from his left hand at point-blank range, but a black hole formed and the gold energy disappeared into the void.

As he parried the Admiral's attacks, Jon couldn't help but notice something peculiar about their arena. He couldn't verify it without lowering his defenses, but he was sure that the surrounding energy lines had picked up in speed, such that they were now pulsating downward as opposed to the steady flow that had occurred before. However, Jon couldn't concentrate on it for long. Instead, he focused back on the fight as Drake drove Berith against Astaroth again and again. Gazing into his opponent's mismatched eyes up close, Jon saw Drake was now the personification of crazed fury.

Driven beyond reason by the perceived theft of *his* victory, Drake broke contact and pivoted to strike, only for Jon to vault away. A black geyser rose around the Admiral. Drake created an energy shroud and drove forward again – he wasn't even teleporting anymore Jon noticed – with Berith set to impale. Jon evaded and reengaged. Only for his attack be parried as well.

Despite his assaults being unsuccessful, Jon focused on putting Drake on the defensive, executing several more strikes that Drake was forced to parry. And just as before, the Admiral's rage and exhaustion had deteriorated his form, allowing Jon to slip in cuts into his left shoulder and leg. Infuriated even further, Drake lashed out with a golden beam shot, but Jon evaded it easily this time.

The Admiral, now frenzied and bleeding, yet undeterred, let out a battle cry as he attempted to cleave Jon's legs, only for the latter to leap over the attack. Jon swung Astaroth overhead, using the momentum to charge his opponent. Drake managed to stop the blow, holding both blades immobile for the moment. Both channeled their respective blades' energies forward, black and gold energy bolts flew out in all directions. Destroyed sections of the arena rained down, but neither wielder noticed nor could break the deadlock.

And then, seething with indignant wrath, Drake knocked Astaroth back and swept around to strike Jon in the waist. Jon repelled the blow, turned, ducked the follow-up strike, and managed to cut Drake across the cheek and across the forearm. Blackened blood seeped from the wounds as flesh began to disappear.

Maddened by his opponent's continued defiance, Drake let out a great bellow of hatred. Gold energy began to blaze around the Admiral. Initially thinking Berith had just possessed him, Jon quickly flipped away, only to be proven wrong. Drake plunged forward. Nearly impaled as his feet touch ground again, Jon defended against the Admiral's onslaught. Slashes, parries, and power attacks swept Jon to the side. Instantly, Drake was upon him, with the pirate barely managing to keep Drake from dividing his head down the middle.

Jon maintained his form and deflected the strikes, as well as those which followed. He was very aware of his exhaustion and knew he couldn't continue for much longer. However, as he watched Drake become more and more erratic, Jon decided he was far from finished. Again he found an opening in Drake's form that allowed him to evade his next attack while striking the Admiral in the back. The shock and pain worked to confuse Drake for the moment. That was more than enough time for Jon to move in, but Drake lashed out with his left hand and seized Astaroth's blade before it could fall. Only the gold energy surrounding the Admiral's hand prevented him from being dismembered. With superhuman strength, Drake threw the blade aside, and the two drove forward once more, clashing their swords against the other, energy surging, as their gazes met. Both knowing that their battle, no matter who won and who lost, was reaching its final stage.

---

The energy was surging around her now, having virtually transformed from a minor rainstorm to a full torrent. Under her power it accelerated with each passing second, converging more and more into the intended point. Such was its flow that she felt she was no longer in actual control of the storm. Rather, it felt as though she were simply guiding it toward its destination as it grew exponentially in strength. A part of her wondered if she would be swept away in the torrent, but that was only a temporary thought as her attention was soon drawn back to the source.

From what was once complete darkness, the briefest form of light began to emerge. A pure white light, shining through the abyss like a single star, seemingly insignificant in its design. Yet, as more energy was drawn to it, that light grew, turning from a single dot against the black into a small sun. One that nearly blinded her as she gazed upon it, forcing her to shift away from it as it continued to emerge.

This was it, she thought as the light expanded more and more. This was what she had sought for so long; the culmination of her quest and lifelong dream. And yet, as she turned back to gaze into the light, she found herself beginning to wonder...

That was as far as she progressed with her thought before the light emerged in full, eradicating the darkness and replacing it with a whole expanse of white. What remained after that was complete silence.

# Predecessor Temple
# Ephesus

With another thunderous clash, the two blades fell upon each other, both Wielders attempting to force the other into submission. It was quite evident that both were at the very last of their strength now, as neither the pirate nor the admiral could overcome the other's force. And yet neither was about to give in.

After a few seconds, both simultaneously brought their left hands out, launching a burst of black and gold energy into one another. So unstable and poorly composed were their respective energy bursts that their impact caused an enormous shockwave that sent both Jon and Drake falling away to opposite ends of the temple. Only by sheer fortune did either combatant retain his footing, though they both slid into a kneeling position.

Suddenly feeling himself choke, Drake let out a sharp cough, which was immediately followed by a splattering sound. When he looked upon the ground, he saw a small amount of blood now laid across it.

*Is this...* his mind railed as he tried to force himself back up. This attempt would prove futile, however, as he was soon back on his knee. *Is this my defeat?*

Growling at the notion, Drake forced himself back to his feet; Jon managed to do the same. Both were at the end of their respective strengths now. As such, they each realized that the next strike would be their last.

Suddenly, both men felt the ground under them begin to shake, just as the energy flow accelerated even further.

"She has succeeded," Jon couldn't help but declare. "Arcadia will soon be upon us."

He swung Astaroth about, preparing. "But that has nothing to do with us," he stated, all the while focusing Astaroth's energy onto himself, thereby generating a black aura. "All that remains is you and I, Raphael."

Facing the elder Flint, Drake glared. "Yes," he seethed, golden light encompassing his being. "That's exactly what it comes down to, Jonathan."

Slowly, as black and gold energy surged around them in thunderous bursts devastating anything in its path, both men assumed combat stances with their respective Devilblades. This was it, this would be the final blow. Whoever stood, whoever fell, it would all be determined in the next attack.

With the crashing sounds of the surrounding destruction, both combatants ran forward, their blades brought out to their respective sides. Time appeared to slow between them as they continued their advance, their gazes holding past the falling debris, shaking ground, the flickering light and onto one another. All while energy crackled around their respective forms, nearly spreading throughout the temple.

And then, contact was made; with a fearsome roar, both Wielders executed their respective slashes. They moved past each other and halted in their tracks, both now assuming the final stances of their attacks. Only then did the perception of time return to them, just as the temple began to shake even more violently.

Neither of them moved. Instead, they held to their stances as if time still eluded them. Then, after the briefest of moments had passed, Berith disappeared from Drake's side. In spite of his best efforts not to, the Admiral lurched forward and fell to the ground, a much larger pool of blood emerging from his torso.

Hearing his opponent fall, Jon allowed a victorious smirk to emerge on his lips, but he knew it was not to last. A deep wound had been inflicted in his own being, and blood was already flowing out of it. As such, he could not prevent himself from also collapsing as Astaroth vanished from his own hand. Only by pure force of will did Jon manage to slump to his knees.

"We won..." he murmured under his breath, as he slowly felt the light begin to fade and his body beginning to fall forward. All the while, the feeling of triumph continued to run through him, even as all thought and feeling gradually died away. "We won..."

With that, Jon fell face first on the ground. All while a great conduit of light erupted from the temple's center. One that bathed the entirety of the temple, the ruined city, and the surrounding space above in a field of brilliant white light...

# <u>Chapter XLI: Aftermath</u>

*It was blinding, the light. So blinding that he saw not the slightest shadow, not the smallest form of darkness. A whole field of white light, surrounding him and encompassing him, seemingly infinite in its scope and depth.*

*As he remained there, holding but the barest consciousness of his surroundings, he wondered if this was what they had been searching for. If it was what* she *had been searching for, had enlisted the aid of him and his brother for. It was possible, perhaps even likely, he thought. Or perhaps it was something else entirely. Perhaps it was the end of the universe, the very boundary of what he and those around him had considered reality. Or...or perhaps it was the afterlife itself, at long last having emerged to embrace his soul.*

*He couldn't help but find a certain irony with the last one, considering how he had been apathetic toward any such conception. It was not that he did not believe in it; rather, much like how he considered the idea of a superior being that watched over his universe and all within it, he had simply not cared whether it existed or not. He had neither believed nor disbelieved that such a realm existed, instead having focused on the reality around him and his brother. And now, he was beholding something of that nature, though he wasn't quite sure if it was, indeed, his final resting place.*

*For a time he could do nothing but wonder, again with as much consciousness of his newfound setting as he could retain, toward whether or not he had indeed past on. The answer seemed all too likely, given the state he was in before the light had reached him, but for some reason, he couldn't be sure. And then, before he could explore the thought even further, he was able to see something else within the light. Something that he had only been able to see at that moment, and yet, through means that he did not understand, he felt had always been there, standing before him.*

*He instantly recognized that something, recognized* her. *Though the light remained encompassing, such that he could only depict the faintest silhouette, he more than recognized her form; a form he had not seen in fifteen years. Without even realizing it, he opened his mouth to speak to her, to speak to her once more. However, he heard no words escape from his mouth. He raised his arm toward her, yet she remained in the distance and seemingly beyond his reach, even as he extended his hand to the furthest.*

*For her part, she simply stood by, seemingly watching him in turn. However, for a fleeting moment in time, he thought he could see an approving smile upon her lips.*

*And then, without any word or warning, she turned away and moved back into the light. Again he called out to her in a wordless cry, all the while his hand grasped at the open air between them. Yet she continued on regardless, her silhouette growing more and more distant with each step, just as he became more and more desperate to reach her.*

*Then, she was gone. Disappeared within the field of light from whence she came. The very same light that soon darkened and faded out, leaving him within complete nothingness...*

# Ryugu Castle
# Kyoto, Ryugu

Eye fluttering open as an altogether different kind of light reached it, Jon felt his consciousness slowly return to him. Along with that, he found himself in an altogether familiar position; laying on a medical bed in what could only be a medical facility, with sharp pain running through his body. The only difference was that facility was not aboard the *Black Sun*. Rather, as he observed the surrounding architecture, he saw that he was in the medical ward of Ryugu Castle, which also meant he was back on Ryugu. The lack of Aquilan masks and icons and the differing alphabet on the surrounding equipment only reinforced that fact.

Slowly, Jon rose up from his position, feeling his body strain against him as he did. Compared to the last time, he hurt a lot more, as though the pain was coming from all over. Of course, there was a good reason for that. This time around, he hadn't merely been wounded in the chest. This time he had new scars on virtually every part of his being, something he verified by pulling back the blanket and inspecting his form. When added to the excessive physical strain, it was only natural that he felt the way he did. He hurt, badly, but was otherwise still alive.

Gradually it all came back to him; all that had transpired and led to his being in medical care once more. The battle over Ephesus, his own second duel and following victory against Drake, the Blue Dragon's intervention. It all came back to him in a steady stream of recollection, all the while Jon proceeded to lay back and feel at ease.

The battle was over; he would not have been where he was if it didn't culminate. He and his crew had triumphed; they had held out against the Imperials long enough for Lord Fuma and his fleet to arrive. Lorelei had obviously succeeded in unsealing Arcadia, and he had avenged both his mother and his earlier defeat against Drake. For all accounts and purposes, Jon felt a great sense of pride toward these accomplishments, a small smile formed upon his lips. It had been a hard battle, and it had likely cost him much, but in the end, it had been won. The Second

Battle of Ephesus would go down in history as a victory for Morganna Flint's successors.

The question now was what had happened afterward. He imagined that Lord Fuma's fleet had recovered the surviving crew, but what had become of them? How many had survived and who? What had become of the *Black Sun*? Had she been recovered as well, or had she been deemed unsalvageable?

Sighing, he realized that he would gain no answer from where he was now. As such, with as much effort as he could muster, Jon slowly rose from his bed and sat upon it, feeling every ache and pain across his body as he did. Once he was adequately upright with his legs over the right side, he took a breath and moved to touch the floor.

He was so focused on his efforts that he only barely noticed a familiar pair of arms move over him, helping him.

"Gently," Apache spoke as he guided Jon forward, then aided him in standing up fully. "Gently."

After a bit more effort, Jon finally gained his balance, "I will probably regret saying this later," Jon commented as Apache stepped back, allowing him to stand on his own. "But your being here is very reassuring to me."

"You should be grateful, Jonathan," Apache replied sharply, then handing Jon a cup of water. "It was no easy task chasing out all of Lord Fuma's medical staff and taking the place over for mysel...er, *your* personal care."

Drinking slowly, savoring the liquid as if it were fine brandy, Jon then asked the inevitable question. "How long was I out?"

"Four days," Apache answered as Jon handed back the cup, which he placed on a side cabinet. After that, he withdrew Jon's eyepatch and handed that over. "Technically, you should still be resting."

Slipping his eyepatch on, Jon glanced over toward Apache with peculiarity. "That's it?" he asked. "No threats? No attempts to physically restrain me?"

Apache let out a sharp laugh. "I'm old for a reason, Jonathan. I don't have a death wish," he exclaimed. "And besides, I know better than to keep you down at this point."

Before Jon could reply, Apache fixed his eyes upon him. "You won Jonathan," he reaffirmed, clear approval coming through with each word. "You actually won."

Jon nodded, allowing a smile of his own to form. "You speak as if you had doubts," he retorted, before turning serious again. "What happened after?"

Apache considered. "Don't know too much about it myself," he explained. "After the Imps retreated, the Blue Dragons gathered us all up, the dead included, and took us all back here," he said, gesturing around the room. "The wounded were treated, and the dead were buried."

"Alex?"

"Alive and bothersome as always."

Again Jon nodded, before asking another hard question. "The *Sun*?"

The doctor shrugged. "They recovered what was left of her," he explained. "But I don't know if she'll ever sail again."

Pursing his lips, Jon decided to put that aside for the time being. "Arcadia?"

This time a gaze of uncertainty came over Apache's eyes. "That's a tricky question to answer," he said as he scratched a talon across the back of his head. "Lorelei succeeded in unsealing it, but..."

"But?" Jon asked.

Apache licked his beak before answering. "Nobody knows what to make of it," he clarified. "It's something that none of us, not even our dear songstress, has ever seen before."

Jon was about to ask Apache to describe it further, but before he could utter one word, he heard the door open from the side. Turning around, he saw Alex standing in the doorway, a myriad of emotions across his face. Slowly, Alex crossed the threshold, allowing the door to close behind him, all while tears began to well up in his eyes.

"About time you woke up," he commented as he moved toward Jon. "I was beginning to think Apache was holding you for ransom."

Jon only smiled in turn. "Let me guess," he replied nonchalantly. "If that had been the case, you *wouldn't* have paid it."

Though the tears continued to well up as he crossed the distance, Alex played along. "Depends on the price," he said. "Figured you're worth about...fifty aurics."

Jon laughed a little. "Just fifty?" he shot back. "My gloves are worth more than that."

"Well, what can I say brother?" Alex retorted as he came to stand face to face with his elder sibling. "I need that money for more essential things."

"Grog?" Jon questioned.

"Exactly," Alex replied, barely holding back his emotions.

A few more seconds passed before Alex, at last, let it all go. He embraced his brother in one swift motion, Jon returning the embrace somewhat more slowly.

"We did it, Jon," Alex spoke into his brother's side. "We beat the bastard that killed Mom."

Jon shook his head. "He wasn't the one who killed her," he corrected. "But other than that, yes, Alex. We beat him."

With that, Alex pulled back, allowing Jon to look him in the eye. "And how about you?" he asked. "From what I understand, you did a remarkable job in command."

Alex chuckled. "Who are you kidding?" Alex playfully admonished. "I nearly got the ship blown up from under me."

"Perhaps, but it would have been on your terms regardless," Jon replied with reassurance. "Drake himself claimed you possessed 'unquestioned brilliance',"" he added. "Before I gutted him, of course."

"Of course," Alex retorted, considering for a moment. "I do have to admit," he spoke amid that thought. "'Captain Alexander Flint' has a nice ring to it..."

Smiling, Jon grasped his brother on the shoulder. "Someday, Alex," he said, squeezing lightly. "For now, however, you're stuck with me."

The younger Flint feigned a disgusted expression. "Way to ruin the moment bro," he stated with false revulsion.

"As I meant to," Jon shot back with a responding sly expression. He then switched back to the subject at hand. "Outside the three of us, who's up and moving?"

"Nice of you to remember I'm still here," Apache quipped from the background.

Alex smiled, knowing what his brother meant. "All of them Jon," he replied warmly. "And they've been waiting for you."

Jon nodded, his own smile taking on a warmer tone. "Then, let's not keep them waiting for much longer."

Moving in slow, deliberate stride, Jon followed as Alex and Apache led him toward the castle's main receiving room. With his body still strained, it was challenging for him to remain upright, let alone to walk. Jon had to proceed more cautiously than usual. Outside a quip or two, both his brother and his doctor understood his plight and moved slowly as well.

Eventually, they reached their destination. There, as Alex had alluded to, eight members of their immediate circle were standing by, presently in conversation with each other. Upon Anna catching sight of their approach, that conversation halted and instantly all attention turned toward Alex and Apache's wounded charge, who could only smile at his crew. After a brief moment to take in the image, the group, save for one, ran toward the elder Flint and moved around him, laughing triumphantly and granting him congratulatory pats on the back and shoulder.

Kaiser, in his own excitement and momentarily forgetting his strength, pulled Jon into a grand bear hug and lifted him off the floor. Instantaneously overwhelmed with pain, Jon inhaled sharply yet awkwardly returned the embrace, as much as he could. Even Barbarossa, who stood more off to the side than the others, found that amusing. His eyes shone with approval toward his 'infidel' commander. That amusement only multiplied as, upon Kaiser putting Jon back on the ground, Davis granted the captain an enthusiastic slap across the back, nearly causing Jon to stumble from his fragile balance.

Watching it all play out from her position in the corner, the last member of the group could only smile in her usual manner as the select crew of the *Black Sun* regaled their captain. For a time she was tempted to join in, but she knew better than to try. It was because of her that they, *he*, had been forced into that battle in the first place. It was because of her that they, again namely *he,* had nearly died. She had no place amongst their number; no place at his side, beyond what was necessary. She didn't need her powers to understand that.

After watching for a few moments longer, she decided to leave the crew to their celebration. Thus, taking a small breath, she turned around and began moving toward the door. Before she could reach it, she felt a firm hand grasp her upper arm, swinging her back around. There, she found a familiar sapphire blue eye looking back into her own.

"Don't think you can walk away that easily," Jon stated, his voice holding no hostility whatsoever.

Blinking in response, Lorelei forced another smile upon her lips. "It's only proper," she replied, somehow managing to keep the uncertainty from her voice. "After all, if it weren't for me, you wouldn't have had to go through all this."

Jon merely shrugged. "I've been through worse," he said, his smile taking on a reassuring tone. "And it's not like I didn't have fun along the way."

Lorelei opened her mouth to reply, but Jon spoke first. "Besides, I accepted the contract."

He then placed both hands on her shoulders. "As far as I'm concerned, it was all part of what you hired me for. Seeing you through to the end."

Minute tears welling up in her eyes, Lorelei could no longer restrain herself. Without warning, she embraced Jon in much the same manner as Kaiser, only this time, Jon was better prepared. Continuing to smile warmly, Jon gently wrapped his arms around her, relishing the moment. The others looked on with interest, but neither of the two paid them any mind.

After a few moments, they separated. Their eyes, however, remained locked for a few moments longer, Jon's single blue eye holding perfect alignment with Lorelei's violet pair. Watching intently, Alex couldn't help but nod in approval.

The scene was then interrupted as a retainer entered the room, bowing toward Jon upon his approach. "Flint-*sama*," the retainer greeted dutifully. "My lord is ready to meet you and your company."

———————————————— ————————————————

Seconds later, Jon found himself moving as the retainer guided him and the others toward the castle's throne room. Again it took some effort on his part to function in his condition, but the retainer was courteous enough not to walk too fast. And though Davis, somehow noticing Jon's plight, offered to support him, Jon appreciatively refused the help. If he were to stand before the Blue Dragon Lord, it would be on his own strength.

As they reached the massive ornate double doors at the center of the castle, the doors opened. Within the chamber, Lord Fuma remained seated upon his throne while Kaguya, now dressed in her original black and blue *kimono*, sat in the *seiza* position below and toward the right. Both watched as the group entered, with Jon and Alex each stepping ahead onto the center platform. Once in the center, both brothers bowed to the Lord.

For a time, only silence reigned in the throne room as Lord Fuma continued to gaze over the two brothers, who remained still under his regard. Neither of them knew what the Blue Dragon Lord planned to do with them, but both knew they would soon get their answer. As such, it was a struggle to remain taciturn.

Then, after a prolonged moment, the head of the Blue Dragon Clan began to speak. "Not very long ago," Lord Fuma stated. "You both came before me as you have now, with but a newly captured starship and the beginnings of a crew at your disposal."

Continuing to observe, Lord Fuma nodded as the brothers remained as they were. "At that time, you had claimed yourselves as commoners, wishing to make an arrangement based upon mutual benefit instead of equal standing."

Upon that, the Blue Dragon Lord stood up. "Today, I see those two same men standing before me once again," he spoke as he gracefully stepped down from his throne toward the center platform. "But no longer do I see them as commoners."

He then came before the brothers, who remained at attention and gazing ahead. "Now," he said. "Now I see men of worth. Men who have gained honor for themselves, and for the name Flint," he continued. "Men, who are worthy of taking up their mother's banner."

The beginnings of a smile formed on the brothers' faces.

"Men, who are worthy heirs to the Gold Dragon," Lord Fuma proclaimed, before stepping back, pride as brilliant in his eyes as daylight. "Men, who I am honored to have taken under my tutelage."

Though they continued gazing forward, that same pride shone in the brothers' eyes, alongside Kaguya's. Again, Lord Fuma nodded in approval.

"And for that, you may hold yourselves up with pride," he said. "For you are indeed the sons of my most worthy adversary."

Continuing to observe as the brothers struggled to keep themselves from breaking formality, Lord Fuma, at last, gave the appropriate command. "Be at ease, my students," he commanded, to which the brothers eagerly complied. "For you have no enemies before you..."

Jon smiled as he and Alex looked toward their teacher. *For now,* he thought, completing Lord Fuma's sentence.

"Your words do us further honor *sensei*," Jon replied, bowing slightly. "We would not be where we are today without your guidance."

"Nor your timely assistance," Alex added with utmost sincerity.

A small smile formed on Lord Fuma's own lips. "There will be some fallout between the Blue Dragon and the Empire over this," he mused, looking off to the side somewhat. "But that is only a minor price to pay."

"Perhaps," Jon interjected, recalling that Drake had acted on his own throughout. Knowing that Lord Fuma understood this, he saw no reason to bring it up. Instead, he focused on the matters at hand. "That being said, I'm afraid we are in need of your services again."

Lord Fuma smirked knowingly. "To rebuild your ship and crew, yes?"

"Indeed," Jon agreed, before glancing over toward Kaguya. "We also wish to retain the services of your daughter."

Hearing this, Kaguya rose to her feet and moved to her father's side. And though she remained formal, the younger Fuma could not keep the exuberance out of her own gaze. "I would be most honored," she answered bowing.

Lord Fuma could only nod his acceptance. He would have stipulated it in any case, as he had before. "We will grant safe haven for you and your remaining crew, as well as a station to gather replacements," he announced. "Your ship, however, I'm afraid I cannot help you with."

Jon suddenly felt a shadow move over him. "Why?" he could only ask, doing all he could to keep his rising emotions in check. Was the worst of his fears realized? Was the *Black Sun* indeed unsalvageable?

This only amused Lord Fuma, who was more than able to pick up on the elder Flint's emotions. "Rather than explain," he said, betraying no emotion of his own. "Perhaps, you would like to see for yourself."

---

Now sitting within Lord Fuma's personal shuttle alongside the others, Jon watched silently as the craft moved toward the starport. For the life of him, he could not remember the last time he had been so nervous, feeling such unease. Nor could he remember the last time he had experienced such an attachment with something that possessed no sentience of its own.

Sighing inwardly, Jon supposed it was only natural. Before, the *Black Sun*, when she was still the *U-7501*, had just been a ship; a means through which he and his brother could at last reach the stars on their own terms. Now, however, she was more than that. No longer was she just an object or a presence, nor even a means to an end. Now she was as much a member of Jon's immediate circle as the eleven beside him. She was their ship, their home, their comrade. And though he could continue on without her, he did not wish to see her life cut short any more than the *Morgan le Fay*'s before her.

Glancing toward the side, he began reading his officers' own faces. Like his, they each held uncertainty in their own unique ways. Even Braun, the one man Jon would have expected to see knowledgeable of the *Black Sun*'s current condition, seemed far more passive than usual. This in itself answered Jon's other unspoken question, regarding whether or not Braun had worked to repair the *Black Sun* over the last few days. Apparently, he hadn't and was as much in the dark about her present state as the rest. Not that Jon didn't understand why, of course.

And then there was Lorelei, who obviously knew what Lord Fuma was alluding to *and* was in tune with the ship, but she too retained her silence. As she was far better at concealing emotions than most, she seemed utterly docile. In spite of his inquisitive eye, Jon could not tell what she was feeling or thinking. For the first time in his life he wished he were a psion. The anticipation was nerve-racking; he would almost rather fight Drake again than have to continue waiting for an answer that he was unsure he wanted to know.

Jon knew he would not gain anything by being anxious. He closed his eye and focused, attempting to relax. Whatever the answer was, whatever state the *Black Sun* was in, he would accept it. And though he had no idea where he would gain another ship, if the worst turned out to be true, he would find a way. With his crew beside him, he would even take a broken down freighter as his new command.

Opening his eye, he saw the starport berthing *Black Sun* was now in view. Taking a breath, Jon waited for a few more seconds before the designated port was reached. However, the view was obstructed by the *Ryujin*, which was also in dock. Only when the shuttle had passed over Lord Fuma's flagship could he gain a clearer line of sight. Jon felt those seconds pass by as if they were hours, as did those beside him, again sans Lorelei.

Slowly the shuttle traveled over the *Ryujin*, just moving above her massive bow cannons. A few moments later, they passed over the last of the *Ryujin*'s hull and cleared the port. Taking another breath, Jon and those around him prepared themselves. Now was the time.

There, as Jon and the others looked on, was the *Black Sun*, in its beaten and battered form.

At first, Jon started to ask Fuma why none of his dock workers were around her, at least looking her over and evaluating the damage. But then, he noticed something in particular. Though he had to strain his eye to see it, he spotted, in one of her breaches, energy being transmitted to the damaged areas. That could have only meant one thing, much to Jon's inward relief. Her Moebius System was online and working.

"I had ordered my crews to look over her," Lord Fuma commented. "To at least fix whatever could be fixed and grant some ease to Professor Braun."

Only then did Lord Fuma turn, a warm smile now prominent. "However, before they could do anything," he explained. "We discovered that the *Black Sun* was already healing."

"Impossible!" Davis let out in confusion. "The Moebius System was knocked offline during the battle and couldn't be repaired!"

Lord Fuma only shook his head. "Apparently it has reemerged," he said, continuing to gaze over the ship. "And now, just like all of you, she is recovering."

Jon looked toward Lorelei, who merely smiled in turn. "Don't look at me," she exclaimed. "I had *nothing* to do with this."

"But you knew," Jon pointed out.

The psion merely shrugged. "I had an inclination," she admitted. "But in agreement with Lord Fuma, I found it more fitting that all of you see for yourself."

She then nodded forward as the shuttle turned around for another pass. This time, it passed by the bridge tower, which had seemingly fully regenerated. The completely unblemished Golden Roger shone brightly upon its side.

"My god she is beautiful," Alex breathed as he looked over his mother's former sigil.

"Yes," Kaguya, who was sitting beside him, agreed. "A worthy vessel to bear the mark of Morganna Flint."

A smile formed on Braun's own lips. "Going by the damage and the rate of repair," he spoke without taking his visor off the golden roger. "I estimate that she will be fully healed by the time we gain our new crew."

"Which in itself begs the question," Davis suddenly spoke up. "When all is said and done, where do we go from here?"

That was a good question, Jon admitted. As far as he knew, he had fulfilled his primary duty to Lorelei, and she never stipulated for anything afterward. In turn, there was a whole galaxy out there, one that only now did Jon and company hold a proper means to transverse. An entire universe lay before him and within, great wealth and prosperity.

Ultimately, however, Jon decided that could wait for another time. For now, he chose to enjoy the peace of the moment. All while the Golden Roger continued to shine brilliantly against Ryugu's setting sun.

# Chapter XLII: Revelation

## Ryugu Castle Gardens
## Kyoto, Ryugu

The wind was slowly starting to pick up. Being a largely oceanic world, Ryugu generally retained colder climates than most other planets of its type, and it helped even less that it was a relatively windy day. However, Jon had little trouble enduring, he merely materialized his great coat over his shoulders. And so he continued his walk through the castle gardens, his eye taking in the beauty of the surrounding landscape.

Now in the middle of the summer season, Ryugu's native plants and wildlife appeared in full splendor. The surrounding cherry trees were in bloom, their pink blossoms seemingly as plentiful as the stars, while various flowers lined the path that Jon was currently walking upon. The wind, despite its slightly adverse effect upon his body, only added to the serenity around him, picking up several of the sakura petals, swirling them in the air before scattering them across the path. All while Ryugu's blue sun slowly began to set over the eastern horizon.

If nothing else, Jon appreciated the calming ease of the moment. It was what he needed now; between the battle itself and the sheer chaos that followed it, he needed a moment, even a brief one, to feel at ease. Yes the *Black Sun* was healing, such that actual repair work was utterly unnecessary, but that was only one part of the equation. Weapons still needed replenishing, equipment needed replacing, new Corsairs needed to be brought in and, above all else, new crewmen still had to be found and recruited. Much had been done over the past two months, and yet there was still more work ahead. To say nothing of the fact that most of the present crew, Jon included, were still recuperating.

Thus, Jon was where he was now, enjoying the present calmness and its accompanying beauty. It probably wouldn't last; something was bound to turn up that required his personal attention. But it would be enough for him all the same, thereby allowing him to return to his assignments with a refreshed state of mind.

As he continued down the path, Jon decided to stop momentarily beside one of the cherry trees. There, he took off the glove of his right hand and, slowly and gently, touched his scarred finger against one of the flower petals. Compared to the leather of his glove or the metallic or wooden surfaces that he was used to touching, the organic and frail petal almost felt foreign to him. That, of course, only emphasized the sensation.

He realized he was no longer alone, feeling an all too familiar presence now standing behind him.

"I hope I'm not intruding," Lord Fuma spoke.

Jon withdrew his hand. "Not at all *sensei*," he replied as he replaced his glove. "I just needed some fresh air."

"Quite understandable," Lord Fuma agreed. "That is, after all, one of the gardens' purposes."

The two started to walk together. "My engineers tell me that the *Black Sun* will be fully regenerated in approximately three more weeks," Lord Fuma stated. "Is that the estimate Professor Braun has given you?"

"More or less. We should be fully crewed and stocked by then as well," Jon then flashed a small grin. "We haven't had any shortage of applicants."

Lord Fuma matched that grin with his own. If nothing else, the Second Battle of Ephesus had solidified the Flint Pirates' status and reputation throughout the galaxy. Possibly even more than Jon and Alex's surnames.

"Yes," Lord Fuma concurred. "Even now, I continue to hear about your exploits. Though I'm afraid, some of them are rather dubious."

"Oh?" Jon let out in wonder. "Like what?"

Lord Fuma smiled in turn. "You are a fine warrior Jonathan," he answered. "But I find it hard to believe that you fought Admiral Drake with only your bare hands. Or that you defeated him by choking him with said 'bloodied hands'."

Jon actually laughed. "Well," he said, raising his hand and causing a small wave of darkness to flicker between his fingers. "There were a few points."

"I'm sure," Lord Fuma replied. "And then there's the role the Blue Dragon supposedly played..."

"Let me guess," Jon rejoined. "You only showed up *after* we had the Imperials essentially beaten."

Lord Fuma nodded. "Some even claim we never appeared at all," he said, smiling at the irony. "That you fought and defeated the entire Imperial Thirteenth Fleet without aid of any kind."

This time Jon scoffed at the idea. "I only wish we were that strong. Not that I would ever turn away your support, *sensei*..."

"Not at all," Lord Fuma waved the notion away. "It is only natural for you to stand upon your own feet and rely upon your own strength. Just as your mother had done."

Jon nodded in agreement. For all of her triumphs and failings, one thing no one could deny was that Morganna Flint had begun with virtually nothing and yet formed both the original Flint Pirates and the Gold Dragon Clan through sheer strength and perseverance. The elements that legends were made out of.

That's when another thought occurred to the elder Flint. "Tell me one thing," he asked, somewhat hesitant. "I sent you that message a full day before the battle began."

He then glanced inquisitively toward his teacher. "Yet considering the amount of time you would need to organize your fleet and then the time needed for arc speed, it would have taken you nearly half that amount to reach Ephesus."

Lord Fuma held no forward emotion toward this inquiry. "Yes," he acknowledged, already knowing what his student was alluding to.

Pushing back his hesitation, Jon came out and stated, "You purposely delayed. Didn't you."

The Blue Dragon Lord paused before answering. "It was necessary," he explained. "I needed to see just how you would fare against your enemy, as well as how strong you and those that followed you had truly become."

Lord Fuma then glanced toward Jon with similar inquisition. "Does this anger you?"

Jon shook his head. "Of course not," he replied with understanding. "It was our battle to fight."

The Lord nodded again, this time with satisfaction. Indeed, his older student had grown into a strong man, though he was not wholly grown yet. In time, additional experience and wisdom would see to that.

The pair were quiet for a few moments as they both crossed a wooden bridge over a flowing stream. It was only when they were midway across did Lord Fuma speak again. "My raiders have covered the entirety of the temple since the battle," he spoke in near monotone. "Yet they never recovered the inactive Berith."

Jon sniffed in response. It was obvious what that meant. "I wouldn't put it past him," he answered. "He probably teleported back to his ship before the Imps retreated."

He then laughed a little. "Apparently, I've made one more enemy *sensei*."

Lord Fuma laughed as well, though with a bit more force than Jon had done. "You've done much more than that, my student. Drake and the Empire with him are but a fraction of the whole."

At that, Lord Fuma stopped and glanced up toward the sky, toward the stars that were beginning to emerge. "By now the entire galaxy has heard of Ephesus and are acting accordingly," he explained. "Your enemies will be stronger and far more numerous, and will include any from the remaining twelve Powers to the other three Clans themselves."

He turned to face Jon directly. "In turn, there will be additional battles to fight, alongside additional adversaries to defeat and additional treasures to take," he said. "Just as there are events in the making that you or even I have yet to realize."

The Lord then glanced back up to the sky. "Whereas the first battle was your mother's last step, Jonathan, this one is but your first, toward a larger and greater world."

Crossing his arms, Jon also gazed up to the sky. Slowly, the stars became more and more abundant as day turned to night, alluding to the enormous galaxy that laid beyond. A galaxy full of treasure and adventure. A galaxy for the taking.

"The first step..." Jon stated with solemnity, inwardly wondering if his mother's spirit were really out there, amongst those stars. "To the resurrection of the Gold Dragon."

A full smile now emerging across his lips, Lord Fuma once more nodded in acknowledgment.

# Maruyama Park
# Kyoto, Ryugu

Letting out a sigh of contentment, Alex continued to move down the street, observing the various booths on either side. Today was *Tanabata*, or the Star Festival, a holiday whose origins hailed back to Ancient Terra. Long ago it was claimed that, once every year upon the seventh day of the seventh month of the Terran calendar, the ancient deities Orihime and Hikoboshi, normally separated by the galaxy at large, would come together and meet within the night sky. While such a tale had long been relegated to mythology, its celebration had remained in practice on Terra all the way to the End Wars and had since been adopted, like many other ancient customs, by the Blue Dragon upon its founding.

And so, for the last few hundred years, the Blue Dragon's citizenry, from Ryugu to Naha, would come together upon this very day to celebrate the lovers' reunion. Cities were covered in lights and colored streamers, while outdoor stalls were constructed to provide food and entertainment. Men and women wandered the streets in *yukatas*, music in all forms and fashions was played across the street corners, and overall jubilee was abundant throughout the air. And, once nighttime had properly emerged, fireworks would soon be exploding within the darkened sky. Overall, Alex could not think of any other place he wished to be. Especially with the woman beside him.

Dressed in a dark blue *yukata* adorned with miniature golden stars, Kaguya looked as radiant as ever. Though she was and would always be beautiful, there was something about her being in non-combat garb that made Alex feel even more drawn to and enamored by her. It was as though she had set aside her warrior princess self, such that she didn't even have her ninjato with her, and was now focusing, though somewhat awkwardly, on being Kaguya the woman. The effect was far from being unique to the Flint pirate; several eyes watched as she strolled down the street, all drawn to her just like Alex. The only difference was she gave no heed to any of them, just as none of their numbers dared make a move on Lord Fuma's daughter. Alex's responding glare only dissuaded them further.

Eventually, the pair came up to a booth that was grilling yakitori. Alex smirked, as a certain memory came to mind.

"Don't tell Apache," he said as he withdrew two aurics, earning a small smile from Kaguya as she too recalled the moment. Smiling in gratitude, the cook immediately produced two yakitori sticks for the pair, with Kaguya reaching with her left arm to take hers. And though she attempted to mask it, Alex was perceptive enough to see her wince as she grasped the stick.

The pair soon began walking again, gradually moving through the crowd, eventually making their way to a nearby bench. "You just can't beat these when they're fresh," Alex mumbled as he took a bite of his snack. "Who knew that a couple thousand years into the future, chickens would not only still be around, but still taste so good?"

Kaguya paused at the question. "Technically this isn't made of Terran chicken," she pointed out.

Alex shook his head. "A chicken's a chicken, no matter what planet it's indigenous too," he argued before taking another bite. "Just as salt is a universal compound, chickens..."

He trailed off as he noticed Kaguya staring up into the sky, a pale blue light momentarily flaring across her features. Alex smiled. He turned to look. The fireworks had at last started.

"Been a while since we saw one of these," he whispered as the lights continued to flicker. "Not since Jon and I were training here."

He glanced back at Kaguya, who despite gazing at the fireworks, was still listening. "You remember that?" he asked. "When we sought your father out to train us in mastering our Devilblades..."

"I do," Kaguya nodded. "Just as I recall you being clumsy about it in the beginning."

Feeling a tinge of embarrassment at the memory, Alex rubbed the back of his head. "Back then I was more of a thinker and less of a fighter I admit. Hadn't been in as many battles as my brother."

"I could see that yes," Kaguya replied, before casually taking another bite of her yakitori.

Alex couldn't help but feel unsure. Was she actually chastising him? "Well, at least I got better," he exclaimed. "Thanks to you and your father."

"Indeed, though it took a fair amount of effort to do so."

"If by 'effort' you mean 'beating into me', then yes, I suppose it did," Alex admonished, inwardly wincing at the memories. Somehow, and rather suspiciously, his training entailed more sparring and less verbal explanation. "And don't say you didn't enjoy it."

Alex wasn't sure, but he thought he saw Kaguya flash a miniscule grin. "It was necessary," she responded as if it were obvious. "The best method for physical training is through the body, not the eyes or ears."

"Right," Alex retorted, not entirely believing. "And I'm sure the broken bones I continually received were also 'necessary'."

"They didn't kill you," Kaguya pointed out. "And they became less frequent as time went on."

"Because I was getting better?" Alex asked.

"Because I learned the concept of 'proper restraint'," Kaguya replied, then taking another bite.

"Har har," Alex let out, snagging a big bite from his treat. Despite the slights, he found himself smiling again.

The fireworks continued to light up the sky as a moment of silence moved between the two. Eventually, however, without looking away from the flashing lights, Kaguya began to speak again. "We have come a long way," she said softly. "Haven't we?"

Alex nodded. "And we still have a long way to go," he answered. "Though God only knows where our destination will be."

Kaguya looked down for a moment, another small measure of silence intertwining. "I..." she started. "I don't want to know it."

This time Alex looked back at her. Kaguya continued. "I'm..." she nearly stumbled over her words. "I'm afraid of what we may find there."

Hearing her voice betray the emotions her face would not, Alex inwardly sighed. "We've gone over this before Kaguya," he spoke reassuringly. "Your father is wise to have you monitor us, no matter what it may entail."

He took her hand in his, "And you're only serving your clan's interests by doing so."

Solemnly, Kaguya nodded. "I know," she replied, just as a specific memory came to mind. "And yet..."

*Silence reigned throughout Kaguya's quarters as soon as the hologram of her father had dissipated. It had been a terse conversation, to say the least; Jon, who was still present, had been direct and formal, not once speaking of her actual role aboard the* Black Sun *nor insinuating her father's subterfuge, while the Blue Dragon Lord had remained cold but diplomatic. Jon had simply given his request, that the Blue Dragon support the* Black Sun *in the coming battle over Ephesus, and Lord Fuma, after listening to the elder Flint's request and overall plan for the battle, acquiesced. The meeting had concluded soon after that accord.*

*Or at least, Kaguya wished it had been that simple and straightforward. Though she appeared as stoic as always, she could not remember the last time she had ever felt such unease, if not outright terror. Nor did she remember the last time she had seen Jon so vehement, even if he didn't show it outwardly. Only his eye betrayed the emotion, and Kaguya, in clear spite of all she was and how powerful she had become, could not bring herself to look straight into it.*

*With the business at hand taken care of, Jon rose back up from his kneeling position and retook his greatcoat, then slowly moved toward the door. As he did this, Kaguya opened her mouth to speak again, but she felt the words die in her throat. What could she say to him now? What was there to be said? Her mind raced to come up with an answer while anxiety began to overwhelm her, yet she could not find anything. However, she knew she had to say something before he exited that door. Before their bond was entirely severed. Before a part of her family was lost forever.*

*With one last sway of his greatcoat, Jon reached the door. It was only then that Kaguya managed to speak. "Am I..." she said in a near whisper, fear emanating from her voice like light from a sun. However, it was enough, as Jon stopped in his movement but did not turn around.*

*She trembled, trying to control herself. It was one of the few times in her life that she felt no control whatsoever; even whatever fear she may have held in battle paled to what she felt now. "Am I..." she spoke again, tears now threatening to fall from her eyes.*

*Then, mustering up enough strength, she asked the question. "Am I... your enemy?" she forced it out, straining out the words as if they had refused to be uttered. And though she had succeeded, she felt no relief whatsoever. Tears were now gleaming from her eyes while her body quivered with near terror. She almost did not want to hear the answer, lest it really was the worst of her fears.*

*For his part, Jon stood where he was for several minutes, continuing to face the door. He had obviously picked up on her fear; her voice alone conveyed it well enough, and the elder Flint's senses were as sharp at picking up emotion as her own. And yet for a time, he said nothing, seemingly standing by as if he were actually considering his reply. A part of Kaguya feared that he was doing so to keep his own emotions in check, lest he really did attempt to deal with her as a betrayer and a threat.*

*Then, after several minutes had passed, Jon at last answered. "No," he said simply, causing Kaguya to look up in near shock. "No, you are not."*

*All at once, Kaguya felt her shaking cease, all the while light slowly began to return to her world. That was when Jon continued. "At least," he said, a tinge of his original fervor coming through his voice. "Not now."*

*With that, the door opened, and Jon exited her sanctum. Only then did Kaguya close her eyes and let the tears, now filled with relief, flow.*

Even in the present, Kaguya felt herself tremble at the memory, almost as if she were cold. "I should never have joined your crew," she spoke, the fear beginning to reach her again. "As long as I'm aboard the *Black Sun*, your lives are in danger."

"I got news for you, Kaguya," Alex retorted. "Our lives have *always* been in danger."

This naturally did nothing to assuage Kaguya, who looked back to him hesitantly. "I am a scion of the Blue Dragon," she exclaimed. "And my father is its Lord."

This time Alex remained silent, allowing Kaguya to look away again. "His orders are absolute," she let out. "And I am duty bound to follow them, no matter what they may demand of me."

She looked down, feeling the tears well up again. Only the knowledge that she was in public view kept her from shedding them. "I..." she breathed, feeling herself shudder. "I really am a *hebi*, poised to strike..."

So badly did she tremble that she barely noticed Alex move closer to her. Once there, he gently wrapped his arm around her, pulling her closer to him, then reaching up and slowly guided her face to look at him. There, she found herself gazing into his deep brown eyes, which regarded her softly and with visible reassurance.

"Listen," Alex spoke as softly as his gaze. "I don't know what the future holds for us either. Nor do I know how your father will perceive us in that future..."

She opened her mouth to speak, but he narrowed his gaze, indirectly asking her to let him continue. She complied. "What I do know, however, is that, if such a time does come where your father gives you that command, you will make the right decision."

He slowly wiped an errant tear from her eye. "You are a scion of the Blue Dragon, yes, but you're also a Flint Pirate, and you know that Jon and I will *never* willingly go against your father or your clan."

Slowly, Alex could see the anxiety begin to fade from Kaguya's eyes. "For that, I entrust you with my life and the life of my brother. You are the blade that has protected us, regardless of your original purpose."

Alex took her hand in his. "But for now, please, don't let it haunt you," he said, a reassuring smile forming across his lips. "For the moment, we are in your father's good graces, and there is no blood to be shed."

Kaguya's eyes shone with newfound peace toward his words. For Alex, it was the most beautiful thing he had ever seen. "So let's just relax, and enjoy the rest of our time before the big meeting..."

"I told you I was sorry!" a new but quite familiar voice shouted, causing both Alex and Kaguya to look up. There, in the distance, they both saw Anna marching through the crowd with a distraught Davis desperately trying to keep up with her. "I really thought you were coming onto me!"

"That will be the day!" Anna snarled back as she made her way through the onlookers. "You ever try that again, I'll cut that hand off and feed it to the first carnivore I find!"

Upon closer inspection, Alex and Kaguya could see that a large bruise now adorned Davis' cheek. "I tried to be a gentleman about it!" he countered. "I mean, I could have always gone for your chest!"

"Goddamned pervert!" Anna shouted back as she moved deeper into the crowd, Davis continuing to follow her at best speed. The two only went on arguing, even as their voices began to fade.

Blinking at the scene, Alex couldn't help but actually laugh a little. "Well," he said. "That was completely random." *Not to mention mood spoiling.*

Kaguya actually laughed as well, much to Alex's relief. "At least things really are back to normal amongst our number," she pointed out.

Alex nodded. "Yeah, I guess so," he muttered, before taking another bite of his yakitori. "Though whether that's a good thing or a bad thing is anyone's guess."

## Ryugu Castle
## Kyoto, Ryugu

Within the confines of his temporary quarters, Barbarossa slowly gazed over the book that he had just received. Though it had apparently taken some effort, his captain had indeed kept his promise and given him a copy of Terra's holiest scripture. At first glance, Barbarossa found it rather plain looking compared to the Tevret; a simple book with black covers and an equally simple golden cross embossed on the front. Barbarossa supposed his captain could only gain him a basic copy, but for some reason, he found the humble and simple design fitting for the scripture. Just as many of its protagonists, or so Barbarossa had heard off and on, had held humble and simple lives before being called upon by their God for greater purpose.

*Perhaps we are not so different after all,* Barbarossa thought as he ran a finger, claw retracted, over the cover, taking in the feeling of the smoothened leather. Though far less elaborate and ornate than the standard Tevret, he could still feel a strange power emanating from this simple book. A power that, for the last few thousand years, even during Terra's Thousand Year Darkness, had enraptured and captivated any and all who gazed upon it, all but driving them to open it, to read and consider its words. A power that Barbarossa, for all of his disdain toward Terrans, could actually find himself further intrigued by.

However, it appeared now was not his time. Just as he was about to open the book and read its first verse, he felt an all too familiar presence enter his domain.

"You're the second to enter my room unannounced," he spoke without turning his head. "And the second to do so without any fear or apprehension."

"I take that as a compliment," Lorelei replied as she stood behind the Leo, her arms crossed behind her back. "Though unlike the first, I'm afraid I hold little knowledge of that book, and so cannot give an appropriate quote or reference."

"Heh," Barbarossa let out as he rose to his feet, placing the book on a nearby shelf. He then turned to face the psion. "What can I do for you, Miss Lorelei?" he said, immediately moving to the business at hand. "I doubt you came here to discuss theology."

Lorelei smiled in her usual manner. "Actually, I came here for something of the opposite," she said, nodding toward the book. "In your faith, is there an antagonist against Aslan's will? Specifically, an equivalent of the Terran Devil?"

Though not knowing what Lorelei was alluding to, Barbarossa answered anyway. "Dajjal," he said. "He was once the most trusted of Aslan's malaks, or 'angels', but disobeyed the order to give glory unto Aslan's creation, and so was cast from the heavens to become the first of the iblis, or 'devils'. Since then, he has worked to corrupt all life away from Aslan's light."

"I see," Lorelei replied. "And I suppose he grants power to those he corrupts?"

"As well as damnation," Barbarossa answered, feeling unease toward his explanation. "What interest could you have in this?"

Lorelei smiled in turn. "I am merely curious," she explained. "If Dajjal came before you now and offered you the power to slay your enemies, what would you do?"

Barbarossa opened his maw to answer, but Lorelei spoke first. "Would you turn him away from the beginning?" she inquired. "Or..."

She then held her right arm out. "Would you be the least bit interested?"

It was then Barbarossa saw what she was holding. A dull grey stone with a curious sigil: that of three lines intersecting at the top to form a triangle, tipped with circles at each end, while two crosses extended from either side.

"Is that...?" Barbarossa let out, realizing all too well what that stone really was.

"Indeed," Lorelei confirmed, quite pleased at what she saw. "And I want you to have it."

For the life of him, Barbarossa did not know how to react. He had heard many things about that stone and the power it contained; power that could be utilized, but at significant personal cost if utilized incorrectly. And then there was the purpose of his having it.

"Why?" he questioned. "Surely, you know what I would do with *that*."

"Take the *Black Sun* for yourself?" Lorelei queried. "Yes, I am quite aware of your agenda, and that you hold to it even now."

"Just as I am aware of your attachment to Captain Flint," Barbarossa retorted. "And yet you are giving me the means to destroy him, at last."

"So it appears," Lorelei acknowledged.

This did little to assuage Barbarossa of his doubts. "So again I ask, why?"

Lorelei smiled, knowingly this time. "Because, as I will soon explain in the next..." she looked at her wristcom. "Thirty-seven minutes and twenty-one seconds, I fear that in the future, we will need all the power we can muster."

A hint of seriousness entered her voice. "Though we have faced and triumphed over much already, there are forces out there that we may yet

293

go against. Forces that, at this time, we are entirely unprepared for."

She again held out the stone. "This by itself will not be enough," she explained. "But it will give us a greater edge, all the same, adding to the four that we already hold."

Barbarossa could barely contain his shock. *Four?* he thought, completely taken back. The captain and first officer were obviously amongst that number, but who were the other two? And why hadn't they utilized their respective powers to this point?

As he considered, Lorelei reached out and grasped his right hand. "It is said that the blade chooses its wielder," she clarified as she placed the stone into Barbarossa's open palm. "And though even I cannot explain how this process works, nor can I determine if this blade will find you worthy..."

She then had Barbarossa's massive fingers close around the stone. "I believe, in spite of your faith and adherence, you are the best candidate to utilize the Devil's power," she said. "The power of Dajjal."

Swallowing, Barbarossa held the stone in front of his eyes, gazing upon its sigil. Like the book he had just grasped, he sensed great power in it, but of an entirely different make. Whereas the book's power was enrapturing and captivating, this power was pure temptation. Ever so subtly he could feel it pulling on him, drawing him into itself while imploring him to speak the arcane words of its awakening. To bring its power unto himself, to utilize against all that stood before him.

Wisely, or so Barbarossa believed, he ignored the temptation and lowered the stone from his sight. "If we are indeed in need of this power," he stated. "Then why haven't you taken it for yourself?"

Again Lorelei smiled knowingly. "Because," she responded as she held up her hand, "I already have power of my own..." with that, Barbarossa could just pick up a glint of magenta flicker between her fingers. "And as I said, I am curious."

She then took a step closer to Barbarossa, who easily dwarfed her. "Just how would a holy warrior such as yourself utilize Dajjal's power?" she asked. "Would you use it for your own gain, as one would expect of his 'corrupted'?"

She then reached her hand out. "Or," she said, brushing a finger against the Star of Aslan upon the Leo's robes. "Would you use it for the light?"

Barbarossa attempted to reply, but he found himself unable to speak. He felt he needed water, yet he was not thirsty. Seeing this, Lorelei simply flashed another smile before backing away. "You don't need to answer now," she declared as she moved toward the door. "Simply consider what I have said while keeping your mind open to possibility."

She smirked as she came up to the door. "That is, after all, one of your primary strengths," she pointed out, before sliding the door open and closing it upon her exit.

Now alone in his domain once more, Barbarossa again gazed at the stone. Again, like the book, it seemed so simple, so unassuming.

And yet under that appearance, he could still feel that darkness ebbing at his soul, attempting to draw him into its grasp...

———————————

Sitting in Lord Fuma's private meeting chamber within Ryugu Castle alongside the rest of the *Black Sun*'s officers, Jon had to admit that he was uncomfortable. Uncomfortable enough that he hadn't touched the plate of food which an attendant had placed in front of him, nor had he taken a drink from his sake cup. Instead, he continued to wait with the rest of his officers for the lady of the hour to appear, as she had during the *Black Sun*'s maiden voyage, to explain her purpose.

And that was precisely what this meeting was to be about, though upon a different subject. Tonight, after over two months of continuous research, Lorelei was to explain exactly what they had found and fought over on Ephesus. The unveiling of Arcadia's true nature and purpose.

With this in mind, the captain silently mused over the events not too long ago. For the briefest moment, after he had defeated Drake, he had seen it; a great light that, seemingly infinite in power, shone over the entirety of the temple until all laid within its field. After that, however, Jon didn't remember anything, as the next thing he realized was he was back on Ryugu. And though he had conversed with others about it, none of them seemed to have a clear account of the event. As far as they could tell him, that great light had shown from the temple and seemingly spread across the entirety of Ephesus and the surrounding space, until at last dying out moments later. After that, details were vague, even amongst the Blue Dragons.

Since then, Lorelei had been back and forth from Ryugu to Ephesus with a Blue Dragon expeditionary force, researching the temple and all the hieroglyphs within for data about her discovery. From what Jon had learned from her in between, Arcadia, or at least that light, was still active on the planet, but even she hadn't been able to glean much information from it at the time. Now, however, she seemed to have gathered enough data, such that she could at last share her findings with the rest of the *Black Sun*'s officer staff.

For his part, Jon almost didn't want to be there for it. After having spent so much energy on tracking down and awakening Arcadia from its long slumber, he wasn't sure he wanted to know what it was. Part of it, he supposed, was whether or not it had been worth it. Much blood, including his and his brother's, had been shed on the hunt for it and even more had been shed fighting for their claim to it. All that in mind, Jon didn't want to be told that none of it was worth it; that the greatest mystery in the galaxy was nothing more than a fool's errand.

And that wasn't even the worst. Now that Arcadia was at last awakened, what would they do with Lorelei herself? At first, Jon didn't even know why he thought that, yet the thought forced its way through his defenses all the same. Obviously, the accord he had held with her was now complete, and he had his own goals to follow, but did that mean it was also the end of their partnership? In clear spite of himself, Jon found that idea disheartening. She was, after all, the *Black Sun*'s matron and scholar, just as she was one of the most fascinating beings he had ever encountered. How would the ship continue on without her? How...how would *he* continue on without her being aboard?

He shook his head at that last part, wondering where in the nine circles of hell that had even come from. As fascinating as she was, Lorelei was simply a client to him, and Jon had long since completed their contract. Where she went from there was of no concern of his. Especially when he had more pressing matters to attend to, such as the resurrection of the Gold Dragon and his mother's legacy.

And yet...and yet for the life of him, he could not keep himself from feeling unease toward the prospect. Once more in clear spite of himself and his best efforts, Jon could not imagine what life would be like without her being aboard the *Black Sun* and taking part in whatever ventures she sailed for. Such thinking went against what he was and how he saw the universe, and yet it was there all the same. For better or worse, the woman who fancied herself a siren was irreplaceable. As was her song, in itself something his crew had long grown accustomed to.

His thoughts ended abruptly as the door opened, revealing the woman of the hour for all to see.

"Thank you for coming," she greeted the gathered with a bit more formality than usual as she entered, coming to the head of the table. "I see that you're all well rested."

"No thanks to you," Davis quipped, which earned a hard jab in the gut from Kaiser, who was sitting next to him. Anna was notably on the opposite side of the table from the helmsman.

Lorelei simply gave off her usual smile as Davis hacked and coughed. "I suppose I warrant that," she acknowledged.

Already Jon felt something was off; her manner was far less chiding than usual. And as he glanced around the table, he saw that several of the others had noticed it as well.

Ignoring Davis' recoil from the pain, Lorelei continued. "Before we begin," she started off. "I want you to know that whatever you may think of me now or in the next few minutes..." she said, trailing off somewhat. "It's been an honor, having sailed with you."

She then looked toward Jon. "And having you at my side throughout this venture."

Jon cast a questioning glance to which Lorelei smiled succinctly in turn. She then produced a datachip and entered it into the viewscreen at the front of the room. "This is Ephesus in its present state," she said. "As recorded by a Blue Dragon satellite."

A second later, the viewscreen lit up, showing Ephesus from a distance. At first, it appeared in its natural state, but as the group looked closer, they saw that something was off; a tiny white beam of some kind was extending from the planet surface and reaching out into space. Seeing that they had all caught on, Lorelei tapped a key and had the image magnify several times.

Upon the last magnification, the group immediately recognized the image. The originally miniscule beam was now a pillar of white light, one emanating from the temple on the surface and extending a certain distance into space before seemingly cutting off. All with magnificent intensity, like an Ancient Terran lighthouse in the midst of a great storm.

"Arcadia," Alex summarized up front.

Much to everyone's surprise, however, Lorelei turned and flashed a more apologetic smile. "I'm afraid..." she said, hesitating a little. "That is not quite correct."

A cold swell moved over the table now as the occupants realized what she was alluding to. "What do you mean?" Boss spoke, a dangerous edge slowly entering her tone.

Taking a breath, indicating that she did not want to explain what she was about to, Lorelei went on. "This.  is not Arcadia."

*"WHAT!?"* Davis bellowed, rising anger dawning across his

expression. This time Kaiser did not reply to his actions, as he too was overwhelmed with shock. As were the others, some of them almost to the point of violence. Even Jon could barely contain his exasperation, but he allowed her to continue all the same.

Taking another breath, Lorelei went on. "As I explained to all of you in the beginning," she said, speaking more calmly now. "Arcadia was not only hidden but also locked away."

She then reached into her pocket and withdrew Aurea and Argentum, holding them up for all to see. "Originally I thought these were the keys to its unlocking, and in a way that's still true," she explained. "But I'm afraid that was a limited analysis."

Placing his head onto his clenched hands for a moment, Jon could only reel from the new information. Were the worst of his fears really true? Had it all been for nothing? Biting back such feelings, he looked up and nodded toward Lorelei. "Explain."

Nodding in understanding, Lorelei continued. "What you see now is not Arcadia itself. It is, however, connected to it in the most literal sense."

She gestured toward the image. "This is a special and highly elaborate Predecessor device. A device that draws upon and channels pure energy, energy not unlike that of the Devilblades, from the base of the temple and into deep space."

She then tapped another key, showing a starmap of the galaxy. Ephesus' position was highlighted with a red icon. "From the image alone, it appears this energy reaches a point within surrounding space and abruptly ends," she said. "However, through my analysis, I found that this was far from the truth."

She then tapped the key again, causing a blue icon to appear. "The energy, after seemingly reaching its end in realspace, is transferred into subspace and channeled further through a complex series of mediums," she nodded toward the blue icon, which then magnified toward open space. "Toward this specific point."

Again tapping the key, the viewscreen magnified around the blue icon, showing what appeared to be an utterly void area of space. Jon almost thought it was a black hole, as there weren't even stars around it. "A point that, in recognition of its true purpose," she said. "I have designated Porta Coeli."

Renewed shock crossed the table, though of a completely different nature. "Heaven's Gate," Alex translated, suddenly looking upon the open space with newfound perspective. "You mean..."

"Yes, Alex," Lorelei nodded, smiling as she saw the group catch on. "You are looking at an interspatial gateway in the making," she confirmed, her smile growing further. "A gateway that undoubtedly leads to the true article."

As the group took that information in, Lorelei explained further. "Ephesus was never the true resting place for Arcadia. Rather, it's something else entirely. It's but one of the keyholes to Arcadia's gate, one of I estimate to be seven in total."

The viewscreen flashed again, showing a new grid image. "Once all seven of these devices are engaged, their combined energy will flow into Porta Coeli and generate a complete gateway, which will then undoubtedly lead us to what we seek," she continued as the image showed seven beams of energy converging onto the single point, causing a full gateway to emerge. "Only at that time will Arcadia be open to us."

Much to everyone's surprise, it was Kaguya who spoke next. "Basically, while we still haven't found Arcadia..." she said in her usual tone of voice, expressing no forward emotion. "...we've taken a great step toward it."

Lorelei nodded. "The first true step that has been made since the galaxy was young. What we've done to this point was just the beginning."

She then shifted the screen back to Porta Coeli proper. "With the Ephesus device engaged, six more remain to be found. Six devices that are virtually anywhere in the galaxy, all with their own myriad dangers and obstacles to overcome..."

"As well as their own enemies to kill," Boss remarked as she casually lit her pipe.

"Keep in mind that we have our own objectives to fulfill," Alex spoke as well. "But I see no reason why we can't complete them along the way."

"Whoa whoa whoa!" Davis hollered in shock. "You guys aren't seriously considering this, are you!?"

"What's there to consider?" Anna remarked from her side. "The whole reason we came together in the first place was for this one venture. It's only proper that we see it through to the end."

Boss puffed out a cloud of smoke. "A lot of people died so that we could make that one step. To stop everything now would be to undermine their efforts."

"If anything, I'm only further intrigued by all of this," Braun remarked, his artificial hand stroking his chin in thought. "After all, if Arcadia had been so easy to find, then it really wouldn't have been anything worthwhile."

"Here here," Gran also commented. "The most valuable treasures are always the best hidden and locked away," she flashed a grin of her own. "And if Arcadia is such that it needs a full interspatial gateway in order to access..."

"Then it can only be the most valuable treasure in the galaxy," Barbarossa surmised, again much to everyone's surprise. "Even I cannot help but feel intrigued as well."

"This can't be happening," Davis stammered in agitation. "After all we went through just to get to Ephesus, you all want to go through that *again*!?"

"Have to admit," Alex smirked at the prospect, as did Kaguya beside him. "It was a helluva ride."

"We took on an entire fleet led by a mad genius Admiral for crying out loud!" Davis pointed out. "Who knows what we'll be facing later if we go through with this!"

Kaiser grinned; Gran translated. "Kaiser says 'that only makes it all the more interesting.'"

"Indeed," Barbarossa acknowledged, eliciting a fanged grin. "Especially if we get to face more Imperials along the way."

"To say nothing of the other Powers," Boss added.

"Or the other Clans," Kaguya pointed out, appearing strangely enamored by the idea.

"Heh," Apache said as he leaned back with a smirk of his own. "Just means more work and coin for me."

Hearing all this and literally picking up on their anticipation, Lorelei couldn't help but smile more genuinely. It had turned out better than she could have hoped. However, there was still one person at the table who wasn't say anything. "Well, Captain," she addressed Jon. "It appears I will be retaining your services for a little while longer."

With that, all attention turned toward the captain, who merely nodded. "It appears you will, Miss Lorelei," he casually answered. "I hold no issue to this."

Lorelei's smile deepened. "Well then," she declared as she sat down at the table and grasped her sake cup. "I once again look forward to our work together."

Nodding, Jon raised his cup. "To our new voyage," he pronounced, prompting the others, including the none too pleased Davis, to lift their cups. "And new discoveries."

"Cheers!" the group recited before taking their drinks.

# Chapter XLIII: Wheel in the Sky

## Aoba Izakaya
## Kyoto, Ryugu

At long last, it had come. The final night before the *Black Sun*'s renewed voyage. With that in mind, the near entirety of her revitalized crew was present. Throughout the various spaces, newcomer crewmen sat alongside original veterans, conversing among themselves in enthused tones. Among the latter, stories were repeatedly exchanged, with the newer crewmen bringing up their backgrounds and past experiences in an attempt to impress their more seasoned compatriots, while the veterans brought up their firsthand accounts of Ephesus, Kurzis and in some cases Rochelle. All the while food and alcohol were steadily consumed, with the Aoba's wait staff making a significant profit from supplying both.

At the head table, Jon quietly sat with the rest of the *Black Sun*'s officers – sans Barbarossa – and watched it all play out with interest. Compared to the other tables, the ten that sat beside him were far more at ease with one another, such that their collective presence was non-intrusive and the words they exchanged relaxed and casual. Jon had long noticed this, causing him to stifle a smile, once again in spite of himself. What had begun simply as a group of strangers, with but a common goal, had become something more.

"Sure are a lot of new faces," Anna observed as she looked over the other tables. "I can't believe we managed to gather them so fast."

"Tell me about it. I've been making off like a bandit since the first shuttle flew in." Davis replied as he glanced over to a nearby table, a grin eclipsing his lips as several women waved to him. "I got to admit, I like being a legend."

Nearly all eyes rolled at this. "More things change, more they stay the same," Alex muttered as he took a drink. More than a few of those newcomers had gone after him too, conveniently whenever Kaguya wasn't around, but unlike Davis, he wanted none of it. "I'm just glad we'll be able to launch on schedule."

"Yeah, about that," Boss spoke up, somewhat urgently. "Is it true that we haven't found the second planet yet?"

"Unfortunately," Lorelei replied as she took her own drink, savoring the flavor. "For some reason, the Circumgressus hasn't responded to my latest inquiries."

"Great," Davis answered with a dubious glance. "So we're going to launch on schedule, but without proper coordinates to follow."

"For the time being yes," Jon replied with assuredness. "Though, going by how the Circumgressus responded in the past, it will likely be a matter of time before the coordinates appear."

He then took another sip of his drink. "We'll simply concentrate on standard piracy until then."

"Nice," Davis nodded in approval. "About time we got back to traditional pillage and plunder."

"Got any leads on that, Captain?" Anna inquired, thrilled at the prospect of doing traditional pirate work again.

Jon nodded with a conspiratory smirk. "A few," he replied. "Convoys to intercept, planets to raid, government officials with valuables to acquire... We'll have more than enough work on our hands."

"Not to mention jobs to take from the Blue Dragon and any other interested parties," Alex chimed in.

Boss raised an eyebrow. "I thought you two were done with the 'pirates for hire' thing. That part of the reason you took the *Sun* was to get away from it."

"Before we could only take whatever assignments came by us," Jon explained. "Now, however, thanks in part to Ephesus, we have far more offerings."

"Which allows us to pick and choose more judiciously," Alex added. "Plus, having the best starship in the universe at your disposal provides a lot of leverage, especially regarding due payment."

"Heh, I suppose it would," Davis let out as he casually swirled his drink glass about, looking over the shifting liquid. "Funny how it all works together."

As Anna took a sip of her own drink, she caught something at the corner of her eye. One of the newer crewmen, one with an impressive array of scars and tattoos, had cast a side glance at the main table before turning back to whisper something to his cohorts. And though they were too far away to be heard, the topic of their conversation was quite evident.

Putting her drink back down, Anna made a frowning expression. "Unfortunately, you're right Alex," she agreed as she glared toward the opposite table. "The more things change, the more they stay the same."

The others quickly followed the line of her motion, again rolling their eyes at what they saw. It helped even less that they caught similar glances from other tables.

"Nothing that we can't handle," Alex spoke reassuringly. "After a raid or two, they'll come to realize their place."

"Sure," Davis spoke up with his usual cynicism. "But after that, there'll still be more like them, waiting and quite willing to take the ship out from under us."

"I think it's rather amusing personally," Gran chimed in, clearly listening in on the surrounding conversations in question. "They've all heard the stories, and yet they still somehow believe they have a chance."

"That they do," Lorelei confirmed as she scanned over the surrounding thoughts. "And with astonishing, if blind, self-assuredness I might add."

"Such is the way of the universe," Jon replied with a sigh. "As Alex said, they'll eventually learn their place. As will any who follow them."

"And the damage they'll make in the meantime?" Davis questioned. "I mean, all it takes is one renegade who knows what he's doing..."

"We'll manage it all the same," Jon stated with the same reassurance as his brother. "We've come this far with such beings in our line. And we'll continue further with them alongside."

Thought still doubtful, Davis nodded. "Whatever you say, Captain," he replied as he finished his drink, and then began pouring himself another. "Just another run around the cosmos."

"Amen," Alex stated as he passed his glass over, allowing Davis to refill it as well.

Smirking, Jon turned back to gazing at the tables around them. So many new faces, as Anna had alluded to; so many different species mingled together, all dressed in uniform black and gold. Just like the crew of the *Morgan le Fay* back in the day, a thought, among others, that only made his smirk deepen into a full smile.

Smiling himself as he saw his brother's expression, Alex couldn't help but ask. "What are you thinking about, bro?"

Smile deepening even further as he saw the rest of the table turn to him, Jon merely nodded. "Just how far we've come," he replied. "And yet how it feels like we're back to where we started."

It took a moment for the group to understand that, but they all came to realize it too. Anna was quick to summarize. "*Black Sun* being refitted, new crew at our disposal, us sitting here celebrating a grand voyage about to begin..."

"Except five of us," Davis said, alluding to Jon, Alex, Kaguya, Gran, and Kaiser. "Weren't here the first time."

"Even so, the effect isn't lost," Anna stated, too caught up in the moment to care. "Nor is it ill-fitting."

"Yes," Gran agreed, a smile of her own across her lips. "I can't think of any better way to start off our new voyage."

She then angled her head toward Kaiser, obviously hearing the Herculeans' internal motions. "'Except with more grog,' Kaiser says."

"Here, here!" Alex let out in agreement. "There's always room for that!"

"And Davis getting his sorry posterior handed to him by Kaguya," Apache spoke with a sneer. "Can that happen again too?"

"I have no issue with this," Kaguya casually replied, much to everyone's amusement.

And to Davis' exasperation of course. "Yeah yeah, laugh it up," was all he could say before taking a long drink. "Since we're all caught up in nostalgia, I'd like to point out another thing that's missing."

The group looked at him confusedly, forcing Davis to clarify. "Lorelei's singing," he said, turning to the psion. "You were on stage the first time, remember? Why aren't you up there now?"

Lorelei sighed, apparently frustrated herself. "Unfortunately, two of my Psirens were killed on Ephesus," she explained. "And though I have replacements in mind, it will take time to work with them."

"That sucks," Alex said, summarizing the thoughts of the entire group. "So we basically have to go without your music for a while?"

"Just until I get the band back up to standard," Lorelei reassured. "Though obviously, I won't be able to do that tonight."

"In that case," Jon offered, already having a tune in mind. "How about a song we can all sing?"

Curious, Lorelei leaned over, allowing Jon to whisper the song in her ear. Smiling at what she heard, Lorelei leaned back and, after a few moments to clear her throat, began.

> *Oh, we'll be alright between the devil and the void*

Instantly recognizing the song, the rest of the table enthusiastically followed. The other tables began joining in, one after another.

> *We'll be alright between the devil and the void*
>
> *We'll be alright between the devil and the void*
>
> *And we'll all hang on behind.*
>
> *And we'll roll the old chariot along*
>
> *We'll roll the old chariot along*
>
> *We'll roll the old chariot along*
>
> *And we'll all hang on behind!*

Alex added the next line.

> *Oh, we'll be alright once we make it around the sun*
>
> *We'll be alright once we make it around the sun*
>
> *We'll be alright once we make it around the sun*
>
> *And we'll all hang on behind.*

Next came Anna.

> *Oh, we'll be alright as our holds are filled with gold*
>
> *We'll be alright as our holds are filled with gold*
>
> *We'll be alright as our holds are filled with gold*
>
> *And we'll all hang on behind.*

Then Davis, his gaining much cheering and raising of cups and tankards.

> *Oh, a cold pint of grog wouldn't do us any harm*
>
> *A cold pint of grog wouldn't do us any harm*
>
> *A cold pint of grog wouldn't do us any harm*
>
> *And we'll all hang on behind.*

Then Gran.

> *Oh, the songs of the stars won't do us any harm*
>
> *The songs of the stars won't do us any harm*
>
> *The songs of the stars won't do us any harm*
>
> *And we'll all hang on behind.*

And then, Lorelei turned to Jon and nodded. Smiling, Jon added his own.

> *Oh, we'll be alright as the wind is in our sails*
>
> *We'll be alright as the wind is in our sails*
>
> *We'll be alright as the wind is in our sails*
>
> *And we'll all hang on behind.*

Upon completion of that last part, the izakaya became overcome with cheering yet again. The night only continued unbridled from there.

# Ryugu Castle
# Kyoto, Ryugu

Hours had passed since the celebration's end, as well as the Flint Pirates' evening retirement. Though it was within their nature to have celebrated until dawn, the fact remained that they were departing in the morning and Jon wanted his crew to be well rested for it. As such, though it had taken a bit of effort – namely in wrangling in the more drunken members of the crew – the party did finally end, and the pirates returned to their respective dwellings. Since that time, Kyoto, and seemingly the rest of Ryugu, had slept peacefully.

At least for the most part. Though he had made a valiant attempt at it, Jon quickly found that he couldn't sleep. Whether it was due to his anticipation, or simply that he had already spent so much time resting and recuperating from his wounds, he was simply too active. Thus, after several fruitless hours of tossing and turning in his bed, he finally decided it wouldn't hurt to remain awake for a while. With that, he got up from his bed, retrieved his eyepatch, and opened the nearby window, granting him a clear view of the outside.

Even now the city of Kyoto remained well lit, a sparse amount of traffic moving around it in both the sky above and the on ground below. However, it wasn't lit enough that Jon couldn't see the stars, nor the fullness of two of Ryugu's moons above, one being quite closer to the planet than the other. A spectacular view all around, Jon sat by the windowsill and found himself, with nothing else to do, slowly drifting into contemplation.

*Even from down here, it seems so infinite,* Jon thought as he looked up toward the cosmos above, dotted all across with gleaming stars. Mostly stars anyway; a good portion of them were also distant planets as well as the arc engines of ships moving about, amongst other celestial objects. And there was even more beyond them, well past the extent of Jon's vision yet present in the universe all the same, up to and including outside galaxies. So many things to see, so many things to reach out for, such that Jon could spend an eternity hunting and only discover a minuscule amount.

He smiled. Up until recently, that was all he could have done; gazing up at the stars as his ancestors had done so long ago, wondering what laid beyond yet never able to reach it for themselves. Now, thanks to the *Black Sun*, he had the means to reach; to explore that vastness and seek the treasures that laid within. Even now, he could hardly believe it. Despite how far he had come since meeting Lorelei on Aurora, it still seemed so much like a dream to him, not unlike how Wendy felt after her impromptu visit to Neverland. A dream that, instead of waking from, he would continue to fall deeper into slumber over.

As if to emphasize the point, he felt an all too familiar presence nearing him, causing a frown to emerge across his face.

"I hope this isn't going to become a habit with you."

Emerging from the darkness, Lorelei, dressed in a dark blue nightgown, only smiled in turn.

"Good, you've gotten better," she mock complimented. "On Aurora, I had to speak up in order for you to know I was present."

He watched as she came up to join him at the window. "You do realize the image you're setting," he said. "Coming into my room at this hour..."

"Let them think what they want," she spoke as if it were no consequence. "Besides, appearing as the Captain's Woman will dissuade the more vile crewmembers."

Jon nodded, understanding what she meant. "Fair point," he replied, then turned back to the stars.

Lorelei also looked out. "Quite the spectacular view," she commented. "I can see why you chose this room for your dwelling here."

"Actually, it was Lord Fuma's staff who chose it," Jon corrected. "But yes, the view is spectacular, if not simply appropriate."

"Hmm," Lorelei answered as she continued to gaze. Though she had no way of verifying, she thought she could see Ephesus as one of the "stars". "It still seems so far away."

Jon nodded again, once more understanding what she meant. "Yes, it does."

She looked down in thought. "After all the effort we went through simply to activate one pillar... I can only imagine what the other six will entail."

"I'd like to think not as much," Jon replied, folding his arms. "Though pessimism would tell me to expect only more."

"Perhaps," Lorelei replied, taking on a smile as she considered. "Though in a way, that only makes the adventure more interesting."

Jon smiled as well. "Indeed."

As she looked up at the sky again, Lorelei couldn't help but wonder. Could one of those stars be the second planet? "It's just as you said Captain," she continued. "We've come a long way, and yet it seems like we're back to where we started."

"To a degree," Jon corrected. "It was just you, me and Alex in the beginning."

"Yes," Lorelei agreed as the memory returned. "Two downtrodden pirates for hire, and a hooded wanderer seemingly in over her head..."

"Somehow meeting up in the very same tavern," Jon finished for her.

"And with a single beam shot heard all the way to Terra," Lorelei added, before laughing a little. "Hard to believe that was just over five months ago."

"Time is relative, as the saying goes," Jon replied simply.

A brief moment passed before the pirate spoke up again. "May I ask you a more direct question?"

The psion's turning to look at him was all the answer he needed. "What made you choose me as your Captain?" he asked. "Out of all the potential candidates you had beside North?"

She smiled. "What made you take that shot?" she redirected. "In spite of all the obvious reasons not to do it?"

Jon closed his eye, allowing another moment to pass before answering. "It just seemed like the thing to do," he claimed, once more, simply.

Lorelei's smile deepened before turning toward the stars again. She knew there was a different answer, but she knew better than to press him. "So it was with me."

Though he knew there was a different answer to that as well, Jon also let it go. There may yet be a time where they could give both answers truthfully. For now, however, they would only enjoy the moment. "I see."

With that, the pair continued to gaze at the stars in complete silence.

## Flint Pirates umbra *Black Sun*
## Kyoto, Ryugu

With a feeling of deep contentment, as well as some anticipation, Jon took his seat within the *Black Sun*'s bridge, slowly running his hands over the armrests. Everything was in place now; the ship was back in full form, her stores completely replenished and her crew at their stations. All that was left was to give the final word.

Gazing forward, he took in the sight of the bridge. Now fully revitalized from the damage it had taken from Ephesus, it looked as completely new as it had at Rochelle. Davis, Anna, and Barbarossa retained their stations at the front, Lorelei and Gran held theirs at his left, Alex and Kaiser did the same at his right, Kaguya was standing by Alex's station as she had the first time around, and Braun, Boss, and Apache stood behind him to watch their departure firsthand. All holding the same anticipation he felt, yet professionally remaining on standby for his command.

Moving further, Jon gazed at the forward viewscreen, which showed the open sky above. It was now the late morning, and Ryugu's skies were as abundantly blue as ever. There were no clouds now, as the storms had long come and gone. Only the white light of the resident sun stood out from the blue, which Jon, in his classical mindset, found similar to a lighthouse on a wharf. The final marker for his ship to pass in order to reach open space.

"A new day," he murmured under his breath, before getting things started. "Status."

"All moorings retracted Captain," Anna reported, her anticipation showing through her voice. "Local airspace is clear of traffic."

"Helm is active as ever," Davis answered similarly. "Arc engine is up and running."

"Starport control reports we are clear to launch," Gran added, her voice holding a more emphasized musical tone than usual. "They wish us luck as well."

"All systems in the green," Alex reported, smiling as he did. "We can launch at any time."

Jon nodded at all of this, all the while preparing his audio player. As before, he had an appropriate track for the occasion.

"Then may the wind still be at our backs," he said, mirroring his own words from the first time. "Take us up, Mr. Davis."

"Aye, sir," Davis replied, carefully easing the controls.

Slowly but gracefully, the *Black Sun* rose from her dock and into Ryugu's open air, gradually climbing higher and higher into the sky. As before, her black hull gleamed against the sunlight, all the while the Golden Roger on her bridge tower remained completely visible to everyone who saw her. From the ground below, many of Kyoto's citizenry looked up in awe to see the black and gold umbra fly over their city, gradually ascending toward their world's upper atmosphere.

As Jon watched the *Black Sun's* continued rise, he noticed Lorelei had gotten up from her station and now came over to stand by him, a hand on the back of his chair and an anticipating smile of her own across her lips. Despite it being a breach of protocol, Jon paid it no mind. In fact, a part of him found it fitting for her to be there, watching the ascent beside him.

Slowly the blue skies receded to the black of space, the white pinpricks of stars gradually becoming visible. The battlecruiser *Haruna* and a few other ships could be seen in the distance, with the former signaling the best of luck with her light. If Jon didn't know any better, he thought the Blue Dragon ships were there to formally see them off.

A few more minutes in, they passed the small contingent of ships and at last reached the full black.

"We have cleared orbit and are entering free space," Davis reported, turning back to face Jon directly with a smile of his own. "Where to Captain?"

Smiling back, Jon tapped his chair arm panel. "Wherever the wind blows," he spoke sagely, before selecting a specific audio file. "Wherever the wheel turns..." At that, the opening tones of *Wheel in the Sky* began to fill the bridge.

Davis nodded. "I think I know just the place," he said before turning back to his station. "Course plotted and set in."

Jon nodded, just as the song's full form began to play. "Arc Five, Mr. Davis," he commanded as the entirety of the bridge centered on the viewscreen.

Thus, the *Black Sun* accelerated into arcspace, returning to the void once more.

# <u>Epilogue: Return to Neverland</u>

## Neverland Tavern
## Aurora City, Aurora

With a steady hand, Thomas Cavendish poured the contents of the bottle of Old Caribbean into his tankard, taking a moment to savor its sweet odor. Though it wasn't the best liquor he'd ever had, it had grown on him recently, and he couldn't deny that it was a good drink. Once the tankard filled with the appropriate amount, he replaced the bottle on the counter and then took a swig, again savoring the sweetness of it.

It was after midnight now, local time, and the tavern was technically closed. Nonetheless, he had developed a rapport with the owner and, so long as he paid the right amount for his drinks and locked up when he departed, he was allowed to remain. This suited him just fine since he was not quite ready to turn in for the evening. There was but one more task for him to complete before he could.

At that, Thomas heard the opening and the closing of the door behind him, followed by the sound of boots stomping softly against the floor.

Without turning to face the wearer, he waited for the boots to continue their trek up to the counter, where they came to an abrupt stop behind him. This only caused him to smile, as he knew the wearer all too well.

"Care to join me?" he offered, gesturing toward the bottle.

"My apologies," the female voice replied. "But it is against regulations to drink while on duty."

His smile deepened. "Come now," he replied as he turned to face his 'guest'. "Surely one of your stature could afford to bend regulations a little..."

"With respect, I'm afraid I must insist," the woman staunchly replied, before withdrawing a datapad. "The scout ship has reported."

Taking the datapad, Thomas was quick to look over its contents. "Well well, they've finally left Ryugu," he spoke with evident interest. "Their heading?"

"They appear to be moving toward the Outer Rim," the woman replied. "At least, that is our scout's estimate."

"I see," Thomas said as he continued to read the data. "To engage in good old fashioned pirating if I had to guess."

The woman was unsure. "Wouldn't it be more likely that they've already found the second?"

Thomas shook his head. "If they have, the Captain is too smart to go after it right now," he explained. "He'll wait for the last remnants of Ephesus to die down first."

That's when another thought occurred to him. "On that note, how is Drake?" he inquired. "Have they got him stabilized yet?"

The woman shook her head. "I'm afraid not," she said. "Admiral Drake has been returned to cryo for the time being."

"A pity," Thomas replied with a trace of regret. "I suppose we'll just have to see how that turns out."

The woman silently cleared her throat before moving on. "The scout ship is on standby at this time," she declared. "What is your command?"

Thomas nodded, deciding to move to the heart of the matter. "Pull it back for now," he said. "Pursuit would be impossible at this point."

He then leaned back against the counter, continuing to scan over the datapad. "We'll let them run free for the time being," he said. "Until they begin their search for the second Babel."

Though still unsure, the woman nonetheless adhered to the order. "As you command," she replied, retaking the datapad when Thomas handed it back. "I shall return now."

"Very well," Thomas replied. "It shouldn't be long before I return to Terra myself."

Nodding in reply, the woman turned on her heel and moved back toward the door. Before she could exit properly; however, Thomas spoke up again. "One last thing," he said, stopping her. "What is that ship's new name?"

The woman balked at the question. "Surely they're not still calling her the *U-7501*," Thomas clarified.

After a moment to recall, the woman replied. "According to the rumors," she said. "They refer to her as the *Black Sun* now."

"The *Black Sun*..." Thomas repeated, considering that name. He soon found himself nodding in approval. "Not bad Jon."

Business concluded, the woman departed the tavern as Thomas retained his tankard. "Cheers," he spoke jovially upon raising the mug. "To the *Black Sun*."

With that, Thomas took another swig.

*Black Sun*
*Legacy of the Predecessors*

www.ingramcontent.com/pod-product-compliance
Lightning Source LLC
Chambersburg PA
CBHW031106030726

47496CB00002BA/411

*9780985250126*